The Litten Path

James Clarke grew up in the Rossendale Valley, Lancashire. *The Litten Path* is his first novel.

The Litten Path

JAMES CLARKE

CROMER

PUBLISHED BY SALT PUBLISHING 2018

2 4 6 8 10 9 7 5 3 1

First published in Great Britain in 2018 by
Salt Publishing Ltd
12 Norwich Road, Cromer, Norfolk N R27 0A X United Kingdom

www.saltpublishing.com

Salt Publishing Limited Reg. No. 5293401

A CIP catalogue record for this book is available from the British Library

I S B N 978 1 78463 146 8 (Paperback edition)
I S B N 978 1 78463 147 5 (Electronic edition)

Typeset in Neacademia by Salt Publishing

Printed and bound in Great Britain by Clays Ltd, Elcograf S.p.A

For my brother Chris. Everyone still misses you.

'. . . And you know, there is no such thing as society. There are individual men and women, and there are families.'
MARGARET THATCHER

PART ONE

The Causeway to the Moor

H IS DAD WAS squatting by the bed directing the Anglepoise into his face. Through the glare Lawrence could smell fresh outdoors, cigarettes masked badly with peppermints.

"*What?*" he said.

"Said wake up."

He turned away from the bother but his eyes were so scrunched that he misjudged the distance and clumped his head against the wall. Cold stucco. He bit the inside of his cheek and kept his mouth shut.

"Kid."

Movement. Then what sounded like his homework being blundered off the desk. When his blanket was peeled back, Lawrence yanked it towards his neck again and hissed "*Jesus*" over his shoulder.

"Not him."

"You're funny."

"Not as funny as this."

The blanket was torn away entirely.

"*Shit, what'd you—*"

Arthur's rough palm smothered Lawrence's mouth. Those beer lips were always so clumsy against the ear.

"*Quiet.* An' watch your lip. Your mother didn't raise a bloody yob."

Even the gentlest moments could turn against you. A

minute ago Arthur's outline had been dimly lit between the doorway and the landing. Now this. Lawrence finished his sentence anyway. His curses emerged as muffled nonsense.

"Calm it."

He prised Arthur's bastard hand off. No one else had a dad like this, the human equivalent to a poke in the eye.

"*Am* calm."

"But not quiet."

"What do you want, Dad?" Lawrence clamped either shoulder and tucked his legs in until he resembled the shape of a question mark.

"I've a job for you, but you need to keep it down."

Dad's grin rictus was like always. Lawrence had a similar face, except his wasn't as grey and there was no blot on his cheek that drew the eye. A pit wound that coal dust had seeped into, tattooing the slash-mark blue.

"*Dad.*"

"I know, kid. But I'll make it worth your while."

A handful of coins landed on the mattress: warm coppers strewn next to Lawrence's torso that was as hairless as a baby's kneecap. Worth getting up for, he supposed.

"Time is it?" he said, sitting up. He'd been sacked from his paper round and needed the money. Sixteen and skint. Gristle, bone and bags under the eyes.

Arthur laughed. "Wrong question."

"Kind of job?"

"*Special ops.* Now get some clothes on and meet us downstairs."

Ten minutes later they were crunching along the strip path around the back of their house on Water Street. It was late

February and the moon was monstrous. It undermined the sodium road lamp flickering on the corner ahead.

"Summat about a carpet?"

"Bloody rug I said."

"Right."

"Cracking rug it is."

"Right."

"You listening?"

Fucking carpet. Never mind all the cloak and dagger business, a bribe in the offing meant Lawrence's mam wouldn't be allowed to find out about all this. Lawrence stumbled in a clutch of weeds, not that Arthur noticed.

When they reached the road they headed north, the opposite direction to Litten centre. Litten was a pit village that called itself a town. Its angled streets were crammed a hill or two away from the rest of South Yorkshire. Factories and works studded every outskirt, chimneys burst out of the ground like raised middle fingers and the clouds of pumped smog were caught still in the daylight. Litten was tired pubs with stone troughs outside that they used for watering the sheep back in the day. It was the odd scrat of grass at the end of your row, an arcade under a metal awning, a roundabout, too many traffic lights, charity shops and an old bandstand in the centre where the brass band from Brantford pit still flogged the dead horse every other weekend.

And still Arthur smiled. His hair looked static-charged against the unreal glow of the street.

"What d'you mean a rug, anyway?" said Lawrence.

"What do you mean, what do you mean?"

"Well, really a rug?"

"Course."

"Then why this hour?" His Casio said half two.

"As this is the only time we can get it."

"But it's freezing, Dad—"

"Bloody hell, you've a coat, and you're always whining about early bed. I thought you'd be up for this."

"I am."

"Well stop acting the fairy then."

They walked on. The sky could have been indigo, purple, black, as they advanced deeper into the sticks. A steeper incline and visible breath. When Arthur put his hand on his shoulder, Lawrence let it stay.

"Could at least say where you're taking us."

"So you know Threndle House, right?"

Lawrence began to say no.

"Course you do."

"Big place?"

"Where Brantfords lived."

"Aye, what about it?

"Well that's where we're off."

Lawrence stopped in his tracks. "It's a mile off!"

"Come on, kid, I did say this were Special Ops."

It was always so funny. Lawrence began to head back the way they'd come, no longer the eternal boy, adding for good measure that there was nothing special about *these* ops.

"*Wait*," said his dad, grasping him by the elbow, his voice so many things; pick your bloody adjective. "I need your help, kid. Them muscles."

"What muscles?" Lawrence was being led back towards Threndle House.

"Well, these for a start," said Arthur.

"Get off, Dad, God's sakes."

"Look, I'd not ask other than it's for your mam."

Now they were getting to it. There had been a lot of overtime in the run up to Christmas, and on Shell's orders Arthur had taken on all that he could get. He'd described to Lawrence the great mound of coal collecting outside of Brantford pit. Perceptible from the road, the pile had to be climbed over on the way in: an immense blackness the men could look at from way upon the gantry.

With his tongue, Lawrence touched his top lip, where hair had started to grow. These were the deep hours, when the bobbins and the sprockets of the mind squeaked. "Why always me?" he said, surprised by the whine in his voice.

"*Because.*"

"You always say that, Dad. There must be a mate or—"

"There's no one," said Arthur. "There is no one."

It took them the best part of an hour to get there, but eventually they reached a grand stone building that loomed like a mural at the end of the road. This was Threndle House, and Lawrence was being pushed to it by his father's hand.

A five-foot wall protected the house from the public. Detached and remote, it was a large property, though still smaller than Lawrence remembered.

"Knows exactly who it is," said Arthur, hauling himself up the wall. "Kind of what I like about the place."

For once Lawrence's dad was right. Threndle House made up in grandeur what it lacked in size. "Watch out or someone'll see you," said Arthur, nodding in the front door's direction. "Swarsbys are on holiday."

"Doesn't answer my question."

"You didn't ask a question."

Lawrence took the hand offered and was dragged up the wall.

"Just trust us," said Arthur. "They're not in."

They sat kicking their heels against the brickwork. Threndle House would have been shrouded were it not for the silver light draping over everything. The place was thick, almost sullen in shape. Across the lawn you could see mullioned windows and doors, curlicues of metalwork and masonry along the roof. Roughly on top of all that was a gherkin. Gargoyle, probably. Though Lawrence couldn't quite be sure from such a distance.

Arthur produced a canteen from his anorak and removed the lid. It was a dented old thing that his own father, Alec Newman, twenty years' coal dust in the lungs, used to keep hot vodka blackcurrant in. Lawrence's grandad was a Shotfirer. He set charges in bore holes and detonated them to make headway in the pit. One morning after a blast failed, Alec went to check the line for a problem in the circuit, only the young man he was training wasn't the brightest spark; he tested the detonation key the moment the connection was repaired. The canteen was the only surviving thing they found left buried in the debris.

"Have a drink," said Arthur.

Lawrence accepted the canteen, smelled it, handed it back.

Arthur screwed down the cap, looking like he was the one being put upon. "See, wi' what's going on at minute—"

"Wi' pits?"

"What else would I be on about?"

"Well, I—"

"Ever hear of a rhetorical question, kid?"

Lawrence puffed his cheeks.

8

"Manvers are striking over snap times, I heard, and . . ." Arthur adopted his daftest, poshest voice. *'The lady's not for turning.'*

Lawrence couldn't help but laugh.

"So I daresay summat's up. They've been chipping at us wages long enough."

The canteen sloshed. It spent most of its time in Arthur's back pocket. Your dad home after his shift for a processed cheese butty, washing it down with some spirit that turned you full-on fruit-loop.

"Union's after donations. They've had everyone out postin' leaflets. I ended up volunteering."

"Good of you," Lawrence said.

"I'm all heart."

They both laughed this time. Arthur had made no secret of falling into the job. *Slaving to heat everyone's baths,* was a stock phrase in the Newman house. *Powering Sunday pissing dinner for the neighbours* was another. One of three sons clumsily named after three ancient heroes, he and Uncle Hector travelled daily in the pit cages, miles underground to the districts of Brantford, treading the same routes as before and deeper still. Vaster aspects of coal, hotter tunnels to work in. The third brother, Samson, hadn't been so lucky, but he was never spoken of. Sam was an awkward discussion no one wanted to have, a picture in the living room of a Teddy boy with a monobrow.

"Weren't like I had much choice," said Arthur. "Het's been saying I won't do my bit. No way were I about to give him chance to lord it over me like usual."

He turned and gobbed over his shoulder. Uncle Het still lived in town. Lawrence saw him and his dad exchange a look when they came across one another from time to time, but the two didn't really speak. He longed for someone to exchange looks of his own with. His breath clouded into the empty space in front.

"You should see him with his hair all slicked. Thinks he's AJ bloody Cook, I swear."

"Who the hell's that?"

Arthur clicked his tongue. "Point is I'd to get involved or have Het and the others to contend wi'. Leaflets seemed an easy enough job."

"So they've had you round posh end?"

"Fat chance. Flintwicks Estate. Not far, is it? After us round I've stopped here. Which leads us to this evening."

"Were gonna say."

Lawrence's dad dug him in the ribs.

"You'd better not have dragged us out of bed 'cause this is the only time you can dump them leaflets, Dad."

"That might come later," admitted Arthur, showing off a batch of undelivered papers. "Like I said, I'm more interested in what's round back here. Want another drink?"

Lawrence hadn't even had any in the first place. The mansion glowed madly, lit special where it wasn't black and total.

He shook his head.

"Suit yourself," said Arthur, then dropped off the wall into the garden.

They stole across the lawn. At the front of the house a tree coiled towards the gables, lending texture to the place like some kind of beard. The tree reached the gutter running under what *was* in fact a gargoyle, its stone face wet with moonlight: a demon grinning down on Lawrence's dad.

"You said Swarsbys."

"Aye, Tory," said Arthur. "Saggy-titted wet lettuce, here for by-election, God help him. Naturally he's buggered off skiing the minute he got here."

"I seen that in the paper."

Splashed all over the Free Press. Derek Shaw, the Labour incumbent for Litten Borough, had suffered a heart attack, so his seat had been thrown open, the Conservatives deciding to contest it. Clive Swarsby was the man they'd sent, only he'd disappeared straight to France on holiday. Lawrence remembered the man in black and white, a skiing politician; the news had made the nationals, a cartoon in one paper of a large-featured, buck-toothed ghoul careering down a mountain with a trail of pound notes streaming behind it in the snow.

"So you thought you'd bob round?" he said.

Arthur looked thoughtful. "Not sure. To be poetic I suppose seeing the house were like stumbling into someone else's head, except for a minute it were my head, not some dream. The sky surrounding were all lit. I couldn't go past wi'out looking. I said to myself: why not? *He's* the one who thinks he can decide what's good for everyone. Why shouldn't the likes of me come see what he's about?"

"That's a yes then," said Lawrence, under his breath.

"So I jumped grounds, had a look and found this. What d'you reckon?"

A long shape was sticking out of one of the bins. So this was the rug. Even poking out of the rubbish it was taller than Lawrence. It could have been a damaged piece of industrial equipment, bent in the middle and having to be propped against the wall to keep from falling on someone. Lawrence felt its coarseness, a fox barking somewhere the moment his fingers grazed the fabric.

"Well?" said his dad.

"I think it's in the bin."

"Aye, well a twat like Swarsby doesn't know the value of 'owt. Mark my words, kid, this is a find."

Consider them marked. The off-white moon was a curdled penny. Lawrence didn't know. "I don't know," he said.

"Oh, shut it – quick scrub and it'll be reight. If this doesn't cheer your mam, nowt will."

"Then what?

"How do you mean and then what?"

It took them a long time to carry it home, a pair of midnight bailiffs, each holding one end of a repossession. They skittered the bins and dotted the rubbish as they dragged the rug out into the open, but the commotion drew no attention and when Lawrence got back from school the next day, he and his dad laid it in the living room whilst his mam was out doing the shopping.

"*Turkish*," said his dad, on his knees, smoothing the ricks from the surface that now covered the entire floor. The rug's pattern was like a jigsaw, and studying its compact spread made Lawrence think of the sea at Bridlington Beach, where he'd visited as a boy, the moment he swam too far out and realised his mam couldn't see him anymore.

"We've done well here," said Arthur.

"Suppose."

"Do you not think so?"

. . . The salt water up your nose. The dread line where the horizon met the sky . . .

Dad started going over the story again. They'd saved up, bought the rug out of town and blah blah. They had to tell Mam something. She'd never accept a stolen gift and a cast off she couldn't help but look down on. Words Lawrence knew to be true, though the fact they had to be kept secret and couldn't be spoken in front of her made them feel like lies.

When his mam finally walked through the door, Lawrence stood well away from his dad. Shell Newman had a frank, open face that tended to hang, but as she saw the rug for the first time, her lips pinched. She wasn't one for taking promptly to acts of kindness.

"What's this?" she said.

"Present, love."

"Kind of present?"

"What do you think?" Arthur beamed. "You can thank the overtime."

Shell chewed a strand of hair broken free from her ponytail. "Didn't think there were any."

"Well there were."

"Right."

"Serious, love."

"Aren't you always?" Shell caught Lawrence's eye. "Oh, I don't know."

"Chap were on his hols," said Arthur. "It were last one and he wanted rid."

Lawrence had to admire his father's gall.

"Suppose it's a nice pattern though, isn't it, kiddo?" There was the slightest lilt to his mother's voice, and in this moment, seeing her not daring to like her gift, Lawrence realised that although he hadn't a clue what the future held for him the last thing he ever wanted was what his mam had.

"Yeah," he said, bringing his mug of tea to his mouth and wrinkling the bridge of his nose so it would look like he was smiling.

"Then it's a keeper," his mam replied brightly. "Thanks, both yous, I'm touched, *proud*, actually. You've worked hard and it's a nice thought. Really, it is."

Arthur looked about ready to click his heels. He aimed a kiss at his wife's cheek but the oblivious Shell turned away and left him puckering at thin air. That was all it took to send Lawrence into the kitchen. He clanked his empty mug by the sink and watched the rigid strings of sleet slanting against the window.

Two weeks later and a wardrobe opened, several tiny moths flying out of it. Truancy was an easy enough trick, especially on Fridays. Arthur was on six till twos so up at five and gone for half past, whilst Mam was on her visit to lay flowers on Grandad's grave and chat to Granny Kelly in the care home. Lawrence had gone along with her in the past but by this stage it seemed pointless. Last memories sent rolling down the pinball drain, Granny Kelly didn't recognise anyone anymore. By now the Topaz stud in her engagement ring would be getting knocked by Shell's unpainted fingernails. By now, Asa Scanlan's Fiesta would have grumbled through town and deposited Arthur at Brantford pit.

Lawrence grabbed the basics from the wardrobe: a pair of shorts, his slippers and a cable-knit sweater. Another moth settled on the door as he closed it. He put his finger on the insect and left a glittery brown smear on a sticker of Mel Sterland.

Downstairs he flicked on the telly. It was March and TVAM was on. He noticed his sweater had finally lost that cloying, second-hand smell as he dragged the neck hole over his head, the thought interrupted by a sharp sound in the cloth and a peculiar give in the fabric.

He tugged the sweater off and held it to the light. There was a large tear under one arm and, elsewhere, sunshine gleamed through it in a series of unnatural pin-pricks. He flopped, bare-chested, onto the settee. Another moth was nearby: he swatted it. He'd lost count of how many he'd killed recently. They were paltry things, barely seeming to move and when they did flying so gently towards the nearest source of light that all you had to do was clap them from the air, or crush them against whatever they were crawling on.

He concentrated on the people on the screen. Some wore NUM badges, most dark colours. Under their soupy sky, each one of them seemed to resemble his father. The protesters rushed into the police, jamming against a fence where a man in a donkey jacket stood. There was a crush as the fence collapsed, people flooding the screen and trying not to stand on the man. The crowd heaved over him, rushing like oil into an oxbow lake.

The camera cut away, straight to an image of a pit, a pit as mucky and confusing as the workings under the bonnet of a car. Headgear spun against the day. Trucks and footprints and smog pipes and bilge pumps, cabins and coke ovens, work yards and brick-yards, girders and timber; equipment, equipment, equipment.

Lawrence almost expected to see Uncle Het barking at someone, neck streaked by that scar of his that looked like a cross-section of salami. The screen emptied. It focused on a close-up of an exhaust, then the car itself, a yellow bug crawling along a road that trickled over the moor, heading south.

Lawrence supposed that was where everybody off the telly went: up the Litten Path.

He switched off the TV and sat back, tugging at the rug's tassels with his toes. They'd had people round to admire the damn thing the weekend before, where it had made a welcome distraction from the pit dispute, which was the inevitable main topic of conversation. Arthur for one was against striking. "What good's taking action on someone else's behalf," he said, "cutting us nose off to spite another lad's face?" which was one of his brasher statements, holding court, as was his custom, causing a stir on an afternoon of chicken drumsticks and paper plates.

Lawrence didn't know whether he agreed or disagreed with his father. He no longer bothered to enter into meaningful discussions with endless men like him and the other heavy-arsed loudmouths in the room. Pissed in the afternoon with their sideburns in need of a trim, vigorously mantled cheeks and noses with snowflakes of blood vessels burst in them, banging on about variety performances or cars or ways of doing things in days gone by, when everything was harder fought for and therefore more genuine.

Another grey Sunday. Mam cracked out the china she'd lifted from Granny Kelly's when she first took ill, and stood behind the settee rubbing Arthur's neck while he talked up the luxury under everyone's feet. Accepting the rug had given Shell such a lift that Lawrence found himself having to make the best of a gathering he'd no one to invite to, answering the same questions about school, giving the same shrug when asked what he was going to do when he left, head dipping when told how much he'd grown, how handsome he was when he knew he wasn't good looking.

The Sunday ladies drank Babycham, the men bitters, can-isters of brown ale that went flat once poured into the plastic cups. Lawrence's hair was combed in the middle like it was ten years ago, as he helped show off the rug and an antique carriage clock to everybody. The clock was another of Arthur's gifts, and so deep had it put him in Shell's good books that he was allowed to smoke indoors, although Lawrence's mam was so busy finishing the cupcakes that she forgot to put out ashtrays.

Arthur tapped fag ash into his hand while detailing the clock's story. A win on the dogs had seen its purchase. "Last minute, like," he said. "I thought I'd use the winnings for another summat for the wife. You're chuffed aren't you, love?"

"Why wouldn't I be?"

"My wife. My only keeper."

Eye contact was to be avoided, it seemed. Arthur emptied his hand into the plant pot then hurried to the kitchen to be loud and overly helpful instead. He could be seen pouring crisps into the plastic bowl on the worktop, sorting drinks and peering into the sink's plughole, staring as if it was some kind of vortex.

In the lounge Lawrence pushed his finger through the chewed hole under the sweater's arm. It had all felt so artificial. The out-of-date fruitcake that was 'still OK', the fig rolls the Scanlans brought and Gordon Lomas' *hyah-hyah* laugh and bald fucking head. Everyone wore pastel or beige, the women criticised Princess Diana and the blokes gathered in ribald groups. The afternoon peaked when Lawrence went to the kitchen to fetch more pop and caught his parents in there, *touching* one another.

But what alternative? Protest and cry fake? His mam would

kill him. This was Yorkshire. Far better to keep quiet than be thought soft. Far better to sit back and enjoy the sausage rolls.

The sweater's tear was now so much bigger that he might as well have done with it. He tugged at its edges until he'd ripped the garment apart completely.

Satisfying to at least ruin something.

Another moth flew past. Lawrence tried to get it, missed. He tried again and slapped the coffee table where it landed, the impact rattling the windowpane.

He looked around the room. On the armchair were moths. The electric fireplace, moths. On the ornaments, the TV and the lampshade.

He went upstairs to check his wardrobe and found more holes in the clothes hanging in there. The culprits crawled over the desk and all four walls. Lawrence swatted all of those that he could see then carried his clothes outdoors, slinging them over the washing line by the brazier Arthur used to burn the litter people threw over their fence, and the leaves shed by the sycamores stooping over their yard. Lawrence would light a fire to smoke the bastards out. Bonfires did for midges; he'd fumigate the moths from his clothes the same way.

But not before he combed the rest of his room, checking under the single bed pushed against the wall, vacuuming the steps of floor space then changing the bedding. Still no nest. Just crawling or flying insects that were crushed as fast as he came across them.

Next he tackled his parents' room. This was not a place to be entered lightly, not because his parents were especially private people, but because being in their personal space made you feel like you had somehow wandered into their brains.

This room was where Mam and Dad became Shell and Arthur, the parts of them Lawrence knew nothing of, ever so close to being revealed. Medicine, lingerie, letters, receipts, private heirlooms, belly-button fluff and toenail clippings. All of it told their secret, human story.

Lawrence only dared search their wardrobe, although it was the same state of affairs in there as in his. He left every item hanging – Mam would hit the roof if she knew he'd been touching their stuff – taking the trouble to vacuum the carpet then the landing, spraying enough air freshener in the bathroom to choke any living thing to death.

Downstairs he took out more moths and cleaned the stains they'd left on the walls by spitting on the hem of his t-shirt and using it as a makeshift cloth. The kitchen was all round edges, vinyl floor and Formica surfaces, its cupboards so packed and regularly used that the chances of a hidden nest were slim. Lawrence went to the living room to check in there instead.

The rug was like a stagnant sea. Lawrence vacuumed its exposed sections until he reached the settee with its fringe that tickled the floor. He lifted the heavy piece of furniture with one hand and went to push the vacuum underneath it with the other, but as he bent to see what he was doing, he noticed a papery movement lurking within the shadows.

The settee thunked to the floor. Lawrence stumbled onto his arse, the vacuum sucking a few rug tassels up and making a desperate noise. Fuck. Fuck. Fuck. Lawrence lifted the settee again and saw the hysterical gathering beneath it. The congregation and the shift. The antennae and the wing.

He dragged the settee into the middle of the room. Revealed where he'd shifted it were thousands of moths, writing and crawling over one another. 'He slid the armchair out and found a lot more where that had been, then lifting the rug he found maggots: cream-coloured puddles of insects squirming in the dust, half-caught by the clumps of hair and the dirt and . . .

"Kiddo?"

Some voices could cut through anything. Lawrence switched the vacuum off, not daring to turn as he heard his mother's keys clattering on the floor. His belly was after gold in the gymnastics and still he had the rug's corner in his hand.

"Mam."

The lines of Shell's face were tight, her mouth an O-shape. She let out a moan of disgust, so soft it could almost have been a squeal.

It made Lawrence let go of the rug, which slapped to the ground, its force creating a ripple that sent a plague of moths flickering into the air. The insects rose and engulfed the living room. They glittered like dust motes in the sunshine streaming through the big window.

"Jesus!" Shell cried, slamming the door to protect the upstairs and swiping at Lawrence. Her nails caught his nape hair as he tried to escape, as she dragged him into the yard along with a wooden chair from the kitchen. Lawrence kept trying to speak. He kept saying her name.

Mam.

Mam.

"Get your clothes off and sit on that bloody chair!" Shell shrieked.

Lawrence did as he was told while his mam removed her denim jacket and wrapped it around her face, tying the arms at the rear of her head. She marched back into the house and opened a window, a plume of moths erupting from the gap as Lawrence listened to her talking to someone on the front desk at Brantford.

"Tell him his wife's on t'phone," said Shell, "and I don't care if shift's about to wash, I want him home, A-S-A-bloody-P!"

Soon Arthur returned, stepping from a taxi in his boiler suit and boots. Lawrence had stripped to his Y-fronts by then. He squinted towards the unbearable sun as his father took one look at the rug, rolled up and smoking in the brazier, spread each hand and said, "Well, obviously. *Obviously . . .*"

Mam's chin was tucked into her throat.

"She knows, Dad," blurted Lawrence.

Arthur stared.

"I said she knows."

"You told her?"

"I had to."

"You *told* her."

"I'm sorry, Dad."

"You never think, do you? About anything."

Lawrence wiped his streaming eyes. He'd slipped his trainers back on because his feet were cold. He liked the way the maroon laces weaved in and out through their dirty eyelets: interlinked and criss-crossed; over and under; the over and the under and the . . .

"Jesus, Shell, I got it . . . I got in a deal!"

That dull sound again.

"The truth, Arthur. For once the bloody truth."

Lawrence's father looked like he might bolt, but he was cowed by the faces in the neighbouring windows, which were themselves bloated and paled by the glass. There were no escapes in knotty little working communities like Litten.

"*All right,*" he said.

"Did you not hear her, Dad? If you just say what happened . . ."

Arthur pinched the bridge of his nose. "Lawrence," he said. "I'm tired of hearing your voice."

He sat on the ground.

"It were all from skip."

Mam's chin lifted. Her chest heaved. "How do you mean *skip?*"

"Frigging bin, all right! From nice place, Threndle House."

"Rug?"

"Course rug."

"Clock too?"

Arthur nodded. The rug had really taken. Its busy flames sounded almost like water running into a bathtub. They licked the air, noxious and declarative, the burned fabric terribly sour-smelling.

"They were both in good nick, like. I mean you saw 'em, Shell."

"My husband the thief."

"I thought it might make a change. I thought it might cheer you up."

"Everything costs summat."

"*Think I don't know that?*"

"It's made a show of us in front of everyone!"

Mam's bottom lip practically touched her nose. With a visible effort, she controlled herself. "Lower your heads," she said. "Pair of yous."

"Why?" said Lawrence. His dad still wouldn't look at him.

"Just do it," Mam said. "As I need to check."

"For what?"

"*Infection*," Mam spat. She strode forward and grabbed Lawrence by his head.

2

I T FELT GOOD to be alone.

Shell sat in the kitchen staring at the light. On the counter was Arthur's dinner: a can of spaghetti hoops set next to a plate of thawing fish fingers and chips. The frozen food landing on the china plate as she emptied it from its packet an hour ago had been the only sound in the house, and since then she had sat.

The familiar whirr of the airing cupboard. Shell had found the note after putting the food out. It said to wait a while, come meet them at Litten Hill. Arthur had specified to come at 'tea time' which might have sounded fine but Shell hadn't been able to work out when was best to leave, and realised it was so typically unspecific an instruction that she could barely give voice to her frustration.

She'd waited on the lip of the bath, firing tepid soap suds down her naked back. She'd waited in the bedroom, towel-drying her hair and letting it hang, and now she waited in the kitchen with her husband's dinner defrosting by her side. The hulking sky spread robustly outside the painted-shut kitchen window.

She made a final patrol of the house. The smell of disinfectant and bleach hugged everything. It was over a couple of weeks since she'd burned the gifts, but vividly Shell recalled the bubbling of the carriage clock, its varnish peeling like skin from a lesion in a fingerprint. Dying time becoming visible through that strange ripple in perspective that heat causes.

The rug took longer to disappear. Shell left Lawrence alone while she went to the garage to fetch the petrol. She'd expected him to have scarpered when she returned, or at least to be pulling his clothes on, but he'd stayed where he was, her son, desolate in underpants and trainers.

She'd emptied the jerry can and tossed the match and as the rug took flame, saw how ashamed Lawrence was, although whether it was for infesting their home, being in thrall to his useless dad, bunking off school or being a party to lying and embarrassing her in front of the whole town, Shell wasn't sure. He was probably just upset at being caught out. The second liar in a house of liars – you'd think he'd been dragged up.

Together they watched the rug burn. Shell thought she'd seen the moths ablaze, rising like scraps of confetti. Again she couldn't be sure. Perhaps dead moths were what she wanted to see. Those itinerant specks of insignificance symbolising the things that plagued her home, all the things that bothered her; the things that weighed her down.

Although burning the rug hadn't ended the infestation, because every day since Shell had vacuumed. Every day she had polished and prodded the crannies with the duster. She had washed the settee covers and the curtains and she had sprayed all the surfaces until they ran slick with detergent, but the insects clung on as stubbornly to things as she did.

There was one now, fluttering towards the light. Shell went for it, missed. Those two were waiting; she didn't want to join them. Lawrence, that teen. Arthur, that husband. It was hard to know how to deal with them. She had nothing much to say to either one.

Especially Lawrence. An accidental birth, was there any other kind? So she hadn't breastfed him and maybe that was why they weren't close. His pincer lips made her sore so she'd used formula milk and become callous with the bottle. Lawrence gorged himself like a little piglet. Shell had watched the milk dribble down his double-chin.

Although she knew she was being irrational, it niggled Shell, not breastfeeding her son. It niggled her every time he puked after he'd been fed, and the memories of how it was always Arthur who rose at night to quell the baby's tears, Arthur who boiled the nappies clean in the saucepan while Shell could only think of shouting to make Lawrence stop crying rather than burp him, take him for a walk or have a bash at a lullaby, all that niggled her, too.

And she wondered about herself, why she behaved this way. Never playing dress-up. Never doing drawing with Lawrence or telling him stories, failing to coax him from his shyness the way the other women did with their children. Things just never *occurred* to Shell, and going back to crouch in front of her son in the playground, putting her hands on his shoulders and saying, 'Don't worry, you go play,' felt like too much of a climb-down once she'd realised her mistake.

Probably Lawrence thought about this stuff too.

She hunted for her jacket, scaling the stairs and carefully avoiding the scrub marks staining the wall. Her house felt that cheap sometimes. The mounted ornamental plates Arthur bought from the car boot sale, the minibar he'd insisted on in the living room, with its platter for mixing the drinks, all of it made Shell cringe.

Boss-eyed walls. Lightweight doors. Shell entered the spare

room and looked at the blow-up bed, which was semi-deflated. There was her jacket lying next to it. Arthur had taken the spare change from her pockets.

She swept downstairs, forcing her arms through the sleeves and that bastard from her head. She'd cut Arthur's bloody hair off the other week. Had to. Fingers like crabs' legs along his and Lawrence's scalps. As soon as she found the moth in Lawrence's hair, she'd crumbled the thing to nothing. There had been no choice but to react after what her family had done, and by that logic if she was going to react in the first place it was better to do it thoroughly if she was going to do it at all. Liars and cheats needed telling.

Gripped by what you might call a fugue, Shell took the kitchen scissors to the main bit of Lawrence's fringe where the moth had been. She disposed of the hair in the brazier then promptly found more hidden moths, snipping where they had been too.

After that she cut the lot off, using the razor while she was at it. She'd get that scalp smooth-bald rather than pie-bald, give Lawrence a head like a light bulb rather than a globe where the stubble formed into misshapen continents, reminders of what she couldn't quite remove with the scissors. Arthur was next; Shell wasn't nearly so gentle, snapping at his hair, focusing in particular on the grey strands shaped like zigs of electric wire, while Arthur stared churlishly at the limp and sooty clothing strung along the washing line. A solitary red tear had dribbled down his forehead.

Shell locked the front door. Yes, she remembered Litten. She remembered her youth, making her way down this same route, glistening today, some parts still cobbled, past the allotments with its plots and its vista of plants and bamboo

27

canes, its benches and sheds, the rectangles of soil looking like recently filled-in graves.

She sparked a fag, sucked as much nicotine back as she could. She'd never been a drinker; she'd always smoked. She liked the kick of it. She liked forcing the fumes out of each nostril. Arthur thought she'd quit long ago. She hadn't. Shell felt like she'd been a smoker long before she ever tried it. Her grandparents had smoked; her dad, Lee – pomade in the hair and Sinatra down the pub – he'd smoked; so did her mother. Shell had always liked the smell. Taking up the habit felt so natural. There is such a thing as fate; it's called being pre-disposed.

She thought of herself at sixteen, poring over those exercise books, maths problems squished as nonsensically as dead ants on the page. Pointless, all of it. Shell had snuck down the shop to buy something to take her mind off things, and there met a lanky streak of piss with a bicycle, leaning against a wall with a roll-up sticking out of his yap. The youngster seemed to think he knew absolutely everything, and although there was the odd sideways look, he showed no real interest in Shell, which intrigued her all the more.

Because she wasn't beautiful. She knew that and was fine with it. Beautiful girls were never taken seriously. They weren't grounded. They rarely developed wit or clever tricks. And in any case who needs looks when you've sex appeal? Shell was clear-eyed: she knew her face was too plump, like an over-filled water balloon, still blokes wanted her. That made it all right.

She had worn the boy down until he offered her the ride she'd hoped for from the start. Astride the saddle with her legs splayed, her groin clenched the leather, her fingernails sunk deep into Arthur Newman's cardigan as he stood on the pedals and clattered them down the rec. It had beaten revision. Shell smoked her first cigarette that day and put her tongue so far down Arthur's throat that he had to pull away and splutter. When she was young Shell was as shy as Lawrence in many respects, but sex or the promise of it always drew her out into the open. Nothing else was important then, not school, family or the prospect of what she'd one day do. All there was, was living and music and boys, in particular that ambivalent lad who'd promised to call on her the first chance he got, whom, as it turned out, she wouldn't speak to again for another six years. Waking up with the world to look forward to, that was Shell Newman's girlhood, and was anything better than being young when you felt as past it as she did?

The wind was beginning to snap as Shell approached Litten Hill. She made her way up the slope, an inhospitable bluff with no grass to speak of, more an abundance of scruff and fern. She pushed through the lengthening sward, ignoring the underwood's snags, following a path taken recently, she assumed, by her hairless husband and son.

She'd never been one for exercise but walked a lot and was naturally hardy, so made good time. She emerged from the scrub and found herself on the summit. Below her the broken woods spread until they reached the borders of the town. A bird glided low, casting no shadow so deeply was the dying light imprisoned by the clouds.

Voices. Shell pursued them, catching her denims on a bramble. Crouching to untangle herself, she spotted the twin domes belonging to her husband and son, who at times felt more like kith to her than they did kin.

They were bent over a sapling whose red leaves emerged

from the bin bag in which its roots had been wrapped. Shell was out of their line of sight, yet close enough to hear their voices carried by the wind.

"You might as well start digging," Arthur said.

"Here?" said Lawrence.

"Course bloody there."

Lawrence knelt gingerly on the ground, which made Shell smile. "Dirty earth," he said, prising a clump of field out and holding it above his head. Shell could see him prodding the muddy roots, the soil presumably showering onto his trousers, because Arthur was saying "Watch them pants or your mam'll go spare. You know what she's like at the mo—"

He stopped himself.

Shell's smile faded.

"Just be careful, will you."

"Whatever you say." Lawrence stabbed the trowel into the ground. Winter was over but the North didn't seem to have registered it yet. The stubborn breeze blew. Shell would have abolished the wind if she could.

She buttoned her jacket at the collar. Arthur, smoking a roll-up, wore an anorak; Lawrence, digging away, was dressed in a parka. Each sported a newly shaven head, warped skulls accentuating open-car-door ears. They must be freezing, Shell thought.

When the hole was big enough Arthur dragged the sapling to it. The sheltered sun had dropped rapidly in the sky and the streetlamps in town and the boxy farmhouses scattered about the hills had begun to emit a bleak, spectral glow.

"Nice leaves them, Dad."

"Soon as I saw it, I knew it were ours."

"Where'd you get it?"

Arthur readied the sapling, missing its bin liner floating off in Shell's direction. Shell stuck a foot out and trapped it, picked it up and stuffed it in her pocket.

Her husband used the trowel to cut around the perimeter of the pot, then began to prise the sapling free with its stem, careful to protect the root ball. He sometimes showed a similar tenderness to Lawrence, and could be careful when he wanted to be. It was one of the first things Shell had ever liked about him.

"Never mind that," he said.

Removing the sapling had caused some damage to the pot so Arthur tore away the broken section and chucked it, the shape frisbeeing past Shell and jamming in the ground. The root ball began to crumble in his hands.

"*Shit.*"

"It weren't?"

"Pipe down. This needs to be in ground by time she gets here."

"You better not have nicked it, Dad."

"You what?"

"Nowt."

"Go see if she's bloody coming."

Lawrence trotted down the scarp. While he was gone, Shell saw Arthur drop the sapling into the hole and heft the earth in. There was no sunset. There was only the space between the daylight and the darkness.

Lawrence returned. "She's not here."

"Aye, well when she is, make sure you put on a show of it. It's for all of us is this. Wish I had a bloody camera."

Bastard would need far more than a camera.

Arthur firmed the sapling in with his boot heel while

31

Lawrence stood a yard or two away, clicking his fingers. Shell knew her husband sometimes found it difficult to look at their son; that thinking too deeply about fatherhood sometimes made Arthur feel like he was going to fall over. She could see it in the way he stamped at the maple's base now, so decided to put him out of his misery.

"What's big surprise then?" she said, marching over.

The pair started.

"How long you been there for?" Arthur said.

"Just arrived."

"Right on schedule."

"Well, you did say tea time."

Lawrence pointed at the sapling, a reedy juvenile that bent midway and sent its branches into parts. "He's got us this," he said.

Arthur reached for Shell's hand. "A family tree."

"Right."

"Maple."

"For us do you mean?"

"Course us. We'll watch it grow. When we need somewhere to think, we'll come here. It'll watch over us, Shell. Symbolic, like."

Shell took her hand back.

Arthur said, "Lawrence and me planted it."

"I can see that."

"So what do you reckon?"

"Reckon it's a nice idea."

"And?"

"An' what?"

"Well don't you want to give it a once over?"

"I am doing, Arthur. It's a tree."

"Oh, but it's more than that, love. It's—"

"So where'd you get it?" Shell said. This was such a pathetic plan. A try-hard thing to do.

"Bought it."

"Where from?"

"Threndle House," said Lawrence, quietly.

"Eh? No," insisted Arthur.

"Did you?" Shell said. "Because if you did—"

"I didn't, love—"

"Cause if you did, Arthur . . ." Shell's guts bunched. He couldn't. He just *couldn't* have.

"Look, I thought it'd be summat," said Arthur. "Cause we need summat."

"And it is."

"Exactly." Shell's husband moved closer.

"But it doesn't change much, does it?" Shell said, making a point of not looking at Arthur and noticing Lawrence doing the same. "An' don't you think there's bigger things afoot this evening? As they'll likely be calling it tonight."

"Oh come on, love. Cause you've no idea—"

"*I've no idea?*"

"No, I mean can we not just think about summat other than the bloody strike for five minutes," said Arthur. "I just wanted to do summat nice. Not only for us, but for Het and Sam and —"

"Uncle Sam?" said Lawrence. "We don't even know where he went."

"Yeah, well . . ." said Arthur feebly.

"Or what happened."

"Don't you bloody start!"

Shell intervened. Better for the boy to hear about his uncle when the time was right. Some loyalties remained. Pity scars covering what had healed badly.

She said, "Look, it's another nice idea, Arthur. Like I said . . ."

"But, love—"

"*But* tea's on. And Lawrence is cold."

"I'm not."

"You are. And it's getting dark."

There was no denying that. Shell took her son by the arm and began to steer him down the hill. Arthur stayed where he was. His head resembled an un-cracked egg.

"Coming or what?" Shell called back; then, when Arthur didn't reply, said "Ballot, Art. Don't forget."

He didn't reply: he simply tugged a leaf from his tree, and the sadness of the act nearly made Shell run over and throw her arms around him. "I'll see you later then," she called, leaving her husband to become a silhouette. The surrounding countryside was cloaked in blue and a slit of moon glimmered over everything. Shell now knew that somewhere beyond the muddle of homes and lives below her, beyond the ballot, even, was the richness of Threndle House and a hole in the back garden betraying where Arthur had stolen that tree.

Back home, she flicked on the telly; there was nothing worth watching except the news. Shell could stand no more clips of Jack Taylor, so thought about calling a friend, Jan maybe. Then again she wasn't sure she could face anyone. She preferred to do her fretting in private. Tonight was the perfect night for that.

She switched the telly off, and from across the room caught sight of her reflection in the dormant screen, recalling the

34

second time she'd seen Arthur, all those years after she first kissed him down the rec, the two of them leant against one of the concrete posts that held the fence up.

He'd been at The Masons. Older, of course, still appealing. His elbow sported a damp patch and his leather jacket hung on a barstool by his arse. The young Arthur had that loose, knowing expression Shell once mistook for confidence: a manner she now knew was born of a detachment akin to panic, like an animal hiding in the hay at the back of its cage at the zoo.

"Remember me?" she'd said.

"Oh, heck."

"You said you'd be in touch."

"Summat came up."

"For six years?"

"How you doing, love?"

"Don't change bloody subject."

"Let's get you a drink."

"He doesn't even remember my name."

"I'm not daft, Shell. *See*, I remember that smile an' all."

"Tell us summat I don't know."

"Drink?"

"Can tha afford it?"

"Two beers please, pal."

"What gives impression beer's my drink?"

"A man can tell."

"Oh, aye?"

"What you doing with yourself these days then, love?"

"Keeping myself amused."

"I'm down pit."

"Quelle surprise."

Shell could spit to think of herself. Daft and curly bobbed, all half-closed vowels and hoop earrings, pissed-up then coaxed into a knee-trembler by the bins while the band played, married before she even knew what was right for her.

She'd been pregnant so it had seemed like a good idea, and in many ways it had been. Not now. The morning after the wedding, Shell awoke with such a sore throat after all the cigarettes she'd smoked at the reception that she ordered milk with her breakfast at the Grey Grebe Hotel to soothe it. Arthur had borrowed a neighbour's scooter – a wedding favour, he claimed – to chauffeur her. They'd had fried eggs, his hand heavy in her lap while she played with his long hair and frowned at the ring he'd bound her with: a pale band of silver with a stone in it. She'd split her yolks and ate as daintily as she could. The milk furred in a moustache on her lip.

It was getting on for eight, still early. Shell took out an old photo album, searching for the parts of herself that had been lost or irreversibly altered. The album was leather bound and had cream padded pages and a date written in biro on the inside front cover that made her feel old.

She tried to skip the nuptial pictures but inevitably ended up stopping on one: Arthur captured in his brown tux, that yellow tie she'd picked out for him. Booze-grizzled and gap-toothed. Those dated pork-chop sideburns, remember them?

Such a kid. Secret smile. Shell's eyes were shadowed blue and her blustered face was all styled-up. She'd worn droplet earrings that her gran had bestowed. Hiding behind the veil she'd felt so mysterious, covered by a perforated cloth that now reminded her of the net curtains hanging in the fucking kitchen.

More pictures. Lawrence when he was a baby. What a

fidget, frantic clapping. It made Shell feel uneasy, thinking of that, and she wasn't sure why. She closed the book and went to the window-sill. Her cigarettes were buried in their hiding place in the tissue box. She lit one up out of the back door and had just about finished it when she heard footsteps coming along the backs.

"Shell?"

"Who's asking?"

"It's Het."

Shell stopped herself from touching her hair. A moth buzzed past and broke for freedom.

"Arthur's broth—"

"I know who you are, daft bastard."

She still couldn't see him.

"So is he in?" Het said.

"Who?"

"Tha knows who."

"Why?"

"Because he weren't out for ballot, and don't you go making excuses for him."

"Well don't you go telling me what to do on my own doorstep."

Het's voice rose, or perhaps he'd come closer to the house. "Most important night in years and he can't be bothered to show his face. Is he in or what, Shell?"

"No he's not and this is the first I've heard of it."

"And you his wife."

Shell's fist caused the door chain to rattle. She stepped into the yard and said "Het you can either come in or leave off because I'm not standing in the cold while you mither me for something I know nothing of."

Silence followed, the sound of gravel. Shell was about to head back indoors when the latch on the gate clicked and Het faltered into view. He was taller, more broad-shouldered and terse-faced than Arthur. Between his black donkey jacket, his dark hair and the night, Het looked stained by the coal he helped cut from the earth most days. A rubbery burn had scarred part of his neck and jaw and the left tip of his mouth. He touched the scar, as he often did when he was nervous. His hair was slicked to one side, Shell noticed, and that suited him. Everything suited Het.

"Sorry, love. It's just—"

Shell chucked away her dog-end. "Don't need to tell me what Arthur's like."

"I know that. I do."

"An' there's no excuse for talking to me the way you just did."

Het made to turn. "I'm sorry," he said. "You're right."

"Oh, shut up. How are you anyway, stranger?"

"Not bad," ventured Het. "Well, been better . . . in all honesty."

In the kitchen she made them tea. Black with one sugar for him, strong with lots of milk for her. The teaspoon clinked against the plate of Arthur's by now completely defrosted dinner.

"How did it go?" Shell said, knowing the answer, and when Het told her the strike was going ahead, said she was glad. Het accepted his drink and blew it cooler, causing the puckered stain on his neck to stretch. Shell was disappointed when he didn't ask *why* she was glad, because she wasn't really.

"Sorry for just turning up out the blue like this."

"You're all right. Not seen you for an age."

It *had* been a long time. Their unfamiliar reflection was reminder enough of that. Caught within the frame of the window, they could have been in a painting: two people with china mugs, one balancing her chair on two legs, the other interlocking his fingers on the table. Het drank his tea. Shell drank hers.

"Good job it were you at the door," Het said. "I might have cracked him one."

"Wouldn't have been first time."

Het chuckled and emptied the tea into his mouth. It must have been scalding. "You've no idea where he might be?"

"Why do you wanna know?" said Shell, her initial surprise at Het's appearance giving way to her suspicious nature.

"Just do."

"Aye, but since when do you ever pop round for a chat?"

She went to the biscuit barrel, opened it and found nothing inside.

"Already said. He weren't at ballot."

"Aye well our Arthur never turns up to half union shite. And let's face it, he'd skip his own funeral if he could."

"Ah, Shell . . ."

"What?"

Het was smiling. Shell sat in the chair closest to him.

"Nothing, really. You just reminded me of what me mam used to say: there's two kinds of people you don't need to worry about if you've not seen them in an age. Those you can't forget, and those who never change."

"An' which am I?"

"Oh, bit of both."

Het's knuckles were terrific things, like bolts, and Shell was surprised at her urge to reach out and touch them. She pinched her thigh under the table and said, "Well, believe it or not, I have changed. Unlike some." She finally succumbed and touched her hair. "Once upon a time I'd have dragged from you what you wanted wi' Arthur. Now I'm not bothered."

She counted to five in her head.

"I just need to know he's on board with everything," Het said.

"What for?" asked Shell, suppressing a smile. "They're only closing a few pits."

"*Serious?*"

Casual shrug.

"Well if twenty thousand jobs is a few I'd hate to think what a lot is. And what about Cortonwood?" Het began picking at the skin around his fingernails. "Perfectly good pit is Cortonwood."

Shell glanced over the table. Het looked unbelievably weary.

"I just don't understand it," he said.

"TV said only Yorkshire's voted yes."

"Rest'll follow."

"They've changed welfare."

"Union'll sort it."

"Frigging union."

"There's power in a union," said Het. "That's why I'm here, 'cause this is important. I need to make sure our kid's up for it, Shell, as if my own brother's not . . . Well, it doesn't exactly bode well, does it?"

"Never had you pegged as superstitious."

"What I'm saying is if we can get everyone on board we'll be fine. Six weeks and done, tops."

Shell had never seen Het like this. She hadn't seen him in years, really, not since she'd gotten married. Het and Arthur had fallen out after Sam was sent to borstal for putting their father in hospital. And who had Shell been to say anything? She was new to the family, just another woman with an opinion.

Het continued. "They'll back down if everyone stands up," he said, "they'd have to. Shutting working mines, it's a deliberate attempt to provoke us. If a pit's not exhausted or unsafe, it can't be shut, let alone wi'out union say so."

"Sounds like they can and not much anyone can do about it."

"There flaming is."

Smartened-up as he'd never been, Het was finally grinning. A working man, far too proud of it. The grin became a nod as he gestured to ask if he could use the toilet. Shell nodded, then, hand flat against her neck, exhaled loudly as Het left the room. Her stampeding pulse frightened her.

Het returned. Shell couldn't help noticing the damp patches on his cords from where he'd wiped his hands after washing them. Or maybe it was piss, she thought.

"So he'll be down pub?"

"Probably."

"Which ones does he go in?"

"All of them."

The living-room door opened and struck Het in the back. It was Lawrence, dressed in his parka, a red t-shirt and jeans.

"Uncle Het," he said. "What's he doing here, Mam?"

Het stared at Lawrence's head.

"He's after that father of yours," Shell said. "Off out somewhere?"

"After us Dad, Het?"

"Right first time."

"Well, he's not in."

Lawrence stepped properly into the room, spotting his trainers under the coffee table where he'd kicked them off earlier. He went over and began to pull them on.

"I can see that," said Het.

"Er . . . Lawrence?" said Shell.

"He's gone out," said Lawrence to Het.

"All right, Sherlock . . ."

"An' I know where he is."

"What? Where?" said Shell.

"I'll show you, Het. S'where I'm headed."

"You've school tomorrow," Shell insisted.

"This is important," Het said, missing the look Shell gave him. "An' I'll keep an eye on him."

They'd only ignore her if she didn't give permission. Shell watched them bustle outside and hurry towards Het's car. After they'd gone she went to the tissue box, extricated the bobble from her hair and shook her curls loose. The fags were finished so it was back to waiting. The bars of the fireplace throbbed their volcanic orange. She could not forget Het's eyes. She pinched her thigh at the thought of them.

She pinched it as hard as she could.

3

THERE WAS A crusted pattern flecked across Arthur's hand. It was too dark to see, but he could feel it.

And his knuckles hurt when he flexed his fingers. He was lying on the grass, in the countryside or maybe a garden, and the stars studded above him like beads. He was damp all over. He hated the damp.

He sat up to rub the wetter target-shapes on his back. He could taste iron, actually, wasn't as drunk as before but still felt it, and how long had he been bleeding for?

There was the gargoyle, the marker overlooking Threndle House. Arthur groaned, sort-of-remembering resting against the warm metal counter of the chippy, dinner out of a newspaper by the bandstand, then the pub. Always the pub. Front teeth clacking the glass' brim, sprawl of empties in front, alone because everyone else was at the welfare for the ballot. Every hand packed bolting to vote yes.

Every hand except his. Withered rollies and then the shop, pointing over the bloke's shoulder at the serious stuff regimented like bottles in a shooting gallery. Arthur must have come here afterwards, wandering the grounds of Threndle House a firmer prospect than home.

He stood up, drunk. Was that smoke nearby? There could hardly be many fires going at this hour. Likely it was just mist.

The burning rug had made its mark. Arthur kept smelling it, its rank scent summarising his past-its-best marriage, *Eau de Shite*, a staleness such as came out of your hair when you washed it the morning after the night before.

When you still had hair, that was. Arthur circled the house until he felt the uneasy texture of broken glass under his feet. This must be the place, Threndle's façade. One of the two panes of glass in the French doors had a hole in it. Arthur put his finger to the nasty edges. Was this his handy work? It had to be. After all, there was nobody else around.

He whistled. Delicious was the moment. They always were, visceral cigarette burns in the fabric of your day. Twisting the aerial from a car, tipping the bins over on your way home late at night, maintaining eye contact for that extra moment; doing something just for the pleasure of doing it when no one was around to catch you almost outweighed the desperate need to deny everything later on if ever questioned about the act. Arthur crouched. Here was proof of his presence: the neck of a bottle of white rum, broken off, the cap still screwed-on tight.

Now he remembered drinking the last of it, tightening the lid then throwing the empty bottle at the wall. Its detonation had zinged his face just as that coal lump at Brantford had done. Just as the firework had done on the 5th of November, 1957, when Het's unforgettable scream tore through the Yorkshire air, seconds after *The Mighty Atom* blasted out of Sam's hand and struck him in the jaw. Arthur was made to pay for that. He'd bought the fireworks and lit the Atom as Sam held it. "*For a joke,*" he'd wept. "I *didn't mean it.*" His dad's fist impacted on the bridge of his nose anyway.

"Fuck off."

You could talk directly to the past when you wanted to. Arthur dropped the piece of bottle, licked his finger and weighed the options presenting themselves. Go home or go further. Bollocks or brains. Threndle House was the ancestral home of the Brantfords, who owned the pit before the whole industry went up the Litten Path, nationalised. Its windows felt almost unreal as he touched their stone surroundings, although he supposed everything felt a little fake when you really questioned it.

There was a longing inside of Arthur, and what could be done about that? He knew all about futility. All his life he'd done his best, and still he was a disappointment to his son. And as for Shell, thanks would be a fine thing. So they'd loved each other; she'd gotten pregnant. She was the one who wanted to do it all the time and hated rubber johnnies. Not to mention Arthur's father always getting at them, constantly telling them how ashamed he was they weren't married. Alec Newman refused to even look Shell's parents in the eye until their children were wed. Shell didn't have to listen to old Alec like Arthur did. She could have said no when the ring came out. And maybe she ought to have, if this was how she was going to be about it.

Fuck it. He pushed his hand through the hole in the French door's window and reached for the key inside, finding nothing there. He belched, tasted rum, vomit and chips. He'd take a look around like he'd done on the night he found the moth rug. See what having the world on a fork got you. Let a politician be on the end of an executive decision for once. See how they bloody liked it.

He had to kick his way inside. This fucking living room was the size of the whole downstairs of his house, that igloo on Water Street. Everything was cast in blue. Arthur's shadow pushed across the room's cloaked features. He put his arms out

45

so that his shadow looked like it had claws: a monster rising up the wall, sneaking up on the settee and the footstool, the sideboard, the piano, the armchair.

Those French doors had been locked tighter than he'd thought and now his foot was bloody killing him. He limped to the wall and managed to switch on the light, revealing an overcrowded room. Fancy wood with swirls in it. Raised wallpaper, dense carpet, a polished candelabra and cut glass. A large painting was there, too, and loads of boxes were piled up. Stacked and collected gubbins in every corner.

Arthur fixed himself a glass of port. He'd never liked it much but it was the kind of thing people drank in places like this, so he thought he should probably give it another go. He sank to the settee, drink slopping on to the cushions. The trick was to let your eyes close and your thoughts run. It was his mansion, his living-room. There was a gruff dog at his feet and the walls could have been made from wedding cake they were that white. Candles were lit everywhere, too. He'd wear a suit if he lived here. All day, every day. No tweed or worsted. A simple dinner black. The missus would be smiling by the piano. Shell. A younger Shell with bigger tits. Arthur knocked the port back and poured another. It tasted like cough syrup. He picked a candle up and put it down again, sparked it up then ran his finger along its length, into the swamp up top. Wax concealed his fingerprint. It was hot for a couple of seconds and then it was fine.

He opened his eyes. Same old Arthur. Couple of hundred quid a week Arthur. Shouting to make yourself heard Arthur. Sweating your tits off under halogen work lights Arthur. He took another sip of port, eased his shoe off and massaged his aching foot. Pain and swirling troubles were his lot, a life that would one day be lost that he'd never really had chance to start living.

After a while he shuffled into the atrium, stopping at the foot of the stairs to inhale the heavy smell of turps and white spirit. Threndle House felt deserted in the same way that schools do when the children have gone home for the day. In the same way that multi-storey car parks do when dusk falls.

There was a noise nearby that brought him back to Brantford, a persistent scrape similar to those made by the pit mice that first arrived in the hay bales when the ponies of old were still in use. Rodents in the districts, white-furred because they never saw natural light, chewing holes in your fucking butties if you ever made the mistake of putting them down. Arthur fumbled for another light switch, managed to find one and illuminated the hall, to be greeted by an ugly sight. Dust sheets bobbled with scrunches of masking tape were twisted into mad plaits up the floor, while padded fibreglass insulation the colour of intestines and a tabloid newspaper were scattered nearby. There were hunks of rubble and all kinds of detritus. The place was a bloody building site.

Arthur ran a hand along a wall covered by a landscape of part-stripped wallpaper, torn into bladed shapes, serrated peaks. Nearby a radio lay on its side with the battery panel open to reveal it had nothing to power it.

Down went the last of the port, only its rich taste mixed with the smell of turps made Arthur gag. He spat out his mouthful, leaving a thick puddle on the dusty tiles, and looked up to see an old mirror propped against the staircase.

He let the glass tumbler break on the floor, then knelt down so he could blink at his own reflection in the mirror and stick his tongue out, that overworked slab of grey meat.

He opened his mouth as wide as it would go and tensed his head until he could feel the blood in his temples going like the clappers and his face turning a boggling crimson. He used to do this in front of the old bedroom mirror when he was a kid after his classes with Miss Bose. Miss Bose, a retired local teacher who had way too much time on her hands, had been enlisted to help on Wednesday evenings because Arthur had a problem saying his 'S', or as his father put it, problems getting his mouth around what needed saying because he was otherwise satisfied getting it wrong.

Miss Bose's services were paid for in kind: the three Newman boys to help her when she needed something doing. This might be a message delivering, a fence painting, her shopping fetching or her yard weeding. Old bird had aspic in the kitchen: a plate of opaque jelly with a boiled egg in it; pork pies or segments of spam. She devoured the Reader's Digest and eschewed home remedies. She'd once held Arthur's head over a can of tar because she said it would help with his chesty cough.

"New York, unique, unique New York," said Arthur. That was one of the exercises Miss Bose used to have him say, walking from one end of her lounge to the other with an encyclopaedia balanced on his head.

"Red lorry, yellow lorry, red lorry, yellow lorry."

That was another.

He'd hated her lessons at the time. Now he enjoyed thinking about them. He liked to think of Miss Bose. The plastic headscarf she wore, her rouge, the way she scrubbed soot from her front step with a donkey stone and swept the dust from the pavement, feathered her ornaments. With her potted aspidistra and her rose petal perfume, the old lady was a throwback to the energy of the past, to having a future laid out for you, to a time when you didn't have to work in the noise and the hot dark, spending your spare moments at the pub, the library or the moor, thinking often of that Larkin poem from your mam's copy of *The Less Deceived*: 'Spring'. The lines about those the female season has the least use for, seeing her the best of all.

On the wall was a photo collage, a boy and a girl in most of the pictures. The boy was a pretty thing, effeminate. The girl always wore sunglasses, had a face you could never truly make out. This must be the Swarsby children. There they were holding a Labrador puppy. There they were by a sports car and there again in a picture with a pretty woman with hair like pasta twirls, a satisfied man in his forties. Clive Swarsby was in only one of the photos. His arm was around another man, a handsome man, severe hair parted, prissy-looking. Swarsby and this man wore waistcoats, bow-ties, cummerbunds. They were surrounded by mist, or was it rug smoke? Each tilted a conceited face towards the camera.

Blink and you're the wrong side of thirty. Never travelled, soft as shit and one day to be deader than driftwood. There was no point in bloody anything, not even your next breath. Arthur punched the photo collage, breaking the glass, then climbed the staircase of Threndle House. As he went, his hand dripped blood into the port spillage. Not that he noticed. He wouldn't really much have cared if he had.

The upstairs was exactly like the downstairs. Dusty, sparse-ly decorated, Threndle's rooms were either devoid of furniture, character or both. You had to laugh, so Arthur did. He laughed drunkenly through this grand old house.

Eventually he reached the master bedroom, which was as blue as the living room and just as furnished. More boxes were stacked against the walls, three wide, four high. There was a bed, king-sized, and the armchair and linen chest were fancily lined. Velvety drapes, a Juliet balcony, a compact dresser, a set of drawers and more boxes. Fuck me, a bathroom. Arthur had grown up using an outdoor bog.

Standing out on the balcony he smoked a roll-up and disposed of the dog-end, watching the ember nicker away in the wind. Swarsby's bedroom looked like an unpacked set from one of those melodramas his mam used to drag him and Sam to. Aged seven and eight at the Odeon in Rotherham, Sam sitting transfixed, fingers belly-clasped, Arthur tugging the loose threads on the armrests and kicking the backs of the seats in front.

He sat on the bed where Swarsby slept: a father whose family weren't forever looking at him like he was a meal that had gone wrong. When you thought about it, a big house was as good as it got, and it wasn't even that good.

He gripped his knees until he'd composed himself, then went to the dresser, rifling through the drawers for something, *anything*, that he could sell that might make enough money to see out this strike. It wasn't like the Swarsbys didn't have plenty already. And if Shell already thought him a thief, why disappoint her expectations?

A jewellery box was in the top drawer, hidden at the back. It was made of sandalwood, uncarved but well-varnished, and had a copper clasp and a vacant keyhole. Arthur had just stuffed the box up his sweater when two channels of light flashed up the driveway and swept the bedroom. He ducked, swearing, feeling as hollow yet constricted as he did whenever he and Asa descended into the airlock at Brantford, speeding in the cage towards the drift tunnel. He tucked the sweater into the waist of his jeans to trap the box, then crawled out of the room, cursing every light as he made his way towards the stairs. He'd had to turn on, hadn't he? Now the house was lit up like a bloody Christmas tree.

The stairs he took two at a time, pain in his toe forgotten. There wouldn't be much Arthur could say to Shell if he was caught. On the other hand it might give him the chance to tell her that he loved her.

He burst outside and saw another vivid moon. The temperature had dropped and the car's brisk light dominated everything, fog light penetrating the March air.

Too many roll-ups: Arthur had to catch his breath. He could see the lawn stretching beyond him like a great woollen pinafore. He felt oddly weightless, had a mind to walk towards the car now that it had finished parking, actually, both hands held out, ready for the cuffs. He might as well, seeing as between the coal board, the government and his family, the whole world wanted to gut him and part of him wished more than anything that it would get a move on.

"Arthur!"

A figure was standing on the garden wall, hands on its hips. Arthur shrank from it, but in doing so was obliged to edge closer to the car, which had just killed its engine. People were climbing out. "Why are the lights on?" said a girl. She wasn't from around here.

"Daddy, look," said a boy.

Nor him.

"Someone's been inside. You two stay in the car while I go check."

Swarsbys.

Arthur crept over the lawn to where the figure on the wall had been. There was no longer anyone there. He knew it was the only exit point, the same spot he and Lawrence had hopped over the night of the moth rug. He was about to make a break for it when a hand slipped over his mouth. He squirmed. Tried to cry out. Driving an elbow into his captor's torso, he was rewarded with a grunt.

Still he was held fast.

Arthur kicked the man's legs but another arm slid around his belly, somehow missing the jewellery box. He was forced upon the grass and pinned. Lips retreated across teeth. The world was soaking and a strange, cushioned piece of flesh was pressing against his shaven head. A weighted mass dug upon his back.

Arthur knew then who had him: whose hand was exerting the pressure. It was the same hand that had held him when he was a boy, the same hand that had stopped him from setting fire to the old tenterhouse on the hill that time. It was the same hand that had clamped to its howling owner's neck all those years ago.

"Get off, Het. Let us go!"

Then came another voice.

"*Dad.*"

Arthur stopped struggling immediately.

"All right, kid."

"What you doing?"

Het let go. Arthur climbed to his feet, and, seeing that his son and brother had come for him, had never felt so ashamed in all his life. He was going to cry. He couldn't stop himself.

A sob came out.

Het shoved Arthur with both hands. "What the flaming hell!"

Arthur tried to speak. Het had him by the lapels now and he supposed he was in for a right pasting when the car's horn sounded from over the way.

"Dad," the girl called, "they're still out here!"

Arthur pulled himself together and led the others into the shadows as Clive Swarsby appeared in the doorway of Threndle House. A squat man, Swarsby moved nimbly enough back to the car, ordering his son out of the way.

Lawrence's eyes were like two whirlpools, a pair of expiring suns. Arthur felt choked, like he might swoon. He didn't know what to do.

"We need to move," said Het.

There was always that.

The Swarsby's car reversed, its headlights beginning to sweep the garden. Just free from view, Arthur hurried behind Lawrence and Het. He was shame. Recycled fear. His bloody foot was hurting and the lights were in pursuit.

"In here," said Het, disappearing into the undergrowth with Lawrence following. Arthur paused, a few steps behind. Maybe things would be better for everyone if he wasn't around. There had to be better role models for his clever lad. Better husbands for his lovely wife.

He sat on the grass. Above him was the universe, Cassiopeia. Miss Bose had taught him the constellations but that hadn't been enough to keep him from her purse. He'd gone to the tinker fair on her pension, telling himself she wouldn't miss the cash and he could stand the different way she began to look at him, because no one else knew where the handbag was. Only him.

Arthur apologised to the dead woman's ghost and lay on his back with one hand spread over his eyes so that he could peer up at infinity through his fingers. To think of the lambent burning Pleiades up there, to see the first green blazes up in the mystics, a panel of night clear on this evening; he began to cry. Shell didn't want the tree. She thought he'd taken it. Electric blue.

Time passed. A couple of seconds. Then a set of arms slipped under Arthur's armpits and lifted him on to his feet.

"No you don't, you're not getting out of it that easy!"

Het.

Arthur was slapped around the face, twice, three times, then dragged by the wrist through the garden.

The headlights had them. Swarsby was shouting. Arthur ran towards a pale hand that he could see at last, a rescue arm dangling from the wall.

Lawrence.

He raised his arms to seek his son, ready to be hauled to safety.

But the hand disappeared.

"Lawrence," Arthur hissed. "*Kid!*"

4

LAWRENCE KNOTTED HIS tie around his neck and drew it up to his Adam's apple. It felt almost like a noose. He slid his legs into their trousers then put on his blazer. The sole of his shoe was coming away and the tots from over the road were being noisy again. David Cairns was saying goodbye to them, barefoot in his dressing gown, holding a bowl of something. The guy looked pretty pleased with himself. The strike must make a nice little break from work.

Mam was going on about something from downstairs so Lawrence shouted back, voice wavering in that half-broken way that always embarrassed him. He was coming, he called at the door. The bus wasn't due for ten minutes anyway.

Shell pushed into the room and dropped a slice of starkly buttered toast on the desk. "Still need to get a move on," she said, missing the sour face Lawrence made behind her back.

"Am doing," he said.

No reply.

Leaving breakfast to go cold, Lawrence stopped on the landing to poke his head into the spare room where his dad slept these days. Arthur wore a t-shirt, yellow underpants and odd socks. He looked like a huge dolly peg, flat across the inflatable bed, face-down on the settee cushion he used as a pillow. The curtains were open behind him, a cold block of daylight causing the scab on his head to glisten, the smell of last night's booze strung powerfully across the room.

It had been two weeks since that night, the crying, the lying on the grass. Lawrence had tried to forget his own revolting excitement as he ran from the Swarsbys but it had been impossible. He'd giggled, actually *giggled*, climbing up that wall. A moment later Arthur had arrived. Lawrence had been about to help his dad up when he spotted the Swarsby girl wandering into the car's headlights. He'd straightened up to get a better look at her and left his father to scramble up the bricks on his own, then act like it was *him* who'd done something wrong. Cheek of him. Shape of him. A sullen lump in the front seat all the way home. Lawrence entered the room, whipped the cushion from under Arthur and thwacked him around the head with it.

He belted out of the house and down the street towards the sticky sound of wet tyres creeping along the tarmac, managing to catch the bus before it left. He paid the driver and stepped down the aisle, but the empty bus was running later than he was. It jolted off before he'd had time to sit.

The momentum carried Lawrence to the back seat, where he fell against a window. There he watched Litten go by. It was almost as if the town was moving and he was the one rooted to the spot.

It took roughly an hour to get to school, seeing as Arthur had forced him to take the test for Fernside Grammar rather than enrolling at Litten Modern like everybody else. Weeks of coaching it had taken. All those Saturdays doing practice papers, Arthur supervising him with the aid of the answer sheet, sometimes depriving you of dinner if you didn't do well enough.

Despite all the revision everyone was surprised when Lawrence got into Fernside, scraping his maths but coasting

English and verbal reasoning. Arthur was over the moon. He bought the school uniform as soon as it was in stock and had Lawrence parading down the welfare in his blazer and shorts, the brass buckle shoes he'd been assured were in no way girly. Lawrence did what he always did: went along with the decision that was made for him.

Although he was never once asked if he wanted to attend Fernside, and had drifted through the years there. The other kids from his primary school grew up nearby, yet distant, the lifelong friends his dad promised he'd make at Fernside never quite materialising. Lawrence blamed himself. He was easily tongue-tied and overcompensated when he managed to break from his shyness, coming across desperate, insincere or plain weird. He cringed to remember the time he claimed to have a copy of I Spit on Your Grave, the time he said he'd kissed all those girls in town and the time he said he'd met Brian Clough on a day out in Leeds. He could hardly contest the stick he'd got when the truth came out, but supposed it had always been in the post one way or another. All his life Lawrence had attracted mean-spiritedness. He was just one of those people.

The double-decker crawled through Litten. It was an old model, one of those damp shithouses where the foam in the chairs was flat from overuse and someone had ripped the ashtrays from every armrest. The back seat was set in front of the engine and it vibrated whenever the bus stopped, sending a stuffy heat wafting over Lawrence that began to judder him to sleep where he sat.

Litten's dozy outskirts. Hills shaped like upturned basins. Sky-striving trees and smoke-stacks of industry, each of the borough's villages dealt its parade of shops selling pre-sliced bread, canned goods and the local paper. Livestock were herded up these roads and the headgear of the pit was always visible. The gas from Brantford coke ovens stank. Brantford the moody animal, blazing out hair perms of sulphurous gas.

And there was the theatre, now derelict, the sullen rec with its swings wrapped over the top bars, the roundabout covered in scrawled names and a single shoe lying by the slide. All Lawrence wanted to do was escape this place, yet at the same time Litten was home, nothing as comforting as home, all your life knowing it, knowing it as much as you wanted to know what lay beyond home's borders.

The bus turned uphill. The route took it past where Lawrence used to have his paper round, where he'd been sacked for stealing the softcore supplementaries from the tabloids. He had thought he'd never be caught, because what kind of a customer was going to complain to the newsagents that the tit-section from their Sunday Sport was missing? Mr Hayden from the corner house on Dearden Fold, that's who.

"Oi, Antwerp! What's so funny?" called a voice. They were a good way along the route by then and the bus had nearly filled.

Lawrence made a show of being engrossed by the boy opposite. The kid was pulling a clod of gum into a vine and letting it swing from his fingers.

"*Antwerp, you cunt!*"

It was Ryan Fenton and a crony peering across the bottom deck from the stairwell. Through the cobweb of smoke drifting down the gangway, Lawrence could see Fenton's gold earring, his prosthetic-looking head leering cruelly at him.

"Fuck knows what he's laughin' at. His slap head's turning blue in't cold. Here, give us a wave, Antwerp."

Lawrence forced a laugh. Since his head had been shaved, everyone had been calling him *Antwerp* because he was the spit of a Belgian war victim from the history text book. It was Regis' fault. The silly twat had nodded and smiled when it was first mentioned in class, and that legitimised everything. Now thanks to a clueless history teacher and a pair of warring parents, Lawrence was stuck, singled out in a way he couldn't lie or joke his way out of.

People were looking – he was going to have to respond. "Blue head?" he called down the bus. "It's March not Christmas, you pricks."

There were '*ohs*' from the people within earshot. Ryan Fenton's face dropped as he shoved through the crowd towards Lawrence, the whiteheads on his forehead livid, mouth parting like a badly-sliced chicken fillet.

Lawrence was preparing to spring over the seats in front when the bus intervened, swerving around a corner and throwing anyone on their feet to the other side of the aisle. He darted from his chair, feeling a hand cuff him around the head as he went to stand by the driver. An *Antwerp, give us a wave*, chant followed him; it was taken up by the entire bus. "That you they're on at?" said the driver. Each hand sported a hazy tattoo of a swallow.

"No," said Lawrence. "I don't know who they're on about."

In part, Fernside Grammar looked like a medical complex. Flat-roofed and monochrome, the new blocks were divided into conjoined buildings, blank windows dividing up the wall space. The old building was mossy and spired. It had a bell tower and a munificent stained glass window, the school insignia carved into a cornerstone above the main entrance. Its approach was a steep wind tunnel with a shaking school sign. The pupils headed under the sign through the main gates. They buttoned and held their blazers, shrieked through the double-doors to seek shelter.

First lesson was Food Tech, and they were making Shepherd's Pie. Lawrence perched on a stool in the kitchen classroom while his teacher, Miss Potts, demonstrated how to chop onions. Cookery was better than CDT and metalwork, which were taught in the winter and summer terms respectively. With cookery you got a second tea, which was usually devoured cold on the bus home.

This was a low ability set and it wasn't difficult to see why. Lawrence always ended up with the duds. Miss Potts had tears in her eyes, her slender fingers gripping the chef's knife, onion peelings littering the table like pencil shavings. The sleek way her lips formed, they could have been made of clay. Lawrence imagined being asked to stay behind after the lesson; it wouldn't take long for total concession to ensue, Miss Potts gasping acceptance. The fantasy was getting really interesting when a paper ball rebounded off the back of his head. He turned around and there was Ryan Fenton, grinning at him.

Merry Christmas Slap Head

"Merry Christmas yourself," Lawrence muttered, scrunching the note up and sweeping it to the floor.

After the demonstration the class busied themselves. Lawrence had asked for cookery money but his mam had insisted on getting the ingredients in herself, providing him with a wrap of mutton, most of a turnip and a can of haricot beans instead of lamb, carrots and peas. A pot of Smash instead of real potatoes.

Lawrence smuggled his meagre lot onto the counter and hid it under a tea towel. Some other items were also missing, of course, so he put his hand up to summon Miss Potts, who grabbed the nearest pupil, Ryan Fenton, and asked him if he could share his ingredients. All Lawrence needed was the stock and garlic.

Fenton duly disappeared, eventually returning with two miniscule cloves of garlic and a mighty blob of orange powder, poorly wrapped in foil. The stock was damp for some reason and smelled bizarre, but Lawrence set it by his other ingredients and set to work.

When the time came, the class stood waiting for Miss Potts to emerge from the store cupboard. She had a habit of lingering in front of a symmetry mirror she'd taken from the maths department and blu-tacked to the wall in there. Lawrence listened to her blasting hairspray all over her head as he secured the tea towel across what remained of his cheapo ingredients. He knew he'd used too much water in his pie, so had added cornflour as an afterthought to thicken the sauce. The turnip meanwhile had been diced so thickly that it had been just about all he could fit on the tines of his fork.

Miss Potts appeared with a dessert spoon and a clipboard with a pen on a string sellotaped to it. She patrolled the rush of cooling ovens, tasting and grading each crackling pie until she came to Lawrence's steaming creation. Hands guarded by oven-gloves, she lifted the Pyrex dish from the worktop, nose hovering above the puttering grey bubbles, then, like an oar delving into a shifting swamp, slid her worn metal spoon beneath the pie's crust.

The spoon lasted perhaps five seconds in the teacher's mouth. Miss Potts began to gag, retching, until, overcome, she hunched over the worktop and coughed out a brown gobbet of pie that shuddered and caught the glare from the striplights in the polystyrene-tiled ceiling.

Nervous laughter began to concuss the room. Everyone was looking as Miss Potts hurried to the sink, filled a glass of water, drank it in one, re-filled it and then drank some more.

"How much *spice* was in that concoction?" she said to Lawrence after she'd collected herself.

"Spice, Miss?"

"*You heard me.*"

"I don't know."

Miss Potts stared.

"Honest, Miss, I don't know!"

There was no time for a reply. Ryan Fenton lunged forward, reaching over Lawrence's station and tearing the towel from what was left of his ingredients. "Antwerp's been on the rations," Fenton cried, presenting the empty stock wrapper to the rest of the class. "An' they stink of fuckin' chilli!"

The whole room erupted. Fenton began to prance about, declaring that *Antwerp's Spicy Smash and Mutton Pie* should be served in the canteen. He had the Smash tube and began waving it in Lawrence's face, so Lawrence leapt for it, accidentally colliding with Miss Potts and sending her stumbling against the worktop, where she knocked his pie onto the floor. The precise shatter of the Pyrex dish finally silenced the room.

Miss Potts made to seize Lawrence but in her haste stepped in the mess and slipped, her foot crunching sideways in the broken glass. She wailed, prone on her back, her lovely hair draped in pie muck. The shock in her eyes was terrible.

Lawrence took one look at the bloody spur of bone jutting free of her ankle and pelted from the room, his loose sole slapping the corridor tiles until he'd reached the main doors and, past them, streets of safety. He could see in his mind the Litten Path. It was a steep finger of stones leading to the moor.

No one would find him in Barnes' Wood, the forest adjacent to Litten Hill. Lawrence crossed the road, skipping between a minibus and several cars packed with men who were probably on their way to a picket somewhere.

Down the scuffed trail, into the forest. Visible through the rafter of branches was the hill, home of the maple Lawrence had helped plant, which should have bedded in by now, its flimsy leaves riddled by the wind's sough, its root-work probing the soil's depths. The family tree had been a nice enough idea but something about the more forceful of Lawrence's parents not giving the gift her backing had made him shrink into himself. He'd left Arthur hanging.

Course he hadn't explained why. Since that terrible surrender at Threndle House, he and his father had hardly spoken. Arthur just tended to sit now, smelling of carbolic soap and stale smoke, often falling asleep on the settee. He never wanted to *go over it all again*, grazed knuckles lifting as he toked another cigarette in the yard, falling again as he reached down to ease the rolled-up newspapers from the legs of his jeans. Shin-kickers, Mam explained, placed there to protect a man from the policemens' truncheons because the officers hit the picketers low, partly so the cameras wouldn't see.

The ground set damp into Lawrence's damaged shoe. This route was silent, broken only by his footsteps, by a wood pigeon startled amid the greenery. He arrived at the River

Ogden, a weak tributary coursing under a scratched metal bridge that had once been painted red. Lawrence climbed the short path to the bridge and paused to look at his reflection in what remained of the river. The woods' tapering branches were mirrored in the water, which had a musty smell. It looked as if there were rips in the liquid, in the sky.

Lawrence picked up a lolly stick and pushed it through the railings into the torn river, where it span gently before catching against the stony bank. He was a veteran of this place. With no friends, a mother glad to have him out from under her feet and a father who never asked questions, this wood was a refuge, a warren of dens within rhododendrons and bogs to sink rocks in; whole patches of puff fungus to kick about and wasps' nests within ruins to provoke. He came to this latticed glade to climb trees. He came here to vandalise things, to swim when the Ogden was high enough and spy on passers-by.

There was no time for any of that now. With the day fast escaping, Lawrence stepped from the bridge, opting for the slope rather than the path, but the incline was too steep and he lost his footing.

He slid downhill, coming to a sharp halt at the bottom. Shoes sunk in the mud, trousers shit-covered and cuffs wet, he lay awhile watching the leaves twist. It would be simple to let this day and all that had come with it slide away. You could do that in a place like this, at least until nightfall. You could probably do it until tomorrow, come to think of it, given that this was an area Lawrence knew well, never mind how long it had been since his last visit.

Two years? Three? There was a forgotten path over the way: a corridor of wild garlic and native bluebell, a ginnel of promise bordering upon the secret. The vernal trail led to a sanctuary Lawrence long thought he'd outgrown; a tree cave formed in the space beneath a cavernous old elm. He got to his feet and headed towards it, a curious excitement flourishing within him. It was as if something neglected was at long last being attended to.

He quickly reached the den and sensed its magic. Spreading its boughs in the clearing's centre was the magnificent tree. It had grown so unimpeded by any obstruction that its crown now resembled a giant brain. The elm's trunk had a split in it wide enough for a man to hide in; fat limbs veered towards the ground like tentacles, dividing here and there, creating crevices to perch in, while afternoon light filtered through the canopy, shading everything by turns a vibrant and sombre green.

Lawrence trailed his hand along the tree's bark, stopping to hang from a branch and lift his legs. The den was surprisingly neat and well-ordered and the fallen log he'd once used as a bench was still here, too.

But someone else had visited. There were the traces of a spent fire and past the ring of dumped blocks surrounding that broad scab of char, a second tree had been painted in pink and blue stripes. Scraps of ribbon and tattered bunting were strung from this tree, linking to the huge elm. Girls must have been here: interfering strangers.

Lawrence dropped to the ground and brushed the gunk off his hands. Now he could see empty beer cans and a take-away box, the remains of what looked like a glass pipe, the transparent bowl stained black. A basic shelter had also been erected. He went over to investigate.

It turned out to be a wrinkled tarp hanging from the trees by a thin cord. Underneath it was a plastic chair, orange, the kind with easily-bent metal legs that you found in factories or warehouse offices. Next to the chair was a blanket with a book on it, face-down, resembling a miniature paper tent. Cigarette butts, too: fag ends everywhere. A ball of cling-film lay next to the book, together with a half-eaten packet of crisps.

Lawrence picked up the crisps. He hadn't eaten all day and cheese and onion were his favourite flavour. He took the book and read the first lines it opened at.

You don't need to tell me what's right and what ain't right. Whatever I do is right, and what people do to me is right. And what I do to you is right, as well. Get that into your big 'ead.

He was about to set the book down without losing his place when a voice made him jump. He dropped it.

"Something funny?"

Beyond the decorated tree stood a girl. She was thin and had green eyelids. A twitch of her mouth told Lawrence that losing her page had not gone unnoticed.

"Taste good, do they?"

"No."

"I'm sorry?"

"Yeah, I mean I like them."

"I suppose you weren't laughing either."

Lawrence shook his head.

"You were smiling."

"That's." Lawrence hesitated. "That's not the same as laughing."

She was about his age. She had bare shoulders and a flat midriff, shoulder-length auburn hair with a fringe and a strikingly angular face. She was attractive in the way that a mantelpiece is attractive; the kind of face you had to try not to find haughty.

"I were just looking," Lawrence said.

"And eating the last of my lunch," replied the girl, sitting on the blanket and returning to her novel.

That accent – it had to be the Swarsby girl. She was a very different prospect up close. The other night she'd been graceful. Now Lawrence could see a shaving rash speckling her shins and thigh bruises that could have been made by someone's thumbs. She was a lot like him: bone pale, bug-eyed and spindly.

"You're hovering," she said.

"Oh. Sorry."

Lawrence didn't move. He wondered what the girl would say if she knew he'd been in her garden the other night, that he'd seen her glowing.

"Some people might interpret hostility as a sign to leave."

Lawrence laughed as good-naturedly as he could. "This is my den you're in."

The girl rested her book against her knee. "Own it, do you?"

"Well, no . . ."

"Does it say *property of scrawny oik* somewhere? I must have missed the sign."

"There's no sign."

"No shit."

"I didn't mean . . ."

"What?"

"Oh, nowt."

"*Nowt*," the girl muttered, aiming her green eyelids at her book.

"Made a friend?" said a second voice. It was a boy, aged maybe a year or two younger than the girl. He was watching Lawrence with a tremendously open expression. He was more conventionally attractive than his sister, but he had a similar lofty bearing.

"Don't mind Evie. She's down on everyone," he said.

"Every*thing*," said Evie.

"It's a great spot."

"Den I found a bit ago," said Lawrence.

"Yes," agreed the boy, making such a sincere kind of eye contact with Lawrence that he felt uncomfortable. It was like gazing into the eyes of those Jehovah's Witnesses that had come to the door that time.

"How old are you?" the girl asked.

"Sixteen."

"And still you're calling it a den."

Lawrence didn't know what else you'd call it. Evie plunged a hand into her brown leather bag, the strap of which was slung over one shoulder.

"Seb," she said. "*Tell* me you've got some."

A pack of cigarettes sailed through the air and landed in her lap.

"Don't call me Seb," the boy said.

They both lit cigarettes.

"You know it suits you."

"It's not my name," the boy explained to Lawrence, who could feel the spring warmth of this daydream on his neck.

"Duncan's all wrong," said Evie, "It's too Scottish. Too matter of fact."

"And Seb?" replied Duncan, shaking his head.

"Is way more you."

Duncan began to smoke. He seemed to enjoy being talked about. By contrast, Lawrence felt conscious of his muddy uniform and bald head. It was that first encounter feeling: never making the impression that you wanted to make.

"There's two things you should spend money on," said Evie to Lawrence. "Beds and shoes. Because if you're not in one you're in the other."

She nodded at his feet.

He tucked them beneath himself. "I expect you want me to say summat clever to that."

"It might be nice."

"Well I won't dignify you."

"I'll dignify myself, thanks. Maybe we can start with something easier, if your filthy shoes have stumped you. What's your name, Mr Den? Mr-I'm-not-in-school-when-I'm-supposed-to-be?"

Antwerp.

Lawrence almost said it, and realising this must have made his face change, because the girl seemed to think he was laughing *with* her.

"My name . . ." he said, trailing off.

Fucking tongue-tied again.

"Where have we moved to, Seb," said Evie, "That the locals don't even know their own names."

Lawrence could feel an excruciating heat flushing up his neck. "Lawrence," he said. "I'm Lawrence."

"Duncan." The boy pointed at himself.

"You said."

"All right, clever clogs," said Evie. "Why aren't you in school?"

She had raggedy hair that somehow managed to shine:

Lawrence had never seen hair like it. "I can't be bothered with it, can I," he said.

Evie grinned.

"I'm at the grammar," Lawrence continued, sure his windpipe was thickening. "Top sets. Too many rules, though. Place is full of wankers."

"And you live nearby?" Duncan asked.

"Kind of."

"We're on the edge of town."

"Bleak fucking House," said Evie.

"I suppose you mean Threndle," Lawrence said.

"Place is practically derelict."

Was that the trace of an apology in her voice?

Evie went on. "There's like three rooms with things in them. The rest of our stuff's in storage."

"Still a mansion."

Lawrence began to scuff a circle in the ground with his finger.

"It's our Uncle Bram's place," said Duncan.

"He's not our uncle, Seb."

Duncan gazed coldly at his sister, then turned to Lawrence, "He hasn't lived there for years. It was supposed to be renovated before we came, only the builders are local. They found out who Dad is and downed tools." He rolled his eyes. "*Honestly.*"

"How come?" It was tiring having to ask questions you knew the answers to.

Evie began fashioning a triangle from the crisp packet. "You're rather nosey, Lawrence."

"Dad's an MP," Duncan said. "Or at least he's trying to be. And not for the party of these parts." He made a curious face, earnest yet somehow staged, as if he'd copied it from someone and was trying to perfect it. "What does your father do?"

"Oh . . . He's a businessman."

"Same as Clive," said Evie.

"Dad's not in business," said Duncan.

"The business of numero uno," Evie said, then to Duncan, "Oh, shut up."

"Why do you call him Clive? You two not?"

"What?" Evie blew a smoke ring. She had a biggity look in her eye.

"Brother and sister?"

"What gives you that idea?"

"Dunno. You talk same," said Lawrence. "Hold yourselves same. Open like."

"*Errrpen*," Evie mimicked. "What's *errrpen*?"

"Just similar." Lawrence blushed for the second time. "I thought—"

"For your information Seb and I met on holiday and now I've come to live with him. He's a *serious* fuck."

"Serious?"

"Oh, yes. He likes to take me from behind. You like doing it from behind, don't you, Seb?"

"You think you're so hilarious," said Duncan.

"No, I don't . . ." Lawrence began, anxious not to lose ground.

"*Nerrr*," Evie went.

"I'm talking to her," said Duncan. "We're brother and sister. The only way I'd put up with her is if I had no choice."

"Right. Sorry. I knew it . . . like I were saying, I guessed, but you can never be sure when you've just met someone, can you," said Lawrence. "If they're who they seem to be."

"And not just when you've first met them," agreed Evie, placing her hand on Lawrence's knee. "I still don't know who my parents are and I've known them my whole life."

Lawrence was elated. He was not someone girls spoke to. He was not someone girls touched.

"I know the feeling," he said.

Evie removed her hand. The way she lit her cigarette, flame angling as she sucked, made Lawrence's toes curl.

Duncan stood up and patrolled the bunting line. "So what do you think of our improvements?"

"They're brill," Lawrence lied.

"Took us a long weekend. We've a lot of those at the moment."

"How come? I mean why's that?" Lawrence glanced at Evie, who'd covered her face with her novel and was lying flat on the blanket.

"Well Evie pretty much just has her exams, and I haven't enrolled anywhere yet. Dad says I'll be off to the West Ridings come September, if things don't go to plan. Or back in London if they do. Till then we're to be home-tutored."

Evie blew a raspberry under her book.

"Suppose it's nearly summer. End of school," Lawrence said. "Would be daft starting somewhere just to leave."

"And let's face it," said Evie, "Clive wouldn't send his darlings to any of the schools around here."

"Why, what's up with them?"

"*What's oop wi' 'em?*"

Lawrence got to his feet. "Here, I know what I sound like, reight. But I'm not the one, it's you who's the new ones. You who sound weird."

"Jesus, I only meant our dad wouldn't just send us *any-where*," said Evie.

"This isn't anywhere."

"Lawrence, that's exactly what it is."

It was funny. Although he was himself allowed to criticise where he came from, the moment someone else cast aspersions upon Litten, Lawrence's hackles rose.

"Oh, darling. Have I offended you?"

"Would it bother you if you had?"

Evie was at last studying him with genuine interest. Only a minute ago, her hand had been on his knee.

"I said would it bother you?"

"No, it wouldn't."

"Well doesn't matter then, does it?"

Duncan offered a round of applause. "Well if you ask me, Evie, I'd say Lawrence has got the measure of you!"

5

A TOTALLED CAR rolling down the hill, a dot-to-dot of blue heads scattering from it. It was fun seeing the silver badges flashing the other way for once, helmets wobbling as the pigs fled. "Bobby's on fucking bob," shouted someone, but Het didn't answer. He was concentrating on the smoke, hoping he wouldn't reach it before the car went up.

Lorries were around the corner and before them was the soon-to-be-torched car the picketers had sent to block the road. "You're a genius, lad," said Chris Skelly, and Het laughed, though he certainly didn't feel like laughing.

Nottingham coalfield. Tan yellow grass country. Fossil grey sky country. The Notts pits were refusing to back the action. Little wonder they'd stuffed things up: a scab county, always had been. Half the pits here were built by scabs during the strike of '26. Better paid, better-equipped scabs. Notts had bought every lie, hook, line, sinker and bait box, yet again finding themselves on the wrong side of flaming right.

Ollerton, where that lad had died a few weeks ago, was scab built. Hit by a brick, they said. Crushed, more like. Het had seen the picket. Now at Tyndale it was how it had been at Ollerton. Kicked off the minibus, police boarding, pointing their batons in your face, telling you to *fuck off*, turn back, just the same.

They were escorted up the M1, accompanied by the police

like flaming royalty over the county line. After that Chris drove them five miles north, stopping at the motorway services to buy a local map so Het could navigate them back south into Notts along the sneak roads, past Bolsover, where they parked the car and supped a recharge in a local pub. The landlord opened early for them. A key in the door and a sympathetic smile for a bloke from scabbing Mansfield.

"You're all right, lads. Come in."

They walked the rest of the way to Tyndale, an hour's yomp through fields that quickly became marsh thanks to a hidden sike that flowed downhill, soaking all their feet. Het was in his element. It was early doors so everything was bathed in that magnificent morning light that crispens up the natural outlines. The cloud was rising from the arrowgrass the way it did on the coated moorland when you walked the Litten Path. *Summer Geese,* his dad used to call it, because of the shapes the steam made when it was evaporating into nothing after there'd been rain on a hot day.

They joined the picket late, them and a few others, some stopping at the shop to get a few tinnies in then singing their way through the housing estate. It was good crack, although it was a different story now Het found himself running behind a timebomb, the winder and shaft at Tyndale dreadful against the sky. Het saw in that fretwork and turning wheel a nightmare, and he hoped he wouldn't end up like Davey Jones of Ollerton.

At the bottom of the hill the police regrouped. According to some local scrotes watching the mounting protest from a street corner, the burning car had been a scab motor. Some of the other Brantford lads agreed it was parked way too close to the pit to be anything but, so they trashed it, tore the radio out and slashed all the seats. Het tried to stop them and was told to *fuck off* for the second time that day. He redeemed himself once the perpetrators had moved on, mind you, hitting on the idea of using the wreckage to stop the lorries. His idea had been to simply roll the car, flaming Arthur's had been to stuff a rag soaked in zippo fluid into the fuel cap for good measure, sparking it with a clipper as it went.

How Het had let himself be talked into that, he didn't know. He cursed as the makeshift fuse did its work, yelping at the blossoming explosion, a popped balloon of orange that roared into the sky and lit the trees, those pine trees, the grainy-looking midlands way beyond him.

All heat bursts were a reminder of *The Mighty Atom*. Het was a good twenty yards behind this particular blast, yet still close enough to feel it, the scorch as good as all over him, reminding him of the stink of burnt hair, the feel of his hand sticking to the raw jelly of his neck where there was no more skin. Thankfully this time the glare disappeared, folding in on itself as opposed to all over his life.

The car was propelled over a cleft in the hill. It dive-bombed onto its nose like a paper aeroplane, rolled towards the road and came to a stop, burning.

That got everyone's attention.

A group of policemen gathered at the hill's base, beyond the burning car, in front of the thoroughfare leading to the pit gates. Het ran at them. So did everybody else. Nothing was more important than stopping those turncoats getting the scab coke. They had to stop the Judases from getting in.

Police faces blurred by heat; a line of linked arms, faceless golems at least three men deep. Het navigated the blockade as the toxicity of the car became a hindrance. He ran towards the pigs; he was really shouting. Boots on the grass. Everyone at it. Voices of hundreds of wronged and angry men.

Scabs. Scabs. You're all just fucking scabs.

The police shouted back. *Fucking come on then.* They steeled themselves, expressions mashed. The lot of them brandished truncheons.

This was the part. This was the moment. Long legs always meant Het arrived first. He ploughed into the police line, waxy head butting into them. Arthur was a few yards away doing the same thing: a brother who he'd forced into this. Plague a beautiful woman like that? Set such examples to your son? All right, an oddball but still a son. A son who didn't deserve the selfish dad he'd been landed with.

The other night Het had driven them all back from Threndle House in the Austin Maxi, switching the radio on because it meant no one would have to talk, Frankie Goes to Hollywood careening out of the speakers; the three of them laughing before going quiet again.

They parked outside Arthur's terrace, then while Lawrence was inside checking to see if Shell was awake, Het told his brother how it was going to be. Arthur was going to back the strike like the rest of them. Every picket. Every protest. Every rally. Do some good for a change. Fight for everyone's livelihoods and stand up for himself. Arthur was coming on picket because Het said so.

Het said, "I want to see you do what's right. I want you to set an example."

"And you'd know all about that."

"I'm serious, Art. You're coming on strike proper."

"Or what?"

"Or I go to the police about tonight."

77

How quickly that bald head turned. *Snap.* Outlined distinctly against the misted window.

"You serious?"

"Like what I said—"

"Fuckin' heard you the first time."

Silence. Arthur drew a curt rectangle shape on the glass with his finger. Several choice flicks turned the rectangle 3-D.

"Look, I'm sorry," Het began. "But this is important . . ."

"Save it. I'll do your dirty work for you, Het, if that's what you want."

"It's not that. That's not it . . ." Het said, trailing off. Their father's flippant malice ran through Arthur and he had never known how to deal with it.

Arthur rubbed the window clean and stared through it, all bruised nobility, acting as if the night's thieving and embarrassment hadn't just happened. "Not what?" he said. "Tell us what it's not."

Het kept it buttoned. Lawrence would be back soon, a nephew who'd already been through one of life's traumatic rites of passage that night, witnessing, as all sons one day must, the moment when their father humiliates themselves in front of them, becomes flawed, fallible, just a man.

Although there had been plenty enough to say and always had been. Because people might like Arthur, they might find him relatable, laugh at his jokes and invite him out on the town . . . that didn't mean for one second they had any idea what being around someone like that was actually *like*. Because all Het's life the bookies had backed the other horse, and all Het's life he couldn't help but wonder how Arthur had got the sweet deal he had. For pity's sake, if Het's scars had been on his body, he wouldn't have minded so much, but the face?

You just couldn't get away from it. The thing about scars is they don't just scar your skin, they scar your confidence, too. Damn near take it away altogether.

Decades spent shying away from cameras. Often, just when Het thought he'd gotten used to how he looked, he'd catch sight of himself a certain way and be reminded all over again of the deformity splashing up his neck and jaw, punctuated by a full stop and a dash, scarified blotch marks on the chin and lip from where the larger bits of plastic had melted on him.

It was no wonder he was always losing his temper. Firework face, dry eyes that felt like they had sand beneath the lids, too much heaviness at the stomach and unwieldy hair he had to lash with wax to do anything with; he ran into the police and he hid himself. He pushed at the cops until he fell over and he got back up again because he was tall enough and he could manage it.

Thinking back to Water Street as you did so. Recalling the silence of your car, sat with your brother, wishing you could trade places with your nephew, because to watch the sleepy peace emanate from Shell; maybe she'd wake and see you, not your face, never that, but your outline, your strong, work-built, toil-hewn frame . . . Het fought for breath. The problem with things you couldn't have was that you could have them if you really put your mind to it, and that made it so much worse. The front door of Arthur's house had seemed to bow with all that resided on the other side of it. It was all Het could do to avoid shoulder-barging through it. Instead he'd shifted in his seat and peeled at the *no smoking* sticker plastered to the inside of his car window, an action which caught Arthur's attention.

"You've a no smoking sign in your car," Arthur said, "an' you don't even fuckin' smoke."

"I'm sorry?" Het said, when indeed he'd heard. He polished his glasses on the front of his shirt, his reflection way too visible in the lenses.

Arthur laughed. "I were just saying—"

"But you'll join us on pickets. You'll make it count."

Arthur sighed, looked at his lap. "Fine, fuck off then," he said, then exited the car, missing Het's apology that was delivered to thin air.

"*I'm sorry.*"

It was no use. As the lights ticked on in the house, Het sped away, vowing to make a good egg of his brother, a man according to the terms set out for them when they were boys. No crying. No mucking about. Be as honest as the day is long and be good to your wife. Be good to the woman in your life. Het would do that. Do it for Shell. Make Arthur play ball just like he'd been made to all his life. Het Newman, eldest hero, told from day one that his brothers looked up to him, never mind whom *he* had to look up to. For who's an eldest son with an abrupt father to turn to when it comes to the business of making your way in a world you don't understand, in a life you didn't ask for but were given anyway?

The police were so many, and such force. It took a certain kind of person to become a police officer. Some good, certainly. Something else too.

Het pushed and leaned into the ruck because they were them and he was him and that line was made to be crossed. A hand bashed his nose, blood trailing down his septum and reaching his mouth. The first lorry was trying to get through. It was nearly at the gates and would have gotten into the compound if it weren't for the picketers. Chris Skelly was saying something but the scrum was too frantic and he was pushed from sight. Het could hardly breathe. Men upon men. Pushing the line and pushing it and the batons reaching in and striking you and pushing it and pushing it and hitting back if you can and pushing some more, trying to get to the lorries and with a yell unleashing that word.

Scab.

Men were being dragged out. Tall Het saw above everyone's heads, these men dragged into the vans. Dogs barked on the outskirts of the ruck and the lights from the police cars flashed a febrile blue, for all the good that did. The day was warm. It was a pleasant afternoon in May. Normally Het would be finishing the early shift about now, off for his crossword and an ale down the welfare and maybe a turn around the dell where the alder leaves hissed and turned, catkins like tresses of hair, hanging ready for the wind to take. But not today. Not in these parts, in this England or in this life.

Feeling faint, he fought for space. Beyond him was the cab of the front lorry. In it sat a driver crossing another picket, a non-union man, probably getting double or triple wages for a job like this, bribed by the government because they wouldn't stump up the cash to keep a few pits open but it didn't matter what it cost to be rid of them.

The guy had a dark moustache and curly hair. He could have been any one of them, so Het beseeched him, on his mind all who were opposing him, everyone he knew and so many he didn't. "*Please stop your truck!*" he cried. "*Please stop your truck, you bloody idiot!*"

The lorry crawled on.

Police reinforcements arrived to force the picket away, and as Het was driven from the pit gates along with everybody else, he despised the man in that lorry for thinking he was any different, for thinking he and the rest of the scabs wouldn't be as for the chop as everybody else when the time came.

More sirens. Here in the midlands the sun seemed to hang deeper and burn with an intensity Het had never known before. It was a government masterstroke to split the industry on closures. They couldn't divide the miners on wages – that had only united them in the past. They were doing it by allegiance instead. Shut a few pits – not all – stockpile as much British coal as possible then import extra from Poland, Australia and Colombia, break the miners' support structures by tweaking the Social Security Act to reduce the welfare payments for the families of the men on strike, pay guns for hire like that driver, bribe anyone daft enough into rolling over by offering them early redundancy pay-outs and somehow keep the midlands working. Not forgetting the police: the nation's forces had been mobilised into an enormous army.

In the crowd he had to admire it. He played football with Sandy Coates and Mick Halsall, the union reps at Brantford. He had their ear. They'd been to Silverwood, the regional strike HQ outside of Rotherham, and later told Het straight. "They've come back to do us," said Mick. "After '72 and '74. They stitched us up to do us proper. But it's Tyndale this week so you and that brother of yours get down wi' rest of the lads an' try an' do some good."

Four white vans screeched signatures into the gravel. Their doors *ker-clunked* and men burst out, this lot in riot gear. The wrecked car was burning and the smoke, the smoke, the smoke.

The squadron waded in, landing blow after blow until the picketers fell away and the rest of the lorries roared into the compound. It was the sort of thing Het saw on his pro-grammes about the crusades, today's skirmish tracing its lineage back to days when battles were won with swords and arrows rather than fists and stones, before bomber jackets and bovver boots; before bricks were thrown.

A policeman loomed into view. "Get back! Fucking get back!" he screamed, clad entirely in body armour. He swung a baton at Het, who was wearing only a t-shirt, blue jeans and his 'Save the Pits' badge.

Now Het thought himself a brave man. His mother had told him he was brave plenty of times, especially when she found out about Dad and the other woman, when Het took her to one side and told her what she needed to hear: her sons loved her, she was important, strong and kind, all the things old Alec had forgotten. But here was a beating and who wouldn't be afraid of that?

He ran, hearing the officer's jeers. He could hardly take exception to them, because what kind of a leader runs? A craven one, that's who. A big man who'd never had his way and was scared of what he'd do if he ever got it.

Shell.

Het made it to the hill. Some lads had broken a wall apart and were using the debris as missiles. Rocks and stones soared overhead, chunks of mortar and nasty bits of car and wind-screen, all other kinds of rubbish. Het spun round and headed back towards the melee, where it felt safer, in time to see a policeman take the full force of something to the brow. The socket above the man's eye was badly caved, blood leaking like a paint splash down his face.

"You all right, lad? You all right?" Het said, skidding to his knees beside the wounded officer. No one liked to see a thing like that. But another officer arrived and smashed Het on the elbow with his baton.

"Leave off him, cunt."

Het clutched at the pain and watched the wounded policeman being dragged away. He and the injured man gazed at one another, nothing really to be said.

Projectiles. A police charge. Now, as the picketers' defeat seemed likely, Het spotted his brother, Arthur, reaching out and stealing a policeman's helmet off his head.

And Het laughed because it was Arthur, Arthur through and through, and Arthur was laughing too, only the policeman didn't find it funny. He struck Het's brother savagely in the face. "Have that then." Then he snatched the helmet from the ground as Arthur was sent spiralling back into the crowd.

Het had almost reached his brother when something stopped him. How would Arthur react? Retreat and save himself, as Het had just done? Or something else entirely?

As if he needed to ask. Arthur re-appeared, staggering wildly in the direction of his assailant. Het was there in seconds, and having been halted, Arthur lost the will to fight, he and Het propping each other up, Het jealous of Arthur's strength, his brother's will to act when he had practically wet himself. It was then that he saw the difference between them, the push and pull of each personality. And what would their father have said, had he been here to witness this? What would Sam say, come to think of it, after all the ugly things Het had called him? He'd been no good that day, full of fear, all his life standing because he was scared to be seen sitting down. Great gusts of shame filled his lungs. "Get off," he said to Arthur, unable to bear the comparisons orbiting in his mind. "Let go." But he was the one doing the holding and his brother's face was a mess.

"Knuckle duster," Arthur said, leaning against Het and bleeding against his shoulder.

"Worst it's been. I'm telling you that's worst I've seen it."

Het was down the welfare. A few others who'd been at Tyndale were also present, but mostly the room, decorated by banners from beams and lodge icons and portraits hanging on the walls, was dead quiet.

Het paid for his drinks and returned to where Shell was waiting, her hair tied back, wearing that sideways expression that always made her seem like she was remembering something from long ago.

The ale was warm and sweet and Het was happy when he was with Shell. He described again how Arthur had been injured. It was a southern policeman that had done it: a man in a white shirt rather than a blue, so it must have been one of the draft from the London Met or Thames Valley forces, heavyweights on extra brass, out of their usual jurisdictions.

It was policemen like this who made comments when they pulled you over, who turfed you out onto the road, roughed you up and called you darling. Het had recently been told by one of these officers that the miners deserved what was happening to them. *You and the rest of the fucking scrubbers,* his face pushed into the jagged gravel of the hard shoulder. There was an Alsatian, the animal's fur collecting drizzle pearls as it barked heat into the miners' faces from no more than an inch away. The daffodils were in bloom by the roadside, your scar stretching as you tried to escape clasping jaws. "That strawberry ice cream?" one of the policemen said to

Het, jabbing his scar with a nail-bit finger. "Fuck off back to Rotherham."

"Well, where's he now?" said Shell, "You must have some idea." She sipped her drink.

"You tell me."

"Well I would only he came back in one of them Phantom of the Opera type things. Fuming, he were, while I fetched ointment and sponge. When I came down he'd hopped it."

"Hospital sorted all that," said Het.

"But I'm his wife."

Shell might be Arthur's wife but it wasn't as if she was out searching for him. Back from her new job at the bakery, acting concerned with a drink. She reminded Het of his mother in that she always behaved how was expected, never mind that she probably didn't mean a word of what came out of her mouth. Another chance and another, one more, always terrified of the alternative, the Litten Path. He watched Shell's lips and wondered what they would taste like.

"He'll turn up. Still if you're worried we could ask around," Het said.

"Give over. I'm not having folk think I can't look after my own husband."

Janice Scanlan approached their table, asking where the latest food donations were to go. Shell would never admit to being the one in charge, but the other women looked up to her and it was obvious she enjoyed the responsibility. She directed Jan to a table at the back where food tins and welfare packages were steadily accumulating. Channelled regionally by the union, the donation and care parcels were flooding in from the locality and elsewhere: the public, via international aid and other unions, other governments and overseas pits.

The comrades in Russia had been especially kind. Although it might feel like it sometimes, the striking miners were not alone.

It was Shell who'd started Litten's soup kitchen. Over the last few weeks she'd also helped design placards, come on marches and when the police charged the pickets, blown her whistle and chanted with the best of them. She packed the snap, made it, too. She poured the coffee, listened to people's problems and helped them mend their clothes. Het was proud to say Shell was as much a part of this struggle as any man, and if you asked her about those who snuck like rats into work around the back of the pits, those who were bold enough to argue it out with the picketers out front or even fight their way through the crowds, never mind those who wormed their way in, entreating those brave enough to come on strike, insisting that they were only thinking of their families, Shell knew the name for them.

Het wondered what she'd think if she knew Arthur didn't want to help the effort: that he might have scabbed if he could. Het was tempted to tell her, wanted her to know what kind of a man her husband was, only she *must* know, more than anyone she must know. Arthur Newman, gap toothed and magnetic. Wind him up and let him go. Offer him a pill and he'll take two of them.

Equally Shell knew about Het's father as few outside of the family ever did. She was young when she first met the Newmans. Het remembered her introduction, having to spend most of the night trying to keep cool whenever she glanced his way, cracking his finger joints under the table and kicking himself for missing that night at The Masons, letting Arthur get there first. He could hardly bear to look at Shell and had to resort to showing her what he was about by seeing to it that she got the best slice of beef. In his eagerness he knocked the gravy boat onto the carpet.

Dad liked her straight away. On a walk after the meal, Shell wasn't afraid to joke and contradict Alec. Het walked with them at a slight remove, the collar of his coat pulled up to his nose. This girl was the bristle of autumn; she was the crunch of your boot heel in a frozen puddle. You don't talk to a phenomenon of nature. You simply step back and watch it exact its force.

A few weeks later it turned out Shell was pregnant, and *how* the news delighted Alec, because it meant Arthur was finally on the straight and narrow, in the relationship for keeps, and wasn't he doing *well*. Het endured his predicament quietly, in that desperate, English way, because Shell would never look twice at him, and even if she did and he took a chance smile up on its potential, it would ruin his father, especially after what had happened with Sam. Above all Alec Newman valued family. He would have been devastated at having to ostracise another son.

Sometimes Het felt like the only person who missed Alec. It was Alec who'd taught him about the pits; the brotherhood and strength of it. If one of you had a problem, you all did. That was the way of it. A repetitive life, perhaps. There was value in that. Het didn't know what it was about hardship that made it so nostalgic over time, but he knew hard lives developed integrity in retrospect. Perhaps that was their ultimate reward: being able to tell people how rough you'd had it was almost worth putting up with the thin end of the wedge.

Because there was no doubting Het would become a miner. It was what he'd always wanted, to be like his ancestors, valorous in the heat, working the rock. Dirty hands, clean wage. Growing up, Het's dad had relayed to him all kinds of stories, stories of the coal face, working naked sometimes owing to the high temperatures before the regulations came in. Miners had worn all sorts of outfits, rag and bone get-ups from home, anything you didn't mind getting grubby. Black snot. Coming to the surface with your socks stiff as a board, dressed in bloomers sometimes, flaming whatever, looking daft in the *arse-loop*, a rope chair used to repair the remote shafts the machinery couldn't get to. The hours could be long and dangerous – you could feel suffocated at the greater depths – earning a crust beneath the crust, pit checks ringing in the banksmens' and lamp room boxes. In those days you were paid by weight. You cut your cash from the earth, life funded by what you dug.

When Het remembered Alec talking about his early days in the pit or his country childhood, a youth of podding peas, harvest moons and autumn equinoxes, he pictured him in the living room with the circular mirror leaning against the fruit bowl. Dad shaved in the late afternoons because he said the light was better at that time, its angle casting a rhomboid of sun onto him that picked clear the hairy filaments sprouting from his skin. The shaving bowl was often so bright that it looked like a basin of cloud.

Work the badger brush. Lather the face. Story-telling while drawing a razor against the grain and down the throat. A father's lessons impacted on sons more than they knew. Even now Het shaved the same way as his old man: in the living room, often late in the afternoon, a wet job, the blade's serrations affecting his scar and occasionally slicing his skin (Alec never cut himself) because memory had enveloped him:

thoughts of home and dreams. What he one day wanted and would try to get.

The pattern on his beer's surface budded, flowered and dissolved. Het was sorry for how influenced by his dad he was; sorry for denouncing Sam as a queer. What had made Arthur show the old man those magazines, no one knew, but a poofter in the house was wrong so Het and his father had let Samson know it.

Still, what you don't know doesn't hurt you. It was Arthur's fault for telling on Sam. Some days later Het had returned to where the fight happened and felt beneath his tread something larger than a stone; it was a tooth left on the pavement. He'd picked it up, the tip flecked with blood, the body yellow-cream, and dropped it in his pocket, rolling the sharpness between finger and thumb. He never did give it back. To this day the tooth remained in a drawer by his bed, a severed piece of his father's mouth.

"I've finished," Shell said.

"Me too." Het downed his dregs. "I'm starved. Off home."

"Oh," said Shell. Was she crestfallen? "Well, if it's food you're after, I might be able to help."

She produced from her bag a set of keys with a pink spongey cat attached, a silly grin practically forcing her face in two.

"We've some stock that's for the bin but still decent. I was about to take it home only Lawrence is out and Arthur, well . . . I've left it. We could grab it if you like. If you're nice I might even let you have a discount."

The snooker balls knocked madly on the baize.

6

THE MASK COVERING Arthur's cheek looked like a cricket box that had been cut in half. Lucky, they told him, he was lucky his vision wasn't impaired. The swelling would go down at some point and he'd survive not being able to bring his teeth together for a few days.

He tapped a couple of codeine out of the packet. Another two to make sure. They were too chalky to neck dry so he had to summon a load of spit to force them down. His rotten grimace was reflected back at him in the bus window. He'd discharged himself from hospital earlier, told them he didn't need any more of their attention and the wife would see to him.

He'd have said anything.

It started to piss it down as he stalked the corridors of the outdoor market. Traders advertised their root vegetables, offered up samples on paper plates, sorting their change under the roof tarps while a fat-eyed dog in a coat yapped and strained on its lead until Arthur wanted to boot it in the face to shut it up.

He reached the high street. Daylight split between the buildings and the cobbles shone through in messy patches where the tarmac had crumbled away to nothing, the town's history bleeding openly into the present.

Now the pavement was putty-coloured and family-run shops lined the streets. There were wire bins, cement-footed benches and beyond those, that emotive bandstand. Arthur was having one of those days where he felt like he knew everybody. He went into the fusty-looking shop to pick up his photographs.

The place smelled like damp towels. Leathery cameras hung from the walls by their straps like wing-pierced bats and glass cases containing lenses and flashes and tripods and photographic ephemera hemmed the sides of the room. There were frames containing black and white prints as well, and racks of postcards and albums. A dirty, cream-coloured booth lurked, portal-like, in the corner.

Arthur waited at the counter for the true contents of the jewellery box to be revealed. He'd forced it open the night he took it from Threndle House, finding inside a pot with a canister of film that he'd stashed in a holdall that had sagged guiltily at the bottom of his wardrobe since then.

Until two days ago. Arthur had been kidding himself he was waiting for the right moment to return the film, when really he was waiting until he got desperate enough to develop the negatives. Any help to see this strike out would be welcome. With Lawrence finishing school, Shell might be more inclined to move if they had some money. If these were pictures Arthur could actually put to good use, that was.

He'd taken to leaving the newspaper out, pages opened to where the college ads were printed like listings in the Radio Times. Shell had thought it was Lawrence being curious, and Arthur hadn't dared tell her any different.

"What's he want wi' all this palaver?" she'd said, shaking her head.

Fuck the pits, Arthur nearly said. "I've no idea."

Over a month on the lilo. A month of being side-stepped.

Shell's first ever job and she was using it to avoid him. Flour-stained trousers, lingering down the welfare, being vindictive. Nothing was good enough, not even the maple tree that had been as nice a thing as Arthur could think to buy Shell to say sorry for the business with the rug. Even going on fly picket hadn't been enough to please her. At least at first it hadn't. As soon as she found out he'd put his name down she'd strode home and interrupted him in the yard.

"Were you going to tell us?"

"Tell you what?"

"You know fine well, Arthur."

He'd put down his bloody book. "I thought I'd do my bit. Same as you."

"Right the way up to this you were saying what's point in going on strike. Now you're all for helping."

"So?"

"So what's new?"

Unable to confess the truth, Arthur watched Shell, the wind tickling his naked scalp. Never mind that, love. Never mind the way you made *me* look.

"Just reckon there's no point being a bit on strike," he said.

"*You* all over the country?"

"I can freeze my bollocks off in t'midlands as good as I can here."

"You've heard what it's getting like . . ."

"Worried, Shell?"

"Am I heck."

"Bloody sounds like you are."

"Why on earth should I be worried? It'll be good for you. If anything, I'm glad."

That had blown her off the scent.

"It's paid work at least."

"Quid a picket. Crack out the bunting."

You had to laugh. Some were getting it in the neck from their wives for not working. Not Arthur. Meeting at three in the bloody morning at the welfare or the pub, arriving at whatever godforsaken pit it was this time for some argy-bargy with the police, then home to an iceberg he had hopes of thawing. "So how were it?" Shell had taken to asking, and whether it was or was not, Arthur would always tell her it was shite. He hated being Het's lapdog and his wife would be easier to keep a hold of if she felt sorry for him. It had come to this.

A typical example:

"Where to today?"

"Broscombe."

"Shite?"

"Messy."

"Tell us."

And so he'd explain.

"What they've started doing is letting a few cars through the roadblocks to find out where we're headed. Then they hit us there later. Happened today, love, they charged us. Didn't think they would. Don't always. Sometimes they just bang their shields to scare you, provoke a reaction so they can make arrests. They like telling us what they're making, eighty a day, some of them, whatever it is. Five hundred a week I've heard some get. Bold as buggery, fifty of 'em giving you shit-eye, rubbing it in about their new furniture and new carpets and tellies while we've not two sticks to rub together. Crowing about what they're getting at our expense. They're cold, love. Really they are."

The way Shell breathed.

"Anyroad, before scabs come this time one of the lads must have said summat back to 'em. Or maybe he said summat first, I'm not sure. Either way, it doesn't take much for pigs to come down on you like a ton of bricks. They flew at us. I fought back, tha knows me. One of the lads even put through one of the windows on their van. It was one of the old ones. Rest had cages fitted. Got a bit hairy."

"Looks sore."

The feel of your wife's fingers on your head. Her lovely, smooth fingers on your head.

"You stand out, Arthur. Something about you attracts attention."

"I wish it didn't."

"But you're OK?"

Eye contact.

"We got chased down track, Shell. Had to split into threes. I must have walked a frigging mile to Chris Skelly's car only he'd gone walkabout by the time we arrived so we had to make us way home on us own, Asa and me."

"An' Het?"

"What 'bout him?"

"Just wonder."

"Well while I were hiding up a tree and half the others were getting chased onto the next bloody bus, sour puss were elsewhere. Fuck knows. I've had to thumb a lift wi' some lad. Nineteen years of age, surface man up pit top. Not much older than our kid."

"Will be our kid in less than a year," said Shell, with a hint of satisfaction. "He's nearly old enough."

There was no way Lawrence was going down the pit.

Sometimes after one of these tales Shell would nod on her

way into the kitchen, ease up on the sighing for five minutes. Because it seemed to be working: finally she was coming round, which made the fact Arthur was against the strike burn more viciously in his guts. Because in his heart he was a scab, a strike breaker in all but the deed itself.

He'd thought it over endlessly. He'd at one point even nearly told Shell he wanted to go back to work, be the first in Yorkshire to rebel against this fucking polarity once and for all.

He'd been washing his face before bed. She'd accidentally walked in. That yellow bruise of Arthur's shining luridly in the lather as he and Shell caught sight of one another in the mirror above the sink. Your wife with no make-up on, about to turn back the way she'd come but stopping once she realised you'd seen her. A sense of something, certain they'd just glimpsed in each other the very thing they'd once had but hadn't spoken of in at least a decade.

"One on your hip looks tight."

"It is a bit."

"You'd tell me if you're hurt, though. You'd say."

"You know I would."

"Liniment's in t'cabinet."

"Shell?"

To see her, those lips; your sore hands in the water and a fucking moth on the fucking wall. Arthur didn't care about the industry. He didn't care.

He tapped the countertop with a coin. Lack of foresight had sent him down the pits in the first place. Brantford had been the easier thing. All Arthur had to do was show willing and he'd gotten for himself a job; turning up at the office, enquiring of the woman in half-moon spectacles as

96

to vacancies. She blew her nose and said to come back the following Monday.

The induction was less than short and within one month Arthur had more money in his pocket than a seventeen-year-old had thought possible, and being able to project an idea of yourself to all and sundry whilst necking Dexamyl and chatting birds up had meant so much to him.

Mainly it was inevitable. Just passes in English and History to his name and his father on at him all the time.

Lads of Litten go down the pit. And over half of them better men than you.

Which was at least part-true. Almost every lad at Litten Modern got a job down the pit, as did many women, and of course Hector did too. Fucking golden child had six years Brantford graft in him by the time Arthur went down that office. Het who he'd shot with a firework. Het who wouldn't talk to him because he'd shown those magazines of Sam's to their dad when he was off his head one night and Alec was going on at him like always about being useless.

Easy to reflect on the breadcrumb trail. Starting down the pit, blowing your wage every week then meeting that girl you'd sort of liked one boring afternoon but had forgotten all about. It wasn't hard for a lad Arthur's age to be struck by Shell's canny smile and open legs. He'd been persuaded into marrying her because everyone else expected it of him. Putting a kid in Shell had probably been the biggest mistake, because a son Arthur would inevitably love. He'd saddled himself with the house on the right-to-buy in 1980. It had made for added security with Lawrence attending the grammar school, and had quickly become an albatross – a pissing mortgage with only one way of paying it.

The bloke was coming with the photos. It had taken Arthur just two years to sign away the next fifteen. *Everyone needs coal. Everyone will always be wanting coal.*

Yeah right.

Outside he stopped to watch the expensive TVs in the windows of the electronics shop. They were blaring the regional news, some weather report depicting skinny teens chucking themselves off a pier, star shapes plummeting into the water. Arthur stared at the screens for ages, thought about things, then hurried to look at the Swarsby photographs in peace.

He chose a secluded part of Litten Hill: a combe hidden from the wind and prying eyes, a hollow where he might sit. Somewhere below, beyond the town, its terraces and its shopfronts, was his home, static and anchored by a family. Partially screening this view was a tier of silver birch. Flushed green, the trees looked like a queue of ragged men gazing past Arthur, ancient figures concerned with things far beyond his understanding. Things that didn't concern him.

It was a bright afternoon, the likes of which you never normally saw when working underground all day. The Codeine had dissolved to become a pleasant drag in Arthur's veins, and the envelope in his hand was neither thick nor heavy. Sometimes it was good being on strike. He lay back and rested on his elbows. Tranquil clouds coasted by, great scooped whorls of clotted cream. The place reminded him of being a kid. He often spent the day up here with Sam, or down in Barnes' Wood, at the elm tree, dressed in sweaters, scarves and hats, smoking singles they'd bought from the mini-mart before coming home to dinner and pudding – often a great pot of stewed pears that simmered like gold lava on the Primus ring.

For some reason it was always winter in Arthur's memory. Salted paths and shards of ice in the milk bottles when you went to collect them from the front step every morning. In Arthur's mind Het was always cleaning his first car with a shammy leather as it stood on the cobbles. Mr Perfect with his Vauxhall Victor and a special place at the top of the house. Het always wore a hat, a deer stalker with the flaps lowered, knotted under his chin. He insisted it was to stem the cold but it seemed no coincidence that the flaps hid the hideous scar on his neck. Arthur was always grateful for those extra squares of padded cloth.

On the day of *The Mighty Atom*, Mam's lipstick had been purple and sticky-looking. She wore a striped apron and a flowery dress, one hand arched across her forehead, middle finger and thumb placed on either temple as she turned away from Arthur because she couldn't stand the sight of him. Dad's hair was always prudently combed, his shirt pressed and tucked, but that day he purposefully rolled his sleeves up so he could deliver the hammer blow to Arthur's nose less than ten minutes after arriving home from the hospital. Blood running down your front while your equally culpable brother cowered nearby, wrongly thinking he'd be the next to get a whack from the old man.

"That's for what tha's done to Hector."

"I didn't mean it!"

"Tha never does."

"You never think, lad."

"I'm sorry, Mam."

"Don't cry. You're a waste of space, Arthur."

"*I'm not crying.*"

"You better not be. Not after what tha did."

The discordant colour of the meadow grass Het lay in, fireworks popping in the distance and everywhere the smell of cordite. *Crack, crack* while your mam watched your dad break your fucking nose. Bonfire Boy, the other kids took to calling Het, although Arthur fought anyone he ever heard say it.

"Lawrence!"

Arthur opened his eyes. The bloody Codeine had nearly made him doze off. He sat up and tore open the envelope, spread it against the stooks of short grass, a stash of black and white Swarsby photographs, of which there were two distinct sets.

The first was a series, a sequence concentrating on one subject: the man Arthur recognised from the framed photo collage at Threndle House. It was the handsome bugger who'd posed with Clive Swarsby in the dinner suit. In these new photos the man was older, clean shaven, hair slicked into a helmet of grey, although he'd lost none of that defiance Arthur first noted when he punched the photo collage all those nights ago, impact decimating the smug twat's face.

The guy was in London by the looks of it, eating in a restaurant with another bloke, then climbing into a black cab with this thick-haired, heavily-built sod. The second man was pale of complexion. He wore a sweater over a tartan shirt and a blazer over that. The two of them were going into a lovely old hotel, *The Savoy*.

The second set of pictures were of the handsome man and a teenage girl who must have been about Lawrence's age. She sported shoulder-length hair and wasn't pretty by any stretch of the imagination. She was more beautiful, like a cliff.

She had been photographed getting into a limo with the

man, who touched her elbow as if pinching a corner of paper. There was certainly closeness between them.

Certainly something.

Her build was familiar, and gazing at her skin's starkness reminded Arthur of the feeling he sometimes got when he was amid the stippled remoteness of the moorland, where the lapwings looped their acrobatics through the dense air, wielding the freedom of the tops.

He stuffed the photos into his anorak. It seemed sensible to head home, but he wasn't sure he wanted to see Shell again so soon after running out on her that morning, and now he'd just heard someone calling his son's name beyond the thorns.

It had to be his lad, so Arthur stood, and between the motion, the pain in his face and the Codeine, he staggered. Groaning, he made his way across the hill towards the voices.

7

I T WAS A strange time. May was surrendering to June and the swallows were returning north. You could see them: tracers skimming low, chasing the afternoons into loft-spaces and empty farmhouses. The summer exams were coming, too, though Lawrence tried not to think about those. He hadn't been to school in over two weeks and doubted he'd see another classroom again.

The business with the pie continued. The school was up in arms: a pretty teacher hobbled by two yobs from the lower sets, Grundy the head-teacher as good saying it, peering over his Roman nose, practically *welling up*, thought Lawrence, looking back on things, facing him and Ryan Fenton from behind that desk.

The air conditioning fan had turned on the ceiling, the breeze fluttering the post-it notes and the A1 pad balanced on its stand. Grundy went on and on. Lawrence had never really been in trouble before but he was a low achiever so it was obvious what Grundy thought. When asked what he'd to say for himself, Lawrence tried to explain what had happened, but was halted by Grundy's raised hand. There was a visible wart on the head's finger above where a wedding band should have been. Miss Potts had told him everything he needed to know.

"It isn't me you owe your apology to. And you realise how you sound, given that you ran from the scene?"

There were filing cabinets, a brown carpet and certificates

on the wall. There was an oil painting of Grundy in his gown, lopsided at one corner.

"Don't shrug at me."

"I don't know, sir."

"I've seen boys like you. Lies prosper, don't they? And what of your fathers, what do they do that they'd raise two sons who'd do a thing like this?"

Grundy's yellow eyes. He had that funny white spit that old blokes get at the corners of their mouths.

"Well?"

"Brantford, sir."

"Striking?"

Lawrence nodded.

Grundy's face hardened. He pointed at Fenton.

"Scrapper," said Fenton.

"Explain."

Fenton's father worked for a company that dismantled and cleaned ovens and fryers from takeaways and restaurants that had gone bust. They turned the equipment round and sold it for a profit.

"A grafter," Grundy said with satisfaction, before addressing Lawrence. "I've seen your lot. Civil disobedience, attacking the police – it's a disgrace! No wonder you've turned out the way you have. I'm thirty years a teacher and never have I seen an injury to a member of staff before. Never mind a woman." He shook his head. "For *Pete's* sake."

The boys stared at the floor.

"But at least Fenton's had the grace to stay . . . *You*, Newman, leaving others to clean the mess, thinking you've the run of it. Thinking you can do what you like. You'll be the death of this country, fools like you."

There was a coffee ring scarring the varnish on Grundy's desk. Lawrence studied its circumference as the old cunt steepled his fingers. It didn't matter that Barry Fenton was a cash-in-hand man for a bent little outfit, that all he did was hose the grease off those cookers into a shallow trench so he could watch it burn; Lawrence was from rabble-rousing stock. You can't wash grease down drains because it blocks them. You can't burn fat without the risk of it getting out of control. Fenton was suspended and Lawrence expelled. Sons of bogeymen had no place at Fernside Grammar.

"You're lucky you're not being reported to the Yorkshire constabulary. Miss Potts is refusing to press charges."

Since that afternoon it had been surprisingly easy for Lawrence to hide what had happened from his parents. Their phone had been cut off so Fernside had to rely on letters, and with the school situated over the borough line the notices and meeting requests were stamped with an identifying postal mark. The letters could be intercepted easily.

Mam and Dad were clueless anyway. They'd hardly noticed the signs of Lawrence not being in school. Days became matters. Matters of staying out of sight and hoping nosey parkers wouldn't grass. Lawrence knew his secret couldn't keep, but until it broke the hassle of his parent's discovering it was easily worth the trouble of keeping the truth from them. It was almost a way of testing them, to see if they thought to give a shit. How big the fuck-you could be when they found out his life had unravelled under their noses.

"*Lawrence!*"

Evie was calling: her voice had filled his summer. Swarsby days: growing older and feeling it, wood smoke and teenage secrets, Evie's slender legs a set of tracks that only a password might part.

"Where you taking us?" Lawrence heard her say. He'd take her everywhere if she'd only let him.

"To the summit," he replied. Since getting in with the Swarsbys, he was careful to speak properly. "There's a great view from up on top."

Fucking Duncan was puffing away by Evie's side, his sister who was apparently never out of breath. Evie was the type to make others wait rather than hurry herself and break a sweat.

"This better be worth it," she said, arms folded and shorts ending so high that her legs looked like those of a bird, some shallow wader in a lake.

"It is, or don't you believe me?"

Evie produced a compact from her bag and examined her face. Her complexion had adjusted now that she spent time outdoors that she claimed would normally have been enjoyed at friends' houses, or her room in London.

"I'm sorry?"

"I said there's a great view from up on top. Or do you not you believe me?"

The little round case snapped shut. "You're always banging on about something, Lawrence. If you're not careful I'll leave you behind and so will Seb."

Lawrence said, "Fine by me if you want to run ahead."

"Just hurry up."

She was only rude because she cared. Lawrence led the way. Since their first meeting he'd waited for Evie daily at the tree cave. She visited after her lessons with her tutor – which she took at home – always with Duncan in tow, barely giving Lawrence the time of day if she could help it, although it was telling that she still came, her need for company as recognisable to Lawrence as his own face.

"I'm tired, Lawrence," Duncan said after they'd walked a little further. "I need a rest."

"Seb's stopping." Evie laughed. "Stop the press."

Duncan touched Lawrence's elbow as he went to sit, hand lingering in that unbearably *close* manner of his. Evie sat too. She picked a dandelion clock and blew the hours of the day up to five. Lawrence hadn't met many people in his life, yet the Swarsbys were like no other. One was as suspiciously playful as a once-mistreated cat, the other had eyes like puddles in the marl pits, who being around made you feel like a stranger had come and sat next to you on a nearly-emptied bus.

"You're always tired," Lawrence said. He was forever wanting to prod Duncan to see what came out. He'd been the victim of cruelty so often that he never thought he'd impose it on anyone else, but supposed some people were just your targets. It was impossible to leave them be.

"I like to take my time," Duncan said.

"That's because you're unfit."

"Where we're from there's better ways to kill your days than climbing hills," said Evie. She had dandelion spores in her hair and the width of her thighs expanded as she knelt to commence work on a bird's nest from dead leaves and grass.

"What, like sitting on your backside? Sounds soft to me."

"There's a difference between soft and civilised."

"You're hardly civil."

Evie grinned.

"Suppose your dad can afford to pay for you to sit about," Lawrence said, encouraged. "He probably sacked the personal trainer."

"Not likely," said Duncan. He was so wet, so willowy.

"Yeah, right, I can see your house. Loads of stuff hidden under a dustsheet in the garage. Croquet sets and golf clubs and . . . boules!"

"*Boules?*" said Evie.

"You know what I mean."

"Don't be crass," Duncan said, his face sharpening as he exchanged a look with his sister. "And anyway, why are you talking like this when you've got *everything* at your place?"

Lawrence had told the Swarsbys all sorts. Arthur was in business, Shell was a teacher. They took him abroad on their jolly holidays. They had a five-door saloon, ate cooked breakfasts and in the spare room there was a hi-fi. Fast, faster, fastest. He was saving up for a motorbike, he was going to America and didn't need school so he'd fucking ditched the place.

"I'm joking," he said quickly. "I'm winding you up. You shouldn't be so sensitive."

"I'm not sensitive."

"You are a bit."

Duncan rose. Even the way he stood was arrogant. "It's just you always make having money sound like a bad thing."

"I never said that."

"You imply it."

Lawrence wondered whether Evie would still talk to him if he grabbed a handful of earth and mushed it all over her brother's teeth. He pictured the black loam pasted across Duncan's mouth and chin. The nest Evie had made was posed in the middle of them now like a cave, ready to suck them if they could only imagine it.

"I don't," he said.

"OK, you don't. Now can we go please?"

The Newman family tree was getting closer. Lawrence was curious to see how it was getting on. The country sun burned. His hair had started to grow back now but it was still downy, so his scalp felt the heat, and when it was wet it formed into imbricated little spikes.

Lawrence looked identical to his dad at the moment. Sorry Arthur with his runny nose, his balsam and his hangovers. Lawrence watched Duncan, who'd powered ahead like he had a point to prove, and had to wonder what Arthur would make of giving up the last word the way he'd just done. His father had a famous mouth, which was one of the best things about him. Picking Lawrence up from school in Asa's Fiesta, nettling Asa for the state of the interior; the fact he was never allowed out for a drink past ten. Arthur was always taking the piss out of Lawrence's mam, too, making her laugh because she knew her brews were too milky and the fact she never dusted the bookshelf despite always saying she was getting around to it. Lawrence didn't want to be like Arthur and sometimes thought he hated his dad, but people like Duncan swanned about, always had done and needed telling.

"Well, seeing as you want to go into it," he said, forgetting his new way of speaking entirely, "I just reckon it's an easier life for people like you, you've had it as set out as Sunday dinner."

Luckily Evie was out of earshot as Duncan bit down on the bait. "Come on," he said. "That's hardly our fault."

"Never is," said Lawrence.

"It's wrong of you to try and make me feel embarrassed, Lawrence."

"I'm not saying you should be embarrassed. Just that you should think."

"I do think. I think we manage. We're well managed." Duncan was pleased by *that*. "And if other people aren't then that's their lookout."

"My dad says rich people are usually rich at someone else's expense," replied Lawrence truthfully.

"Oh, everyone in shitholes like Litten has an attitude like yours. My dad works bloody hard."

"So do most people, but they still don't get paid a bomb for doing fuck-all like them in parliament do."

"Dad's not *in* parliament."

"Still reckon he's no idea what real world's like."

"And you do?" said Evie.

Lawrence buckled at the sight of her, his beams and buttresses seeping dust.

"Well . . . no, but I'm a lad aren't I . . . a young man."

"So you say."

Duncan came down the hill to stand with Evie. It would always be the two of them, Lawrence realised.

Duncan said, "There's a bigger picture than most people see. It's not just about them, it's everyone. If this country's going to compete on a . . . God, listen to me trying to explain this. The best way I can put it is Clive knows about things, and that's why he's where he is, and your dad's where *he* is, wherever *that* is. The point is our families are basically the same. All families are."

"You seriously reckon we're the same?"

Duncan raised his voice, yet still managed to maintain his smug overlord manner. "Politics isn't about making money. It's about helping people."

"I thought it were about helping country."

"People are what make up this country."

"You ask the miners if they feel part of this fucking country."

Were they swallows Lawrence could see, or were they swifts?

Soon he was relaxing, taking in the view spread unevenly past Evie's dark, mysterious head. This landscape seemed so personal, with its enclosed fields, the tractor busying itself above the broadness. Lawrence could see the Litten Path. It made him think of his family.

From her bag Evie produced a litre bottle containing some bright, evil-coloured liquid. "We call this a shit-mix," she said. "Every spirit we could find in the house. Stir in a bit of water and as much blackcurrant as it takes to make it taste all right."

Lawrence took a swig and managed not to gag. "Normally I get cider."

"A babyface like you can get served?"

"Too right I can."

"It's funny what you can get away with in the countryside," said Duncan.

"Police aren't too fussed," replied Lawrence, "Usually if you've been up to something it's the locals you need to worry about."

Evie didn't even wince when she drank. "The countryside's too small," she said. "No one here's looking for anything new . . . Clive's words, though for once I can't say I disagree. You got to admit it's pretty boring here."

It was strange hearing what you felt coming out of someone

else's mouth. Lawrence supposed people in Litten were going through everything, just like they were in the south, yet their lives felt drab by comparison. Being alive was surely different elsewhere. It just had to be.

"Would you stay?" he asked the Swarsbys. "If you had a choice."

Both shook their heads.

"Where would you go?"

"Guess," said Duncan.

"London's your home."

Duncan nodded. "And Litten's yours."

"No . . ."

"I'm going to run if Clive makes us stay. Seb and I will disappear."

"Yeah," said Lawrence, absently. He'd always wanted to see the capital. The tubes and umbrellas and bowler hats.

"Have you even been to London, Lawrence?"

"Course I have."

"You haven't." Evie nudged him playfully.

"Have."

"When?"

"When I was younger."

"Younger than now?" She had such cruel eyes. "What was your favourite part?"

". . .Westminster."

"Oh, Westminster, Westminster, wherefore art thou, Westminster? Name another place you went to. Give me a street, a central station."

Lawrence took the bottle and swigged from it, this time failing not to gag. If this was how Evie wanted to play it . . . "It was ages ago," he said. "And my mam took me, she's from

III

down there. Like I say, I were young, I can't be expected to remember every part. What's happened to your mam, Evie? You hardly talk about her. She must be coming to join you all at some point."

The bereft expression on Evie's face made Lawrence feel terrible. "Oh she'll be in her kennel somewhere," she said. "Clive's well shot of her."

"Mummy's still in London," Duncan offered.

"Bram's setting her up," said Evie.

Her brother's eyes were fixed and stony. "Bram's dad's best friend."

Evie made a vomiting noise. "It's his place we're staying in," she said, "His family owned the colliery. What's its name again?"

"Brantford."

"That's it."

"Sounds like a nice guy."

Neither Swarsby agreed.

". . .I'm sorry to hear about your mam, Evie."

"She made a tough choice," said Duncan.

"So very tough," Evie said.

Lawrence wasn't sure if she was being sarcastic or not. "Are she an' your dad still together then or what?" he asked.

"Oh yes," said Duncan.

"Well why isn't she here then?"

Evie piped up. "It's Clive, he's—"

"Had his problems," Duncan interjected. "He needed a break and so did Mum."

"Luckily we had Bram," said Evie. "Our hero."

"*Evie.*" Duncan glanced at Lawrence. "The opportunity arose to come here, so Dad took it. It's as simple as that. A fresh start, new fight. That holiday in France was good for him."

"It was in the paper," said Lawrence.

"Dad says if he finds out who leaked the story he won't be held responsible."

"Jesus, Seb, who do you think leaked it?" Evie sneered, rolling onto her back and kicking her legs in the air. "It's the lesser of two evils. Release a small story to hide a bigger one."

"Evie, could I speak to you for a minute?"

Duncan led his sister away without waiting for an answer and spoke at her while heat blared against the hill. When the pair returned, Evie looked so wretched that Lawrence felt he had to say something. "I know what it's like," he told her quietly. "To be disappointed."

It was as if he'd shone a torch in her face. Seconds passed, stillness. It got so that Lawrence became afraid Evie was going to say something horrible to protect herself, like she usually did, so he stood up to kill the moment. The trick to lying is believing what you say in the instant that you say it, thus making what you're saying at least partly true. But there was no trick to truth, and therein lay its power.

"Come on, Slowcoach," he said, "I'll race you to that red tree."

Without waiting for an answer, he sprinted across the grass, listening to Evie calling after him. He didn't stop until he reached the family maple, where he was met by a tall figure bumbling through the furze. This stranger wore one of those clinical masks made out of white plastic. He looked horrific, like Frankenstein's bleeding ghost.

8

BEING DRUNK WAS hardly a new feeling, but it was always welcome. Evie wondered whether she was too young to enjoy it the way she did, then again her mother had never thought so. They used to drink together when they lived in Muswell Hill, gin and martinis like proper ladies. If Clive was doing well he treated them, splitting the cost across his expenses to justify the west end eateries. *Perks*, Fiona winked, perks. The Jaguar drove them to lunch. Early maturity meant early refinement, so Evie was allowed to drink.

She'd learned the big lessons early: men were despots, life was flawed and money mattered. It took her longer to learn that in the business of self-preservation there are no equal measures; parents would do anything to have you reflect well on them and pretty much everybody is a hypocrite.

Not a second thought had been given to marooning her in this backwater canal. She, a woman trapped in the body of a girl, forced to doggy paddle past the submerged trolleys and traffic cones of Litten.

As far as Evie could tell the north was bare limestone hills, brusque towns, and lurking beyond them, savage country ruined by concrete and heavy industry. Pragmatic shapes dominated everything. Power station cooling towers and factory chimneys, the gaunt shadows of metal: hoists, cranes and parades of pylons massive against whatever skyline she happened to be driven towards.

They said it was pleasant around Harrogate, Ripon and Wetherby, but down here there was nothing but a village, surrounding villages and yet more villages furnished by works, land and the pit. Litten, where you tucked your hands under your armpits to keep them warm, where the before-morning darkness – so really not darkness at all – flooded the halls of your borrowed home and isolated you in profounder, more unfamiliar ways.

Evie had complained, complained, but as far as her parents were concerned she was old enough to know better if she made a mistake, yet too young to be allowed to follow her own mind. She squinted now, the grass beneath her still morning-damp, the sun ahead bothering the view, then shielded her eyes with her hands, careful not to smudge her make-up. Making an effort was something she could still do. She always wore coloured eye-shadow, always the lips were clad in red. Clarissa Swarsby had been the same: an octogenarian made up like a dog's dinner to the very end.

Duncan was talking. "Is he coming back?" he said. The endless mottle and chimneys fanned out in front of them.

"Evie?"

"I heard you."

"Well?"

"Well how should I know?"

It took him three dandelions to realise he had to apologise. "Good for you," Evie replied, once he had.

"You were saying too much."

"I wasn't saying anything."

"Evie, you nearly told him about Dad."

"So?"

"So are you mad?"

"What would you find more suspicious, Seb, me playfully skirting the issue or you acting like there's something to hide? Actually, don't answer that. I don't care."

"You'll care if Lawrence blabs. And what were those hero comments about Bram?"

"You mentioned him first."

"No, Evie, I didn't."

So what if she *had* raised the subject? Bramwell Guiseley was impossible not to discuss, the man who cooked her devilled eggs in his flat above the wharf. A branch belonging to the dogwood on the balcony had tapped at the window, as if asking if it could come in.

"Take it from someone who knows, Pup. The older you get, the more damaged women your own age are."

"How do you know I'm not?"

"Damaged? But how could you be?"

So exciting. Together in Bram's second or third apartment, which was full peculiar corners and ungainly points. Bram was never without company when Evie was growing up. He was the friend of her parents whom she sought to listen to above the others, ears to the crick between the door and the frame when it was agape, eavesdropping on the dinner parties, the gossip from White's and The Cavalry and Guards Club, the reminiscences of pitiless conquests and ribbings gone by. Those were the days of cottoning onto the reality of men who could generate their own social climate, for Bramwell Guiseley's moods could affect entire rooms. Evie admired that. One catcall was all it took. Handsome even in his forties, Bram was the kind of person who would have been carried in a palanquin in another era. *Probably cries paisley tears*, she'd heard someone say once, although Evie didn't think Bram capable of crying.

"Lawrence doesn't know his Ps from his Qs," she said.

Duncan smirked. He could always be lured with a snide remark. "Have you ever noticed that everything he wears looks like it's from the penny rail?"

"I think that's exactly where it comes from."

"He doesn't convince me."

"Doesn't know when he isn't being funny."

"Or when to shut up."

Evie stopped laughing. There was scorn in her, and it had a tendency to break through when she wasn't looking. "Still, he's kind of sweet, though," she added, not daring to look at Duncan, whose eyebrows she could practically *feel* rising into his hair.

"That's rich, you've been like a baby with a spinning top."

"Well, he still feels . . . decent."

"So you want to play with him."

"I don't!"

"Evie, I can see you doing it."

"Shut up."

Shut up shut up shut up.

Duncan took the bottle and said, "He's changed his accent and you don't even say anything about it. He's desperate and full of shit – I don't know which is more pathetic. God, that's strong." He put down the bottle. "If you believe even a shred of what Lawrence says then you're more naïve than I thought. It's obvious he's from an estate."

Evie had never been to an estate and had no plans to visit one. All you had to do was look around Litten to see where Lawrence came from. From the mothers here chained to their prams, to the seagulls that had somehow found their way inland, everything in this place seemed so lost that she could never imagine it found, a death of great insignificance awaiting it, a death it was at all times Litten's job to avoid. Evie would run if she were made to stay into the New Year.

"I don't think he'd say anything about Dad."

"You *are* more naïve than I thought."

"Don't call me naïve, Seb."

"And you stop calling me Seb!"

"You were apologising a second ago."

"Now I'm calling you naïve."

"Oh, fuck off."

"No, why don't you. Go find Pinocchio." Duncan pointed. "I think I can see his nose poking out of the bushes back there."

Fine. Evie headed in that direction. It wasn't so long ago that her brother had cried so much after his first day at school that their mother had the maid lubricate the histrionics with TCP. Duncan's whole bedroom had stunk of the stuff. Evie had to hold her nose when she went to ask him what the matter had been. He'd just flung his arms around her, sniffed about people reading his thoughts, being alone. When had that tender boy been replaced by this brass tack?

The grass was matted here, deep green but trodden to tracks. Sure, it was pleasant enough at these heights but it was still just glorified scrubland. The Swarsbys were in exile, Clive removed from protean London: sent away to fight a dead seat. He'd confessed as much while they were in France, Chamonix white outside and a burgundy on the table between them. Slurring his words through the cigar smoke, pistachio shells scattered across the tablecloth.

"Naturally they've pushed the writ through. The bastards couldn't have me lurking around."

"I thought you had their ear. And I know you're not elected but you still have friends, no?"

"Allies disperse, darling."

"I'm not a child."

"I still don't expect you to understand everything, Evie."

His greasy fingers in the olive dish. All her life, Evie's father had thought little of her. "Try me," she said. "You could even trust me."

Clive licked his fingers and poured more wine into his mug. He'd smashed all the glasses that week. "The easiest way of putting it would be to say I made a call that cost," he said at last.

"Personally? Financially?"

"The latter. Although one could make a case for the former."

"So, you're guilty of . . . ?"

Clive raised his hands. "A man should never have to admit a thing like this to his little girl . . ."

"What?"

"Culpability."

"I'm no girl."

As if in agreement, Evie's father presented her with his smouldering cigar. His hair was bushy, mane-like round the edges, balding centrally as he clung to what was left in that pathetic way some men have. Evie's mouth filled with smoke.

Clive said, "Best you think of this as a chance to regroup."

But she wasn't letting him off the hook that easily. "It's been worrying Duncan," she said gently. "He's been moved away from all his friends. He keeps talking about being held back at school. I don't know what to say to him."

Clive shuffled to the settee. "My boy," he said, touching

the sleeping Duncan's toe. "Do you know, Evelyn, you started calling me by my first name when you were eight years old. You said it suited me better."

"You never corrected me."

"It's important for women to be allowed to stick to their guns."

She could have struck him.

"You'd wriggle out of my arms every time I tried to hug you. I thought there was something seriously wrong."

And maybe there was. Evie remembered hating to be touched, and now that she was older she hated people thinking they understood her. She was the spawn of such a regrettable soul, a corpulent liar with a coloboma of the left iris. Her father's shirt buttons looked ready to burst as he sat back down and reclined in his wooden chair.

"But you will have it your way," he said, smiling at her, then adding abruptly: "I was approached."

"How do you mean?"

Clive's laugh was sodden and asthmatic. Evie poured the remains of her mug into his.

"An opportunity. Blasted friend of Bram's. Irishman." Her father belched.

"You're excused."

He didn't thank her.

"Sheehan. Point man for a consortium named Atlantia. They've bought land in and around High Wycombe. A regeneration project."

"What, for housing?"

"Yes, good." Clive nodded at Evie's perception. "Low cost abodes, very profitable. But they've longer-term margins in mind. Ever hear of Chandigarh?"

Evie shook her head.

"North of India. Designed by Corbusier, laid out in sectors. Skelmersdale, Milton Keynes?"

"Do I look stupid?"

"No comment." Clive flashed his top teeth. "Point is, they're all new towns, planned cities. Atlantia are trying to develop something similar. Sheehan laid it all out: they want to build a mega-complex for the nineties, a new conurbation but done right this time. Wycombe's close to London, it's voted blue since the fifties. Prime candidate, really, reward its loyalty. First they plan the housing, generate the capital, then the contracts will be up for tender. Good news for the shareholders . . ." Clive rubbed his index fingers and thumbs. "As long as they invest the right way."

He winked at her.

"And Sheehan came to you?"

"Bram pointed him my way. We scratch each's others backs, as you know."

Not the only thing Bram scratched.

"Still, it's not just out of loyalty. I do have *some* uses, despite what the women in my life might think." Clive licked the corners of his chapped mouth. "I know the relevant councillors," he said. "Nigel Burt's the chair of the committee. He's the green light man for the county and I know him from Brasenose." Clive pursed his lips. "A boat club man."

"*Another* club?"

"Piers Gaveston isn't for everyone, dearest."

The two of them shared an amused raising of eyebrows, then Clive said, "But before you start complaining, it's always been like this in Britain. Things only happen when somebody who knows somebody makes a call."

"I suppose clubs are only a bad thing if you're not a member."

Clive nodded. "For those that belong come the spoils, and those that don't . . ."

He didn't need to finish his sentence.

"You might also consider the possibility that I believed in the project. *Believe*, I should say. I think it'll be good for the economy."

"You mean your cut was good enough to convince you as to the merits of the cause."

Clive's face was impassive.

"Yet here we are in France," said Evie.

Her father made a butterfly out of his hands and flapped its wings. "The planning committee refused the Atlantia bid. Opportunistic and aggressive, they said."

"So much for Brasenose Burt."

"The man's a shit."

"Couldn't Bram have a word?"

Clive went into the kitchen, where Evie heard him selecting another bottle of wine from the cupboard. When he returned she went herself, sloshed some wine into her mug then hid the bottle. She ran a glass of water and placed it on the table in front of her father.

"It wouldn't do to have a visible link," Clive said. "Silent investors in projects like this can't have ties to cabinet. You should have heard the committee's response. The proposed Atlantia Project will impact on flooding and spoil the view in an area of outstanding natural beauty."

"Is that not the case?"

"Who gives a fuck when there's that much money at stake?"

Evie shook her head. "Their very words?"

"It wouldn't surprise me. I suppose the people of High Wycombe might like adders and whatever the hell else lives there. Newts. They're endangered, aren't they?"

"Life getting in the way of profit."

"Quite."

"Well that's laudable," said Evie. "Though I think what you mean to say is the committee turned the application down because you weren't as persuasive as you'd thought. What happened to the money, Clive?"

That butterfly again.

"I thought the nature of a bribe was it bought you what you wanted."

"Well, if you must know, I gave Burt half then stuck the rest on an each-way in the autumn weekend at Ascot. Christmas was coming and your mother wanted a new dress."

"Fucking hell."

"The rest was supposed to come out of my winnings. Don't forget, another person in my life's almost ready for university. The money to keep you in knickers and baked beans has to come from somewhere, you know."

So it was her fault. Anger rising, Evie thought of the snow outside the chalet, its weight settling, a gust stampeding down the gradient of Mont Blanc as if forced by a great drover on the other side of the valley.

"What possessed you, Dad?"

"Dad now, is it? I didn't think I was going to lose. The rest of our income went on trying to get the collateral back."

"They fixed the race?"

"Let's just say I was led to believe the odds had been consolidated one way in advance."

"Jesus, you're not giving an interview. Who gave you the tip?"

Clive crossed his arms.

"I said *who?*"

"This is what you call a pointed silence, Evie."

"Meaning you don't know."

"Meaning I know who it came from but I'm more interested in finding out why it was wrong."

That strange eye was hooded by the drink. "For the record," Clive said. "I have always won far more than I lost."

"Noted and accredited."

"And I hope someday that you'll do me the courtesy of being as candid about your own life," he said. "Darling, *too wit . . .*" God, Evie *loathed* his lawyer shtick . . . "I also hope you'll be as transparent with your own progeny, should you be unfortunate enough to have any yourself."

This was why he would truly never be Dad. They drank until he fell asleep. Once Evie had grown tired of the snoring, she roused Clive to the bathroom and stood in the hallway listening to him piss. She peered around the creaking door to check he was OK when she heard him gagging on his toothbrush, noting that his trousers were falling down. Even old Etonians had builder's bottoms.

Finally alone, Evie visited the chalet window. The Alps appeared paranormal in the dimness; each hump could have been Bram lying next to her on a snatched weekend afternoon, when he was bored and she was desperate to be complicit in something secretive and adult, considered as a woman, attended to. That bastard had said nothing about any of this.

She'd pleaded with her parents to be allowed to stay at home but hadn't been able to say why. This was because the reality was that London was all she knew, change can be horrifying and she was lovesick. None of which are easily articulated sentiments.

"*Daddy, please,*" she'd said, abasing herself with the informal noun.

"*And stay where, Evelyn? You have met your mother?*"

So had everybody else. Fiona Swarsby was a size six, aged sixty, who had owned a walk-in wardrobe since the age of fifteen. Evie's mother had discarded her played-out husband and children like a used tissue. Divorce wasn't the done thing, far too public. Bram set her up in Highgate. Suitable digs, Evie often thought, for a woman who might as well have lived on a distant volcanic island of velour, sequins and purple drapes, her diet consisting of fox, boar and venison, the cutest children from the villages of the supplicating natives.

So Bram was coming to Evie's mother's rescue. Handsome Bram. Dependable Bram. The motorboat had glided up the river while his moisturised hands rested against Evie's hips, that final time. Evie remembered their silence in the quiet, certain Bram didn't want to cuddle yet still vainly trying to clasp a moment of closeness before it was time to get dressed again. Bram's forgotten damp became a gel on the insides of her thighs, his sticky disdain plastered up the uneven shape of a curve-less body that embarrassed her. She had run to the toilet. Nauseous, spent.

She might as well have been moved to the North Pole. "*Oh, Evelyn,*" Fiona had said to Evie. "*You can't seriously expect me to be looking after you at my age.*" Then she let Bram help her to the car, Bram glancing up at Evie from below: a strung-out face in a Muswell Hill window. He'd smiled. Smiled! Although it was Evie who laughed last, because not one of them expected the vodka and paracetamol:

Not Duncan with his fingers down her gullet.

Not Clive clucking in the taxi to St Thomas'.

Not Fiona, calling her a silly girl.

Nor Bram, ignoring the phone call, never receiving the letter Evie wrote to him, threatening to go public about their affair. The letter was found the next morning, folded inside the front cover of her copy of *Catch-22*, rather than mid-way, saving the page as she had originally left it.

"What's going on? Why aren't you in school?"

Next to the little red tree, Lawrence was being confronted by a man. The man had his hands on Lawrence's shoulders. Evie headed over. She was drunk, she realised. She was also furious.

Lawrence spied her first. His face was flushed, mouth as gormless as one of Clive's Koi carp the day Evie saw them disappear down that heron's throat. She tapped the stranger on the arm. As the man let go of Lawrence and whirled round to face her, Evie's heart skipped. The stranger wore a plastic mask that only part-covered his bloated face. He had a convict's shaven head, the roughness of which was exacerbated by a scraggy beard and a blue stain dotting one of his cheeks.

Evie stepped back. So did the man.

"*Jesus*," he exclaimed. "*No way.*"

She could have said the same thing. He was absolutely ghastly, a guy let loose from its bonfire: the Yorkshire bloody Ripper. He was about to grab her, he must be, so Evie drew her foot back and kicked him between the legs as hard as she could. The man made a funny exhalation and folded over, sinking to his knees, forehead meeting the ground as if in prayer. Evie felt like a little girl again, back on Brighton pier, watching the pennies spewing into the cash flow after she'd shoulder-barged the coin pusher's glass. The arcade attendant coming her way, scooping her booty into her pockets before escaping to the yielding terrain of the pebbled beach.

You win!

"Come on!" she cried. Lawrence was trying to speak to the man, but it was hardly the time for gloating. Evie pulled him by the hand. "Hurry up!"

"That were my dad!"

"What?" They were really running. Their shoes beat the trail that wound into Barnes' Wood like a huge unspooled tape measure. Yard by yard, they hurried, through the bracken stage ahead of copse and shade, skipping through leaf and fern, the very air exciting. What was anything? It was everything. Evie slapped Duncan around the head as she passed him, and he fell in behind her and Lawrence, both the boys deadweights in her wake. Because no man could hold a candle. Evie was the renegade of Litten Hill.

PART TWO

Flattened Stones, Scrambled Heights

9

WELL THIS WAS certainly different, buzzing in a loose convoy down the A1 towards Sheffield, in the front seat next to Joyce Stride, of all people. A few other girls were in the back, boards between their knees, handwritten slogans on sticks and collection buckets gaping in the footwells. Shell had her finger pressed against the A to Z to stop it wobbling on her leg, pressuring the kinked channels meshing colourfully across both pages. She murmured odd place names as the carriageway flashed by outside. Tilts, Blaxton and Hickleton. Levitt Hagg, Micklebring and Maltby.

"Regarding the issue of the name," Joyce was saying. She was a stuffy sort who could be found making comments at the back of the welfare on Friday nights. "I think it's worth noting that Barnsley ladies are the B.W.A.P.C. And I think it'd make us sound more official if we came up with something similar."

"What's that stand for again?" said Shell.

Joyce tutted. "Barnsley Woman against Pit Closures."

Shell tutted back.

"Womankind it must mean."

"Get off wi' you. I always said they were odd in Barnsley, an' no wonder if there's only one set of tits to go round all them blokes."

"Shell!"

"Oh give over, Joyce. You're a hair splitter yourself, half the time. Climb off your soapbox and have a laugh."

Joyce had a sickly face. It was her veins, they were so prominent that on a cold day she could have been sculpted out of blue cheese. Today her neck was strained, tortoise-like, with nerves. It was because they'd taken her husband's crappy hatchback without permission. Although Jed Stride was a public milksop who'd hardly give Joyce the grief she was expecting for taking the car, she was practically in bits over it. Shell angled the oblong mirror in the sun guard but none of the others thought to meet her eye in it.

"I've said before," she said. "I'm not against giving ourselves a name. Fact is I think it's a good idea. But we'll have to come up with something better than B.W.A.P.C. Hardly rolls off the tongue now, does it. I'll get my thinking cap on, come up with something snappy."

Olive Butterworth, cramped in the middle of the back seat, piped up. "As long as it's better than *Scargill's Slags*, I'll be happy. That's what police called us at the rally. Never damped us spirits, mind."

Motherly, currant-bun Olive had attended the big *All Women's* do earlier that month and wouldn't stop going on about it. Pretending not to hear, Shell made a show of changing the radio station. Scritti Politti were more like it. She turned in her seat and winked back at Jan.

"I'll just be glad when all this is over," said Joyce, shaking the fringe of her mushroom haircut from her eyes. "I've better ways to spend my weekends than begging for loose change."

"And there were me thinking you were enjoying a day out with your mates," said Olive, nudging Linda Parkes, who'd fallen asleep. Linda stirred, sounding like she'd a mouthful of glue. Olive giggled and so did Shell, covering her mouth with one hand.

Joyce said, "Why should I value that? I must live half a mile from the lot of you. I can pop round any time I like."

"Assuming we let you in," said Shell.

"I could come admire that carpet of yours while I'm at it, Michelle."

"An feel the back of my hand an' all if you like."

"Girls," simpered Olive, winding down the window. "You're hardly being ladylike."

Joyce got all huffy. "Try telling *her* that."

Olive's ginger hair blew prettily about her face. A pattern of corny badges were pinned up the front of her cardigan, which, though buttoned up, failed to conceal her pronounced belly. She went, "You needn't worry, Joyce. Jed won't mind you taking car."

"I'm just not supposed to. Not on us own."

Other people's marriages irritated Shell, perhaps because she was in the throes of one herself. Skinny Joyce and her beige life. She was only allowed to sit in the front seat when there were no other men in the car, only drank white wine when she and Jed went out. A lifetime of rearranging the cushions and pillows, weeding the patio and doing the Wordsearch in the Mail because the Crossword was too hard. Green Gartside was singing *absolute, absolute*, and Shell couldn't keep her feet from moving.

She leant over and clapped the poor cow's knee. "Don't worry, flower. I'll enlighten Jed if he says 'owt. I mean heaven's sake, he'll get the message if we can't hand him his food-parcel come Monday. He'll shut his trap then, the silly fool. The prickly bugger."

"Is that supposed to make me feel better?"

"What do you reckon?"

"It's always a question to a question with you, isn't it, Michelle?"

"Well how else would you like me to be?"

The rest of the journey drifted by, the sky a blur of cirrus, cat's eyes punctuating the asphalt. It felt stirring to leave the borough. Needed and on a mission, older than she'd ever been, younger than she'd be again, Shell was in such a good mood that she didn't even criticise Joyce's parking as they pulled in horrendously on a residential side street outside of Sheffield centre.

They walked into town, Olive wittering on about how they were like chartists and suffragettes, nurses in the Crimea. Shell stuffed her hands in her pockets. She had never thought about it like that.

Soon they'd be on Queen Street. Shell had been on quite a few marches and stood on the line outside Brantford she didn't know how many times, but had never been anywhere like this without Het. Course it was no fly picket; it was still the coal board's office in the belly of the country, and no one could predict anything in times like this. Arthur had been injured only yesterday. It was just like him to get himself hurt. No doubt he'd be up on the moor today, mard-arsing through the brindle and whinstone.

While his brother was off picketing Selcroft. Het would have set off before sunrise today. Nearly every day the men were picketing in Notts. Shell had been there herself at the start of the strike, seen the good side of the dispute, the honest talk, debate, one day witnessing her Arthur, out of all the men there, convincing the front driver in a retinue of lorries to turn around. It had brought that old flush back to the pair of them. The two of them had understood one another again.

Then things went mad. The NCB obtained their injunction to stop any miner picketing outside of his own county, and every region was cordoned off by the police, sandbags stationed to prevent any more of the strike's floodwater getting in.

They must have had Maggie on the run, because the bitch threw the kitchen sink at it. The entire country was now encircled by sirens, a circuit board of blue, men no one knew from Adam given dispensation to do whatever they bloody . . . Arthur's face. His poor, swollen face.

"Shell?"

Little blonde Jan was pointing down the street with her rose-tattooed arm. Shell had been so engrossed in thought that she hadn't noticed the voices, the women's voices: a chanted song.

> United by the struggle
> United by the past
> And it's here we go, here we go,
> We're the women of the working class

It gave her the jitters. A huge procession was herding towards an even bigger crowd, the whole lot marching towards the town centre. Shell's instinct was always to scoff, but as she and the others joined with the masses, the looks on everyone's faces stopped her short. People were so buoyant. They were alive. She'd barely noticed it was summer before today, yet here the mood highlighted the weather, or maybe vice versa. Shell lifted her face to regard the same firm warmth that washed the slates and the lichen on the mortar between the bricks. 1984 was heating up, showing off its dazzling shark's teeth.

Outside the NCB headquarters Shell re-tied her hair and pointed out the TV cameras to Jan. She could smell cooked meat – a barbecue? – and people were handing out copies of The Miner and The Morning Star. She had never been one for communal feeling or public togetherness, and for that matter tended to dislike people whenever she first met them, but she felt a synchronicity with everyone here. She supposed it was because for once she actually cared about what was happening.

Countless placards and lodge banners were waved as the women pushed through the crowd. On their way towards the stage, they passed a cardboard coffin balanced on the shoulders of five or so men. *Reserved for MacGregor*, it said, though as it went by, the angle made it look as if it just said: *Reserved*.

Able to hear all sorts of regional accents, Shell felt like she'd put her hands together for any one of these people if they asked, and they *were* asking. She linked arms with Jan. There was hope in these alien faces, and it made her think of Lawrence and the family she wanted him to have one day, their lives rayed out in the decades ahead. What would become of them if the miners lost this dispute, if the industry was downsized, shelved, even? Shell was afraid, and she could sense that same fear around her, easily as much fear as hope, and it made her well up in the instant that she recognised it.

She gulped the lump back. Very little could make her cry. Generosity of spirit was one thing, clarity of vision was another, but the reality of things was something else entirely.

"Sorry we're late," she said, nudging Cherry Cairns as they met the others on the concourse outside the cathedral. Cherry had bags under her eyes, lived across the road from Shell and had four kids. She was one of the few women who had never thrown the rug business back in Shell's face.

"Here she is. Mad out there, isn't it," said Cherry.

"We've been waiting ages, Shell," Joyce said.

"How do you mean?"

"Where you wanting us, boss?" Cherry laughed. "Don't play coy, duck. What's plan?"

Shell had wondered if they'd have organised themselves. Naturally it had been left to her. Everyone was staring but they could bloody well wait. She rummaged in her bag for her fags and popped one in her mouth. Lighter, lighter, there it was.

She sparked it first time, thank God. "Well, have we us buckets?" she said.

"Present and correct," said Jan.

"First speech is half-twelve so by my count that's two hours' collection time."

No one disagreed.

"So . . . four groups? Different parts of town. Meet here at twelve for tally and total."

"I were thinking we could do half and half," said Joyce. "Split in two."

"There's twelve of us here."

"Aye, I can see that, Michelle. We could—"

"We'll do four groups, like I said. Cover more ground." Shell glared at the others, prepared to argue.

"We'll have no strength in number that way," Joyce insisted. "Needs solidarity does begging."

Shell ignored her, split everyone into threes. Crown Court. Quays. High Street. Uni. People divided into groups as she'd instructed.

Joyce raised her hand, her whole arm as thin as one of those joke back scratchers you got at the seaside. "Crown Court?"

"Aye, what about it?"

"Oh, forget it."

Joyce had been like this since school. Shell went over so the others wouldn't hear and said, in a quiet voice, "So what's wi' slapped-arse face then?"

"I just don't think you'll have much luck at the crown court is all."

"Stop being a pain, Joyce. I've hardly seen us wrong so far."

"Oh, have it your way then, *Lady Muck*."

Shell was going to say something Joyce would regret when she felt a tap on her shoulder. The rest of the girls were grinning at her.

"What?"

Laughter. Shell pinched her thigh. Fucking Joyce was saying nowt and Smug-Arse Butterworth could hardly contain herself. Had any of them seen her and Het coming out of the bakery the other night? Because they'd been spending an awful lot of time together as it was. Lo, if word got back to Arthur . . . a breeze-fire swept through Shell's chest.

"Have I summat in me teeth?" she said.

"Don't talk daft," said Jan.

"Well, for crying out loud, put us out of us misery and don't make us ask again."

"So you've got the whole gang here an' geared up, right?"

"Well, aye, yeah . . ."

"But tha's forgetting summat."

Shell could only shrug.

"A uniform!"

"What you on wi', Jan?"

Jan's gigantic blue eyes were practically popping from her

head. "Well, there's been a great deal of talk of a name, as tha knows . . ." she said.

"An' I know you said you'd get *your* thinking cap on," said Olive.

"But we chose one anyway." Jan yanked a white cloth from her bag and threw it at Shell. "Reckon tha'll like it."

"Since when do I wear t-shirts?"

"Oh just read what it says, Shell."

There was the poppy red lettering. "Litten Ladies . . . God, this is daft . . ."

"No go on, Shell, read rest!"

Shell sighed. "Litten Ladies fight to the end. We support the miners."

"Again!" cried Olive.

Shell read it again.

"Now, look!"

The girls pulled apart their jackets. They all wore identical t-shirts, even Joyce.

"Tha's a Litten Lady," Jan yelled above the cheering. "So you best start dressing like one!"

Shell spent the morning with Olive and Linda, trying to collect money on the crazy paving near the crown court. She dealt with the public all the time in the bakery, but beseeching them, discussing her business? That was a very different matter.

Less than a pound in silver about summed her efforts up. People were so very *nice*. They sympathised – or patronised was probably a better word. Still, it was gin-clear they were glad they weren't her, involved in this unfortunate and bitter mess.

Shell just didn't have Olive's way with people. She was too forthright, and though she tried to appear natural when she cornered folk, she couldn't get over how her *Litten Lady* shirt outlined the fact she'd no bra on, and it was far too hot for her to put on her denim jacket.

Course it was nice to be outdoors, and Shell could bear a little embarrassment over important matters, but she couldn't resist sticking her tongue out at a baby sitting in his pram, and when Olive managed to persuade Linda to join her in singing like Pinky and Perky at people as they hurried by, Shell slipped away to watch the River Don instead.

Relieved to find a quiet place, Shell stared down at the murky water from the concrete embankment. The river could have been a patchwork of parcel tape, caught and creased, its numerous irregularities winking in the light as if hundreds of mini crescent moons had been collected and jumbled together in a colossal trough.

A barge cut its way through this soft ink, the dank bouquet of sewage and industrial works nearby making themselves known, too. A stockyard stretched on the other side of the river. Figures sat there on their pallets, scoffing their snap amid the pig iron. Above the barge's engine and the clanging of the factories could be heard the spontaneous lap of the river. You'd never think this wide outflow with its gloop and overlay drew its sources from the becks and rills of wild Yorkshire, from the ghylls and ravines of England's Pennine spinal column. Yet beyond it, beyond this carbon city, the landscape was rugged enough to suggest that this was so.

Shell gazed at the distant country, an irresistible sight that gave her comfort. Here, for once, she felt free, free of her reckless family and her stunted existence, free of the welfare with its bowl of 10p's, the tower of Weetabix and enough teabags to last until October. She was free even of Het's laugh that made things go as thick and fuggy as winter mist. And this peace made her hope to one day find the answer she was in search of, although she couldn't remember ever posing life a question.

She looked at her watch. Quarter to. Lawrence would be on his dinner soon. How had he even got to be sixteen? He'd managed it so quietly, dashing along the skirting boards towards his O-levels. Finding the paper with the college ads the other day had been an eye opener. There her lad was, thinking about further education, and there *she* was, not even knowing when his exams were, let alone that he was considering working somewhere other than the pit.

She was useless not knowing that. Mind you, you had no chance with a teenager, especially one like Lawrence. If only he could be a kid again, even for a day, now that Shell had more of an idea what she was doing as a parent. Kiddies told you everything; they were little cupboards you could open whenever you wanted. Now she'd never know what was going on in her son's head. It was what she imagined missing a plane to be like, watching Lawrence's feelings jet off while she was left stranded on the runway.

She chucked her dog-end in the river and returned to the streets. Olive was waving and Linda was tapping her watch. Shell couldn't resist sneaking a final look at the way she'd come. For some reason she was mesmerised by the distant hilly range and the thought that every city, every citizen petered out before something like it, a vastness she'd never understand, such mystery. She could see the way to Lawrence bound up in that feeling.

The route was a single track.

༝

To Joyce's satisfaction they divvied only five quid shrapnel between the lot of them. Shell ignored her snide gaze and led everyone to the main stage to hear the speeches.

The crowd was swollen. Shell could see two women in primary-coloured business suits interviewing groups of miners who themselves had small crowds of people surrounding them. There was a makeshift stage where couples handed out pamphlets. A preaching student was gesticulating, standing on some milk crates with a karaoke microphone in his hand, the microphone connected to a boxy guitar amp.

It was so busy that the Litten Ladies had to stop a fair distance from the front and spread out in the crowd, two or three abreast or single to a gap. While everyone waited for Arthur Scargill to arrive, a chant began to do the rounds. Call and response. Shell smoked through the entire thing.

A huge cheer went up when the union leader finally showed his face. He stepped confidently across the stage like a rock star. Shell couldn't see a thing so went on her tiptoes, putting her hand on the shoulder of a man in front, who gave her a dirty look. There was a lot of clapping and cheering as Arthur – he had to be called Arthur – said how proud he was to be here. But what good did pride ever do? Shell had learned that one the hard way.

So many police, each of them a blue danger point lined up along the NCB building with its stripe of grey brick spanning it like a belt strap. The police resisted the crowd as it poured forward at something Scargill had said. Shoved people regrouped and steadied themselves, creating the space Shell needed to escape from Joyce and get a better view of the stage. Jan called after her – she didn't turn around.

She found her way to some steps. From the top, a sight like

nothing she had ever seen washed ahead: banners and placards, flags and people perched on each other's shoulders, a thousand heads, a human stew. Shell stuck her fingers on either side of her teeth and blew a piercing whistle across the square. Plenty of people stared.

Bloody look at me then.

Scargill didn't turn; he had his hand raised. Too kind, you're all too kind. He wore a blue suit, which somehow felt out of order to Shell, as if the guy had come straight from the set of a Saturday night quiz show. Shell had never seen anyone in the flesh who'd been on TV. Yet here was their ashen chief, and he had that same combed hair, side-parted, coarse as donkey mane, that same neck with no chin as he had in real life. Her dad used to call men like Arthur Scargill chinless wonders; and not that it was their fault, but, no offence, it sort of *was* their fault. Shell thought Scargill was OK. His sideburns looked authentic, he cleared his throat like a working man and thanked people the right way. He *felt* like one of them, and that was important because if he wasn't one of them, he was doing a damned good job of faking it and what else would he be lying about?

He talked of counties, negotiation. He talked of unity and strength. Everyone lapped it up, and why wouldn't they? You don't come to these do's to be told what you don't want to hear. You come to have your lily gilded, to be grouped together and buttered-up, glazed merrily in your kiln.

The speech went on. They'd win because they were the good guys, only there was talk of what a win might mean, and Shell didn't trust that. There was always a catch. Then again perhaps the catch was that she was always looking for one. Shell chewed her hair. This was another benefit of the strike. Her mind felt open as it never had before.

Some pissed lads behind her were acting all giddy.

"Do you mind?" Shell said.

"Who pulled your chain?"

"You lot, I can't hear nothing."

"Oh calm down, Doris."

"Aye, shouldn't you be back at home wi' t'kiddies?"

"Some of us are here to support the effort," said Shell, wrinkling her nose at the stink of beer.

"She must be on t'blob. Decorators in."

They were laughing and Shell couldn't stand being laughed at. "Oh, shut yer traps," she said. "I've not come all this way to listen to some babbies who've just crawled out from behind their mothers' skirts of an afternoon. You're pathetic."

"How's about *you* be quiet," someone else called from nearby, which made the lads crease up with laughter. Shell searched for where the voice had come from and saw Joyce Stride watching her, scowling.

She tried to concentrate on the stage. It was no good. A kernel of unease had taken seed in the veiled uncertainty in people's faces earlier, in the bags under Cherry Cairns' eyes and her Arthur's damaged face, and now it was in flower. She would never confess to anyone how relieved she'd been when her husband wouldn't let her clean his wounds that morning. It was hard enough to feel attracted to Arthur these days. A cracked plate for a face, she just wouldn't have known what to make of.

The three behind her were jostling again. Shell huffed at them once more and wished for Het.

"Go on, Trev. Go on, dare you."

A hand darted below Shell's waist like an eel snapping out

of a wall, grabbing at her behind. She'd been expecting the louts to try something, so managed to get hold of the wrist, dug her nails into the exposed section of skin and tugged hard, forcing the hand's owner to tumble off the stairs into the crowd.

He landed like a rock dropped into a sandpit. People were knocked sideways as the lad's beer bottle flew from his hand, smashed on the pavement and became a wet asterisk.

Scattered folk picked themselves up as the police arrived, four officers varying in size. They roughed Shell's aggressor to his feet. He was winded and making desperate *huck-huck* noises. Shell tried to keep calm. She was tempted to go and see if the young man was OK, but one of the officers had hold of him. "*Man up,*" the officer said, forcibly straightening the lad upright by the collar. The copper was fair-haired. He had pretty eyes and one of those cruel, playful mouths. "What the *fucking* hell you doing?" he said, loud enough for everyone to hear.

The blond officer let go of the youngster, shoving him in the back so he could bend over and catch his breath. Scargill's voice was at this point unintelligible. Everyone in the vicinity was facing this way.

Shell gripped her wrist but kept losing count of her pulse. The shortest of the four policemen stepped forward. He had stripes on his arm and a beard encircled his tight little grimace. "Someone better own up," he said. "Or we'll cordon the whole area and take the lot of yous in."

No one responded. Shell picked the cameras out on the other side of the rally. She was about to whistle for their attention when Joyce caught her eye, shook her head and mouthed the word: *No.*

"I'll give till five for someone to tell us what's happened," the bearded sergeant said.

No one spoke. The blond officer aimed his radio at his mouth. He twisted Shell's assailant's collar like a wet flannel.

Three.

Four.

The youngster's nose bled. Serves him right for touching her up, thought Shell. Then again, these bastards were the police, the same police that had smashed her Arthur's face in, and at the end of the day it was about direct action. Scargill would be proud and so would Het.

She hopped off the wall. "It were me," she said. "It were my fault."

"Right then," the sergeant said, signalling for his men to come and take Shell. The third officer looked about ten years old, the fourth had an Adam's apple that made him look like he'd swallowed a ping-pong ball. As they took Shell by either arm, the sergeant addressed the crowd. "I'm not having a few idiots disrupt a peaceful rally. Listen to your man, clap your hands and get yourselves home." He turned to Shell. "And frankly, Miss, I'm surprised at you."

He was little, probably soft as anything.

"Why's that?" said Shell.

The policeman stopped.

"As I mean, you hardly know me."

The sergeant came closer, podge nose practically grazing Shell's cheek.

"What the fuck did you just say?"

Shell's legs nearly went. These bastards had knocked her family about. They were ruining peoples' lives. Stop and search every time she wanted to go anywhere. She took a deep breath.

"I said, I don't know how you're surprised."

The policeman lowered his voice further. Pantomime of it. Burl of it. "Have we a problem?"

"I were just saying—"

"You causing a disturbance?"

"You can see I'm not."

"Jeff, is this one causing a disturbance?"

The blond officer laughed. "She's a pest, Sarge. She can deny it all she likes."

Shell knew all about pests, silken specks that incubated in your dreams and infested everything you knew. "I'm just pointing out the generalisation," she said. "As I'm a woman, you're surprised. What if I were defending myself? What if it were an accident?"

"Madam, I am telling you to calm down."

"Why does everyone keep saying that? I'm perfectly calm."

"If you don't calm down, Miss. I will arrest you."

Shell grit her teeth. She'd come this far. "Well that's up to you," she said, "but I hoped you'd at least see sense and let me try and explain what happened."

It was as easy as that. Shell's arms were cranked painfully behind her back, her name was taken and her rights read while they fitted the cuffs. The metal clicked and pinched, and then she found herself being led through the crowd. She could see Joyce disappear. Shell didn't even have chance to shout after her, so quickly was she lost.

"Just goes to show," she called out to the people around her, "It just goes to show what they're really like."

"Button it or we'll do you for resisting arrest."

"I'm coming willingly!"

"You're coming how we say you are."

As Shell was steered onward, a stranger appeared from the multitude and walked by her side. "Go quiet," he told her. "Say nowt. South Yorks can be bastards when they get you on your own."

"That's enough," said one of Shell's escorts, shoving the stranger in the chest. The man held up both hands and backed away.

Shell kept her trap shut after that. She was brought towards a line of police transit vans parked outside a command point: a small marquee behind a Heras fence erected in abuttal with a Portakabin that had metal shutters covering its windows. She could hear laughter. Arthur Scargill was joking up on stage.

Joyce suddenly appeared, stepping into Shell's path. "Officers *please*," she said. "May I have a word?"

The policemen paused. Shell's mouth was as dry as anything as Joyce began to speak, her plummy church manner made all the more convincing by her puritanical pudding-bowl of self-snipped hair. She was pale, tremendously so. "I'm afraid this woman's not right in the head," she said.

The officers laughed. "Back away, love. This is an arrest."

Roughly, Joyce was ushered out of the way. The policemen frogmarched Shell on. Joyce hurried with them, pushing in front again, this time holding a hand before Shell's captors as if she was herself an officer of the law, halting the traffic.

"*Listen*," she said, "I can testify with absolute certainty that this woman is an incorrigible eccentric, and not responsible for her actions. Officers, *please*. What happened was an accident. I saw the whole thing."

One of the policemen stepped towards Joyce with his hand on his baton, but Joyce stood her ground. "Really," she said. "Let me introduce myself. My name is Joyce Stride and I am the chairlady of the L.W.A.P.C. Litten Woman against Pit Closures."

"Hold on! Hold the fuck on."

It was the blond policeman. He stomped over and shoved his truncheon directly under Joyce's nose. A polished thing, sensual looking. His chalky fingers nestled in the grip.

"Say your name, please," he said briskly. He could have been ex-military.

"I . . . why?"

"You lot and your questions. When you get an order from someone in uniform, you don't say: *Why*, you say: *Yes*. Understand?"

"Of course."

"Don't you mean fucking yes?"

"Yes!"

"Yes fucking what?"

"Yes, officer."

"Now we're getting somewhere." The man pointed his truncheon at Shell. "You, Mouth. Following?"

"Plain as day," said Shell.

"Halle-fucking-lujah." The truncheon whipped back towards Joyce, who, to her credit, didn't cry out as the weapon stopped a centimetre from her eyeball. "Now, say your fucking name. Or are you refusing to tell an officer of the law your fucking name?"

"I just told you my name."

The blond policeman pushed his truncheon hard against Joyce's cheek, forcing her head sideways.

"It's Joyce," she said. "Joyce Stride."

"Well done, Joyce Stride. Now who do you think you are, that you'd try to obstruct my colleagues in the engagement of their duties?"

"I . . . I am a member of the L.W.A.P.C, a friend of this woman, and I can assure you that she has done nothing wrong."

Now the truncheon switched to beneath Joyce's nose, pushing her head back almost ninety degrees. The blond man in uniform could barely keep from laughing as he said "You're a member of fuck all, love."

Shell felt that old crescendo, but the officer just grinned at her. "You'd better shut it," he said, "before you make this any worse."

"You're all right, Shell," Joyce said, her voice pressured by the angle to which her throat had been forced. "I said, *sir . . .*" she said, batting the truncheon away and facing the officer boldly. "That this woman has done nothing wrong. She's quite mad and incapable of holding her tongue, but that's it. She shouldn't be arrested and if she is I shall be making a complaint to your superiors."

"I'm sorry, I might have misheard, Miss Stride," said the officer. "Did you just say you'd like to make a complaint?"

"I did, sir. Your conduct has been shocking. You're an officer of the law and as such should wield your power with the same respect you expect us citizens to abide by it."

Shell was certain Joyce was going to be struck. Her hands still secured, she broke free of the men holding her and stepped up to the blond officer, his slate-coloured eyes. "You leave her alone," she began, but was stopped, partly by the large hand that reached out and grabbed her by the cheeks, and partly by the tempting smell of toffees that she could smell on the officer's breath as he brought her close, the scent washing sweetly over her face.

A LOAF OF bread and a jar of potted beef in a plastic bag. Arthur made a point of not looking at the garish orange frontage of the job centre.

Saturday and no idea where the wife was. He'd just stopped at the bakery, opening the door and setting off the funny klaxon. Course she wasn't in. Si Gaskell was serving customers instead, long hair tied under that daft white hat, ponytail stuffed into one of those nets that look like they should be full of bird seed. The sleazy prick had no idea where Shell was. He'd stared at Arthur's wracked face and refused to give him a discount on his loaf.

Walking to save on bus fare, Arthur arrived home and entered the kitchen. From the plastic bag he removed the bread, swabbing two slices with margarine and another two with brown sauce. Out came the butter knife Lawrence used when he was a kid and his hands were too small to hold the main cutlery. Arthur stabbed the knife into the jar of potted beef – it was the perfect size – and spread the meat paste thickly across each buttered slice. These sandwiches he split into neat triangles, piling them onto a plastic plate and carrying the whole lot upstairs on a tray along with a mug of claggy-looking, terracotta-coloured tea.

Outside Lawrence's room he fished the key from his pocket. It slotted noisily into the padlock and popped the hook. Last night, home from the hill and the second attack on his person in a month, Arthur had unscrewed the galvanised hasp from the coal shed and fitted it to Lawrence's door. When, as expected, Lawrence arrived home and snuck into bed without so much as a word of apology to his old man, Arthur rose from bed and locked his son in until the next morning. He was no pushover, not like he used to be.

"I've lunch," he said, shoving the door open with his foot. "Kid?"

Little bastard.

Arthur hurried to the open window, tea soaking the sandwiches as the tray clattered on the desk. Judging by the dents in the old toilet and coal shed roofs, Lawrence had done a circus act off the windowsill then escaped into the backs. By the back gate sat a pewter-coloured cat that Arthur could swear was smiling at him.

Into the yard. His balls ached – that girl had really clouted him one – as he glared over the blunt wall at the sparrows twittering in the sycamores. This was him officially lumbered with a pair of AWOL's now. They were selfish bastards, his family, the bloody pair of them.

He should have known something was up when the noise died down earlier; the booted door panels given respite, the spherical handle ceasing to rattle. He should have known when there was no reply after he told Lawrence he'd be back with lunch, that they'd talk about what happened then.

It was a mistake slipping into town in search of Shell. Ten minutes wasted, half an hour, forty even, because of her. Just the time it took to get to the mini-mart and the bakery, just the time for Lawrence to escape. Now the lad could be anywhere and Shell was off gallivanting about.

Arthur tried to think logically. The kind of places he'd

seek if he were in his son's position had their synonyms, and *these* were the places he should check. For the library read the market. For the moorland read the woods. If it was Arthur running away because his friend had just attacked his father, it'd be no contest, he'd take the Litten Path, go down the street rather than up it, defying the little peat canyons and the sinkholes left by the pit ponies, heading past the abandoned Land Rover, sky-blue, rusted and paint-peeled, the springs bursting out of their seats like the components to a broken jack-in-a-box.

There was nowhere better than the moor. Always Arthur could feel it: a mental space as much as a physical one, everything made remote upon its stretch. He'd half a mind to go there now, wading through the bog cotton, up the steeps, buffeted by the weather, witnessed only by the lozenge pupils of the sheep grazing on the bare flat of purple and hazel. But it was out of the question. He set off for Barnes' Wood. The forest would be perfect for Lawrence to hide in. It was where guilt's fugitive could disappear beneath the undergrowth like a serpent.

The Ogden was at low ebb. Sludge banks on either side tilted toward the surrounding woods and tracts of milky sunlight glazed through, broken simply by the knuckle, peg and beam of the trees, one of which had a cache of beer cans stuffed in it.

Arthur's trainers sank in the bog, and he almost slipped on the distorted pages of a porn magazine that lay twisted, sodden in the muck. The paper skin of the naked woman was torn and she had a black stripe hiding both eyes, stars concealing each nipple. She couldn't quite smile in the direction of a plastic bag woven around a tree root. Arthur stopped for a piss. Silence otherwise.

He arrived at the ruins on the south side of the wood. He'd come exploring here with Lawrence in the past, for the odd tryst with former girlfriend in days gone by, bare arse chafing the cold as he fucked and rocked on the brick, spit collecting in that heavy after-moment. Blinking and becoming yourself again. Pulling out and returning gratefully to being separate.

But that was an age ago and now everything seemed smaller. Two of the ruin's four walls were gone and nettles as tall as corn sprouted in what could once have been the kitchen. The structure was crumbling until one day it would cease to exist at all.

Further past the ruin Arthur came to the track that fed the tree cave that he and Sam used to visit. He wondered if the elm had gotten any bigger. His mam used to say elms are associated with death because they drop branches without warning and their wood is a preferred material for coffins. Perhaps that was why Arthur liked them so much. The river bridge was nearby. The stretched verticals of the beech trees looked like they had faces in them. There was no chance of going to the den now. Too much of the past was sealed within its boundary.

Traffic. There was a lot more of that these days. It made a steady sound that crept steadily as might a glacier. Lawrence wasn't here. Maybe Arthur didn't know this place at all. Maybe he didn't know his son and never had done.

He headed for home, kicking a stone towards town until a red car sounded its horn and drew in some yards ahead. Arthur approached, drew to the wound-down window, passenger side, bent so he could see the driver and said, "What you doing, you? You're wasting petrol."

"Bored," said Asa Scanlan.

"You're always bored."

Asa leaned over and opened the door. He was a compassionate and volatile man with a big round head and a bob in the bridge of his nose; his cheeks were bristled and his arms were taut. "Frame yourself," he said, revving the Fiesta's engine.

There was the waiting seat and there was waiting wood, and here was the open door. "You're a sight for sore eyes," said Arthur, climbing into the car.

"Got any cigs?"

"I said you're a sight for sore eyes, *Moonface*."

Asa braked in the middle of the road. "What'd I say about calling us that?"

"Calling you what?"

"*Does tha want a lift or what?*"

Asa was so easy. Arthur switched on the pilot light and made a silly face under it that was murder on his broken cheek. Thankfully it was enough to get Asa chuckling.

"Just don't call us that, all right?" said Asa.

"What, *Moonface?*"

"Funny." Asa set off again. "Face is the last thing you can chat on wi'."

Arthur passed Asa the tobacco and thumped him on the arm. His old friend spoke the language of assent ninety percent of the time. He was all *go on thens* and *why nots* and *you're not wrongs*, but you could rile him into a no when you had a mind to. Winding Asa Scanlan up was as easy as setting a mousetrap off with a pencil.

They drove on a bit. "I'm sorry, love," Arthur eventually said.

"You're all right, lass. Thought you'd be on t'march today."

"Not fit for service," Arthur said, pointing at the mask still covering a portion of his face. "And if you must know, I'm out looking for me lad."

Asa changed gear. "Why, where's he gone?"

"He's gone and got himself in hot water."

"Well how's he done that then?"

"What's this, Spanish Inquisition?"

The sun reached its zenith as Barnes' Wood disappeared behind the Fiesta. The truth was that between picketing and not forgiving being dropped in it with Shell, Arthur hadn't a clue what was going on with his son. It was high time that was remedied. Skipping school and knocking around with a maniac: the boy was out of control. The bewildered look on his face when Arthur found him with that girl yesterday beggared belief. Lawrence hadn't been able to believe that his old man had showed up, seeming to forget that Arthur had been young himself once, and had in fact been a seasoned skiver in his day. And although Arthur didn't condone missing school – there'd be words on *that* – didn't Lawrence know not to hang around town afterwards? It was common sense. As, for that matter, was not standing like a lemon while your girlfriend kicked your dad in the fucking balls.

Arthur gobbled another four codeine and felt the Swarsby photographs in his pocket. They were his only copies. He'd been too scared to put them down in case he lost them.

They were soon near the Brantford side of town, not far from Threndle House.

"What march you on about anyway?" Arthur said.

"Sheffield. Jan's there with your Shell and a few others."

"Oh, right."

"Tha didn't know?"

"Course I bloody did."

There was nothing to do except drive. Without work, a picket or any money, aimlessness was what life often boiled down to these days. Arthur semi-watched for Lawrence while Asa drove. The day's heat was in ascension. They coasted along the textured, marked road, past the rec, pausing at the lights next to the bus stand where the night bus still picked people up on their way home from The Bluenote most weekends.

"Many's the eve spent swaying at that stop," said Arthur fondly, turning to watch the metal post, wonky in its cement foot. Takeaway boxes spilled from the mouth of the bin strapped to it.

The bin's jumbled outline faded as they drove. "When we were lads," said Asa, and Arthur smiled. So many evenings had begun with the two of them sat on opposite sides of the 273, heading straight from their shift to the welfare then hitting The Bluenote, an old club that had swollen banks of lights next to the mobile disco, and a dancefloor filled almost exclusively with girls.

Upon arrival Arthur always went straight to the bogs to take the black socks off the outsides of his shoes – he had to disguise his scruffs somehow – then pushed back through the crowd to find the shitfaced Asa. In those days the candlewax floor had just been replaced by the hard material that made your feet stick, and the club turn sang in their own accent. Three to four hours on the piss then home to Shell, rubbing the corduroy of her spine. "Your hands are freezing," she'd say.

"You look so bloody good, love."

"It's the light fooling you."

So what if it was? Sometimes Arthur's mouth wouldn't

feel like his own as he kissed his wife's neck, as he sank to her lower regions, the coarse nature of her legs. Sometimes it could have been anyone in bed with him. He could have been anyone himself, a perfect stranger to Shell. Their curtains were often lit from the street below, each flower of the fabric's print assuming new life the harder you squinted at it. Altered roses. Living foliage.

"Leathered in the Bluenote." Asa laughed. They were driving towards the Grey Grebe by then. "Bloody Nora. You on that lamppost." He adjusted his weight in his chair. "One handed pull-up's from t'top."

"Them birds were having kittens," said Arthur.

"Bugger me, what were their names again?"

They turned the corner. The two of them had been friends since they were first partnered up at Brantford. A couple of years older than Arthur, Asa started at the pit after it held a recruitment drive across the borough. The management bussed lads in from the local schools and impressed them with the machinery, the struts, joists, coke houses and brick houses, the various ovens and stories of the spoil pile that lit up every now and again thanks to overzealous piling, combustible pouches of air trapped all too dangerously.

Mining life was known for this kind of unpredictability as much as it was known for its sense of community, and that, coupled with the prospect of rising wages and a house paid for by the coal board, appealed to lads like Asa who were done with school the minute they got there and anxious to start tucking into their lives.

Asa put his name down for a job that day and six months later was working with Arthur on the fetch and carry. Typical new starters, their first duty was salvaging scrap down the

Grafton Belt, a spent seam of coal in one of the oldest Brantford districts beneath Litten. Their job was to scoot around retrieving what was left down there, 'On the wood' or 'on the metal', depending what you were after that day, barely able to see a few yards ahead, collecting the shite left behind by old crews, pre and post war, in times when it was almost as muggy above ground as it was below, before the clean air act stopped the atmosphere on the streets from feeling like a willow curtain you could part with your hands. Like a brattice partition, even. The controller of the gas.

Lads the same age who labour together can get close in a matter of days. That doesn't necessarily mean they're alike. Asa's eyes were without curiosity. They were passages into a mind occupied by the sporting pinks, the weekend and the next morning and not much else. His friendship with Arthur was subterranean. Patina of dust over their lamp glass as they shared their snap. Some people are chucked together, others are drawn. When Arthur and Shell Newman met Asa and Janice Scanlan, Arthur was wildly jealous. There were no bottomless lakes in the Scanlans' marriage. There were no dreams of wolves or plague doctors or past lives. Meeting the other couple had made him realise for the first time that the simplistic measure was the better yardstick. That the Newmans had saddled themselves by reading meaning into everything.

"We took them up the moor. Oh, what were their names, Art? When you found that skull."

"Hang a left here, Scanny. Is that him?"

"Where?"

"Going up Flintwicks."

On their way towards the Grey Grebe, the Fiesta turned up the estate. Flintwicks was a puzzle of streets built to retain pit workers after Litten was declared a manpower deficiency area back in the fifties. For some reason its streets were named after towns on the south coast. Horsham, Arundel, Tonbridge, Swanage . . . Up one of these closes strode a narrow youngster in jeans and t-shirt.

"Fucking down there. Turn left, Asa."

The car swung crazily down Rudgwick. The windscreen was so mucky that Asa had to put the wipers on as he said it didn't look like Lawrence, he had too much hair.

"It's grown back loads. Now slow down, I don't want him spooked . . ."

"Jackie and Pauline."

"Eh?"

"Them birds."

"Bob on, lad. Now I remember."

Though Arthur had never really forgotten. Jackie possessed a hefty nose and teeth that in the right light had looked like rock, calcified deposits in her gums. She'd been fending off the advances of a slippery little man in the Bluenote so Arthur had stepped in, then, at closing time, let Jackie persuade him into a night walk. The pair were splash-lit by street-light, looking almost radioactive, thought Arthur, as Jackie said she thought he was dead brave, when in fact he knew he was one of the biggest cowards who had ever lived.

The Morse Code wink of an aeroplane's lights. The lull of the dark. Side by side, strolling the uneven camber of the Litten Path. "It's wet," said Jackie. "I said it's wet out."

"Have us coat, if you like."

"Oh, warm us, will you, Arthur. Come here."

She wasn't a patch on Shell. Arthur let her take his arm anyway. Asa and the other one were laughing as they picked their route behind, the sky looking tender to the touch, a shifting honeycomb as Jackie leaned in for her kiss. Why the fuck not? Arthur was so pissed he'd have agreed to anything. Colour. Fireworks. Het. Arthur was leaning forward, listening to Jackie's nostrils, the weird whistling noise they made, when he heard the crunching sound.

He pulled back. "*Jesus.*"

"What is it?"

"I think you've stood on summat."

It had misted. Jackie peered at her feet and saw that she had trampled on the body of a dead badger. She leapt away. Arthur picked up the beast's skull. The moment felt profound. He had stumbled upon the remains of the most English of all creatures, and it was dead. Eventually Jackie must have left him to it, or maybe Arthur left her; he could forget so easily what wasn't relevant. He jogged home, walked home, floated home to his dozing wife and sleeping son, the tiny augury stowed inside his anorak pocket. He'd watched his family wake up. He'd made them breakfast.

"It's him, Asa."

The subsidiary drag of Flintwicks stretched beyond, with enough road for Asa to put his foot down and speed towards the figure a hundred or so yards away, the figure who turned, saw the car and broke into a run.

"Only a lad of yours would run for nowt, Arthur."

"Well get after him, Scanny. Carpe diem."

"I don't speak French."

"Just fucking drive."

The Fiesta hurtled up the macadam, following the dirty soles of Lawrence's shoes that blinked in sequence. They were going uphill and the car managed to catch him easily.

Arthur wound down his window and told Lawrence to stop. When the lad didn't he told him he was grounded until further notice.

He pulled his head back into the car. "Get on t'curb. Scanny."

"That'll do tyres."

"You're not on a penny farthing!"

"I need this motor, Arthur, I'll not risk it!"

Arthur was about to grab the wheel when a ginnel emerged to the car's left. A walkway with cement-panelled walls and waist high railings at either end. Lawrence headed straight down it.

"Fuck's sake, pull over."

Arthur jumped out of the car, vaulted the fence and sprinted down the shortcut after his son. Tall weeds sprouted between the paving and there were several white dog turds, NO SURRENDER spray-painted up the length of one of the sidings.

Hard to gain on a young man. Although Arthur lived a physical life, giving chase meant a different kind of fitness. Step. Step. Step. His beat on the pavement sent jagged bolts of pain up his fractured face.

"Stop, lad!"

Lawrence kept going.

"Lawrence, please stop!"

Little bastard.

Arthur had a stitch. He watched his son go and was about to call after him when the end of the ginnel flooded red. It was Asa. He had driven around the block and barred the way with the Fiesta.

Arthur hurried as best he could, while Asa stood at the

passage's exit with both arms crossed. Realising he'd been bagged, Lawrence leant, breathless, against a wall. Arthur was about to give him what for when he realised the boy was crying.

"You're all right, kid," he said, putting his arms around his son. "Your dad's here."

The front door opened directly into Asa's living room on Winchester Close. A picture of Ken Scanlan smiled above the wooden mantelpiece. Ken had been a banksman at Brantford, hauling back the cage gates, responsible for the loading and reloading of men and tubs of coal. He'd bought the house from the NCB and passed it on to Asa and Janice and the girls. Their very own home that they now couldn't afford to pay the mortgage on.

Arthur had shielded Lawrence long enough for his face to dry. He sat him down while Asa went to make the tea.

The long minute, the endless second.

"State of that shirt. What you been ironing it with, an hot brick?"

Lawrence didn't reply.

"You needn't have run."

"*You* needn't have locked us in last night."

Asa was whistling in the next room. Lawrence had always been like this. "If anyone should be angry, it should be me, kid."

Another shrug.

"Skipping school, you'll end up like me, let alone that we're at risk of having Education Welfare round. They'll have us up in court, lad, then what will your mam say?"

Lawrence fiddled with the laces of his trainers.

"Can you at least look at me?"

Rubbing the tears had left Lawrence's eyes inflamed. His defiant expression suggested he knew this would be something Arthur hated to see. He was dead right about that.

Arthur's voice cracked. "I said you were out of school again, weren't you?"

"Aye."

"And that's a poor do."

"Suppose."

Fuck me, what did it take to make the lad budge? It was bad enough having a son, one that looked so much like you made you feel like you were telling yourself off in situations like this. Shell was better at this sort of thing. Discipline, dinners and the day-to-day were her territory. Advice, schemes and homework were Arthur's.

He decided upon a different approach, pointing at himself with both thumbs. "You've not even asked about the face."

"You've hardly given us chance. I mean I did wonder . . ."

"*Jesus*, I weren't pissed-up if that's what that look means."

"Well, what were it then?"

"You're as bad as your mam, you are!"

Asa entered, carrying the tea. "Jan's had some shifts at Masons so's splashed out," he said, tossing Lawrence and Arthur a chocolate biscuit each. Arthur could smell the whiskey in his own mug. Asa winked.

"Another thing not mentioned is that girl. Calamity Jane an' her size twelves," Arthur said.

"Has Seabreeze got himself a bird?" Asa rolled his sleeves up.

"He wishes."

"What d'you know about it, Dad?" Lawrence snapped.

"I know she's not all there." Arthur tapped his head. "Bad influence. You're best getting rid."

"Why, what'd she do?" said Asa.

"*Nowt.*"

"You don't get it," said Lawrence, hands scrunched in his lap.

"No, I don't," replied Arthur, though definitely he did.

Their eyes met. "I'm sorry, all right?" Lawrence conceded, which choked Arthur. He blamed the hangover for this mimsiness. He always felt fraught the day after a bout of drinking.

"I should bloody well hope so," he said, downing the last of his hot, splendid tea. As it slipped down his throat, quick as mercury, he had the feeling of a glorious neon fluid being poured over his brain, coursing into every rivulet, every artery.

"Any chance of another, Scanny?"

"Course." Asa left the room and a moment later the kettle could be heard.

"Still ran though, didn't you. Couldn't help yoursen, leaving your old man in the lurch."

The kettle was getting louder. Lawrence was so soft.

"First the rug, then the tree, now this. As if I don't have enough on us plate. Never mind your bloody mam."

"None of that were my fault, Dad."

"Never is. Never has been. You don't care 'bout school. He's not fussed, my grammar lad's not bothered about making summat of hisself. All he wants is to muck about and drop his dad in it. Standing there while some loony attacks him."

"Dad, I didn't—"

"Oh fucking own summat for once, will you, kid?"

Lawrence set down his own mug. "You what?"

The carpet at their feet was some imitation Afghani thing,

a crystal pattern surrounded by acanthus leaves. At home they were back to the old floor and whose bloody fault was bloody that? A pessimist wife and a feeble fucking kid who refused to make the most of the opportunity gifted to him. All those nights going over the practice papers, all that encouragement, fuck's sake. Lawrence was on the wag and making out to Shell that the tree had been nicked and Het was one nil up and as for Shell that ungrateful sack of spuds. Arthur realised he was standing. "You're weak, lad, moaner like your mam! Look at you, shy as fuck. You're a liability. I used to be able to rely on you."

Lawrence stood too. "That's rich coming from you!" he shouted, and maybe he was right. Maybe in a lot of ways he had a right to say such a thing, but as a son there was no way he was getting away with talking to his father like that. Arthur slapped Lawrence around the face.

Have that.

The two of them glared at one another, breathing heavily. When Arthur looked away, Lawrence flopped so heavily into the armchair that the poker set fell over by the fireplace. The sound of the ringing ash pan and sweep was the sound of something broken between the two of them.

In the shrinking that followed, Arthur retreated to a framed photo mounted on the wall. It was another one of Ken Scanlan. This time Ken was holding baby Asa in front of a huge drill rig. Arthur removed his mask. Within the sheen of the glass, he could make out the motley patch of grazing on his cheek. It spread from the main impact point under the socket of a marshmallow eye, a bruised hump like a spoil heap.

"Mess, isn't it?"

Lawrence had his head in his hands.

"I said it's a mess, isn't it?"

Silence.

"Kid?" Remorse marched its challenge. Arthur went over to crouch by Lawrence's knee. The greasy antimacassar behind his son's head was badly in need of a wash.

"I shouldn't have done that."

"You're a flaming hypocrite!"

"I *know*."

"You can't blame us for everything, Dad. I said I were sorry."

"Me an' all."

"I couldn't stop her."

"You weren't to know she'd do that."

"She didn't know who you were . . ."

"Well . . . likewise."

"She thought you were some nutter."

"Well, that were one thing she were right about."

That got a laugh.

"She's my friend."

"Who, Lawrence? Who is she?"

"Evie Swarsby."

Course it was.

"Swarsby?" said Asa, who'd chosen that moment to re-enter the room. "That prick's had the nerve to be posting Tory leaflets through us doors."

"Aye," replied Arthur, re-setting the mask against his face and tugging the elastic over his head. "An' what you doing knocking around with her when you should be in school, kid?"

"Because I've been expelled, Dad. They've gone and expelled me."

11

NO ONE LIKES having to apologise, it's a horrible thing to have to do.

Lawrence was in the lounge listening to the familiar metal scratch of the key pushing into the lock. "I'll do the talking," said Arthur, acting as if he cared.

"Do we really have to tell her?"

"You've sat on it long enough. I'd start getting yourself straight if I were you. Tuck your shirt in. Do them laces."

The front door opened. Lawrence scrunched his toes. He could hear the muted rustle of his mam's denim jacket being hung on the hook. He assessed how quickly he could make it to the back door. His hair had only just grown back after the last disaster.

She pushed into the room. "*Oh . . .*" She laid a hand against her heart.

"All right, love."

Shell glanced at Arthur, who tried to act as if he couldn't recognise the way his wife was deliberately keeping her distance from him. Lawrence knew better. He watched the removal of the mask. How it was laid on the armrest with great care.

"Sorry, love," said Mam, setting down her handbag. The cloud out of the open window looked like bubble wrap.

"'Bout what?"

"Nowt."

"You're back late."

"Am I?"

Mam apologised again.

"Not to worry," said Arthur while Lawrence waited, the awkward plaintiff, the scent of honeysuckle coming at him through the open window.

His dad tried again. "So were the march—"

"I did hear you, love. It were fine."

Knotted fingers and swimming eyes, Lawrence's mam finally noticed him. He held her gaze long enough for her to know what she could do with it.

"That's good then," his dad said, glancing at the sky breaking through the cloud like a blueberry splat in a bowl of semolina. Lawrence and he were nearly the same height these days, neither gangling, simply sizable, though Arthur, hewer by trade, had broader shoulders from hefting the drills and the picks and what have you. Lawrence didn't know much about his dad's work. He didn't care to know. This might be the worst day of his life. He could practically hear the gush of blood in his arteries and veins. The pastel day was terrifying in its stillness.

"Aye," Mam was saying, a blistered feel to her voice. "But nowt to write home about."

She addressed Lawrence directly. "You all right, kid?"

It was an old trick of hers, coming at you sideways. The best thing to do was answer quick. "Not bad," replied Lawrence, thinking of those sooty hands clamping his skull; the fervid swish of the kitchen scissors.

"Good," said Mam.

Lawrence thinned his lips.

The truth had already been discovered, yet it was about

to be revealed again, which made it something of a paradox: a secret that had already been told. Lawrence could sense Arthur gearing himself up to pass on what he'd heard at Asa's. It hadn't been pretty earlier; Asa had to hold him back: a father who had always been so proud of his grammar school son. But at least Lawrence had been allowed to say his piece. His dad had the courtesy to stay quiet most of the way home, too, perhaps understanding failure for the ugly subject it was: one of the hardest things a person ever has to face.

It was Mam who was the unpredictable one. She'd defend you in public but had no time for excuses behind closed doors. Once when Lawrence's goalie gloves were stolen by one of the Champion lads from around the corner, she'd called round, given Cath Champion and her sons what for then come home and had a go at Lawrence for not standing up for himself. He was grounded in the ensuing argument, which was ironic, given that he was at that point giving an account of himself as she'd wanted him to in the first place. Irony was never one of Shell's strong suits. Spite was. Later, Lawrence found his gloves with the tip of the pinkie snipped off each hand. He got his own back by taking the batteries from his mam's alarm clock so she missed her appointment the next day at the doctor's.

He watched her at the door connecting to the hallway. She held it open with her elbow and bothered at the wall-hooks, removing a large piece of cloth from her jacket, balling it up then dropping it in the waste paper basket by the minibar.

She held herself stiffly, brown curls unleashed and her forehead seeming to stick out plainly. Lawrence craned to see in the bin. There was a t-shirt there.

"Love, we've something to say," said Arthur, his inflated face yet another thing to behold, so distended that it made Lawrence think of the grotesque cherub the Threndle House gargoyle had probably once been. With its dying fall, petrifying into stone.

"I said, Shell, me and the boy have news."

Here we go. Lawrence had been over this moment many times, and whenever he got to the point where he told his mam none of this would have happened if it weren't for her, that broad, adamant mouth dislocated and she devoured him.

He couldn't move. He stared at where the rug used to be, the scrubbed boards, tessellating under the furniture, slot-complex, imperfect, up to the walls that penned them, the bone surface of . . .

"Can it not wait?" Shell was saying. "I'm tired."

Yes!

"Well, love, not really, no."

"Well I'm afraid it'll have to. I've had a long day, been on my feet hours and . . ." Shell stopped. Lawrence didn't know where to look. "I'm just done in, OK? I need to get my head down."

She left the room dabbing at her eyes.

The door eased back ajar. When he was sure his mother was out of earshot, Lawrence asked what was up with her.

"How do you mean?" said Arthur.

"You didn't see?"

"She's tired, kid."

"She were nearly in tears, Dad, I swear."

"Get off wi' you."

"She were."

171

Arthur hesitated, then went to the foot of the stairs. "Sure you're all right, love?"

Mam yelled back that she was fine.

See, Arthur said, without words, adding as he re-fitted the mask. "Another of her moods."

"Go see her, Dad."

"Hark at you, trying to get rid."

"Come on," said Lawrence. "It's not that."

"You must think I came down wi' the last shower, lad."

"Honestly, go speak to her."

"Give me one good reason why."

"I just have done!"

Arthur's single eye was kind of horrifying; the plastic of his mask picked out the ochre in its iris, giving the impression of some dreadfully revealed ulterior consciousness.

"It's obvious," said Lawrence. "She didn't say anything when she saw us standing here like a pair of wedding ushers. She didn't seem surprised."

"Women, lad." Arthur chuckled. "She weren't bothered about my face neither."

And nor were you, is what Lawrence supposed he didn't say.

"*Fine*. What now? Can it not wait? She'll only want to go down school when she hears." Lawrence could picture his mam bursting through the swing doors at Fernside, through the cloakroom and up the steps to the foyer, demanding Grundy take her son back. It would never occur to her that Lawrence didn't *want* to go back, that without school was the broader palette, and painting with it, Evie Swarsby. He was a man now. This was life.

Not that Arthur appeared convinced. Old jaw-face, a man

smelling of booze when all he'd been on was tea. A nasty trick, using that padlock. It had made Lawrence miss his meeting with Evie. He'd resorted to climbing out of the window and nearly killed himself.

Course Evie was gone by the time he arrived at the tree cave. Ages he'd waited, listening to the helpless wood, starting at every movement, scratching Evie's name against a rock because he was too weak to carve it properly into a tree. Scribbling it out in case she ever saw it.

As the crow flies he'd left for Threndle House. The day had boiled and a police van thundered by, as they seemed to more and more of late. Crisp white shirts and a motley pack of yowling dogs. "Pit's that way," one of them called out of the window as the van went by. He was pointing at a muddy puddle.

Then came the arrival of Asa's car, red peril bursting into your line of sight. Lawrence was embarrassed about breaking down after being corralled in that alleyway, but you can't fight cumulative tears, and he didn't think Asa would tell anyone. He knew his father certainly wouldn't.

Here was Arthur now. "You're not getting out of this," he said, as if that was the only thing on Lawrence's mind.

"Maybe I'm not trying to, Dad. Maybe summat's up with Mam and it's obvious to anyone but a fucking sieve-head like you."

Lawrence had the Swarsbys to thank for a direct comment like that. He and Arthur had shared their differences over the years, but Lawrence didn't think he'd ever sworn *at* his father before. The eye in that mask had boggled wonderfully. A single finger had jabbed him in the chest.

Bastard should never have hit him. Lawrence stood outside the chipped door of his parents' room and prepared to knock-on. He regretted what he'd said but was also thrilled by it.

Mam wasn't asleep – Lawrence could hear her moving about in the room. He lifted his hand, belly scooped out with nerves, thumped the door and pushed it open without waiting for an answer.

His mam was standing at the end of the bed wearing only her bra and knickers. A bruise as dark as an oil slick spread up her thigh, a sheen of stubble emerged sternly from her armpits and, to Lawrence's surprise, she had a torso that was far from doughy.

She whirled around. *"Did I say come in?"*

Lawrence stuttered sorry and backed out.

Minutes later she summoned him. He was leaning against the landing wall by then. He never knew his mam had varicose veins. They meandered from the summits of her ankles and weren't far off in colour from the coal mark on his dad's face.

The room smelled of air freshener and there was a swatter on the drawers, speckled with moth corpses. By Arthur's side of the bed, unoccupied for weeks, was a Perspex framed picture of Lawrence as a boy, aged maybe seven, cracked from where it had been knocked on the floor and trodden on. The wardrobes were built into the wall and the curtains were drawn to keep out the summer. Mam's hair had been tied back into an almost militant ponytail as she lay down, her face isolated against the canary-coloured bedding.

"Mam."

"Kiddo."

"Dad's worried."

"Is he now?"

Lawrence took a deep breath, noticing for the first time how little of his mother he could read in this room. There were no pictures, no mementos or keepsakes, not even any books, not like Arthur. Shell must do her saving in her head. She must have had a cavernous trove in her, a smuggler's cove accessible only by underground passage.

"You look all, I dunno."

"I just had a big day, love."

"Where'd you get to?"

"Sheffield. An' I already said I'm not talking about it."

That was just one of many things Mam wasn't talking about. She had set off so early that morning that Lawrence hadn't heard her leave. He'd certainly heard her the night before. He'd finished the last of the shit-mix with Evie and Duncan, then, after they'd staggered home, Evie supporting her vomiting brother, dodged into the phonebox near the bakery at the sight of Uncle Het. The last thing Lawrence needed was to be caught out drunk in the evening.

Through the closed door he'd watched that unmistakable figure. Hector had been huge to Lawrence as a boy and was large even now. More round-shouldered than broad, he was shaped like an Egyptian sarcophagus, and had at first blocked the person walking by his side with her arm linked with his. Lawrence recognised his mother through damaged glass. Shell was laughing in the last of evening's light. It would have been a nice sound to hear in different circumstances.

She was looking at him now without her usual eagerness. He'd try a yarn, get a headstart and try not to lose it. The trick was to think past or even *through* the expulsion. Without school he could pay his way - that might oil the wheels - although thinking about it, the working road's corollary was to stay forever in Litten where the only jobs were at the pit. And what could Lawrence do while the strike raged? Work elsewhere? Even if there was a job for a boy with no experience or skills, he was far from ready to start earning. He'd only just begun to live; to consider what he wanted, like the Swarsbys did.

"Is that why you came, love? To check on your mam?"

She was almost smiling. "Kind of," said Lawrence. "But there's summat I need to tell you first."

Her benign expression faltered. Perhaps she'd sensed the approaching half-truth. After all, she'd had over a decade's experience of them from the master of the art himself, downstairs.

"So I know you said Dad'd have to wait with what he'd to say, Mam, only—"

"Give me *strength*. I'm positive your father appreciates you as his messenger but, *Lawrence*." The final bit of his name was all sibilance. "I don't know what it is wi' you two that's making me have to say everything twice today. But I just want to be left alone. So will you *please* just listen to your mam."

Well, if that was what she wanted. Lawrence's hands went nervously to the buttons of his shirt. It wasn't every day you were granted time, let alone opportunity. Together the two felt like gift horses liable to bolt and leave you on your arse if you didn't saddle them right.

"I'm sorry, Mam," he said, staying where he was. Mam's eyes clicked open, little pink cogs. Lawrence had never seen her display sustained vulnerability like this before. He wondered what had happened. This was as open as she'd ever been. He was afraid.

"If you still want to chat, come back later," she said softly, burrowing into her pillow and turning her back, the matter closed.

Lawrence opened the door and shut it again so she'd think he'd gone. He couldn't explain why he wanted to watch this fickle woman sleep, her shape as it rose and fell. The picture of him on Arthur's side felt a thousand years old, and looking at it made Lawrence think about how he might feel one day, remembering *this* moment, *these* minutes, *this* stay of execution. Would his future self be as different as he was from the boy caught unawares in that damaged frame?

Then the door flew open to reveal Arthur with a panicked look on his face. "What's going on? You've been ages. What you been saying about me?"

The slatted blinds bled zebra stripes. Shell rolled over in the light. "What you on about, Arthur? I'm trying to sleep."

"Fucking Lawrence has been expelled."

"*What?*"

"I've been trying to tell you."

The metal canteen was in his dad's top pocket. Booze breath and heavy hands, a square fucking head and gap front teeth. Arthur stepped into the room and blocked the door. Lawrence was trapped between either parent.

Mam sat up and put her palm against that cornice of a forehead. There was nothing to do but wait, take in the pattern of the covers and the chintzy wallpaper. June and still cold, only in Litten. Lawrence wondered if he could make it out of the window.

"What do you mean?" Shell said.

Arthur always pointed when he had the bit between his teeth. He was doing it now. "I mean why doesn't Lawrence stop gossiping about his old man for once and admit what's happened, if he hasn't already, which I'm guessing he hasn't, given that you're still in your flamin' pit, Shell . . . Go on, kid, tell your mam what you've gone and done."

A discarded pair of Mam's knickers was under the bed. It had been hard enough confessing what happened earlier, shuddering home from the Scanlan's as the abandoned bleach works rose on the skyline. Appearing to sense this, Arthur had boasted about trespassing in the barren factory with his brothers, leaping over the open shaft for the guide rails on the third floor. Where were those considerations now? Lawrence looked ashamedly at the floor and hated his dad.

"Our son has been expelled. Now will you listen, woman?"

Shell leapt out of bed. She wore a long red t-shirt with a picture of a bear on it. "He's not. Lawrence, tell your dad about the paper. Why'd he be circling college ads if he's been chucked out of school, Arthur?"

"Never mind that," said Arthur, going the colour of the nightie. "It's true, love. I've caught him yesterday. Weeks back this has happened and he's not told us."

Mam put her hands on her hips. "Lawrence?"

"An' all while we've been caught up wi' strike, the selfish bugger," said Arthur. He looked frantic and catty, an impulsive loon, assuming the worst and blundering in on the assumption his son was betraying him, when it was his wife doing the cheating.

"I want to hear it from him," Mam said. "Kiddo?"

This was it. Get it over with. "It's true," Lawrence answered quietly. He was relieved to get the words out, actually, shed the layer. "I were kicked out of school," he said. "A few weeks back."

Mam snorted. She put her hands behind her neck and

clamped her tongue between her teeth. So it was confirmed, Lawrence's failure had been established. And of course she'd shoulder none of the blame and nor would Arthur.

"Don't look like that," said Lawrence.

"Like *what?*"

"Like what you are doing!" He tried to leave the room, only for Arthur to block his path.

"You need to face this, lad."

Face it? Lawrence could finally see his father properly, see behind that convenient plastic *thing*, the pupil of a good eye reduced to the size of an insect: like a blood-filled tick left drowned in an empty teacup. The eye said it all: Arthur was terrified of Shell finding out about the break-in at Threndle House. In spite of her rudeness, her coldness, her directness, he was afraid to lose her, a wife his brother had already taken. And what a thing it was, to pity your father and how he fooled himself.

"You better tell us what happened," Mam said.

"He'll tell you," Lawrence replied, "Won't you, Dad," and this time he managed to battle out onto the landing where the lampshade hung above the stairs like a wasp's nest. He could hear his parents going at it behind him, arguing over the things they wanted for him, which were really just projections of what they wanted for themselves. Mam was calling him stupid, her own son. *Who else knows?* she was saying. *Who have you told?* Thanking her lucky stars Lawrence had been sent to the grammar school rather than Litten Modern. People might have thought them snobs sending him there, but it was a blessing in this light. The explosion had been controlled, like a warhead on a distant reef.

Lawrence hurried to his room to pack his things. He would

head to his grandmother's, which was a short walk through the cherry blossom specks blowing out of the grounds of Cottonlea Retirement Home, past the weathercock turning on the spire of St Michael's. He loaded his pack and headed out, stopping on the landing to listen to his mother one more time. Through the bedroom door he heard her. He could forget about school. Brantford was the best place for him because heaven knew he didn't listen to his parents.

"No way," Arthur was shouting, "No son of mine . . ." and this sent Shell storming out of the room.

Here she was, saying the words, probably the worst thing she could ever have said to Lawrence:

"Soon as this is all over, your uncle will put a word in for you down pit. He knows people, does Het. He'll sort it like always."

"Not the only thing Het sorts though, is it," snapped Lawrence.

He was out of the house and down the road within a minute.

12

HET PULLED HIS scar tight and brought the razor to his face. Then he drew the blade through the froth. Iron filings of stubble floated in the bowl of pearly water, collecting almost deliberately at the edges.

This routine every morning. Het actually liked the look of himself in the mirror, masked by a soapy beard. Sometimes he felt like he should just let it grow for real.

Too far in to back out now though. He mowed clear lines of skin down his foamy cheek and for once didn't cut himself, then it was done and he was getting dressed. The radio chittered the news; it was only on because he found mornings without another human voice eerie.

It was a short journey to the petrol station. With money getting tight, he'd been driving the Maxi to pickets himself rather than forking out for lifts from the other lads. Taking the risk was preferable to dipping into savings, plus he preferred driving to being driven. Some people were born to be driven. Not Het. He liked being the one behind the wheel. It was a question of ability, of natural indifference when you got to the county lines. The others were better at crouching in the back or lying under the blankets, and usually there was some unfortunate hidden in the boot.

"Duck down, boys."

Slowing it. Staring ahead like all you had behind you was a set of walking boots and a raincoat. Only once had they been caught when Het was driving. They'd been chased and had their names taken, mind you, which was something to think about. When he'd been stopped in the past, Het had been sent on his way with a scare and a story to tell, but this cataloguing of dissenters made him nervous. The government were building profiles, getting clever.

Het also liked taking the men home after a picket. Long quiet drives. You dropped one guy off and then two more until it was just you and the last man left. You get to know someone when it's just you and them in your car. Sometimes the wives would invite him indoors to stretch his legs, and there he'd see how they lived, smell their personal smells, note the accoutrements, the mannerisms and various kids.

Families were hell on him. They also spurred him on. Local and otherwise, those on and off picket reminded Het why he was doing all this in the first place. For every day now it was another pit, another town or cokeworks, steelworks, power station, hoarse throat, muscles sore from hefting bin bags of paint off the sides of bridges onto scab lorries and police motorbikes, upending barricades, using trails of barbed wire to block compounds, sabotaging machinery and running, always charging, a big man at the tip of the flying-V, breaking the police lines and earning bravery ales at 72 pence a pint, calming his brother down whenever Arthur tried to run the other lads at darts and kept losing his brass.

So maybe Brantford wasn't closing. Others were and the employees of those pits had jobs just as worth saving. This was how Het did things. How all people worth their salt behaved. As long as wide was the case. Examples had to be set. They had their codes.

Picketing was his only income. It was a quid a day for

flying, two if you did a double. You and a car full of guys after the extra money, flying in to picket one place, falling back to do another. Het had made twenty quid petrol since that messy afternoon at Tyndale back in May.

Most recently he'd done a run to Port Talbot to picket with the taffs at the steel docks where they'd been shipping in American coal. He and about ten others had spent the night in sleeping bags on the living room carpet of a local ventilation engineer. Het had already forgotten their host's name, but he was a NACOD so still getting paid, so what did it matter? And not that it was necessarily the man's fault that his union was a part of the industry yet not bothering to strike, but it must have made the struggle something of a holiday, no?

No one said anything. It would have been rude. But Het suspected the bloke made everyone bacon butties out of guilt. Because it must be a bit of all right, getting paid to sit on your backside for months on end while the NUM were out fighting for a cause your union were a part of yet failing to commit to. Pressed shoulder to shoulder with the others, Het hardly slept because he was stuck on the end of the row, where it was colder, because of his height. The engineer's carpet was orange and he had a fancy record player. Het's head had lain beneath the table it perched on. He'd bumped it waking up – a knock on the bonce to raise a soul come morning. Then to the wife after shuffling into the kitchen: "Ta, pet. Black with one sugar for me, please."

He arrived at his mam's. In '83 there'd been a heatwave and now, one year on, it felt like there would be another. Morning of mid-June. Blazing hot already. Het wished he had the time to make the most of it.

He'd taken to his mam's more and more of late, started

checking in on Lawrence, who'd come to stay after a falling out with his parents. Not that Het possessed a great deal of interest in the little tyke, but Lawrence was a good enough reason to grab a free dinner whilst trying regain enough of Arthur's favour to see Shell again.

Because she wouldn't see him anymore, not for love nor money, two things he'd never had a great deal of. They'd been getting on so well recently, too. Course tongues had wagged; Het had set them straight. It should have been fine. He just couldn't understand what was going on with Shell.

Perhaps it was that night at the bakery. The shutters had been lowered and locked and the shop's spotlights flickered off, leaving the two of them alone in the back area. Somehow they'd gotten onto his being single. The how and why of it.

"I'm lonely," said Het.

"So get a dog."

Moving closer. There was always something to Shell, some breach in her wellbeing she wouldn't share with him.

Het said, "That's not what I meant."

And Shell said she knew that. "I'm not daft, you lunk."

Smiling, also serious, Het stuck his hand out and rested it upon Shell's, accidentally-on-purpose. She returned the sentiment with her thumb, dragging the digit from under his palm then pressing the back of his hand with it, *firmly*, before drawing sharply away to face the bread shelf with its base of bronzed, angled poles.

No more of anything. No more of that. The disturbance of the paper bag as Shell filled it with buns. The fuzzy honey light of the hatch in the oven being switched off. Het picked up a roll; it was hard in his grasp. He pierced its crust and found it was still soft in the middle. Shell was watching him,

184

he could feel it. He daren't look back. She'd appreciate it more this way, because the curtain of possibility was drawing shut. To call attention to what had just happened, to have it acknowledged, Shell would only deny it. It was her way.

"You're always so solemn."

"It's just my face. People think I'm crabby or in a mood when it's just the weather on us mind or last night's telly."

"Must be nice to be thought mysterious."

"Am I really that mysterious?"

"Aye, Het. Unfortunately you are."

A heave in him. Was it to be how it had been when the bakery door closed, when they'd gone around the counter together with what felt like the same intention?

"Aren't we all though?" Shell added. "I mean, heck."

Het adjusted his glasses. Shell led him to the door. He didn't understand why she was holding her hand out, a moment later he clocked.

"You're having us on."

"You've your tea, now cough up."

Het made a show of looking for his wallet, pulled an old receipt out and placed it in Shell's hand.

She smacked his forearm. "So what am I to tell Gaskell then?"

"Tell him tuna butties of a weekend for Newman. H."

"Drop dead wi' your tuna."

"I've refined tastes, me."

Down the street, Shell's arm linked with Het's as she laughed at the thought of him as refined. It was nice when people had an idea of you. Shell told Het about tomorrow's trip to Sheffield on the way home. She was so excited. Much later, Het sat alone in his flat, got as drunk as he dared then woke up on the settee in the small hours. Arthur had showed up as soon as Het returned home from picketing Selcroft the following morning.

Now he waited for his food. It wasn't so long ago that he'd been served here twice a day. He'd temporarily moved in with his mam to let her care for him after his dad was blown up. Neither of them had wanted to talk; they weren't those kinds of people. It was more of a practical arrangement. Mam adopted him as her point of focus. Het allowed it, needing to feel useful, such a thankless situation was his grief. So tangible the impact his presence had on her.

He was always more of a dependent than his brothers. He'd only moved into his own place a couple of years before his dad's accident, leaving home after overhearing a loaded comment at work one day about mummy's boys.

Mam was fussing now in the kitchen. More pumice stone than pebble, Helen Newman refused to pander to summer protocol and was serving hotpot for breakfast in the middle of June. The kitchen thumped with heat. Every window steamed and the smell of chopped thyme and sweating onions surrounded them.

"Smells great," said Het, flapping his shirt. He'd long since learned where questioning his mother got him.

"You sound surprised." Helen approached with a wooden spoon loaded with hotpot. "Where today?"

God, the heat of that mouthful. "Orgreave," Het said.

"Speak up, lad."

"*Orgreave.*"

"Be careful, won't you."

Wincing, Het swallowed the burning wad of mush. From

the moment *The Mighty Atom* had struck him, his mam had been overly protective of him. She'd only worry if she knew the extent of things at Orgreave cokeworks, so Het told her there was nothing to worry about. "The press have made mountains out of molehills," he said.

Which in a way was true. The NUM had permitted the plant to use enough fuel to keep their boilers running, thus protecting their expensive ovens, only British Steel had persuaded Orgreave into supplying them with coal behind the union's back. With Orgreave scabbing, every union was up in arms. ASLEF and NUR crews had refused to ferry anything to or from the plant by rail after the Treeton men picketed one of the nearby road bridges. Now the site was accessible only by car and lorry.

This had let to relentless fly picketing, police and batons, bricks and the bramble run for Het just the other day. For two weeks they'd been going up to Orgreave. Two weeks of sunbathing, sharing a laugh with the police (some of them were all right), then fighting whenever the trucks showed up. Missiles and batons. Het had been chased into the woods and taken a nasty whack that left him with a jaundiced patch that was currently becoming a lump on the back of his neck.

"Molehills," his mam said.

Course every day Arthur wanted to go up to Orgreave. So did a lot of lads. If you wanted a scrum you went up to Orgreave. Flying out then falling back to Orgreave. Mansfield, Orgreave. Derbyshire, Orgreave. Yorkshire and the approximate Midlands.

For a bloke who'd never even wanted to strike, Arthur was certainly throwing himself into the pickets of late. Het wasn't sure what to do about it. He'd never actually planned to report the break-in at Threndle House; he'd just wanted his brother to do the right thing for once. Put up or shut up. Like most men of principle Het found it hard to laugh at himself even though it often meant he got birthed backwards trying to grit his teeth through life's contradictions. Take now. On the one hand if Arthur didn't strike, Het would never have forgiven him, on the other, he wasn't sure he wanted his brother picketing now at all. The monkey had been given a gun and the means to fire it, and it felt like every day they moved closer to a reckoning.

Het wouldn't call saying there was no trouble at Orgreave lying. It was just underplaying it. His mam might be a miner's wife from a mining family, she was also from that law abiding post-war generation who'd been conditioned in the belief that there were some things you simply did not do, fighting with police coming pretty high on that list. Not only could Helen not bear to think of her sons in trouble, she also couldn't grasp that these days if you were against public disorder you ended up sitting on your hands while the authorities stomped all over you.

"Whole union'll be there," Het said. "From across country."

"You're like Gandhi, lad."

Het suppressed a smile. "Summat like that."

The egg timer trilled. Het's mam opened the oven and checked inside. She stepped back, her spectacles steamed. She removed them; her exposed eyes looking a little like raisins. She said, "But a mother still worries."

The bowls were spaced out, ready to serve. Mam was shrinking with age. Unusually for a woman her age, she kept her hair long, cascading freely over her shoulders, and she wore a dark smock and amber-coloured beads, brown stockings and ballet pumps that she said helped her go on tip-toes to reach things. The back end of sixty. No goals beyond completing the next day and then the next day and then the next.

Het said, "Best off putting that out of your mind."

"Not easy when you see the state of them pickets."

"Telly's full o' rot, Mam"

"Well what about the papers?"

Het had been surprised at how the media had rallied around Thatcher. How did they think it was going to go, the way the police carried on? If anything, all the violence was the governments' fault – in '74 the miners had been allowed to picket where they liked. Things had been comparatively sedate back then. "Them too," he said.

"People have died."

Het snorted. "All the more reason to keep going."

Mam ladled some hotpot into the bowls. Beige swill with bits in it. The government were claiming all this nonsense was to streamline the industry and save money, never mind it cost money to shut the pits, it didn't save. It was obvious to Het that if the NUM backed down over this then the government would think they had a green light to do whatever they pleased, boss the unions over anything. They'd send it all up the Litten Path. Gas, bus, rail, post, health, prisons, you name it.

"Well just remember you don't have to bark every time NUM says so," said his mam. "Last time they tried this we got stuck wi' a three day week. Streets full o' rubbish. Never mind the fact most of our brass goes straight into their leaders' back pockets."

Het left the table before he said something out of turn. Union corruption was a thing of the past, and occasionally over-stepping the mark in the name of what was right didn't mean every union wanted crushing. Up the stairs and to the left, he went, into the blandest of all rooms, the pensioner's spare. Lawrence's smell shocked Het: teenage sweat and teenage spunk, cheap deodorant failing to mask it. A pair of hairy feet stuck out from under the blanket of the usually well-made, single bed.

"Lawrence?"

"Time is it?"

"Six."

The lad groaned.

"Breakfast's ready," Het said.

"I can smell the mutton."

"Well that's better than nowt, which is your other option."

"In that case I won't dawdle."

Het waited. ". . .I'm not seeing much movement. Come on. Up."

Lawrence rolled over, squinting through a gap in the quilt. "Are you wearing them gegs of yours or what?"

Het was wearing them all right. The pictures on the wall were of the moorland, the sky, a forest. The linen chest was open, contents ruptured everywhere, and the egg-shaped rug he'd bought his mam for Mother's Day a few years ago was doubled in the middle from where Lawrence had obviously skidded into the room, rucked it up and left it.

Het tried yanking the covers from off the bed. "You're not my dad," Lawrence said irritably, grabbing the sheet and pulling it up to his neck. "That's his trick you've taken up."

"Five minutes," Het replied, letting go. He went downstairs and began setting the table.

Lawrence soon joined them. The kid might have been in a rotten mood after being turfed out of school, but of late he'd barely a civil word for Het, and it was getting tiresome. It was probably Arthur's fault. After Het got back from Selcroft his brother had shown up. Shaking he was, asking for a drink of water. Arthur didn't manage a single sip. He just lobbed the entire pint at the wall the moment Het passed it to him. The glass smashed. Het's pullover was soaked though.

Arthur flew at him. "You've to stay away from her!"

"Who?"

"You've not even the nerve to admit it!"

Quite so. Het would deny everything if he had to, his heart especially. He managed to roll Arthur over and pin him down, accidentally busting his nose, and eventually sent him packing with an ammonia phial stuffed up his nose and the assurance nothing was going on with Shell.

How could anyone think Het would do a thing like that? Although he might have feelings for Shell, he would never act on them. Had somebody said something? Had Arthur spread the gossip on to Lawrence? Likely the two were in cahoots. Curse their closeness. Het could smell the lad's B.O. wafting sourly across the table.

Eyes shadow-ringed and girlish. Hair scruffily the same length all over. Lawrence clearly got as much guidance about his appearance as he did with everything else. Someone had to pick the pieces up for Shell. "Got a job yet?" Het said, buttering his bread. He'd burnt himself on the hotpot before and now the middle of his tongue felt dimpled and sore.

"No, Uncle Het. Have you?"

Lawrence held his hand out for the salt shaker, which Het slid down the table, with satisfaction watching it stop out of the lad's reach.

"So what's plan of attack? Cause from what I can tell you've room and board and no means to pay it."

"Gran, will you tell him?"

"Oh, leave off, Het. Let him eat."

"Has Arthur even been round to ask about this arrangement, Mam?"

Had he heck been round.

Helen swilled down her hotpot with a glass of Tizer and frowned. She'd always been soft on Arthur. "He'll stay as long as he wants," she said. "He's having a think, aren't you, love?"

Lawrence didn't answer.

"Of that I've no doubt," replied Het. "Though what's on his mind is a flamin' mystery."

Lawrence was always shrugging. His gran said he lacked confidence. Het thought he had it in spades.

He said, "Been up to much wi' all this free time then?"

"This and that."

"Summer eh."

No answer.

Young lads needed three things to feel self-assured: a sense of direction, to be included and never to be made to feel small. Het had been young himself once. All he had to do was let his wisdom bleed through. Avoid condescension.

He cleared his throat. "Seen this one, Mam?" he said, expanding the broad chest of his that he was still dead proud of. "Bright lad. Strong lad. Could be of great use one day." He wiped at a clump of hairwax he could feel behind his ear. "Capable of big things in the right job, you, Lawrence . . . So I want to know." He lent himself a fatherly manner. "Have you started thinking long-term? Cause Brantford will gladly take you."

Pine forest quiet, Lawrence shook salt on his buttered bread, hotpot untouched.

Het tried again. "As it'd be a shame to end up scratching on. No kidding, lad, if I'd even half your brain an' it were being put to waste the way yours is, I'd never forgive myself."

Still nothing. It didn't matter if it was half six in the morning or half six at night. Het banged the table. "Knock, knock! Earth to Lawrence—"

"Obviously, Het, obviously it'd be a shame!"

"Well . . . glad we're in agreement."

"Fancy taking us down Brantford to scab tomorrow, do you?"

"*After*, lad. I mean after."

"After they're mothballed the pits? Do you think that's my plan? Sitting on us arse until the end of time?"

"I should hope it's not. And there'll be no mothballing!"

"Oh, get gone, you've no idea what it's like. Sixteen and stuck living in this shithole wi' nowt to do except walk about, no jobs except down the pit or a poxy few quid's training scheme bloody miles away."

Sixteen was a working age, always had been. The edges of Het's scar bristled as they tended to do whenever he was blushing. This indignant *cub* was another one who was always trying to make him feel past it, acting like he was visible from several miles away. Lawrence was one big afterthought. He'd say anything and tell himself it didn't matter.

He made *shoo* signs with his hands. "I'm fine, all right."

"I just want to help, Lawrence."

"And what if I said I don't need your help."

Het's mam interjected. "Oh, come on," she said. "Why not hear your uncle out? What can it hurt?"

Het almost thanked her out loud. When she nodded at him, he cleared his throat as gently as he could then adopted the same tone he used when collaring newbies at the complex's gates or on the wooden steps leading to the pit entrance, making sure they knew who to address and on what team. How to press their point and when to do so.

He said, "So I can put in a word for you, reight, get you a job. Course it won't be now – for obvious reasons. But *after*, when all this is over, and it will be, mark my words, kid . . . we'll be going back to work. You could come for a chat then. Think of these weeks as a last hurrah. Hang out wi' your mates. Sit in't sun. Then I'll take tha down Brantford so you can see how it feels. You know us Newmans have always been miners, Lawrence. Every one."

"Every one?"

Hold the look. Don't back down. Sam had never gotten as far as the pit, as Lawrence well knew.

"Every one," said Het.

Lawrence didn't reply. He looked frightened, the silly lad.

"All I'm sayin' is a chap like you can make management within five to eight year."

"*Eight years?*"

"Less . . . if you're lucky."

The kid was bottling up like usual. "Somehow I doubt that," he said.

"Who you trying to kid, grammar brain like yours. Your mam's always saying."

"No I've not, an' I don't know where you've got her saying that from. Though I bet she tells you all sorts, you and her . . ."

It was lucky there was food to concentrate on. Arthur *must* have said something. It was mortifying to think of Lawrence

194

grading the design upon design, the muck rake and compost of the affair Hector had been having in his head with the lad's mother for the last decade and a half.

Seize it. Seize the rope.

"Listen, I dunno what you mean by that . . ." Het said.

"I even heard her," Lawrence said, voice freighted with feeling. "Having a go at Dad, saying I know how to get inside peoples' heads and say what I have to, just like him. She thought I couldn't hear her. She said new school won't change a jot. She just said what were a lad like me going to do wi' a grammar education in the first place? She always knew it. Always knew I were for the pit."

Het's mam placed her hands on Lawrence's shoulders. They were wrought things, fragile as bird's wings.

"Dad said I can do what I want. He said Mam weren't being fair. She just went, '*What's fair got to do with it.*'

Shell hadn't pulled her punches – Het admired that. When you were soft on errant lads you ended up with men like Arthur. He carried his empty bowl to the sink while his mam gave the boy a flaming cuddle. On the sill below the steamed glass were jam jars filled with soil. The shoots of baby sunflowers poked optimistically out of them. The last time Het had seen Shell she'd told him about the family tree Arthur had planted. She'd been so scornful of the gift, but Het's mind had striven for the maple, as it did now. He envisioned a tremendous thing, red-leaved, helicopter blade branches. Newman lore spoke of goblins living in the whorled boles of such specimens. Button milk bastards that peeled the bark away like it was cellophane, climbed out at night and stole from you. If you came across a horse spooked at night, it was said the goblins had ridden it across the fields, visited the land of death.

Helen was still talking. "Newmans have always been pit men. And tha father never wanted it neither," she said. "Although it did our Arthur more good than he'll dare admit. And tha's so much of him in thee, Lawrence. Really there is."

"He's a useless bastard."

Het strode over and clipped Lawrence around the head. "Don't talk about your father like that."

"*What I'm saying*," Helen went on. She always knew when not to say if she disagreed. "Is Brantford could be the best place for you, for time being, anyroad. Pits are where young men make 'emselves. Always have been."

Lawrence was so thin. Het had seen him coming out of the bathroom only the other day: he had a pigeon chest that looked like a nose from certain angles. Add to that a tendency to goggle or shrink, and you had to feel for the boy. He had been made a pawn of. He would always be the one to pay the price.

Het said, "Your gran's right."

"I am, love. So listen. Tha uncle's away to Orgreave today. Why don't you go wi' him?"

"Hang on a sec . . ." said Het, only for the ferocious look his mother gave him to shock him quiet. Had Arthur spoken to her too?

"Make a day of it. See what's what."

Het tried again. "Mam, it's really not the place for him . . ."

"Oh but tha'll keep an eye out, Hector. You said it yourself, it's a quiet do. You might even have a laugh. What does tha say, Lawrence?"

Het was sure he could hear the wind filtering through the leaves of the maple.

13

T HE MAXI NAVIGATED the quiet streets. Lawrence
rested his head against the front passenger window. The
morning was really with them, its sun bled upon its stone, its
birds went about their business and there was a glow through
the mixture of trees. You could hardly ask for better weather.
The air smelled almost sweet.

Pulling in outside the Grey Grebe Hotel, Uncle Het tooted
the car's horn at a large man in a flat cap and a younger man
in a Sheffield Wednesday shirt with hair straggling all over his
shoulders. This was Bob and Darren Roach, Het explained,
a couple of Brantford miners.

"Tardiness is ungodliness," Bob said through the open
window, scratching the hair under his cap. "Everyone else
has gone."

"I were held up," said Het, nodding accusingly at Lawrence.
"My nephew."

Lawrence couldn't be bothered to defend himself. He
shook hands with either Roach and slumped in his seat while
they clambered into the car. The two men smelled of sweat
and the pub. They were of that Irish blood that spawns pale
and hairy, hard-drinking types.

"I've a youngster trying to have me sunburnt," complained
Bob, showing off the damp blotch on the back of his grey
t-shirt. "It's frying out there, lad."

Lawrence didn't know what he was supposed to say. Bob

was wheezing a typical fucking pit cough. They were typically fucking indignant about everything, men Bob's age.

"I suspect you'll have found ways to pass the time, Robert," said Het, smirking along with Darren, who was miming 'drink' at him.

"Oh, aye," said Darren with a wink. "Give you time to work on that tan an' all, didn't it, Dad."

"Least now no one'll think us a scab." Bob chuckled. "Pale-skinned buggers."

With the lorries due at eight, Het drove above the speed limit rather than his usual granny-pace. After about a mile Bob said to Lawrence, "You'll be for Brantford then?"

"Thinking of it."

"Your grandad'd be chuffed."

Het was such a milquetoast, and a secretive one at that. He appeared to be concentrating on the road but Lawrence could tell he was listening in. So although he couldn't deny that it was a nice idea, making his grandad proud, Lawrence didn't answer Bob.

Darren leant forward. "What about today then, you ready for t'scrap?"

"Don't know about no scrap."

Het broke in. "Lad's been dying to come on picket."

"I've not."

"He wants to make a difference. See us at it." Het laughed his firm, fake laugh. "This is our Arthur's lad."

The Roaches exchanged a look.

It was another fifteen, twenty minutes' drive to the coke plant. There were hardly any police about. They received not so much as a single stop or second glance all the way there, which was strange, because, as far as Lawrence knew, it had been pitched battles right the way through May, the police doing whatever they could to stop the pickets. Now there was nothing. He supposed this was yet another thing that his uncle was completely wrong about.

This way, please. Drive safely, lads. They followed the police instructions and the arrows and signposts directing them to the working men's club down the Catcliffe end of the plant, parking a fair distance away still because Het was being precious about his bloody car. The picket was building this far back too. Hundreds were gathered here. Union brass with their fuzzing walkie-talkies. Maybe thousands. Maths was never Lawrence's strong suit.

The police numbers had also swollen. Down the drastic Orgreave Road Lawrence could see them lining the way, reaching the fortress of the coke works and those menacing columns, the scorched chimneys intruding madly upon the sky.

Lawrence didn't know what was going to come out of his mouth if he opened it. He stuck close to Darren Roach and ear-wigged on the men's conversation.

"You all right, Het?" Bob was saying.

"I always get like this on picket," Het replied, failing to lower his voice. "And I'm aware for the lad."

Bob said, "We'll look after him." As if Lawrence was some kid.

"Ta, Bob. You been coming here recently?" Het said.

"Our Darren has."

"You've to come expecting a hiding."

Het pointed at the urine-dark bruise spread across his neck.

"Aye," said Darren. "That's why I were surprised you brought him."

Happening to glance over at Lawrence, Het changed the subject. "Reminds me of Saltley Gate," he said.

"Saltley?" said Darren, cottoning on. "How old *are* you, Het?"

Lawrence's uncle had to think about it. "I must have been twenty-nine, my first strike. Scargill were leading from up front. Dad were spitting feathers, you should have seen him. It changed our lives, a win like that."

"Goodbye Teddy Heath," said Bob.

"We did ourselves proud."

Bob said, "They must be mad scabbing here in strike's heartland. Bloody death wish. Sandy Coates were only saying the other day that Maggie'll crack if we can stop her steel. This could be it, lads. What do you reckon, Lawrence?"

Lawrence nodded vaguely at Bob as Het and Darren swigged from their tins of beer.

The police directed everyone towards the junction at Poplar Way, where the lorries accessed the Sheffield Parkway. The noise was enormous here, the topside in front of the cokeworks. All the crowds.

Lawrence had to stare. Had a factory ever looked so massive? Had there ever been as many police waiting in one place?

"You all right?" said Het.

"Aye."

"Stick close to me."

"I said I'm fine."

At last he knew what the pickets were like. Police everywhere, more police than Lawrence knew existed. The protesters reached the back end of the huge field, to what Bob said was a steep embankment ahead of some train tracks and a narrow bridge leading into Orgreave village.

"We'll stay here then get at them from afar," said Bob, his thick hand resting on Lawrence's shoulder. Everyone felt like they had a right to touch him. "You best keep your wits about you, son."

That much was plain as a pikestaff. In the heat of this day there was zero wind. Ahead of the ranks of picketers was a land of dying grass. Then the navy blue began, swathes of police officers that must have been at least ten or twenty men deep. An even greater horde waited on the other side of that, while to the left of the enormous coke plant was a command post, police forces busying themselves around a marquee with what looked like refreshment tables inside, tents beyond, Portakabins and horseboxes dotted further away. The edges of the field, lined against the woods on one side, were guarded by men with dogs. On the other side, guarding the hill, were yet more men with yet more dogs. Uncle Het was rubbing seriously at his scar.

TV crews were also arranged throughout the tophill. Postings of focus aimed cameras at the miners. One crew carried their equipment down the lines, filming until they arrived at a blimp of a man with his top off, holding a placard. The camera focused, rotate and pivot. It was the first time Lawrence had seen a TV crew.

A cheer went up as the camera was struck by a football. One of the crew picked the ball up and tried to remonstrate in the direction it had come from, but his voice was overwhelmed by the profuse hacking laughter of working blokes in a pack.

One of the crew kicked the ball into the air. Arcing, the white sphere was camouflaged against the delicate cloud before re-appearing, *thud*, upon the grass.

Boiling. Loads of people had their tops off. Tough blokes with broad shoulders, sinew. Soft blokes with round shoulders, belly. Plenty of folk were sunbathing, chatting. There were women here and the odd youngster, too; it was pretty convivial, actually. Union men patrolled the field's limits, directing picketers. And there was a megaphone, it must be Arthur Scargill's. You couldn't hear a word he was saying. It was like he was shouting into his hands while someone pinched his nostrils.

"Is my dad here, Het?" asked Lawrence, but Het and Bob were chatting and Darren Roach was ahead, smoking a cigarette. Lawrence scanned the crowd for people still wearing their tops, because his dad never took his shirt off. Arthur was embarrassed about the tattoos he'd had done when he was younger. A domino on the left shoulder. The huge march hare illustrating his back.

The crowd edged forward, front lines of police and picket drawing closer to one another. Although it wasn't time for the lorries yet, Lawrence felt nervous. He twitched his toes. A stone lay temptingly in the grass.

As if the police forces had read his mind, a cry went up, the emergence of the thunderhead.

"What was that?" Lawrence said, coughing to disguise the nervy way his voice teetered.

"Reinforcements," Bob replied, staring ahead, his neck mizzled hideously with sweat.

A clutch of police officers bedecked in riot gear arrived, the jogging phalanx sending a charge through the crowd. There was cursing and defiance as the main bobbies in uniform stepped back to form second and third rows, and the armoured squad took their place up front.

"What's that lot doing here?" Het said.

Replied Bob, "Fucked if I know."

Bob leant against Lawrence's ear, his damp breath warm on both lobe and neck. He said "This is where they give it the Zulu, son."

No time to question what he meant. The new riot police began to hammer their large rectangular shields with their batons. They yelled and pounded them, and the noise of it drowned everything out. Terror squad. Intimidator. It was like when two trains pass one another in a tunnel.

Missiles were the pickets' response. Bottles and rocks were hurled from disparate parts of the crowd, projectiles searing overhead and landing near the police huddle some forty yards away. The picket seemed to swell. Yawning, it covered most of the field. Lawrence was also being pushed forward. The current was sending the canoe towards the precipice.

Het reached out and grabbed him. Lawrence tried to shrug him off, but this only increased the strength of his uncle's grip.

"Come here. We'll not get dragged in. We're just here to persuade them flaming lorries to stop."

"How can we do that if we can't speak to 'em?"

"That's police's line of thinking."

"Are they allowed to just block the way like that?"

"No, but they do it anyway."

Chanting. The words were no doubt meant to inspire, but the way they were sung, Lawrence supposed it was the venom of it. A sentiment pitched somewhere around the defiant mark was emerging in more dangerous terrain.

We're miners, united. We'll never be defeated.
We're miners, united. We'll never be defeated.

It was hard not to think that in the middle of more conflict that this is how it would always be. It had been a year of bleached bones, where every day had been reduced to what felt like varying stages of confrontation, relationships boiled down to nothing. Lawrence washed daily in the shower. He drank the searing water that rained into his mouth.

The lorries must be coming – this didn't feel real. Het's scarred lower lip moved as he chanted quietly along with the rest of the picket. This squaddie-looking interloper had necked Lawrence's mother with that mouth. Maybe it was gravity Shell saw in Het, because you strove for what you didn't have as much as for what you couldn't. Even at sixteen, Lawrence understood that much.

Everyone was pushing towards the gates, blocked by that dense wave of policemen. A merry *here we go*, football chant repeated, over and again. Lawrence began to chant, too. Words could boil up in him, even if he didn't know whether he meant them or not.

"I didn't think there'd be so many," Het said. He looked worried, apologetic. "Stay close, lad. We'll stay where we are, keep hung back."

"You must've told me that five times now."

"Aye, well take another look at them gates, they've directed the whole picket to this field. We've to be careful."

His arm slipped over Lawrence's shoulder, across the chest. Holding his tongue, Lawrence went on tip-toes, staggering as even Het was barged forward by the picket's urgency.

Ahead was the grime-coated edifice of mighty Orgreave. Darren Roach piled into the crowd and was swallowed up. A hundred men must have been in that section alone; a younger set in their twenties and thirties. Darren and this lot aimed for the riot police, who were a short way beyond, brandishing shields. This force stretched lengthwise as far as Lawrence could see, deeper still. A plastic horizon. Tasked domes winking in the sun.

Now Het and Bob had their voices raised. It felt safer here amongst the second or third division of the picket. Het even smiled, perhaps not sensing what Lawrence could: the untethering visible on people's faces, those faces topped with callow-looking hair.

"Lorries are yet to arrive. Five minutes I make it," Het said.

"Where they coming from?"

"Behind all that lot, then back out the same way. Down the road up side of the plant."

"Never seen this many police."

"Nor this many picket. This is it, Lawrence. This is how much we care about one another."

When Lawrence didn't nod, Het gave him a big, important nod and said "Can you not see now who you are?"

Lawrence wanted to shake his head. He disliked, could never handle direct questions like that. Though thankfully Het wasn't waiting for an answer.

"You're a part of this community. Working folk, fighting to make a living."

That arm was searching again – Lawrence swerved out of its way. He found it pathetic, absorbing your job until it became all there was about you, your every virtue bound in it.

"Pits aren't just a career," Het said. "They're a sense of self and that alone is worth its tonnage. A man defines himself by what he does. Show us one person on our side of this field not proud of his job, his history and where he comes from."

"Me."

"This is what makes them them," Het said. He was getting animated now, casting an eye over the crowd. "They think we can't see it. Think they can say a multi-million pound industry's past it. Selby super-pit's most modern in t'world, and they've just spent a fortune at Gascoigne Wood. This is about us, lad. They can't stand *us*."

Blunderbuss though he was, Het might have a point. Why should Lawrence resist this ready-made life? Sixteen and going on sixty, he had never worked in the pit or ever wanted to, but he couldn't deny his roots or who his people were. In a sense their voice was his voice, and in a sense it had been waiting for him to listen to it his whole life. Its shades had fought through before. Defensive things said in heated moments that felt at the time as if they'd come from the mouth of some other person, words Lawrence recognised later as his own, deeply his, his duty to say all along, feelings that might have been making their way towards him for centuries. Maybe some words were yours before you ever thought to say them. Maybe finding your way towards them was what growing up was. Lawrence shut his eyes and sought the sun. Because maybe everyone had a role to fill and it was best to waste no time filling it, because sooner or later it would end up filling you.

"Lorry push," said Bob. "Give it what for, lad. Here they come."

The convoy was inaudible above the crowd. Lawrence saw it, the armed escort. Each fabled truck was empty, heavy in a motorcade with not a scratch on it. The mobile pickets en-route must have failed, or perhaps they hadn't bothered to stop the trucks at all. Rather they were here now. It seemed as if every miner in the country was here today. Lawrence could see the front driver wearing protective goggles. And as the grille of the man's truck revealed itself in all its glorious detail, the entire tophill of Orgreave went fucking mad.

Scab! Scab! Scab! Scab! Scab! Scab! Scab!

The glaze of that first windshield, those cute round headlights, were lost in the crowd's tide. Lawrence went with the push. Impossible not to. The picket hit the police. Here we go. There had never been a crush like it. *Crack.* Men butted against police shields, the whole picket at work. Lawrence struggled to breathe. Even this far back it was tough. So many people. So many at it.

Maggie Maggie Maggie! Out out out! Maggie Maggie Maggie! Out out out!

Lawrence tried to stay upright, he tried to think. There was so much noise. So many bodies. Stink and din, thrill of it. Adrenaline zoned his focus. He managed to pick Het out, turning the air blue. His fucking uncle who never swore.

Lawrence gave it some, too, and that felt good.

The police line held steadfast in spite of the picket's numbers. Kicked-up summer dust, smack of fear and spray of spit. Shouting, shouting, shouting. Then some curious shapes appeared, an enormity that surged above the lock-hold up front. An unnatural movement drawing into view as if storm clouds had gathered above the human landscape.

"Hoss," Uncle Het said, eyes as wide as 50ps.

"*Hoss!*"

The police line split, and from it, as if emerging from the

surface of a lake, burst the muzzles and powerful haunches of many horses, tons of mounted force entering the morning and making its charge into the protest.

People started running. Oh God. Horses chased the crowd. Oh shit.

They were destriers. Their riders wore white helmets. They carried sticks and transparent shields. Het was calling; Lawrence tried to get there. He and Bob retreated back the way they'd come, neither able to go faster than those in front would allow.

Each horse was huge and Bob was too slow. Lawrence grabbed his arm. It felt like burger meat. Bob was telling him he was a good lad. Thanks for helping. Wheezing away.

"Het!"

His uncle turned back. Het must have been the only one going that direction. Horses gunned at people. Officers struck people, herding whatever came into their path.

Het arrived to help Lawrence and Bob through the crowd, which had thinned now in retreat. They were no longer the pursued. The cantering had slowed as the horses began to return to the cokeworks. Black tarmac became yellow grass. A sweat runnel creased down Lawrence's face.

"I'm getting you home," Het was saying, "Stuff this." He was sweating and Bob had his cap off and his hands on his knees.

"Did you not see that?" said Lawrence. "Did you not see what they did?"

"I'm not blind, lad. We need to get going."

Lawrence followed, looking back the way they'd come. He was old enough and he could take it. Evie would be so impressed when she heard about this.

He shaded his eyes, wanting, in a weird way, to laugh. Marauding picketers were attacking the police. The horses had retreated and Lawrence couldn't see where the trucks were. Perhaps they'd made it into the compound already.

A small man in uniform with a Clark Gable moustache appeared at the front of the police line, holding a megaphone.

"Clements," said Bob. "Assistant Chief Clements."

That made Het turn.

Chief Clements spoke clearly into his megaphone. He warned everyone that if the picket did not disperse itself it would be dispersed by force. It was a little late for that. Lawrence broke into the laugh that had been threatening him and turned to his uncle for approval, but didn't get it. Typical. Het was nothing but a big man with a stone face and such an unwillingness to acknowledge life's absurdities that he had become absurd himself.

Het began to clap. "Wi'out fear or favour," he shouted. "Wi'out fear or favour, Tony. Lest we forget."

Stones fell. So did many of the nuggets of coal people had brought with them as an ironic statement. Lawrence kept missing where they went. He found himself urged closer towards the front lines. A lot more police on horseback now contained the field, as did the dogs, the barking dogs. It was back or forwards only. The picketers had been rounded up, penned here and then attacked, and Lawrence saw the heat as a living, sentient thing, a palpable screen through which the clamour of the hounds chasing him into the trees might be heard, their merry jaggeds tearing his shins and the fleshy beanbags of his calves.

Close now. Close enough to see the detail. More megaphone. More Zulu. The noise was horrible. We will hurt you if you try it. We will put our boot on your windpipe and increase the pressure.

Lawrence was to the side of the main ruck, set apart from Bob and Het, who appeared to have forgotten all about their plan to leave, so caught up were they by shouting at the horde of police officers.

Then it was happening.

The horses came again.

People screamed. Lawrence did too, he couldn't help it. An armoured rider came at him, massive astride its saddle, twelve-foot tall and lit by a sun halo, baton raised, using it to scare the picketers away from Orgreave cokeworks.

Back home you saw beasts like these. They came plodding for their feed, docile heads hanging over drystone walls, fluid lips and fringes that wouldn't have looked out of place on a character from Dallas. It was so easy to take for granted their power, so easy to forget what they might look like bearing down on you. This one rippled with sheer weight. You don't hang around for that. The horse was a velvety, dark chocolate colour and had a pale kite of felt midway up its muzzle. Its mounted officer wore a clear visor and a black coat, zipped up to the chin, implacable as he cantered by to urge on the picket, only Bob was too slow; he turned at the wrong time and took a baton to the face.

Blood flecked Lawrence, or was it sweat? The police horse reared, making that squealing noise you heard on Westerns, and that was all it took. Lawrence ran. He ran the contents of his veins to water. It was enough. More than enough. Up the field he ran, swinging a left in a full-on panic. A TV crew were getting everything. At least that was something, he thought.

He reached the end of the field. They'd agreed to meet at The Plough pub, down the Catcliffe end, if they were split up, but Lawrence had no idea where that was anymore. Without Het he'd be stuck. He'd have to go back. He was not the man he'd thought he was. He was just a boy.

He retraced his tracks. Past the fighting elements he went, past the milling groups and those cowering in huddles, returning to where he'd been. The picket was getting into the police here, a smaller group who'd become bottle-necked. It was nasty stuff that took reinforcements to break up. The offending picketers were being beaten, dragged away. The season's heat, 1984. All that's solid melts into air.

There was a slight incline. Enough hill to stand on and search for Het. Lawrence could see horses. He could hear their hooves clattering in the turf, rucking clods of grass up and leaving behind rutted channels of roiled sod. He moved on. At his feet were the indentations the hooves made. Impacted U-shapes that would have collected glassy pools of water if it was raining. He finally spotted Het, the green shirt, the black cords, the soles of his Doc Martens on display as he knelt next to the dazed Bob.

Relieved, wild, Lawrence skidded over. 'It's me,' he began to say, but stopped. Because over Het's shoulder he could see police emerging from outside the factory. A lot more police and they were coming this way.

It was a mass of officers holding circular shields. These men carried long batons and marched in protective gear. Behind them was a battalion of yet more bobbies in their helmets and their caps, spread across the vaulted diameter of the tophill. The front shield patrol wore round helmets with the same clear visors as the men on horseback. They wore dark gloves, too, in which they gripped their weapons and the transparent shields that stated: POLICE. As if they were in some way unrecognisable. As if anyone could forget the sight of them in woollen sweaters and smart ties, coming to mop this protest from the field.

Uncle Het followed Lawrence's line of sight, and what he saw made him force Bob Roach on to his feet. The older man had a huge bump on his forehead. He was bleeding, asking for his son. Darren was nowhere.

"Where did you go?" Het grabbed Lawrence. "I said to stay close!"

"I thought you said to Gran there'd be no trouble!"

They commenced their escape. The police advance was forcing the picketers away from the cokeworks towards the bottom end of the field. Depth charges of action took place everywhere. Squads of officers barrelled at random to seize people from the crowd and carry them to the command post. One agent tended to do the selecting. Red shirt, go. Bald head, grab him.

Whack.

Of course there were missiles. These served to wind the police up even more. Most of their detainees resisted arrest; it was taking several officers to bring a picketer down, and they weren't doing it gently. In some instances the arrestee would be aided by the picket. Lawrence saw one man dragged down by four officers, only to be freed by a gang of picketers. Men punching policeman. Lawrence had never seen that. He had never thought that he would.

Halfway up the field a camera crew arrived. A blue camera with a stumpy robotic lens, pointing at them. "Steve, get this . . . get the guy's blood."

The furred boom hoisted, the TV crew ignoring Lawrence, filming tall Het, his hair out of kilt, glasses midway down his nose. They filmed Bob: rusty bloodstain marking his face, limping badly.

The crew stalked backwards, filming. It wasn't far to the village end of the field, the only exits an embankment with an acute plunge down to the railway tracks, and the packed bridge leading into the village. Lawrence led the way towards the bridge. There was an immense jam of people there but it seemed a better option than the hill, especially now that he and Het were supporting the dazed Bob.

But the shield units were coming and the horse-torn grass, the din around and the gulf inside. It was the complacency of it all, the efficiency, and so what if Lawrence was suddenly gripping the TV boom? He wrenched the pole, which came out of the sound man's hands easily enough. The guy was young, blonde, ginger. What did it matter? Lawrence hit him in the face, hard enough to make him stagger.

"No!" cried Het.

Lawrence grabbed hold of the camera. It was heavy, shockingly so, which gave it momentum, even if you couldn't throw it very far. He launched the camera and sent it rolling in the grass.

The third man, the director or whoever it was, stood there. Lawrence punched him too. He didn't know why. He did it anyway. The fucker gawped at him, cakehole open, stumbling onto his knees with a bust red lip. See you later.

Then Het was on him. "Get off!" Lawrence protested, fighting free, shoving his uncle and punching him in the chest as hard as he could. God, it hurt.

Bob, the shiny sidekick, waded in. Lawrence shoved him

to the ground as well. "Don't fucking touch me!" he cried, and Het was begging him to calm down but it was way too late for that.

"Am I one of you then, Het? Am I one of you?"

Lawrence ran towards the embankment and hurried down it, only it was steep. *Jesus*, it was steep.

He nearly fell.

He did fall.

He rolled.

He rolled again.

It was OK. Grass in his mouth, he lurched, stumbling towards the chippings and shale of the railway tracks. He could feel the stones and then the metal underfoot as he steadied himself on the rails and panted, facing back the way he'd come. He could see Het at the hill's crest, pausing with madness bubbling behind him. Noise was everywhere. Noise of it. From the top of the embankment hundreds of people were flowing downhill. Before they got to him, Lawrence bolted over the ridge and into Orgreave village. It was still early in the morning and he was his father's son, he was a Newman.

14

B Y THE LIGHT of a Davy lamp lit by a match, the cavern in the hill glows. It's a pot, really, a haunt of biscuity rock. Odd drawings are etched up the cave's walls and globs of paint colour the sand from where you've painted your model soldiers from World War Two, and there's toy Messerschmitt's and Spitfires, a dismantled Meccano set. When the time comes you exit on hand and knee, stretch to however tall you are then notice the sky's vanishing point has merged with the high ground, and above you are stars, many punch holes blazing fiercely in the galaxy. Soon it'll be the traipse home to the snick of the key in the latch, catching sight of the moon, *God's fingernail*, Mam calls it, as you peer over Sam, his window beaming, no curtains to quieten it. The moon is always falling, it never hits the earth. Until one day it breaks orbit, picks up speed and comes down in a ball of fire.

Arthur's eyes clicked open. He was wide awake almost straight away. His shallow breaths grew deeper and *yes*, Shell was lying by his side. He didn't dare to touch her. He knew better than to try.

He would always be the one to do the seeking. When he'd wanted to trap off with his wife in the past he was obliged to rub against her and head inland if she'd only allow it. Why should things be any different now? He was only just returned from what had been the almightiest doghouse of his marriage.

There was no other way of putting it, he had bargained

his way back into the bed. Guilted Shell, for which he was certain now that she was grateful. Because after those first few aloof nights, Shell came close now when Arthur was under the covers, and no surer a sign could there be to signal that things were getting better.

It almost reminded him of when they'd first started courting, easing into bed to be welcomed by that drowsy arm of hers, brought up close before his raging body warmth drove her away again.

"You're a radiator, Arthur. You generate heat."

Shell was always saying how boiling he was. She'd said it again only the other night. "I forgot about that. You running on high."

She had no idea how much saying that had meant to him.

None of this was an accident. After Lawrence left home that day Arthur played his hand as best he could. "What did he mean by that?" he'd said.

"*Nothing.*"

"I said what did he mean, Shell?"

"What are you on about, Arthur?" Shell called from her hiding place out on the landing. She was trying to play dumb, which of course meant she was lying. The door handle. Her frightened face. Arthur speaking in the over-controlled tone of someone managing badly. "Lawrence said, 'Not the only thing Het sorts, is it.'"

"He didn't say that."

"I heard it in our room, don't know how you didn't out here, Shell."

Shell mumbled something about not knowing. Screwing her eyes tight, she headed to the bedroom, collecting strewn clothes and fetching them downstairs in the laundry basket.

Arthur followed, waiting for her to empty the washing machine, which was last year's birthday present, and barely a word of thanks had it got.

Next she bustled into the yard, scene of the bloodiest haircut Arthur had ever been given. His hair was finally starting to look normal, but the face, he could forget about the face for the time being.

"I'm going nowhere till you explain what he meant," he said, to which Shell might have looked exhausted. It seemed as if that's how she would have looked when Arthur replayed the conversation in his head again over the following weeks.

"Oh, for heaven's sakes, I don't *know*."

"But you can see what were hinted. You can see that."

"I don't *know*."

"Stop saying that!"

The clothes and sheets were pegged on the line like costumes the day after Halloween. "So what am I to think?" said Arthur. "First this, then Lawrence. Where will he go?"

"He might not have run away if you hadn't blundered in the way you did."

"First Newman to go to a grammar in I don't know how long."

"I didn't say a word in front of him."

"You didn't have to."

The sound of things picked up and put back down again. Always with the heavy breaths, the hurrying to be getting on with something. They were going the long way around the isosceles triangle, all right, but Arthur would get it out of her.

He didn't leave it. He picked at the shore of his wife, picked at Shell, stone by stone, her only break the hour he afforded her when he went round to his mother's to see if

Lawrence was okay, although the boy wouldn't speak to him. Arthur stopped in at Het's on the way home (*'I swear to God, we haven't. Swear on Dad's ghost and the rest there's nowt to it!'*) before stomping back, bleeding, finding Shell hadn't the nerve to flee, which was her all over. Back until she cracked. *Yes*, she spent time with Het. *Yes*, she knew things were said. Not by her though. Nor him. Rather it was the busybodies: Know-it-all A and Sideways-look B, nattering in your ear while sharpening a pig sticker behind your back.

"And has he touched you?" said Arthur. "Promise me."

"What?"

"You'd tell me."

"If we?"

He nodded with great difficulty.

Shell started to cry.

And maybe it was the easy melody of the past playing Arthur false, but he could never once remember his missus doing that. He went to hold Shell, and she sank so hard against him that he nearly staggered.

Where a torch has once been lit, a remnant will always be. Arthur put his mouth to Shell's forehead and wished he could go back in time. He wished so many things. There are restless spirits surrounding each of us. They grope and hold us captive. He was his wife's prisoner too.

"What's wrong, darling?" he finally said, all those unfathomable looks he'd been getting beginning to make an awful kind of sense. A patch of damp was spreading from where Shell's face rested on the pocket of his shirt.

"It's just been a bad morning," she said.

"Tell me about it," Arthur replied in a glib tone that Shell missed, which was so unlike her. In so many ways she was like a forgotten language to him now, New Testament Greek.

Next Arthur was led into the living room where for once not a moth flew as Shell told him about her arrest for breaching the peace in Sheffield that morning. Arthur stood there, blinking dumbly while his wife told him about being taken to the police cells. Shell was a proud woman with not a mark against her name, and the police had done that to her. They'd locked her up, threatened her with the riot act. A life sentence Shell could have got and Arthur hadn't been there.

She had been strip-searched. Pig hands all over her. The police had removed her clothing, bit by bit, checked her thoroughly for what they knew wasn't there. The methodical nature of so personal an invasion was one of the most difficult things Arthur had ever had to hear.

Because Shell had been defiled. First her mouth and then the pen torch shone against her throat. Then under her tongue, on her teeth and gums. They'd also checked her shoes, removing the inner soles before handing them back to her, telling her to get a fucking move on and slide them back in again. Jacket off. T-shirt off. Chin up. Standing topless in her jeans and trainers while some officer wearing latex fucking gloves checked underneath her breasts. You can put that top back on now, Mrs Newman. Then once you've done that can you hand over them trousers? Nothing there. Now turn around, drop them knickers and squat.

A good few nights since then.

A long few days.

Arthur had laid up in the spare room until he found his mettle, insisting on joining Shell in the marital bed. Within a week of reminding Shell he was the husband and if nothing was going on between her and his brother, she'd to prove it, Arthur was permanently restored to the bedroom, even making love to Shell on a couple of occasions. Or perhaps it was just fucking. After all, a long-married pair can commit to the solitary act as they can't with their child in the house, until it becomes something they almost don't have to think about, and few things are more impersonal than thoughtless sex in the dark.

Everyone goes on about the eyes but it's the lips that can't lie. Arthur was tempted to turn the lamp on so he could check on Shell's mouth, to see if it was relaxed or not. Because her kisses had felt staged. And where did she go to, his wife? Why could he never get to her? Was her loving him an act of charity? When had a vital component departed from their marriage?

He cricked his neck and swung his legs to the floor, feeling the sweet bobbles of the carpet under his feet. The room was awash with peace. As if Shell and he were collaborating, breathing in tandem.

He entered his son's room and bore witness to the mute sadness of the empty bed. Behind the curtain, on the sill, were the stacks of magazines Arthur was looking for. Beanos and Dandys, a few footie mags that were as yellow as pre-war foolscap and fuzzy to the touch. Arthur selected a wedge of comics and couldn't resist putting his nose to the pages. They smelled like badly-dried woollen blankets, the insides of a pencil case. A forgotten something, perhaps, that had taken a weathering in a local park.

In the kitchen his feet stuck to the vinyl. The room felt bizarre as rooms often do at night. The groan of pipes and contracting woodwork. The mass of the airing cupboard describing shadows in which a burglar might hide. Someone like him.

Arthur set to work with the very scissors that had separated him from his hair in the spring. He cut letters one at a time from the straplines of the magazines and glued them with a Pritt-Stick to a sheet of paper torn from the tablet in Lawrence's desk drawer. The message was for Clive Swarsby, and when it was completed it was wiped clean of fingerprints and the next day popped in an envelope.

Asa kept the car running while the letter disappeared into the box affixed to the gates of Threndle House. For the attention of Clive Swarsby, it said, because it wouldn't do for young Evelyn to open any funny-looking note, discovering that it was for her that her father was being told to hand over three grand. Arthur had *some* morals.

The photos were dog-eared now, a thumbprint captured on every bottom right corner from where they'd been pored over several times a day. Arthur's personal mark that caught the daylight, caught the sun.

It had taken him long enough to work out what he had. Eliminating scenarios, chalking off what you knew. For Clive Swarsby had left the negatives undeveloped. These were far from sentimental snaps; they were evidence.

But of what?

Of who, more like. A friend. An acquaintance, probably a lot of things, seeing as this man was with Clive Swarsby's daughter, then with another man, too.

Every picture suggested intimacy, visible closeness. The hand on the small of Evie's back. *That elbow pinch.*

Then there were Evie's clothes. In the photo she wore a braided chain outside of a designer V-neck T-shirt over growing A-cup breasts. She was adoring of the older man's profile, fawning while he stared at something out of shot, all statuesque, the perv. And there he was with another man, two fat-heads knocking their fat skulls together in a fat café. It was the same again in a restaurant, the two laughing into their pâté, then later, under the awning of the Savoy.

The Savoy.

Everything pointed towards Swarsby having dirt on this man.

Now Arthur had it too.

He made his way to his mother's. He was getting fit as a flea walking everywhere, which was one of the few advantages of being skint. Picket money went on the bare essentials, snap was taken care of at the welfare while Shell's wage was devoured by the mortgage and the swollen coffers of their friend the good old YEB, though they were behind on both sets of payments. With the strike raging and the overdues mounting – Hate Mail, Arthur had taken to calling it – there was no choice other than to get this Swarsby racket off the ground.

He arrived at the slate path. He hated coming here. Once, just ten minutes up the road, he had seen his older brother's boot striking their father's face. Arthur dragged Sam off beneath the burgeoned mop heads of a neighbouring hydrangea, and Sam bit him, the incisors of the person you were closest to in the world indenting your wrist. That was what you got for spilling the beans. That was what Arthur deserved, all those years ago.

Mam answered the door. It was difficult, her old person's big nose and ears, the punctured slashes through which her earrings hung. Her liver spots were like crop circles of butterscotch spattering her hands and neck.

"Arthur," she said, looking blank. She must have forgotten what he was here for: another stab at solving the perpetual problem of his son.

He nodded.

"What a way to greet tha mother."

"Morning, Mam."

"Now he says it. Shut door, you're allowing a draft."

There was no wind whatsoever. "I'm here for Lawrence," said Arthur.

"Your little walk."

"Could you send him down please?"

"Will you not—"

"*Mam.*"

The old dear slunk away with the same guilty eyes she'd had after phoning the police on Sam. The same eyes that were absent when she let Arthur's dad break his fucking nose.

Lawrence appeared. Funny how time can blur someone. Arthur leant on the door and said, "How we doing then?"

"Good, yeah."

"Cracking day for it."

"Is it?"

"See for yourself," Arthur said, spreading both arms but feeling hurt. Lawrence just shrugged. It had as good as happened overnight, this growing up, and it would likely be as quick in the reverse. Coming to the end of your life just as your child was beginning theirs. Somehow it just didn't seem fair.

He took Lawrence to the Ogden. The indolent river had taken on a syrupy glaze thanks to the shards of summer sun. As the two of them picked their way through the wood, a tawny owl called, emitting its rich, billowing thread. Arthur stopped at the sound, put his fists together, thumb against thumb, and blew into the gap between them, mimicking the owl's song. After a moment the bird duly called back. Lawrence smiled.

They sat together on a bed of rock, a chthonic door of industrial-looking grey.

"Why am I here, Dad?"

"I want you to tell me about this Swarsby lass."

"And here's me thinking you were going to ask us home."

"That goes without saying," Arthur said.

"How come?"

"Because you're old enough to make up your own mind."

"No, why do you want to know about Evie is what I mean . . ."

Lawrence began to construct a tower of pebbles. He built it up then knocked it down. Repeated the action. Meanwhile, Arthur bided his time. It was important to be careful around the lad. At least with his cheek healed and the mask gone, he could convey a truer honesty. A tender welt remained on his face and his eye was still foxed with purple, although Arthur didn't mind the eye so much. Black eyes have a certain appeal. They aren't called shiners for nothing.

"Because I'm guessing this disaster wi' school happened thanks to her," he said. "Least in part. An' I need to know what's going on wi' you. I'm your dad."

Build those stones. Knock them down. "What do you want to know?" Lawrence asked.

Arthur reached out and ruffled his son's hair. He'd missed doing that. "You're like your mam you're so guarded," he said. "Just tell us how the two of yous met."

Gently does it.

"None of that were her fault," Lawrence replied, after a while. "Evie's amazing."

"I'll bet."

"No, really. Her family came from London. You'll have heard of the dad. I met her in the woods. Bend of circumstance, I suppose you'd call it."

"But you're being careful . . . You know what I mean . . ."

Lawrence blushed. "We're just friends."

"How come? She have a fella or summat?"

"Don't think so."

"She never mention no one? Someone from her past?"

"Not that I remember."

"Old bloke, posh? Tell me who he is."

Lawrence stood and said sharply "Why don't you ask her yourself if you're that bothered?"

Arthur thought fast. "Sit down. Reason I ask is I worry. Your dad does. 'Cause I know girls like her . . . No, wait, don't look like that. Girls like this Evie. Not pretty girls, as such . . . I mean the compelling ones, the ones with summat beyond their looks—"

"She's not—"

"Lawrence, you're forgetting I've met her." Arthur paused. Lawrence was finally listening. "And I know for a fact that ones like Evie are the ones you watch. Take your mam. Why else do you think I'm wi' her?"

Lawrence fixed him with a pointed stare.

"*Because* of that," Arthur countered. "Women like your mam have dimensions no matter which way you turn 'em. Diamonds. They're the ones you'll come back to when you're an old duffer like me. I mean who wants to spend the rest of their puff running around with someone who'll do anything you say?"

Arthur had the impression Lawrence was just going along with this conversation, still, he'd say his piece - experience was worth nothing if you didn't make use of it.

"Evie'll have a past," he said. "It might give you an angle."

"She doesn't tell me nowt."

"Nay, you just need to speak to her the right way." Arthur threw one of the stones from Lawrence's pile into the river. "Try that, and, if you want, when she opens up, tell us what she says . . . I'll advise you."

"She thinks I'm an idiot, Dad. Daft and ugly."

"Oh, don't do yourself down. It's the eternal fortune of men that women aren't that bothered about our looks."

It was a joy to see the way Lawrence's face crinkled. "Course they are."

Arthur clapped him on the shoulder. "On the contrary, it's your flaws they find appealing, kid. Which is part of the problem." His smile faded. "As if you're anything like the rest of us it's your flaws you can't get over and what will destroy you in the end."

The stones were knocked over for good. The owl called again, that mercurial silver tone. Arthur had long since realised the trouble he would have been saved if his own father hadn't been too embarrassed to discuss some of this stuff when *he* was a boy. "I'll tell you summat, Lawrence. As I've lived," he said. Out came the canteen. "It'll come in handy, whatever you might think of me, I never lie to you."

There was nothing Lawrence could say to that.

"If a girl's not got her face on around you, it isn't because she doesn't care, it's because she feels that comfortable around you that she can be herself. If a girl says she doesn't mind

227

when you do summat wi'out her, she's lying. If a girl says she wants nowt from you, she's testing to see what you'll do."

"But that's—"

"Shut it. You're never not being tested, an' you'll never know what the pass mark is either. Fail though and you'll find out. None of this a lass will admit to. Least at first."

Lawrence messed with his socks and swept the remaining pebbles into the Ogden. "They're impossible," he said.

"Aye." Arthur laughed. "That's what keeps us coming back."

The following Monday, with Shell at work, Arthur dressed in black and chain-smoked in the kitchen, aiming the smoke at the open back door. The way he went through with questionable plans was to first convince himself of their pragmatism. He'd once stolen the Yorkstone from a vacant house around the corner from his mam's and spent the money he made on a family trip to Bridlington. He'd lifted up the underlay, levered the slabs out with the crowbar and carted them away one by one in the wheelbarrow, cursing his pit-ravaged back and telling himself that if he didn't do it, someone else would. Later, watching Lawrence paddle in the sea and Shell lick melted ice cream from her wrist, he'd felt so distant from the choice and terms that had forced it that it was as if some other idiot had stolen the stone and no way would he ever do a thing like it again. And as it had been then, so it would be now. Arthur went to the front window when he heard the car arrive: Asa's Fiesta. There was no greeting for him as he got in. Asa just shifted gear and drove them away.

There are comfortable silences and friendships that can withstand silence. These are two different things. Then there

228

was the quiet of that little red car. It was Sunday-dead, all the way to Threndle House. Asa and Arthur parked near to the property then hurried to its outer wall.

It was six o'clock, no sound save their shoes scuffing the brick, tights capping their heads and a cricket bat shared between them. Asa and Arthur slid down the wall like a pair of tom cats and landed in the barked flower beds of the mansion.

Dew flecked against their bare arms from the leaf tips. The two men crouched, hidden against the wall by a large, pink azalea. Surely no one had seen them. They were on their haunches, breathing. Arthur's heart boomed. It was bright as anything today and he still had the lawn's splendid fabric to navigate.

Asa had his tights pulled over his face already, but the material was nearly transparent and hardly disguised him.

"I can see your face," said Arthur. "I said I can still make out your bloody face, Asa."

Asa squinted. "How's that?"

"How should I know?"

"Put yours on so I can see."

Arthur did.

"What denier are they?"

"Denier?"

Arthur still had the tights' cardboard sheath. He drew it from his pocket, handed it to Asa and followed his friend's chipped fingernail down the item's description. *Denier 10*, it read.

Asa stared. "You've bought the sheer ones."

"Have I?"

"*Arthur!*"

"All right—"

"Fucking idiot."

"I'll sort it, Scanny. Calm down."

Arthur yanked the waist lip of his own tights until it stretched to his breastplate, then doubled the fabric up over his face. Next he yanked the bunny ears of the legs, wrapped them around his head and tied them in a knot under his nose. The elasticated waist rested on his top lip, only half his face covered, mouth free. "Job's a goodun," he said.

Asa said nothing.

The two men peered at the greenish building. Asa seemed to have calmed a little, but Arthur was still worried. For a tried and tested yes man, Asa had taken a good deal more persuading down the Grey Grebe the other night than Arthur had initially thought necessary. He'd been forced to call upon fictional relatives who had been cruelly reduced to the alms houses, for good measure reminding Asa that he also had a wife and two young mouths to feed. The plan was to scare Swarsby shitless then drive him down the bank, and Arthur had told Asa they were getting a grand each for their trouble. His friend was a man of simple tastes, a lower share of the spoils would surely do him.

"But how legal is it?" said Asa.

"Shove off illegal! After what we've seen on picket, don't talk to me about illegal. This cunt's blackmailing another cunt over his own kid, you know. Never mind that it's his lot what started this mess."

Asa nodded.

"An' if I've the measure of him, Scanny, he'll hand over the dough, no question, then that's me, you and ours sorted till this strike blows over. Trust us, pal, MPs don't want stuff like this coming out. You remember Profumo?"

"Not really."

"Well, put it this way: it didn't work out for Macmillan. And Swarsby's not about to call the pigs. And before you say 'owt, if it makes you feel any better." Arthur laid a hand against his heart. "I'll donate some to union from what we get."

He sprinted across the lawn to the French doors, where he was surprised to see the window still hadn't been fixed. A wooden panel covered where the glass had been. Arthur forced it open with ease.

The lounge had been allowed to breathe now the extra boxes had been unpacked. Daylight made the piano gleam. The oil canvas on the wall could have been freshly painted and the breeze clinked the chandelier, which resembled a crystal jellyfish suspended from the ceiling.

Arthur was admiring it all when Asa barged past. The far-right door led to the atrium and then the staircase. The master bedroom at the front of the house was located up top, overlooking the grounds and the countryside leading to Brantford pit, whose disused Grafton Belt was rumoured to stretch this far. Arthur could actually see a hairline crack in the nearest wall. Subsidence might be the death of this place, which was an irony not lost on him.

They reached the stairs. Although the atrium was still undecorated, at least the mess Arthur remembered from the other month had been cleared away. The cricket bat felt horrid and heavy as he gave it a tester swing. He led the way upstairs to the master bedroom.

All the doors on the upper floor were closed, thank fuck. Arthur arrived at Clive Swarsby's bedroom, the door making a rustling noise on the carpet as he pushed it open, finding an empty bed waiting for him.

He stopped in his tracks. He stowed the cricket bat under his arm and made a shape with his hands, as if holding an imaginary rugby ball. Asa tapped him on the shoulder. *What?* Arthur wanted to hiss.

Asa touched the bed, signalled for Arthur to do the same. The sheets were warm.

Arthur cocked his head and left the room, sliding, flush against the corridor wall, listening at every closed door he came to.

He heard a noise, a rustle of paper on the other side of a third door to his left. Arthur held the cricket bat low, the first outing the willow wood had enjoyed since his declaration with it on a hundred and five in the summer of 1981. With grass stains on his whites, Arthur had been the king of the cricket pavilion that night.

The door swung open to reveal Clive Swarsby, rotund in winceyette pyjamas, slippers on his desk, reading a newspaper. Arthur made a floorboard creak as he entered the room. That got Swarsby's attention. The man leapt from his seat, sending his chair rolling on its casters until it struck a radiator fitted against the wall. That big sarcastic face didn't even seem shocked by Arthur's arrival. If anything, it looked resigned.

15

S HE WORE A denim shirt with both sleeves rolled up. She wore black leggings and a chain of fool's gold, flopped and gathering sweat in the crook of her neck. Clive's credit card was paying for this hot box. Bold enough to turn her nose up at a coach, Evie had still been reticent to splash out on first class train tickets.

Dabbing her brow with a tissue, she wished she could crack a window. No such luck. She amused herself by noting the sheepish happiness of a middle-aged woman aiding a toddler down the aisle; by listening to a man in the seat behind remarking on things only old people noticed: the amount of spires prodding between observable houses; a murmuration of starlings pulsing above the olive-coloured rooftops.

Clive knew all about this trip, he just hadn't been willing to pay for it. In fact it was his idea to begin with. It was best Evie and Duncan visit their mother. It was the summer holidays, and besides, it was high time Fiona lent a hand. "Only you'll have to ask her to foot the bill," Clive said. "Your mother's still not talking to me."

Rather than ask anything of her mother, Evie had lifted the Mastercard from her father's wallet and used it to purchase two open returns to London. She was a dab hand at forging Clive's signature, having used it to fund various indiscretions in the past, and fortunately her face had boiled into such a contagious smile as she paid the man behind the counter at the station, that he didn't look at the name on the card. After all it was the first time in months Evie had been allowed home. No wonder she'd been nearly overcome.

In the aisle seat Duncan slept. He'd slept since they left Doncaster. Slept Britain by. Now there was one hour to go. One hour until the hiss into King's Cross, the station's clock tower rising above semi-circular windows that looked like amused eyes: a frontage that seemed to know something you didn't.

When they finally stepped onto the platform their mother was waiting for them. She wore a teal-coloured outfit and red-trimmed sunglasses. She was so thin Evie could have broken her over one knee.

"What's she doing here?"

Already Duncan was tall enough to look down on Evie. "I called ahead," he replied as they hurried towards Fiona. "Why slum the tube when we can have a lift?"

Evie quickly wheeled her luggage ahead so she could impart a brisk hug upon their mother. The rims of the pores on Fiona Swarsby's nose were highly visible thanks to the over-slap of foundation they had received. She was a woman in her fifties. Growing up, Evie and her friends had called her *The Versace Bag*.

"Why on earth didn't you tell me you were coming?" said Fiona.

"Oh come on, Mummy, that was always Duncan's job."

Duncan arrived, flinging himself against Fiona's shoulder pads. "I've missed you," he said.

"And I you." Fiona sighed. "Oh, Duncan." She glanced from Evie to the ceiling. She shut her eyes.

They arrived at the car, which was parked on double yellow

lines outside a taxi rank, its hazards flashing. Evie wished for cigarettes. It had been four hours without a smoke and now it would be at least another two. She had forgotten what heavy traffic was like. Buses coursed along the Euston Road and a set of sirens wailed nearby – at least that was familiar from up in Yorkshire – and there were so many people. The oblate tarmac shone.

"Ready when you are," said Fiona to the driver. "My babies are home for the fundraiser, what timing."

"Fundraiser?" said Evie, shifting in her seat. "What fundraiser?"

Duncan chuckled. "It's the garden party tonight. Mummy's taking us."

Summer was in full flow in the south. It was summer up the Cally Road, summer en route to Holloway and summer in steep Highgate, where their mother was now based. Not far from the car park situated beneath Fiona Swarsby's apartment complex, the flat level of the bus lane had been heat-manipulated into a strange and unsettling wave shape.

"Tony Dallas is living around the corner, Evie. Clem's always asking after you," said Fiona. "Why don't you pop round and say hello while Duncan and I catch up."

Clem was an old associate and would make a better time-killer than most. All the way back from King's Cross Fiona had blathered on about Bram. How good he'd been to her, how kind he'd been to put a roof over her family's poor heads. There was no way he wouldn't be at the donor club party that evening, therefore Evie had to be looking her best. Clemmie Dallas had always been good at preparing for big occasions.

Evie rang the doorbell of a palatial cream-coloured house

located ten minutes' walk from her mother's flat. A stout-armed maid answered the door, demanding to know what business Evie had there, but before she could answer, a teenager strolling through the vestibule stopped in his tracks.

"Swarsby," he called, sliding a hand through his hair.

"*Felix*."

"How are things?"

"Oh, still standing," said Evie.

"And home without additional fingers, I see."

"There are no external changes, at least."

"I'll be the judge of that. Turn around."

Evie laughed, complying readily.

Felix smirked. "And no sign of a tail."

With haste Evie was returning to the places she had missed.

She was shown upstairs – built from eighty thousand pounds' worth of solid oak, Felix said – and was soon smoking and drinking wine with Clemmie Dallas as if they'd been seeing each other on a daily basis for the past two years.

Clem's domain was the top floor of the house. Her room was split into two levels: a lower chamber where she slept when she wasn't boarding at Cheltenham Ladies College, and a mezzanine area extending deep into the loft.

Evie rested her elbow on the lip of the low window that opened out onto the mezzanine roof, admiring Clem's fairy-tale hair and pertness. Her old foe reclined on one of the sofas, a foot resting on the head of a teddy bear the size of a small child, as she filled Evie in on the latest comings and couplings and embarrassments. Clem seemed only vaguely put out when Evie failed to engage in this commerce with any enthusiasm, angling a condescending look from the other side of the room.

"What's wrong, duckie?" she said. "You don't still need to act like you're a million miles away, you know."

The nib of the joint glowed enticingly in Clem's mouth. So let her look. The fact was that the reputations and pliant victories of Evie's old friends and their Tatler aspirations, together with the gossip she had been so eagerly awaiting, had meant almost nothing to her. So there had been another launch, another suppressed liaison in an alcove somewhere. It turned out that the happiness of others was dull and invasive. "I'm fine," said Evie. "I just haven't smoked in such a long time. I'm not as easy with the feeling as I used to be."

Which was apparently Clem's cue to send over the joint, sniggering as Evie took another drag and exhaled a long plume of grass smoke, barely managing not to cough.

A brass tin lay on the floor between the girls, packed with exotic-scented sativa skunk. Evie picked at one of the dense little buds, her toes kneading the luxurious rug. "God, your room's huge," she said at last. "Is that your horse, Clem?" She pointed to a watercolour painting of a child astride a mare. A mustard rosette was pinned on a blurred lapel.

"I *think* so," said Clem. "Although I don't ride anymore. It makes my groin look like a pair of cooked steaks."

"God," said Evie. "Your own horse. A room like this . . ."

"It isn't as big as Felix's."

". . . Marble dresser, walk-in-wardrobe." Evie gestured at the array of tapes and records arranged in columns about the room. "You're so lucky."

Clem blew her own twist of smoke into the compact London air.

"What?" said Evie.

"Nothing."

"What, Clem?"

"*Nothing.*"

Clem rose to the desk and fetched a copy of *The Face* magazine. She began to leaf through it, showing very little emotion as she digested a piece on Marvin Gaye's funeral, all the while rotating with one foot a pleated ring she wore on the big toe of her other foot.

Accepting the dismissal as once she never would have, Evie returned to the window and its vista of Mary Poppins rooftops. Here, as far as the eye could see, were the jagged barbicans protecting London from the rest of the country. She might well have shown too much esteem then; she was hardly dropping her aitches. Perhaps the grass was making her more conscious, more observant, or perhaps nothing fit any more and she was only just beginning to realise it. She knew Litten had changed her, but even listening to her Walkman and running a hand along the psoriasis of flaking wallpaper at Threndle House hadn't made her feel *this* poor. Clem's lovely profile. This fecund city. How easy it was to lose yourself. How the bottom could fall so totally out of everything.

Although even Evie could see that Clemmie wasn't the fairest of comparisons to make with herself. Clemmie was the eldest daughter of Tony Dallas, *the* hedge fund manager for AGP, an asset management firm with offices in London, Hong Kong, New York, Jersey and Sydney. Tony Dallas was a prominent member of the Premier Group, the Conservative party supporters' club responsible for tonight's fundraiser. For an annual fee and subsequent donations, Premier Group members were invited to dinners with senior party officials, post-PMQ lunches, drinks receptions, events and important campaign launches. It was said Tony Dallas was a shoo-in for a knighthood.

And *her* father? The patsy, the dupe, the stooge? Evie had to laugh, and so she did.

"What's so funny?" Clem said, finally shutting her magazine.

"Oh, nothing. Nothing's funny."

"Actually, everything is."

"You're probably right."

The girls giggled, the ice between them seeming to liquefy at last.

"I can't believe your timing. Are you sure your mother didn't tell you about tonight?" Clem said, rolling another joint.

"Honestly, no." Evie shook her head, the grass she'd already smoked causing her to stray closer to the shuttered trapdoors in her head. She didn't believe she had ever met anybody like Bram, and was currently picturing his tanned knees, wrinkled at head height as she awaited him on the bed. How she loved to hate what she loved. Feared she'd never be happy. Wouldn't let herself.

"Any survival tips?" she asked.

"Haven't a clue. I don't keep up with things like that." Clem was supine on her side. "I only turn up for the cocktails."

Now it was Evie's turn to deliver the condescending look.

"*All right*," Clem shot back. "I do like to dress up, and laughing at those walruses and turkeys is a hoot . . . But as for the gossip, I'm nearly as out of it as you are. I'm only just home from college."

Even more since she'd moved away, Evie had gleaned that when you live in any world it begins to permeate you: it's a kind of seepage. For example, she had a soft spot for the sincerity of the country now that she had never had when living in the city. And similarly, as a child of a politician, she had spent her whole life steeped in the illusive rites of omission, ambition and indirection, so this thinking was embedded in her, too. Which was why she could spot falsehoods from a mile away, and why she was certain now that Clemmie was lying.

The speed with which Clem changed the subject confirmed Evie's suspicions. "The party's at Archie Wethered's," she said. "Do you know the Wethereds?"

"Never heard of them."

"God, you *have* been out of it." Clem raised the joint. "To the bucolic life. A purer way."

"I'd like to see how you'd do up there."

Clem arched an eyebrow. "Fuck that. Arch is in retail. He's just branched into pharmacies. You should see his house."

"Influential, then."

"They say half the cabinet's been round. Even the prime minister."

"Bloody hell."

"I could tell you a thing or two about Arch."

But Evie wasn't bothered. She felt snugly high, so much so that she wasn't particularly interested when the next joint came her way. She set it on the corner of the coffee table, balanced diagonally so each tip hung above the carpet.

"*He's* stepped up to the crease," she said.

"He's paid to join the Premier Group and annual membership doesn't come cheap. Plus he's hosting the garden party, so I'd say Arch hasn't so much stepped up as is captaining the team entirely. Is it that dead where you've been that you wouldn't have heard of the Wethereds? Have you been trussed

240

up in a dungeon all this time or something?"

Barely an hour into the visit and already the asides were coming thick. Still, Evie couldn't deny that the hidden arbours like this, the world of the Dallas's and the Wethereds, were where things happened, where things felt safe. And who wouldn't want a slice of these generous comforts?

"I suppose all the *Who-do-you-know* stuff does feel slightly immaterial these days," she admitted.

"*Immaterial?*"

"You know, petty. It's old-fashioned, isn't it?"

"Jesus," said Clem. "I'll call the doctor."

Speaking of old-fashioned, Evie had once asked Bram about his background. He'd told her that his father *Gerry* was a farmer, which her own father had found hugely amusing, because Sir Greville Guiseley was actually the eighth holder of a baronetcy that could be traced back to the seventeenth century. His stock was worth upwards of ten million pounds and included two thousand acres of arable land, Threndle House itself – inherited from his deceased wife, Margot – a stately home outside of Harrogate, his house in London and a hall near Whitby; all of which went to Bram upon his father's death. The hereditary peerage must have come as something of a bonus, Clive joked.

"So is there any cock up there or what?" asked Clem, when they were a little drunker.

"God, no."

"You hesitated."

"Didn't."

"You've found some sport, Evie. I can tell."

"Really I haven't."

"Balls," said Clem. "I can still read you even if you have

been off getting a farmer's tan. Which suits you, by the way. Manure-brown."

"You do realise we don't have to look like Victorian dolls any more, Clem."

Clem finished and docked out the second joint. Her room was hazy, smoke filtering from the skylight rather than into the house. She removed her t-shirt and shorts and faced Evie in her bra and knickers.

"Give me a hand with this, would you."

Clem slipped her lingerie off and went to select a dress, now naked. She was so decisive. While she stepped into a coconut-white halter-neck, Evie stole a handful of grass from the tin and shoved it in her pocket.

"Breathe in, so I can do it up."

"Breathe in," said Clem, playfully slapping Evie's wrist as her zip was fastened. Her figure was sickening in its way. So it was with pretty people.

"What do you think?" she said, popping another bottle, red.

"There *is* someone, actually," Evie said.

"Go on." Clem began her make-up.

"Someone local."

"Horse and cart? Build walls?"

"No—"

"A brooding landowner then. Ha ha."

"Oh shut up. He's a year younger than me. Just left school. He does brood though."

The fact Lawrence was a schoolboy seemed to surprise Clem. "That dress suits you," said Evie.

"What're you wearing?"

"I didn't bring anything. Everything's been a bit slap-dash."

"That's the best way to approach it. Take your pick from any of these if you like," Clem said, entering her wardrobe and flicking through the hangers like a rolodex, removing dresses and laying them on the beanbag. Evie recalled Duncan remarking on Lawrence dressing from the penny rail at the market.

"Do you like him?" said Clem.

"Who?"

"What did I say about being coy? Your rustic. Tell me about him or you're going to the party as you are."

"He's a miner's son."

"*Shut up.*"

"Really."

"Evie, that's bloody brilliant."

"I can't decide if I like him or if I'm just bored. Probably a bit of both. Maybe neither."

"Maybe all of the above. What does he look like?"

"Well, he's not really my type, but he has a quality. I think he'd do anything I asked."

"Oh, *why* didn't you bring him?"

"I'd have had a hard time. I don't have his number and I don't know where he lives – we've just been meeting in the woods. I think he's embarrassed. Besides, I haven't seen him for ages. We were supposed to meet up the other week . . . I didn't show."

"Cow."

"He hasn't been back. I'm not sure why I didn't go."

"Washing your hair, I expect."

"Washing Duncan's, more like."

"You always did make me laugh."

"Pass the wine. Thanks."

"Certainly sounds interesting," said Clem, brushing her hair. "Tell me something else."

Lawrence. There wasn't much Evie knew about the only person in Litten she had allowed herself to meet, which made it all the more strange that she found herself telling Clem about him now. She said, "He lies all the time, and he has this spot in his head, a cubbyhole he goes to. It's absorbing, really. He just goes silent. He's desperate, really."

"He sounds almost as much hard work as you."

Evie threw a pillow, giggling as it ricocheted comically off Clem's head. Clem collapsed dramatically onto the carpet, laughing too. It was refreshing to be a teenager again. As the taper of Clem's dress reached the stairs, her dark wine left tidelines up the inner slopes of her glass.

The Swarsbys and the Dallas's shared a car west across London. Evie wondered how her mother had been promoted to this social stratum. In all the time her parents were together, they seemed only to mix with other low-level party members and civil servants. Bram was as high as they ever got. He and Clive were at Brasenose together, although the way Bram treated her father – Evie grew to realise – made the friendship seem like more of an act, an avuncular benevolence on Bram's part. Yet here was Evie's mother, living in luxury and flirting with millionaires.

Evie wasn't sure if the venue they arrived at was Archie Wethered's house, or if the property had been hired for the occasion. Either way it looked fit for a ducal residency, a stately home garlanded by magnificent wisteria, an enormous glass cupola protruding above the lobby and significant acreage for grounds.

Duncan led the way towards the main doors. He looked very grown-up in his dinner suit, striding along the rouge carpet fastened down by brass runners, up the stairs to be greeted by the staff.

They were served champagne and directed towards a marquee around the back of the property. Orbs of light were strung gaily from the pine trees, crystal balls that told no future. The band played swing-time even though it far was too early for dancing. All the women were layered, lithe and shoulder-draped. They held large purses and let their necks show, their men tucked and pressed, crisply defined in black and white.

Far less shapely than Clem, Evie had snacked before departing but was terribly aware of her conspicuous bones, her exposed clavicle. The chicken fillets felt strange against her breasts, fleshy beneath the turquoise dress. She ate a ruthless number of canapés, partly to compensate, and partly because she was so bloody stoned. It was also, in part, for the anonymity of purpose, to give herself something to do, because being high made her feel like everyone was looking at her. It made her think that they knew the things only *she* knew about herself: the things she had done that made her dislike herself the most.

She touched her hair. It was crunchy. She had another drink. Thankfully Duncan was coming this way, because *there*, down the other end of the shingle path, was Bramwell Guiseley.

Evie ducked behind a bush that had been clipped into a double spiral. Bram wore a cummerbund similar to the one in that bloody photo that was still cracked after the break-in back in March. Evie swallowed her wine; it was sharp. She turned to face her brother.

"What are you doing behind the topiary?" said Duncan.

"There's Bram."

"So he is."

"Do you think he knows we're here?"

"Mummy told him we were coming."

"You've spoken to him?"

"Course I haven't."

Evie would never cry over Bram, but something nearly happened as she monitored him now. Pallid as winter, even in summer, she had never been paid attention to before, never truly considered, not until Bram. He had given her books and blended compliments into their conversations. He had listened to her, written expansive letters in response to her own juvenile salvos, offered her his opinion on intimate matters, his advice, crediting her with the sort of intelligence she had not known she possessed, making her think of herself and regard herself, become aware. And then there were those times at his clandestine flat, Bram's hot tongue upon her neck mere moments after she first put her hand on his knee. She had been more grown-up than ever, a woman who knew her own mind. The skrike of gulls on the Thames. That single white hair sprouting amid the otherwise dark thatch on Bram's chest.

Evie realised Duncan was staring at her, and knew that she had revealed a part of herself, a visible wound, and that her brother had no respect for people who gave away everything.

"You're on something," he said.

"I'm not."

"When are you going to stop letting this family down, Evie?"

She didn't know.

It was a short walk to the toilet to cover her mouth and scream. The swing doors fanned her face and then she was entering the end cubicle under the frosted window. Feeling this way about Bram, it was as if she'd been mugged and couldn't go past the spot where it had happened. A consensual fling should not result in such self-loathing. Sex Evie had occasionally instigated, even if she never finished it, was still under her control. She rested her head on the cistern and breathed. Developing feelings was crude and childish, becoming entrammelled with the first person that ever made her feel understood even more so. How obvious she had been. Clemmie and the other girls took lovers. They were never taken themselves.

She returned to the garden. Everyone was clapping as Archie Wethered finished his welcome speech and stepped aside so the auction could be set up. Glossy programmes had been arranged on a nearby lectern. The auction lots included vintage posters from victorious Conservative elections gone by, a luxury chalet holiday in Austria, a grouse hunting trip to Scotland, a night's exclusive use of a private members' club in West London, a bronze statue of Winston Churchill and numerous items of jewellery. Evie was interested to see that activities with various powerful government officials were also on offer – afternoon tea, dinner dates and shopping trips – all of them available to the highest vested bidder.

After that would come dinner, speeches and dancing. The menu had been displayed on a side table: grapefruit stuffed with crab and avocado, consommé, roast sirloin of beef, Norfolk turkey, breaded lamb cutlets, cider-glazed gammon and vol-au-vents. Green salad, tomato salad, Waldorf salad, French bean salad, sweetcorn salad, something called *pilaff*, new potatoes, the whole lot followed by a dessert of orange sorbet, strawberry gateaux and black cherry flan. After that came cheese and biscuits, tea and coffee and wine, wine, wine, wine, wine.

Another drink, another, why not? Evie watched the auction proceed and thought of the world she had left behind, a place where the cloud canopy never seemed to part for very long. Every day in Yorkshire there were processions of police vehicles on the pit road near Threndle House, battalions of urgent white and blue heading towards the locals who stood together outside of their place of work and other pits like it. These picketers staged protests and held their banners aloft. They claimed to fight for their jobs when, for the most part, it wasn't even their pits that were being threatened. It seemed absurd that these people would put themselves through that for one another. Although that was the immensity of it, Evie supposed, the power of collective action. No wonder the government wanted to stamp it out.

One day she and Duncan had gone to spy on the miners and their families queuing for their meals at the welfare. It was surprising how chipper everybody seemed. The news outlets reported dawn raids by pillaging miners, hoodlums damaging public property and carrying out violent raids on the police, causing trouble both in the centre of the country and its extremities. Yet they were just *people*; Evie knew that now. She had also realised that there were twin planes of reality in this country, and the closer you looked the more blatant their divergence seemed to be. She swooped upon a platter of food then helped herself to more champagne. Ahead was a marquee and in front of that was an ice sculpture of a hand with a torch. It was the Conservative herald.

Feeling sick, she went to find the others. How easy it was to be alone in a packed place, stumbling between rooms without belonging. Evie tried the indoor and outdoor bars, eventually finding Duncan at the edge of the dancefloor in the marquee. He was deep in conversation with Felix and Tony Dallas, so Evie lingered at his shoulder and tried to listen in, gaining neither a word of acknowledgment nor an opportunity to speak. She was privy only to the sound of Duran Duran. A man in a dinner suit and a woman in blue were the only people dancing. They moved together, all hips, and began to kiss with tongues. Evie watched them until the song had finished, then went in search of Clem.

She couldn't find her friend anywhere, so knocked back another couple of drinks and people-watched before leaving the enclosed area and heading to the main grounds. There she could smoke and think in private.

Exiting via a side gate, Evie shed her heels and walked, barefoot, which felt pleasant, then dropped to the ground and slumped against a corner where a laburnum-covered pergola protruded from the wall.

A mellow mat of grass rolled ahead. So did the tree line, and in front of that was an unyielding sallow mark that could have been a lake. The smoke purled from Evie's lips, the grateful smoke, and the sky above formed an overcast roof.

She was about to wander further into the garden when she heard a noise coming from the gloom. Being outdoors was making her feel very drunk, but she could just about see a figure standing a few yards away, almost hidden by a net of branches. Maybe it was Clem.

Evie made her way towards the pale shape until she could recognise the unmistakable contours of Clemmie's face. "I've been looking for you . . ." she began, but stopped as she noticed Clem's dress tumbling in corrugations over the sides of her legs, and a man's head nodding between the space there.

Clem's mouth was slack. Her eyes finally focused upon Evie, who stood but two steps away. Nobody spoke. The chasm of Clem's mouth became huge as her hand wrenched the crouching man's hair. He gripped both her thighs; Clem's teeth were clear, bared at Evie now, as, still watching her, she bent to kiss the man, fingers fanning the back of his skull. Evie could make out the face. It was Archie Wethered.

She hurried to re-join the party, fighting a sob and unable to explain quite why. She could see her mother's beehive hair standing out in sharp relief against the ice sculpture. Glazed, Evie felt glazed. She helped herself to another drink and drank another to chase that, which steadied her. Fizz always went down so bloody easily.

Her mother was chatting to a man. Dark of complexion, he was recognisable from the business pages, some party or other: one of those easy, old-money types who brushed thinning hair over bald spots and drank more than they ate because they were secretly making sure their man-boobs didn't get any bigger.

"Evie!" said her mother. "Evie, meet Harry. Harry, this is my daughter, Evelyn," Fiona said.

"Great to meet you," the man drawled, liquid. "How lovely."

He had an amused face, a louche posture, and Bram was nowhere to be seen. Evie would slip behind her lover when she saw him. She would drop a hand in his pocket and grab him where he couldn't wriggle free.

"*Evie?*"

"Hi. Sorry. S'good to meet you," she said. "Who's this, young man? Tell us what y'do."

"I'm in property, mainly," Harry said.

Evie hiccuped. "I've just finished school."

Fiona's cheeks were thoroughly rouged, but Evie could still see them colouring. She gave her mother a desperate smile disguised as a sneer, then wiped her nose with the back of her hand, knocking her chin with the shoes she was still holding. They clopped against one another, left and right.

Harry said, "Your mother tells me you've been staying in Yorkshire."

"Yes, and frankly, it's fu—"

"*Evelyn!* Please excuse my daughter, Harry."

The man's hand alighted on Fiona's waist.

"Sent north . . . I did ask to stay. Y'would, wouldn't you?" said Evie. "Ask for help."

Fiona was doing that wobbly-head, tongue-stuffed-behind-her-bottom-lip thing.

Evie said, "But Mummy sent me to a warzone."

Fiona forced a laugh, mouth opening so wide that Evie was surprised bats didn't fly out of it. "Don't be so dramatic."

Harry's papery eyelids narrowed. "Ah, you mean the strike. An unpleasant business."

"Unnecessary, too," said Fiona.

"If you ask me, Keith Joseph had the right idea," whispered Harry.

Fiona set a hand on Harry's arm, then touched her chest.

"Y'should meet a friend of mine an' tell him that," Evie said.

Harry craned to see across the room. "Is he here?"

"It's not his scene."

"But a warzone?" Fiona raised an eyebrow. "You're going to have to back that one up, Evie."

"Put it this way, now I know what a Black Maria is."

They both tilted their heads in approval.

"This one's come home familiar with all sorts of earthy language," Fiona said. "My son is more realistic, probably too realistic for his own good. But Evelyn . . ." – she shook her head – ". . .has always been more impressionable."

"Surely not," said Harry, and smiled at Evie, who parted her lips and showed him her flat, welcoming tongue.

"I'd say she's more like her mother," said Harry, raising his drink.

Evie wanted to put her head through the nearest pane of glass. She made a noise. She wasn't sure how it sounded, as if she was tickled, perhaps. In any case it summoned Fiona's hand to her wrist. Snapping tight, the nails dug in.

"My daughter is drunk."

"It's an occasion for drinking," said Harry kindly.

A large plant was visible to Evie's left, a maple in a copper pot. There was a wonderful purple tinge to its leaves, which were like emblems. "What's that tree?" she said. "There's one like it on Litten Hill."

"What *is* she talking about?" said Fiona. "A friend of mine was like this at Ascot this year. Delusional with drink, she was. Babbling."

"Ascot?" said Evie, perking up.

"Why don't you have some water?"

Fiona summoned a waiter, who arrived with a platter from which Evie swiped another glass of wine and downed it.

Ascot. *Of course.*

"How were the races, *Mummy?*"

Fiona snatched the empty wine glass. "You've had more than enough."

"You're quite right."

"She's delirious."

All of them laughed. Fixed races and duff tips. Fascinators and top hats and carnations for all.

"I confess I was fibbing when I said Harry's name is just Harry," said Fiona. "Would you mind if I told her, Harry? It's *such* a grand title."

"Oh, not at all," said Harry, clearly delighted.

"Evelyn, you won't have realised it but you and I are now in the company of—"

"Viscount Digby Alexander Halifax *the fourth*," said a voice.

"Bram!"

"How're you doing, Harry?"

The rest of the conversation was lost upon Evie. Bram seemed to stand at ten feet tall, and his eyelashes were like tarantula legs. Evie thoughts seemed to multiply in size. She could do nothing as she felt Bram's arm slither around her waist.

"Hello, Pup."

His voice. Evie's vision was swallowed. She was in the charnel house and the outdoor light had gone all wrong, becoming indistinct, yet piercing, while her mother, Harry and Bram and indeed every other guest seemed to distort and solidify until they weren't really people at all, but waxworks, malformed, beset by radiation, perhaps. Melted mannequins.

Then they weren't waxworks at all. They were simply an image of waxworks, a life-size photograph of waxworks that behaved as if it had been held over an enormous flame. The image's silver nitrate bubbled, pock-holes opening, corners furling inward. Evie couldn't tell who was speaking. There was only Bram and that hysterical phosphorescent glare. She stumbled backwards and heard her name as she knocked a glass from someone's hand in a bid to steady herself on the ice sculpture. Evie just had time to think how cold the herald was as she buckled in the shingle, the sculpture toppling from its plinth and shattering on the ground. As chips and splinters of ice skittered across the path, those wonderful orbs of light strung above the garden party winked out, one by one.

Then there was nothing.

PART THREE

A Deeper Prospect, and Rugged Scenes

THERE WAS HIS domino, old snake eyes. Shell wouldn't touch it, that pair of ones. She'd been in the green soap-scented parlour when Arthur first got the tattoo done and would not forget the look on Alec's face when he saw it. They'd been daft enough to go round for tea, and Alec had spotted it poking from under the sleeve of Arthur's t-shirt as he helped wash up. "Does tha know about this?" he'd said, all batty-eyed, presenting Arthur's shoulder to Shell as if he owned it.

"*Michelle?*"

Course it had been her idea. A joke at first, then a dare. Arthur never backed away from a dare. They were the domino, him and her, two black spots for two bound hearts, made of bone, or on a good day, ivory.

"I couldn't resist," Shell had said, drawing Arthur close the next street over, breathing against his sideburn.

"Tha never can."

Worth it in them days. Back in the flat she'd rubbed Germolene on the domino while Arthur told her how he felt. Rarely did she say it back. Love was to be understood rather than declared. I mean, Shell often thought, just who are you trying to convince, always saying the words to me?

The India ink was faded now. Autumn and so very wet out. Shell had to crack a window – she was always roasting with Arthur lying next to her. She rose, tip-toed across the room and fiddled with the catch. Through the window gap, rain. It sounded like thawing ice. Daylight the colour of puddle water seeped around the edges of the blinds, and now that Shell was back in the bed, Arthur wheezed away, his chest so pale you could practically see the organ beating in it. This tobacco man, her husband. After lying awake for a long while, Shell went downstairs to make the tea.

At the kitchen table Shell rubbed the sleep from her eyes with the sleeve of her dressing gown. It had taken her son's departure for her to realise once and for all that the chemistry of her marriage was gone. That what she and Arthur had been left with was an uneasy replica.

Even before the rug fiasco Shell had been measuring how things were against how things used to be. She knew that the past has a tendency to appear easy, and that looking back too fondly upon it was dangerous. That had never made it any easier not to do so.

Then had come Het. Shell pined for those heady first weeks of the strike. Discreet days, threading her arm through his when no one else was looking, when he wasn't expecting it, that beat of their smiles meeting: the shyness of things between them being at their thinnest.

She was cheating on Arthur then, she knew. She had taken to phoning Het up to see what he was doing – *that* you didn't do as a married woman – went with him for the free dinner at the community centre in Strepley, saying it was so they could talk when really it was so they could be alone. She'd even let Het take her to his personal spots: the alder dell, his flat, painted only the year before, the detail of Het's bad decorating job obvious: the paint paralysed in pleats down the wall to the extent that Shell could have picked them off if she had a mind to. She'd chided him about cleaning the place, then been taken out in his car, having a go at driving the bloody thing, stalling it before nearly hitting a telegraph pole. No wonder Het got carried away that night in the bakery.

It had taken Lawrence's rebuke to make Shell realise, as much to herself as anyone else, how she was being. She was some kind of woman. How she could hold her head up when she was as bad a hypocrite as that, taking her family to task the way she'd done, carrying on the way she had? She'd darted away from Het, let Arthur harry her into giving him another chance. It was the right thing to do, the correct thing, and might even have given her some peace of mind if the quiet moments weren't when the volume in her head was turned up the loudest.

She slapped a moth. The noise wouldn't stir Arthur, who'd risen at four am to get to the Kellworth picket for six. Shell washed the dead insect down the sink, gave the room a spray with the repellent she kept handy these days, then took her tea to the door so she could watch the rain fall on the yard step. She loved this time of year: its scent, the colours. But Arthur was waiting, so as soon as her cup was drained she'd go to him like she was supposed to. For you could make yourself ill on solitary mornings, letting yourself wonder and wish.

He was in one of his spacy moods when she woke him a little later. Bearded, hair messy and face bloated with sleep, Arthur sat in his t-shirt and underpants, hand absently resting on Shell's wrist. She was aware of its weight, the closeness, wanted to shrug him off and did so.

He didn't register.

Noon, no breakfast, Nescafé instead. They were out of

food, the weekly parcel due, so they both smoked – she'd stopped hiding it – and enjoyed the silence. Shell had learned to stop pestering Arthur, for the things on his mind were likely the same as those on hers, and she was sick of thinking her own thoughts, let alone discussing them.

Six months of this and now Christmas was coming. Six months without a full-time wage. The NUM had misjudged it calling everyone to strike as early as they had. You don't enter into action in spring, you do it in winter when the country needs coal. The idiots had leapt at Thatcher's provocation like a dog after a ball, and now that the government hadn't backed down, people hadn't even two sticks to rub together at an important time of year. No end of this in sight. Bored witless, Shell had spent the last few afternoons pulling the weeds from the bottom of the wall in the yard and between the stone flags, scrubbing the outside of the coal shed and doing the house's outside windows as well. Of an evening she'd been working her way through Arthur's poetry anthology. Verse that had seemed daft to her at school now unsettled her with its relevance. Life was tactile these days as it had never been before.

Bored, bored, bored and poor, poor, poor. The record player and telly had gone the way of the washing machine, and, only the other day, Shell had taken the bus into Rotherham to pawn her mother's silverware and china. There wasn't much to look at in the house now, just a whole lot of nothing. Shell wished she'd never pushed to swap the range for the electric fireplace. Piss take it was these days, unusable.

Least they still had the gas. They could ignite the hobs to heat the kitchen for the time being, do a bath. Shell had the bakery's rota memorised. She'd begged all the shifts she could, knew when she was on, how much she'd get and when she'd get it. It wasn't going to be enough to cover the mortgage, which was badly in arrears.

"How were last night?" she asked Arthur. She still liked to hear the stories; she was a sucker for heroics, bravery's groupie.

"Shite."

The customary response, although Shell was sure Arthur wasn't tempted to scab anymore. Even *he* wasn't mad enough for that.

A handful of scabs had somehow been persuaded back to work in Yorkshire. Those two at Silverwood arriving with coats over their heads every day now. Through the gates the bastards went, presumably to sit around indoors while thousands of their colleagues and at least the same number again from across the country went ballistic outside. It was hardly an option for Arthur to follow suit. He kept saying he was picketing to avenge Shell's honour, never mind the fact that she didn't like to think of it having been taken from her in the first place.

The contusions pasted across his knuckles looked like eczema and there was a phlegmy just-woke burr to his voice. "Got lift to Kellworth for early picket," he said.

"Wi' Asa?"

"You know not wi' Asa."

"All right," said Shell. "No need to rip my head off."

Arthur glanced at her sideways. "Sorry," he said. "I partnered up wi' Gordon and a few others. David from over the road an' Alan Hopkins who were my chargeman when I first worked Grafton Belt. We lucked out for once, got near fire for a warm. Right under the tarp on the settee. Played a bit of brag for matchsticks."

"Sounds alreight."

"Were till we'd to move on. Police had been tipped off so most of us went up picketing Woodthorpe instead. That's why I were grateful for the extra pair of socks, love."

Shell also used to pack extras for Het, back in April with its showers. He never had the nerve to pat her on the knee as Arthur had just done. Het was happy to be thought of rather than seeing it as Shell's duty to save him the effort of thinking for himself.

"Many police?" she said, washing the mugs under the tap with her finger. There was a huge dispatch force billeted past Strepley, not far from Fernside Grammar. Each bobby there was on a pocketful of twenties a day, Hertfordshire police in this case. Since they'd managed to persuade those scabs at Silverwood and elsewhere – Allerton and Brodsworth were two pits that sprang to mind – various billets like this had been stationed across the county now that the whole of Yorkshire had exploded.

"I'll give you one guess," said Arthur.

Shell didn't need to guess. How much must it be costing the government to subject its people to this? No one around here had voted for them, yet they were the ones picking up the tab. They said Thatcher was the daughter of a grocer. Well, Shell couldn't walk home with her own groceries these days without being pulled over by the police. *Where you going? What you doing? Who you married to and where is he?*

The bloody law with its bloody hands on her bloody hips, spinning her this way and that. There were stories about the dispatch forces. Only last month, in Armthorpe, there'd been hundreds of their vehicles stashed in the pit grounds, and quite rightly there had been a picket to try and stop it, only for the protesters to be charged, chased into town. You'd have thought that'd be the end of it but no, the police descended on the picketers, attacking them wherever they found them. Any householder who tried to help out was set upon, their home besieged, smashed up, civilians dragged to the vans along with the picketers, pulled through their own gardens, chucked down, beaten and detained. They said it was seven police-men to every prisoner. Armour, truncheons, the lot. Horses in front rooms. Dogs on the lawn. Saliva on the footstool and fat bastards in uniform stepping on Nanna's hot water bottle.

Straight after that the police held a victory march through Armthorpe centre, half those responsible for the carnage dressed in boiler suits with no ID numbers, just as had been at Orgreave that day. There, the most violent had been dressed the same, a brutal lot, more army than police, like them in Belfast got. One minute Maggie was parading all over the Falklands, sinking her ships. The next she was giving the same treatment to her own people. Truly, these were strange times Shell was living in.

Arthur said, "Considering there were supposed to have been a tip-off at Kellworth, there were a hell of a lot at Woodthorpe an' all. Whole set of police waiting at the bridge to Settle Lane. We've ended up running a mile or so back to try and get to the pit another way. Still pitch dark, love, lot of rain about. Here, mind fetching us another of them?"

Shell put a second pan of water on the hob. There was another moth. She opened the drawer to fetch a fresh teaspoon and saw the kitchen scissors, which took her back to the fetid rug and the fatty smell of its burning that day. Why did every memory become such a stone in her shoe?

"You keep your head down, don't you?"

Arthur glanced at her. "Aye can't have more than one of us wi' form in cells. Lawrence'll never come back."

Not even realising he'd put his foot in it, Shell's husband carried on as brazenly as a bluebottle. "We went through the forest instead. Mad in there, it were, we could see only ten yards in front, if that. We've come to the compound and bumped into another lot on picket who've had the same idea. They were waiting outside engine house when we found 'em, so that made a good few of us waiting for this sergeant to move on.

"We had to wait till he'd passed on his patrol, stripes on his arm, right here, clear as day he were that close, Shell, only Gordon's taken his time in the woods, he's slipped on his way to meet us and made a noise. Sergeant turns his head, blows his whistle. Next thing we know there's a gang of forty coppers in riot gear coming our way. There were nowt to do but hold us hands up. They've had us rounded up in a circle and marched down the pit exit. Anyone lagging got an hiding, those that were making good pace an' all for that matter. Then just as we've got near the main road, another load arrived. Bloody trap it were. Half the lads legged it into the car park only it were that dark and wet you could hardly see where you were going. They ran straight into a third squadron waiting wi' batons. I managed to run the other way. No chance of going back to help bloody rest."

He came with her for something to do. The welfare was full of the latest breakdown in peace talks. Things had been nearly sorted in July before Thatcher intervened, demanding the coal board toughen its stance, thus ruining any chance of a resolution. Two months on and no surprises. The Trade

Union Congress had backfired so there was no chance of a general strike anymore, no coordinated support from the other unions that might have turned the tide. And now the dockers were back at work the ports were open, which was all the government were really bothered about. Winter was on its way. People said Thatcher had ordered millions of pounds worth of candles.

Shell left Arthur having a game of snooker and went to join the queue for the food parcels. The rented truck had visited that day: SOGAT were responsible for this latest regional donation. The NUM had been given a hundred grand at the start of August, and all over the county it had been feeding folk. Though, when that was totted up, it came, per Yorkshire miner, to less than two pound a family.

Shell stopped on the way for a nosey in the kitchen. Her peering through the serving hatch alerted Olive Butterworth to her presence. Olive was pouring water into Styrofoam cups arranged across a tray like an army of model soldiers. She wore a Litten Lady t-shirt that must have shrunk in the wash, Shell was tempted to say, as she tried to see what soup was brewing in the vat.

"Shell," Olive cooed, blocking the hatch. She wore a ton of badges. She had been speaking at some of the local meetings, brandishing her puce son Matthew, who, if Olive had her way, was destined to become the latest in a line of fitters, the next generation of Brantford Butterworths. Easy to picture Smug-Arse's bottom lip wobbling while she garnered all the applause. Palsied and quick, Olive's eyes teary, the epicanthic robes of worthiness that at all times she draped herself in, plain to see.

"I wonder what we're in for this week," Shell said, nodding towards the parcel queue.

Olive handed her a cup that might as well have been a thimble. It contained orange squash. "Same old snap, unless you know something I don't," she said. "A rare delight having you show your face, Shell. Things picked up round yours, then, I take it?"

"Not especially, but I'm grand and ta for asking."

"I heard your Lawrence is living at his gran's."

Shell didn't rise to it.

"And Joyce is here an' all." Olive gestured across the room.

"Well, good for Joyce," said Shell, automatically searching out Joyce's mushroom head. Unlucky enough to make eye contact with the woman, she glanced at her shoes and raised her hand a touch.

"Seen Het of late?"

Olive's nose wrinkled.

"Like you say, it's been a while," Shell added, too quickly.

"Comes in enough. On his own now an' all, I see."

"As well he might."

Olive sprayed the hatch jamb and began to wipe it. "You'll have heard he was nicked the other week."

"What for?" said Shell, having to put her hand on the wall.

"Unlawful assembly."

Shell couldn't speak.

"Oh, aye. He's made bail but you know how it is, they'll have you confessing to all sorts. A mate of our Johnny were arrested up Orgreave an' now he's been charged with conspiracy to riot. Dragged out of picket, beaten black and blue. Now they're charging *him*. What's up, love?" Olive said. "You've gone all quiet."

Shell joined the parcel queue. The woman at the front was going on about the rigmarole with the social. So far below, she said, were the families of those on strike shy of the forty pounds a week it was supposedly sufficient to live on, that it was almost funny. Shell blotted out the noise as best she could. Her food parcel, when it came, contained potatoes, a loaf of bread and some jam. It tended to vary. Some days you might get a bag of sugar and beans. Other days it was soup, Yeoman pie filling tins and a tub of margarine. God, what Shell would have given for normal butter. It was the little things you noticed, in between the big stuff. A good job Arthur liked jam sandwiches, a good job it wasn't raining and a good job Shell had a decent night's sleep in her for once, otherwise she didn't know what she'd do, she might have to sit down for a minute and be sick.

Het.

She touched her trimmed hair, cut for free the other month on a barstool set on a donated bedsheet here in the welfare. That was the last time she'd been seen out in public. Since Sheffield, Arthur had been collecting the food parcels, so how else was Shell supposed to know about Het? Probably Arthur had kept it from her, the conniving bastard.

She set aside those thoughts for the small hours. She was tired and poor Het. Done in and poor Het. And she missed her son. She'd shaved Lawrence's head then upset him after he'd been kicked out of school, the poor thing. She was pretty sure he had no idea about what had gone on in Sheffield. No one knew about *that* apart from Joyce and Arthur, and Shell wasn't about to broadcast it – people thought little enough of her as it was.

But she had to wonder if he'd heard. Why else would he act the way he did every time she went to see him? On her visits Lawrence acted so off, in fact, that Shell feared he still harboured suspicions as to her involvement with Het. Course Arthur had sworn to her that he'd convinced Lawrence of the truth . . . Shell didn't believe him. Their boy was so morose, and he'd stood her up when she went to see him on at least three occasions now. There was no other way to explain it. 'He just goes out,' Arthur's mother explained, looking so bloody pleased with herself, never mind that it was some way to see Shell being treated by her own flesh and blood. Never mind that it was some way to grin at your daughter-in-law, who was clearly upset while you polished your worktops. Lawrence could be dead in a ditch and all Helen could do was act high and mighty, informing Shell that three of her own she'd raised with the same freedoms and no harm had it done any of them.

No comment.

Shell had given Lawrence time. A season of his own accord before the strike finished and he signed up at Brantford, as she was certain that he would. In the meantime his departure was just another thing for her to endure, so she crouched by the convector heater and warmed herself like some vagabond.

The hot air comforted Shell's exposed ankles, and for a moment there was nothing in her head, nothing at all. Then she realised this was exactly how she'd been made to crouch in Sheffield, the torchlight shining up between her legs.

She stood up so fast it made her feel faint. *Now turn around, drop them knickers and squat.* A teasel in her thoughts. She and Joyce in transit, rattling in cuffs. "Cheer up, ladies," that blond copper had said, straight-backed, tough hands on tough knees, like some granite statue. His badge had a white rose on it, hung in the middle of a star.

DoB and fingerprints. Echoing corridors. Unflattering light. Shell had grown up trusting the police. They were supposed to help people, look after their community and protect what's right. She was relieved her father would never hear about what happened; he was buried under a sober knoll by a neat red path at St Michael's. She had laid tulips at his polished headstone the day after her arrest and confided to the grave about how embarrassed she was by the whole ordeal. She said she didn't want any part in the strike now. She didn't want to see people, hated her weakness, her place in the world.

Dad said not to fret. He always said what Shell needed to hear now that he was dead. Shell had touched the earth that covered his body, letting herself snivel a bit, her legs beginning to ache, kneeling down, but, *for crying out loud*, getting the knees of her jeans wet.

"Not a word Joyce. Serious."

"But, Michelle!"

"*You know what folk'll say. Do you want everyone gossiping behind us backs? I've worry up to my eyeballs as it is.*"

A cheer pitched and splashed now on the other side of the room, which seemed a far more worthwhile thing to dwell upon, better than the hollow walk to the bus stop, Joyce Stride's sobs ringing in your ears. Arthur had his snooker cue raised, so Shell went over to him, joining in with the applause, on the way spotting a notice Sellotaped to the wall. They were running a charabanc to Skegness on Saturday and if anyone was interested in going, they should put their names down. She took the biro from her handbag. The Costa del Skeg. Arthur could bring the suncream.

Saturday.

Shell stuffed the blankets and towels into a rucksack along with some jam sandwiches and a flask of coffee, and carefully slid some magazines she liked into her handbag so they wouldn't spoil. Under her arm was a beach windbreaker, in her purse the money Si Gaskell had advanced her. He'd agreed to knock it off her wage, which was good of him, so when he brushed past her on his way to the oven as she was cashing up at the till, she let him get away with leading with his crotch: his rotten reward.

The family time would be worth it. The plan was for Arthur to fetch Lawrence from his gran's, while in the meantime Shell would catch the bus to Wolton where they'd all meet. A number of families were already in the WMC car park by the time Shell arrived. They hadn't the weather yet, though at this hour you couldn't be sure of what was in store. The optimistic had their swimwear with them but Shell didn't fancy the water. Thinking of all that space below got on top of her.

The mustard and white charabanc arrived, an old fashioned thing. She tried to see if anyone she knew had scratched their names on the backs of the chairs as the driver started to load people's bags into the hold. She wouldn't let him touch her luggage. There was no way a stranger was handling her family's stuff.

Soon the vehicle was full and people were impatient to be setting off. No sign of Arthur and Lawrence. Shell stood by the front doors and scrutinised the road. She'd specified the time. She'd definitely told them.

Wolton was on the other side of the pit, smaller than Litten but larger than Strepley. Shielding her eyes, Shell could see Brantford's headgear, the stilled winder and the corner of the massive hopper, the dust-slaked cableway that ran skips of spoil to the looming heaps on the other side of the valley. Although the pit wasn't operating, the smell of methane, sulphur and coal smoke still lingered, and Shell could feel the prickle of coal dust on her skin. She glanced at the coach and spotted some nosy hag staring at her, which was all she needed. She stormed over and knocked on the window. "I know very well the time," she called. "Think I can't see you crowing there, you old bat?"

She spat on the kerb weeds and sparked a fag. Fluctuating light refracted off the windshield of the coach, reflected no son, no husband and certainly no apology. The driver asked if she was coming or not. They'd to get a move on if they were to miss the traffic. Shell said she'd be with him, her family had been held up.

"Would you mind giving us another minute?"

"I'll give you two."

Shell barged into the WMC. One for the synapses, the place reeked of bleach, had a pine-effect tiled dancefloor, seating round its edges and a tan haemorrhage staining the ceiling, from either damp or cigarette tar, Shell wasn't sure which. A pair of dart boards were hung on a wall. Shell tripped on one of the board's rubber runways in her hurry to ask the barmaid if she could leave a message in case anyone called for her.

Another repeat of them showing her up. She was getting that laddered feeling again and had to breathe through her nose as she wrote:

> *Dear Lawrence and Arthur*
> *I've gone on my own*
> *Sort tea yourselves*
> *Mam.*

The nib of the pencil broke as Shell drove it into the paper to impress the full stop. "Two blokes, about yea big," she told the barmaid. "Same face, one grey, one a boy: hesitant buggers when they want to be."

She handed the girl the note.

"Tell 'em I were here. Give them that."

People clapped her onto the coach and the engine battled into life. Shell shoved her things down the aisle and propped them in her lap as she dropped into the only available seat and tipped her head back to catch her breath. She was so angry and disappointed she could cry.

"You look flustered."

It was Het.

"Well shift over and let me chase my breath then," Shell managed to say, then stood up so he couldn't see her face.

She hoisted her belongings into the overhead compartment then sat once she'd composed herself. Het fit uneasily into the space next to her. He looked as cramped as a Great Dane in a Wendy house.

"I've Racing Post if you need a fan," he said.

"Must be desperate times if you're resorting to that."

"It were already on the seat." Het smiled, handing it over.

Shell wafted herself with the paper. It had been spilled on so was crinkled funny. "When did you get here, anyway?" she said.

"About a minute before you."

"Did you see us name on t'lists or summat?"

Het didn't answer. As he took the bag Shell hadn't been able to fit into the overhead compartment and set it on the floor between his feet, Shell grit her teeth. Her mouth wanted sewing shut sometimes.

"Just a shock to see you," she said.

"Been an age since I've seen the beach," Het replied,

changing the subject. "And as I can't picket, I thought why not."

"I only just heard."

"*Don't worry*," he said swiftly. "I've been looking forward to this actually. Bit of sunshine." He might have lost weight, and his hair had less wax in it. "You not wi-?"

"No."

"Well you've brought enough stuff."

"I don't want to talk about it."

They were as bad as each other. The coach departed, and in almost no time Shell felt all resistance slip away. She rested her head on Het's shoulder as the ignorant, selfish wilderness drifted by. They'd be through Gainsborough soon enough, traversing Louth and the Lincolnshire Wolds. Then they'd reach the shifting metal sea, where, how did that W.H. Auden one from Arthur's anthology go again? Where all that you are not, looks back on all that you are.

Something like that, anyway.

The charabanc's windows wouldn't open so it was an uncomfortable journey whenever they hit traffic; they might as well have been sitting in a greenhouse. Shell feigned sleep but the other passengers were making too much noise for her to pull it off convincingly. The youngsters especially. They were all kinds of excitable after being treated to spending money by the union, who had funded the trip with money raised from a Trades Council gala earlier that summer. Everyone was terrifically excited by the first break they'd enjoyed in months. Thankfully the noise meant it was hard to talk over the racket. Shell simply watched Het point out a few sights: the Scarborough Hotel she knew he'd once stayed in; the site where

Seeley House used to be, the former miners' convalescent home.

Last off the coach, they headed to the sand, where already the mining families had dispersed amid their handsome happiness. Shell could see the shrieking scaffold of the roller coaster and the bulb-studded spokes of the Ferris wheel in the amusement park. Men had their trousers rolled to the knee and shirts removed to reveal dimpled, onion-white flesh. One old boy had twisted his hankie at the corners to cover a sensitive head.

Het carried the bags as they wandered through. "Shall we sit a bit?" he said, content to stop anywhere.

"In fact can we go along?" Shell replied. She wanted to be alone on the marzipan, watch the breakers and the mudflats, listen to the waves smash themselves apart.

Along they went. All the way Het gave Shell goosebumps, or at least something did. Maybe this was how she could finally define love, or at least what she felt when she was alone with her husband's brother. She wanted to confide in Het. She wanted to show him her mind's vaulting outlays, the false peaks and promontories where her thoughts seemed to sprout oily wings and stare crazily back at her. She had never let Arthur see any of that.

Skegness, so bracing. Shell wanted well away from all the Butlin's, Jolly Fisherman shit. People were tearing into their ice creams like cows with salt licks. Long burgundy tongues flicking Mr Whippy. She walked on, worrying about this sort of imagery, the caustic analogies that sprang so readily to her mind. What was wrong with her that in a heartbeat she thought this way, summoning a head full of alley cats, Whitsun slags and chimneypots full of ash? To think as she did. It was cruel to doubt her marriage, cruel on Lawrence and cruel on Het, who she'd all but strung along these months, refusing to acknowledge what was between them or perhaps spending too much time acknowledging it on some subconscious level, and not wanting to flag it up to her responsible self because the moment that she did it would have to stop.

Until today. She didn't know if she could rein in her tendencies anymore. She and Het strolled by the ocean, took their shoes off and waded in time through the freezing, fizzing water. After a while the crowds were gone. It was just them by a dune, which they descended so they could pitch the windbreaker up.

"Will you tell us what happened?" she said, once they'd laid out the towels.

"About what?"

"Don't try that wi' me."

By concentrating on unpacking the bag, Shell gave Het the space he needed to explain what had happened. Two weeks ago, he and a few others had ventured out past curfew. Their plan had been to picket Braithwaite Main then head home for lunch, flying elsewhere that afternoon. Chris Skelly still had his phoneline up and running and had been receiving silent calls, probably from the police seeing if he was in or not. He'd got a call that morning and been daft enough not to answer it as he was leaving the house.

"I should have known then," Het said. "I should have thought."

Het, Chris, Gordon Lomas, David Cairns and Darren Roach all convened at The Masons, went up the pit road then drove up the M180 to Braithwaite, an older pit than Brantford, where people had worked the High Switch seam for nearly sixty years. Never had Braithwaite had a problem with scabs, yet chief constable trickery had fooled some of the desperate strikers there into going back to work. Fancy being one of the only people in Yorkshire scabbing, especially at a famous pit like Braithwaite. What happened to the traitors' wives, Shell thought. A name change, a new life. Where would they go? Who would they know? It would be awful.

Het was present for the arrival of the scab bus and its escort. A lot of men heaving, fainting in the crush. Some picketers erected a barricade, tearing down a row of saplings and nearby street signs and piling them up – all sorts of garbage in the road. Over the pile the bus went, having to slow, giving a lad with an automatic centre punch the chance to pop the windows in the doors. The driver's lap was full of glass after the picketers tore the cage off and smashed his windscreen. The poor bugger didn't know what had hit him by the sounds of it. And serves him right, Shell thought. Serves him bloody right.

Yet the police resistance was too strong and into the maw of Braithwaite went the scabs, Het, as ever, pushed front due to his size, face to face with an officer, so close that he could still vividly describe the plaque on the man's teeth, the condensation on the insides of his visor, the leather chinstrap and the pimple on the bridge of his nose.

When some of the picketers lit a fire Het and the others returned to the Austin Maxi, the police getting hold of Darren Roach and giving him some hammer. The Litten men had a bruised flight home. They discovered Het's car had been reported and its plates recorded, when, on the way back, they were stopped by a Leyland police van. The van overtook them, braking sharply in their path, a turn that left skidmarks on the road.

276

Four bobbies leapt out and knocked Het's wing mirrors off, smashed his front and rear lights and then the windscreen. Before the police had chance to drag any of the miners out, the men scarpered. Het was the one they followed. He navigated the stile and drop fields at the base of Withens' Peak, tracked all the time by the Leyland, which from some distance he could see was still after him. The police must have been using field glasses, because when Het ducked into a farmyard they caught him nearly straight away and chased him on to a pigeon shed. Terrified, cornered, Het opened all the hutches and set the pigeons free, the spooked birds flapping like feather dusters into the policemen's faces. In the melee, Het somehow managed to get away.

He arrived home to a patrol car; the authorities knew he was a picketer; his name had been taken in the past and they had his beloved car as evidence he'd broken curfew. Taken to Doncaster station and booked in, Het was locked up for hours then moved on because they needed the cell space for more prisoners arriving from another picket. Back at Strepley nick they kept him in the communal cells until midnight. They threatened to charge him with assaulting police. Told him all sorts.

"They were like, you're not so hard wi'out your mates, are you," Het said, his sandwich untouched. "Drove me past them Swarsby posters on the way to the station an' all – funny what sticks in the mind. Charged me wi' unlawful assembly when all I've tried to do is save us jobs. Arrested, Shell. I've turned up to God knows how many pickets and not so much as chucked a stone. Not once. I've just *been* there."

They watched the water. The malt breeze retreated and went another way.

"Condition of us bail is I've to report to police station every morning now for eleven," Het said. "Have us name signed. Stuck indoors for a curfew all of my own: seven at night till nine in the flaming morning. Banned from any property belonging to the NCB, Central Electricity Generating Board and British Rail, amongst others."

"It'll be fine, love. I'm sure it will."

"Will it?"

She couldn't say.

After a while, Het remarked that the rocks beyond looked like Conisborough Castle, and did Shell fancy having a look? She'd been deliberating whether nor not to tell him about what had happened in Sheffield and was grateful for an excuse not to. "Course, love," she said. She took his arm.

The prospect of rain made the day feel potent. It had been so long since Shell had been anywhere, and here she was with Het. The huge rock appeared to move the more she looked at it, and way beyond it sailed a ferry, a pale monolith transporting passengers to another country. She blinked into the wind. It was a pleasantry, this day: a humid privilege before winter on the coast. Back Shell lingered, enjoying the moment, leaving Het to continue on to the rock. Her fringe tickled her eyes, as did the piquant sting of the salt. Her hood snapped and blew against her shoulders, front and back. Cairns of stones lay in the sand everywhere. It was as if someone had been performing rituals.

Shell picked a wary route towards the water's edge until she stood on the precipice of a rock pool. Captivated by the miniature stalagmites, the vivid reds and blemished qualities of the rock, she called to Het, pausing as she saw how far ahead he was, and wishing he'd respond.

She watched the pool, for how long she didn't know. Its blank surface was so windblown that it created wavelets the eye couldn't focus on properly. These textures grew more hypnotic the more Shell observed them, the rippling water with its pure, blank sheen and beneath it: vibrancy, only one perspective or the other visible at any one time. Never the two at once.

Shell loved the sea then, and felt as far beyond herself as she'd ever felt. In her mind was the Litten Path. She could walk it and join Het. She could return to the windbreaker and grab her bag, easy.

So what was it going to be?

She called his name.

"Het!"

And he must have had some idea what she was going to say, because he said, "I've something to tell you," when he arrived, appearing quite shaken.

Shell didn't want to hear it. This was what she wanted, and it was so very fair.

"Can it not wait?" she said.

She took Het's hand and placed it against her breast.

17

THE CASTLE ROCK turned out to be sea rats, hundreds of them crawling over a stone hillock. Hard to believe, yet there it was: all that brine-sleeked fur. Het watched the creatures idling and scurrying over the kelp. Vast clouds had built into smoky turrets beyond them, and the acrid rodent smell supplanted the fresh coastal air.

It was lucky Shell hadn't seen them. She'd lagged behind as Het got closer to the rock, missing the despairing noise he made as he realised what the shifting mass actually was. It had been like looking at things through a pebble glass window, then it had made an awful kind of sense.

Shell had been spot-on before: he *had* decided to come to Skegness when he saw her name on the welfare list, taking a punt on Lawrence being too far gone, too grown-up and too angry for the trip, and Arthur being, well, *Arthur*. Het registered and hoped none of them would see.

It was easy, lingering out of sight until you were convinced Shell was alone, then boarding the coach while she was in the WMC. The practiced expression Het wore for when she sat next to him went completely unnoticed. You couldn't second guess her. The quickest, bluntest mouth he had ever known had been practically silent up to this point.

Talking now though, wasn't she. Het answered Shell's call. He was ready to say the words. *About that husband of yours . . . well, it was me who had him picketing in March. So ask me how Arthur turned considerate, Shell. I'll tell you why.*

But how to put it? She was so fragile. Her head resting on his shoulder all the way here had told him that much. Surrounded by witnesses, too. Shell must have known what people would say, she did it anyway. All those weeks wondering how she felt. Couldn't phone or go round. Wrote a letter and binned it. Wrote another and binned that too.

Shell was grinning, curls blown about everywhere. It was unfair how drawn to her Het was. He kept thinking about those rats, their tang, the sea's undercurrent. They were omens, and this terrified Het. He tried not to let Shell see how shaken he was. He did a good job of it, too, because as he arrived and stood before her, she gazed at him and said, "Can it not wait," when he tried to tell her about Arthur.

He'd expected nothing, so got everything. Shell took his hand and totally levelled him with it. Her nipple grew bold under his fingers, and she touched his scar.

No one touched his scar.

In that moment Het belonged to his brother's wife. She could have torn his heart from his eye socket for all he cared.

All there was to be done, it was all to be done. Het let himself be guided to the towels. The windbreaker was driven into the sand, and beneath it, to the sound of rippling canvas, he kissed Shell for the first time. He was a virgin in that he'd never made love to anyone he cared about. A virgin in that he'd never gone with someone spoken for. The sand was rough and damp and there was a great lurch in Het's guts as he removed Shell's pants and slid them down to her ankles. Accelerate into the bend. The overbearing jangle of his belt buckle. The rapid moments of a cumbersome morning. The pair of their bodies clicked.

Millions of damp craters began to appear in the beach. Rain pelleted Het and Shell's bodies, the back of Het's head, Shell's face. Het felt hideous and wistful. They'd hardly finished being together and already they had to separate. He patted sand from himself, went to do the same to Shell, then thought better of it: it was too fraternal a gesture. Plus the wind had started to blow east and everyone knows that means there's been a change in luck.

Shell re-packed the bag. She was already acting weird, so Het tried to put his arms around her.

"We shouldn't have done that," she said, rubbing her wrist as if she'd been stung.

"We had to."

"Were wrong."

"Couldn't be helped and you know it."

Her palm was on her forehead, the other hand flat on top of that. "We've to get back."

"I'll come wi' you."

"People might see."

"We've all afternoon —"

"You might, Het. I'm taking train."

She wouldn't let him help her with the bags. Het watched her leave then once she'd gone, went to where everyone from the beach was hurrying to escape the heavy weather. Alone, Het watched the whitecaps come and go, before heading to the arcade to dry off. The coach wasn't leaving for a couple of hours yet anyway.

He spent the rest of the day thinking. Orgreave refused to be forgotten. Losing Lawrence and having to go after him that day rated as one of the scariest moments of Het's life. It had been madness amid those Rotherham houses. Tons of horse, dog and foot soldier coming at you down residential streets. Bob Roach insisted on coming to look for Lawrence and got clattered a second time for his trouble. The police tried not to go for your head in case it showed, in case they did damage they couldn't take back. A snatch squad hauled Bob topside.

Het had taken cover in a garden before escaping into a snick between two houses. From there he saw more beatings than he thought possible. The police went absolutely mad and Lawrence was nowhere to be seen. Back home and frantic, he journeyed to his mother's, but the kid wasn't there either. Banshee tyres screeched around the corner of Water Street next, but no one was in at Shell's, thank God. Welfare, no. Streets, no, and the woods, where Sam and Arthur used to exclude him? Forget it.

He even tried the police station. Hospitals. Nothing. Arriving home and thinking: Sack it, I'll head back to Orgreave. He'd known what he was in for and damn well got it. The Catcliffe end was full of bleeding men, The Plough car park was like the aftermath of a warzone. It was civil war when you thought about it, though, wasn't it? Civil war.

That horrid jog tophill. There had been relative calm after the push of the short shield units into the village, police and picketer alike recharging their batteries; only Arthur Scargill went and got himself arrested and sent the entire afternoon up the Litten Path. The usual bombardment ensued. You name it, all of it was hurled at the police. Savage heat pumped from a watery sun and horses, horses, horses.

The cavalry had attacked the picket and forced it into Orgreave village and the nearby industrial estate for the worst carnage of the day. It was all over the place by the time Het arrived for his second serving, going man-to-man, describing Lawrence to anyone who'd listen: as futile gesture as there could have been. With Orgreave Lane blocked by chaos, Het was forced down that rotten slope again, making the acute journey to the train tracks, practically in tears. His was no rebel heart. If anything had happened to her son, Shell would never have let it go. He had no choice at all that flaming day.

That was a few months ago, nearly three. Lawrence turned up later that evening and acted as if nothing had gone on, ruthlessly shrugging Het off when he tried to hug him and see if he was all right. Kid was bloody Arthur mark two.

Since then Het's savings had been drained and to top that, as a condition of his bail, he was banned from picketing so couldn't get his fly money anymore. There was what the union could offer – it wasn't much. With the government mounting a challenge against the legality of the strike, pursuing the NUM's brass in court, it was dead broke. The priority had to be local families. Therefore Het relied on the soup kitchen for his snap and his wits for everything else. His flat had mostly emptied, the valuable commodities gone.

He'd tried to find work. He'd done the pubs and gone out of town to speak to building companies, services. Nothing doing. He'd even left a card in the newsagent's offering his services as a handyman at a knock-down rate, receiving not a call, just a few comments when it was brought up in the food queue come Friday.

Naturally he told anyone who wanted to repeat what they'd

said to step outside. They might act like he'd forgotten who he was and what he did, but Het was the same Het he'd always been. He was, had been and always would be a miner.

His craft certificate was proof enough of that. It was mounted upon a nail on the wall next to a picture of the queen and a photo of his mam and dad cutting their wedding cake. Below it had been Dad's wireless. Het still had the TV but was never in the mood to watch it. The programmes seemed trivial now and the news, well, Thatcher was right for once when she said the violence was disfiguring their screens. Het would never have thought the media such liars. If it was two hundred picketers to eight hundred police, you could guarantee the news would tell the world it had been two hundred each. That headline in The Sun after Orgreave was a disgrace. The BBC claimed it was the miners who'd charged first.

Het went to collect his post. It was the morning after Skegness, he was exhausted from lack of sleep and no surprises why.

More bills. He was behind on the rent and everything else. He leafed through the letters until he reached a final one he couldn't explain, his name and address typed neat, no post mark, nothing. Thin as that.

He tore the envelope open. The letter was from Clifford Briscoe, the pit manager at Brantford.

Dear Mr Newman, blah blah . . . It has come to light . . . gross misconduct . . . arrest . . . terminated.

He'd been sacked.

Fireworks. Your brunette years donated and the grey ones coming for you with no chance of a reprieve. Het thought about breaking something but couldn't bring himself to punch the wall or smash any of his stuff. He set a fist against the armrest and began to push. You put down a twenty-six year shift and now your P45 was winging its way towards you. He'd be for the blacklist if he was convicted, never mind prison.

Water Street was cold and impersonal. Its russet bricks were damp and the muck between them worm-holed and loose-seeming. Het tried to see through the front window. Although there was no sense of Arthur being in, he wasn't hanging around to make sure. He went around the back of the house and thumped the door.

Shell had either been crying or was badly allergic to something. Frail golden flies were all over the place as she answered Het's knock. They crawled on the lightbulb and over the table. Upon everything.

"What you doing here?"

"What's wrong, love?"

"I said what you doing, Het?"

"I've been sacked."

The door was pulled to. Shell reached for Het's scar, a gesture that made him duck away.

"I'm sorry," he said. "I shouldn't have come."

He almost took flight but didn't, his clunking legs carrying him down the backs beneath the sycamores until Shell grabbed him.

"You're not going off on your own?"

"I don't know," Het said. "I don't know."

They ended up at the dell. It was a short way past Barnes' Wood, a glade irrigated by the River Ogden that encouraged damp loving alders to grow. The trees' bark was hoary and fissured and their pear-shaped leaves were bruised and had started to wither. There was no dramatic colour to an autumn alder. Their leaves simply dropped away.

They sat where it was dry so Het could explain the letter. He couldn't keep the emotion from his voice. He didn't know what he was going to do.

Shell had only the comfort of herself to offer, which worked all too well, the smallest surprise of the day. She kissed Het so hard that he thought she might have cut his mouth. And as they happened then, as they would, over and again, at least for as long as they could, Het opened his eyes and saw at the base of the nearest commanding alder tree distorted roots emerging from the netherworld like giant mutated chicken's feet. October days and things were changing, and if the choice was to betray your own feelings or those of a brother who'd blown his chance, then really, that was no choice at all.

Shell became Het's occupation; he had little else to do. They were direct if they bumped into each other. Cordial nod, retain the distance, nothing suspect. When they met later it was different. Thrown together in the stolen deep at Het's flat; breaking curfew come evening or at nightfall, at the dell. They even did it in his car once with the back seats down. Flesh sticking to leather. No room for anything except them.

Shell hardly spoke during these brief meetings, and that was fine. There wasn't a great deal to say when you were getting everything you wanted. All Het had to do was concentrate on owning it. Not messing up.

Under Het's encouragement Shell re-joined the Litten Ladies. Any fool could see what that did for her. Illuminated, she was a confident speaker. Rational and passionate, she got people's hopes up; not a strident bone in her body. Het was proud to watch her. She was and wasn't his, but that didn't matter.

It didn't.

Because Shell hadn't been complimented, she said, in such a long time, when Het congratulated her after another of her speeches. Hers just hadn't been that sort of marriage. That justified everything. Shell sat down with Arthur and finished her drink.

Het's brother was another matter entirely. It was all the sleeping Het was doing, each empty day leading to an early night followed by a late lie-in, the odd nap in between, his mind a nomad of the furtive trail, right up until the moment when Het would stun himself awake, thinking Arthur had twigged what was going on, thinking Shell was going to end things, sustain her marriage rather than him.

Mid-month. NACODs were due on strike on the twenty fifth and Het was letting his hopes get dangerously high, because without the manager's union on board, every pit in the country would have to stop. There would be no power available for any industry. No power for the country and its voters. Not a single thing would be able to function. That would make the government listen – they'd flaming have to.

Talking of fantasy, Het and Arthur were on speaking terms again. They'd done a grand job of avoiding each other since the break-in at Threndle House, yet after accusing Het of getting too close to Shell that summer, Arthur had been almost genial. Probably he felt guilty. It was so like Arthur, sauntering into Het's flat then chucking his drink at the wall. If Het failed to spring across the room he didn't know what would have happened. It must have killed Arthur. Never once had he physically bested Het. No matter how quick his mouth was,

Arthur could never drop his older brother one. Het had fixed his nose and sent him home to Shell.

Then it had gone and happened, becoming guilty of the very thing you'd been so hurt to be accused of. Het had met his brief and told him about himself – long-serving worker, no record of arrest, paid up union man – and been tempted to confess what he'd been up to with Shell, just to get it off his chest. Sly pints with your sister-in-law over a plate of chips drenched in vinegar and burger sauce. Having it away every spare minute. The days were getting colder and so was Het.

The thing was that with Lawrence at his gran's and Arthur never in, Shell was easy to get away with. Arthur had to be up to something: he certainly wasn't picketing like he was supposed to be. Het resolved to have a word. Although it was easier to steal Shell with his brother out of the picture, he still wanted to see Arthur put right. While they were at it they could work out a plan for Lawrence. That would please Shell. It might even slow the hawks from swooping over Het's life as they did every day now. One for each problem, an entire cast.

The front door opened. Het could smell the pissy reek of old fags. Shell was there, face on her. She was always so off with him at first.

Het said, "I'm here for Arthur."

"What do you want wi' him?"

"We've things to discuss."

"You know I don't like being sprung upon." Those marauding eyes. The day sounded like a seashell against Het's ear. "He's having a bath," Shell said. "You're best not coming in."

"It's fine, I'll wait. *Look* . . . is everything?"

"*Shut up* . . . It's fine." Her cloistered face turned coy.

"Gives us chance to tell you the news, actually, Het. Hang on a tick."

Shell went inside then returned with a scrap of paper grasped against her chest. "I saw an adviser at Job Centre," she said quietly, refusing to let Het take the note. She held it up for him instead, displaying a phone number under the name of some meaningless college, decreed in cursive script.

As usual, something in her expression was lost on Het. "I thought you already had a job," he said.

"Well, aye. But it's had us thinking, why stop there," Shell replied. She took a cigarette from its box and lit it, hand, box and lighter disappearing back into the stash under her armpit. "Why stop at all?"

Women shouldn't smoke. It was uncouth and filthy. Het said "Tha's spoke all over the borough – you've hardly stopped. Isn't that. You know . . ."

Shell's eyes did something magic. "*Exactly*," she said. "An' all the years before, nowt. Since I started on all this . . . you know, going on stage and that. Organising the kitchen an' that, well, I've asked for details of a course."

Het had the urge to say that his mam and thousands like her had never needed school and turned out fine. "Can tha put that out please?" he said, indicating Shell's cig. "It's going in my eyes."

"I beg your pardon?"

She was frowning at him.

". . . I'm chuffed, Shell . . . It's dead great."

"Do you really think so?" She had that measuring look now that made Het wonder if he'd been convincing enough, so he told her it was great again. That did it. Shell started whispering at him, never mind that it was all well and good for her, well and good for kids like Lawrence. What about a bloke a few years shy of his forty-fifth birthday? Het had only ever worked in one place. He was Imperial not Metric. He'd been one of the last people to do national service, remembered shillings and baths heated with kettle water. His dad and grandad had fought Britain's wars and supported its posturing and now he'd been sacked, a supposed enemy of the very economy he'd spent his life helping to build, perusing plastic window wallets for unskilled factory jobs twenty miles away – most of them taken – and now listening to Shell explain herself away from him. Fifty percent of his life was gone and the rest was going with it.

He said for a flaming third time what great news it was. "Industrial Relations. Sounds promising."

"Aye. Now listen cause I'll only say this the once . . . but, well . . . it's thanks to you, love. Making us go back. I'd never have thought I could apply for something like this."

Het pretended he hadn't heard. He was readying to make his excuses and hit the dell when the door opened.

"Well bon-fucking-jour."

"Arthur."

Shell stuffed the paper into her pinafore.

"Brother," said Arthur. "To what do I owe the pleasure?"

All teeth. All ornery swagger. Arthur wore a dinner-flecked t-shirt, a towel around his waist that stopped at the knees, and odd socks, one of which a little toe poked out of. His shins were noticeably wet and his damp, slag-coloured hair was towel-dried and at odds and ends with itself. Arthur had grown a raddled beard recently that almost disguised the blue mark on his face and the scar the knuckle-duster had given him: a line under the eye that made him look permanently exhausted.

"Well?" he said.

"Come to see us little brother."

"Well I am blessed. Am I not blessed, Michelle?"

"Be nice, Art," said Shell. There was a look of naughty amusement on her face that drove Het mad. He had never once been able to make her look like that.

"Down pub, if you'd join."

"To recite another yard of us mistakes, I suppose."

"The opposite, actually."

Arthur looked suspicious, as well he might.

"My treat," said Het.

"Well if you're footing the bill then that sounds like a bobby dazzler plan."

They sat under the lodge banners near the snooker table. Arthur drank at twice the pace of Het, nodding *Slàinte*, before each pint and raising his glass. Het played along but could only stretch to one more round of drinks so just came out with it about half an hour in.

"I want to talk about that night at big house."

"Well, don't be shy," said Arthur, that famous late night air about him. "As I'm in a fine mood. Gratis pints will do that for a man."

Het took a breath. He could not stop staring at the flatness of his beer.

"Been playing on us mind that perhaps I could have handled it better," he said. "The other month. Forcing you on picket."

Arthur kicked his legs out and crossed them.

"So I wanted to say sorry. Sorry, Art. There's no need to keep at it, not if tha doesn't want. I'll not repeat a word of what you did."

Het was practically shaking. He didn't need to say he still expected Arthur to be on strike. That much was understood.

Arthur started to laugh, a sound that might have been jagged and slashing if it were visible. "Well, bugger me . . ."

"What?"

"*You.*"

"Me, what?"

"You know, Het, I don't ever think I've heard you say sorry before."

Sure he had. Course he had. Arthur was just forgetting because he amounted to one big apology himself.

"Aren't you good?" said Arthur. "Letting us off."

Het waited for his brother to say something else. Nothing was forthcoming. "That's as well then," he replied.

"Well indeed."

The Lurcher over the way barked. It shivered, its sabre ribs and black lips all-too visible. Meanwhile the rain made a racket against the welfare windows. The ground at the bar was sodden, entrance floor slippery, mellow light flooding the snooker balls. Arthur's roll-up made Het cough.

"I suspect tha's heard—"

"What, that you've been given your marching orders?"

Het put down the beer mat he'd been tearing up and tried to compose a response.

"*Sacked.*" Arthur grinned. "An' everybody knows."

"Well, I wouldn't put it exactly like that . . ."

"How else to put it?"

"It's a mix-up, I'm appealing the decision."

"You should have taken redundancy, or gone back to work. So should I, for that matter. Maybe I will now you've deigned to stop blackmailing us."

"Arthur, you're not . . . *You'd go back?*"

"Reckon they'd make it worth us while to get Brantford going again. Or I could work elsewhere. Markham or summat. Bet they'd take us."

"You'd be a dead man."

"We're all dead men. Might as well get paid." Bastard had that look, started going on about being sick of holding on. "What's point?" said Arthur. "I'm on the verge of going down the butchers of an evening asking for the last bloody bones reserved for the dogs so my family's got dinner. An' all for a few pits I don't fucking work at."

But it wasn't just that, it wouldn't be just a few. Het was about to say so when Arthur cut him off. "Save it," he went. "If the pits close, they close: I'll do summat else. Eight months an' no wage, thanks to you." He pointed to his scarred face, his sorry hands. Het couldn't deny it. "We're nearly losing the house."

"Well that's your own fault for getting a mortgage – that's the idea of the flaming things – scare you into working for fear of endin' up homeless."

Arthur had nothing to say to that because there was nothing *to* say. You couldn't get around facts. Het pressed his point.

"Zero times zero equals zero, Art. We'll not walk into another job. What jobs are there? Only jobs are at the pit. All round here it's pit country. What they gonna do, comrade, build us some mystical new place of work?"

"*Comrade.*"

Another of those white-gold insects was on Arthur's sleeve. Het watched him crush it under his thumb. *Arthur,* making out like everything was everybody else's fault. *Arthur,* acting like Het was some bully beyond a man trying to do right by everyone.

"Whole point of a union is if there's a problem in one bit of the chain, it's organised so the whole chain stops." Het coughed, losing track of his old spiel. He touched his brother's arm. "Do you not see . . . ?"

Arthur was no longer bothering to hide his disgust. Able to finally see that he was being goaded, Het's voice rose. "And another thing I want to say is . . . I want to have a chat with you about Lawrence."

There was no laughter on that potted wreck now. "What about my lad?" Arthur practically spat.

"It's just . . . Look, I think it's high time he was home wi' his mam, don't you? You need to do summat about it."

Arthur necked the last of his beer, picked up Het's glass and began to drink that, too. He had weak, bovine eyes, jellied balls that saw nothing the way you did. The space between those front teeth could hold a cocktail stick. It had been one of Arthur's party tricks in happier times.

"Oh, you do, do you."

Het snatched his pint back, spilling a load. "Shell's upset. And you must—"

Now it was Arthur's turn to raise his voice. "Oh right, well, when've you been seeing her then?"

Het steadied himself, still seated, first and second fingers on the ruins of the beermat. "Just in the bakery, like . . . I stopped in."

"An' what you doing buying bread from my wife?"

"Oh, here we go."

Arthur started putting on his coat. "Don't you think to give me one of your sermons after the way you carried on wi'

Sam. After taking my son to that thresher up Orgreave. That's right, he told us. An' I'll tell Shell an' all if you mention that fucking do at t'big house one more time. An' while I'm on the subject of *my wife*, you've never put the puppy eyes down for her, from day one I've had to watch it, bloody shameless, you are, an' she's not interested. So get under wi' the idea once an' for all or I'll bloody flatten yer!"

Het would like to see him try. "If you won't speak to Lawrence, Arthur, I will."

"He thinks you're as much of as tosser as I do."

"Scabbing bastard!"

Het swept Arthur's tobacco off the table.

"Stay away from my family, Het. I'm serious."

Het was already on his way out of the welfare door.

Straight over.

A crow cawed. Het could never work out how they didn't get sore throats. Forget Arthur, he was striding the Heap Road looking for Shell's son. Mam had said the lad was putting up posters for the by-election campaign, which had surprised Het. There had been so much going on recently that he'd completely forgotten about the impending vote. How Lawrence had got in touch with Neil Jennings and the Labour team, he didn't know. But at this rate they'd have him in the union yet.

Swelling with pride, Het climbed the lower bluff for a better view. With a host of chimneyed connections spread in front, Litten looked like a toy town. It was drizzling; Het pushed the damp hair from his eyes. The violence and splendour of the hilltop wasn't far, with its scars of rock and uneven outcrops with certain endings.

A car cruised by.

Another.

It was chucking it down. Het spotted something through the prism of rain, so clambered across to it: a poster by a drystone wall. Perhaps Lawrence would be ahead with his paste bucket, brolly and brush.

The poster was stuck to some chipboard, the first in a series tied to every other lamppost along the road. Het approached it, removing his glasses and wiping the lenses on the thighs of his jeans. The poster's edges were freshly glued, the paste still gloopy. It wasn't for Jennings and Labour at all; it was for Clive Swarsby and the Conservatives.

All Het's strength nearly left him. He bent double, then after a long while, straightened up, sighing at Litten. On the other side of the valley was Threndle House, a burrow of smoke emanating from its chimney. One of the lights clicked off and on again. It was as if the mansion had just winked at him.

It took twenty minutes to get there. Pressing the buzzer on the gate, Het wasn't exactly sure what he'd say to these damn people, but he'd think of something.

He hadn't been here in months, and in daylight, not in years. He could smell burning. Autumn was always like this, the most sentimental season – even in the wet, that blue smoke smell, the discordance of leaves trapped in the gaps between park railings, the memory of having your lamp checked before escaping for your shift down in the safe warm balm of the ceaseless earth.

There was no answer so Het walked around the property, peeping over the wall where he could. The mansion was actually pretty dilapidated and maybe that was fitting because as far as Het could see, the fires of a cosy Britain were stoked in places like this. Here was a living manifestation of the English fantasy of church bells, jolly spinsters and sunsets edging over country clubhouses. Here was an England that had never really existed outside of dreams and fiction. All that golly gosh, picnic hampers, tweed, brown leather and gingham, spaniels and yachts and steam trains, mulberry bushes, initialled hankies and kids in boater hats. It was no wonder a politician lived here. The house embodied the sorts of ideas they could publicly aspire to whilst laying waste to the organised working class.

Het returned to the gate and gripped one of the bars, causing some of the paint to come away and leave rusted orange wounds behind on the metal. He knew this was a daft idea but he was going to do it anyway: make a gift to Shell of her wayward son.

He stepped on the bottom-most iron helix but as he set all his weight on the gate, it swung open with him standing on it. The thing hadn't been locked in the flaming first place.

The wide front door had one of those un-buffed brass knockers and no one to answer it. Het had better luck at the postern entrance, his call answered first-time by a boy Lawrence's age: a young man, really; dark-haired and keen.

Het didn't recognise him. "Evening," he said. "Name's Het."

"Hello."

"It's about . . ." Het stopped. "I'm here . . ." He stopped again. "Fancy me not getting us words out. Any chance a lad's here? Your age, name of Lawrence. I know it's odd me askin'."

The sensitive boy's face was in flux. He began to laugh, not loudly, or at Het; more as if he'd remembered something funny. His top teeth found his bottom lip and he said, "Why, yes, come inside. You must be Lawrence's father."

Het didn't set the boy straight. He stepped into the house and wiped his boots on the steel mat. He had been shown into a scullery. Its tiled floor was chequered and an old-fashioned drying rack was suspended from the ceiling by a pulley system. White clothing draped over that and there was a sink and a washing machine and a dryer. An ironing board was propped tipsily in the corner.

Het was led down a wood-panelled corridor. The boy hadn't introduced himself; he'd just snapped his fingers, not a question asked. He did glance back a few times, probably to see if Het found it a bit of chuff coming to a place like this. Het wasn't about to give him the satisfaction.

Promptly a door was opened and voices could be heard on the other side. Het was taken into what turned out to be an auxiliary living room, tucked away from the main parts of the house: an old servants' quarters, perhaps. Lawrence was sitting by a kindly-looking fire.

He'd been folding leaflets, collecting them in a pile and wrapping them with elastic, and now he stared at his uncle. Het was speechless. A girl was there too, her Barbie legs resting in Lawrence's lap. She wore a hard-to-describe expression. This was a hot-potato friend if ever Het saw one. Tough to hold. Easily lost.

"Het," said Lawrence.

Het managed to laugh, a terse laugh, more a blast of air than anything. He might as well have come on crutches with a cap in his hand. He wondered if the girl knew what type she was. He guessed she did: he could see it in her manner, her ready mouth. He could feel the dark lad staring at him, so cocked his head. No, he wasn't Lawrence's dad, and that was just tough.

Het selected a leaflet from the table. The fire in the hearth popped and made his clothes steam. "Working hard, I see."

"Just lending a hand."

Het pinched the bridge of his nose under his misted glasses. "Mind if I sit?"

"Yes."

"So you're one of them now."

"Just helping my friends."

"Promoting *that lot.*"

The dark boy piped up. "Dad needs all the friends he can get at the moment."

"It's backs to the wall time all right," said the girl drolly. "Who knew the locals would go on strike as soon as that back-bencher's ticker stopped?"

Het ignored her. Derek Shaw had been a proud leader of this community for thirty years, and who was this Swarsby that he'd enlist a daft-as-a-brush kid like Lawrence to his cause? There'd not been a rally nor a meeting for this campaign, and no wonder. Even if by some miracle Swarsby were to win, he'd be one of those distant representatives who never answered a letter and only visited the constituency once a year for harvest festival or some such. Het tried to smile at Lawrence. No smile came.

"I'm surprised Dad's bothering to make a go of it all," the girl added, then, as if she and Het were friends, said, "Are those coal scars on your wrist?"

"I need a word, Lawrence. In private."

Lawrence looked to the girl as if asking permission. For some reason Het thought of the pink heat of the coke ovens.

"Anything you want to say to me, Hector, you can say in front of Evie."

This *Evie* didn't bother to conceal her glee. Out of the corner of his eye, Het could see the dark lad shaking his head. He also knew what Het had recognised: Evie was destined for a destruction of her own making.

Het just came out with it. He wanted Lawrence to go home, speak to his mam. "She misses you, lad. Won't you think on it?"

"Oh *Lawrence*," the Swarsby boy said. "Have you not a care for those who raised you?"

The posh little *poof* – though Het didn't say it – had a point. As Lawrence blushed, it was all Het could do to keep from saying *listen* to this imp. But Lawrence was embarrassed enough as it was and it wouldn't do to attract further attention to it.

"Your mam loves you. Whole family. An' you've a place down Brantford . . ."

"Oh, Het, for once just *shut it!*"

Both Swarsbys were taken aback. So was Het. There was a lot going on in Lawrence's face as he said, "To be honest, I hardly know this guy."

Het beckoned with every finger. "Come on, we're leaving."

Lawrence looked as wild and red as a horsefly sting. He didn't move, so Het addressed the Swarsbys. "Where's your father? I'd like a word please."

"I don't think that's a good idea, do you?"

"On the contrary, Miss. I think it's a damn good idea."

"Really? Because as far as I can see you're trespassing on private property, despite being asked to leave. And if you don't go this instant we'll be calling the police."

That was all Het needed. He implored Lawrence one more time, with his eyes, as close as he'd ever get to begging.

The kid kept on stacking his leaflets.

18

F OR A SUPERSTITIOUS man Arthur was desperate-
ly short on luck. He was born short of it. Had to be.
Like most people he had rituals to preserve good fortune.
He never opened a brolly indoors, he kept a forelock from
Lawrence's first haircut and he covered the mirrors in the
house during storms to keep the lightning from getting in. He
used to do that, anyway. He was constantly on the lookout for
black cats.

And still it was all going to shit. His first family outing in
months and Clive Swarsby had chosen today to get in touch.
Talk about bad luck. This was the kind of timing that saw
championships lost in the dying seconds.

Weeks checking the Free Press, checking it every Thursday
when it came out. There was to be no word from Swarsby
until the end of August, but Arthur still hadn't been able to
keep from checking the paper and now it was nearly the start
of September.

It was lucky he'd even seen it earlier. On the way to pick
Lawrence up, he'd stopped at the newsagent's for matches
and realised the new edition had been out since yesterday.
Crouching near the door at the bottom shelf of the aisle,
Arthur licked his finger and leafed through the copy on top
of the stack. He swore to see it. Made the other customers
look. There was the ad: a cleaning job at Threndle House,
contact listed as Guiseley: the instruction he'd been waiting

for. There can have been few people who'd waited this keenly to make a call.

He borrowed a pen from the shopkeeper, scrawled the number on his palm and went to the phone-box around the corner. The tone purred once he'd jabbed the sticky metal keys. A cardboard tray of cold gravy and chips were on the kind of floor that was cold all year round, the knowledge someone had pissed in here recently preying on him.

Eventually Swarsby answered. "Hello?"

"I'm calling about the cleaner ad?"

Silence.

"I'm the right man for the job?"

That was what he was supposed to say.

"The advert's been out over twenty-four hours," said Swarsby tersely.

Arthur smiled, opening the phone-box door and booting the chips out all over the pavement. "I had a lot on."

"I've had a huge number of calls about the position."

"Look are we meeting or what?"

"What the hell do you think?"

"Time?" Arthur crossed his fingers. "I had plans today."

"Well, you'd better reschedule. Be here in an hour."

The line went dead.

No bloody way to contact home and no time to head to Wolton to catch Shell and tell her he wouldn't make Skegness. Arthur double-checked the bakery, left a message with Gaskell to say something had come up, then went to the phone again and used what change he had to try and get in touch with Lawrence.

His mam's phone rang and rang. He tried it a couple more times. All that chat for nothing, greasing Lawrence into spending the morrow with his parents, swearing there'd be no mention of school or the pit. The things you did to make the peace. After the pub, Arthur had walked Lawrence to the cottage bought with the compensation money bought with his father's death. The house reeked permanently of mildew and brown paper. It had a picture of Arthur and his brothers positioned on the sill in a constant suntrap. 'Well done,' his mam mouthed at him from the top stair. Where was she now? Arthur held on until he heard the no-answer tone bleeping down the line then smashed the bastard receiver back into its bastard cradle. There was nothing else to be done. He'd take his family on a real holiday after this. He'd take them on two.

He took the municipal bus as far as he could towards Flintwicks because it was spitting with rain, then walked the rest of the way. He still found Threndle House imposing. Its dinted gargoyle leered from its gritstone perch, weathered by time and hunched by design. Shaded, ear to ear.

Arthur's shoes made shredding noises in the asphalt chippings as he went to put his hand on the nearest wall and feel the chill of its architecture. To the side of the property was a gorgeous old Jaguar XJS. Although he couldn't drive, Arthur cupped his hands on the windows and peered longingly at the dashboard, the wooden-topped gearstick, the gliding binnacle. A couple of minutes later he was at the back of the house letting himself in via the tradesman's entrance. Every window was turbid. Shadow was everywhere.

The Swarsbys kept their coats and things in the scullery leading from the trade door. Arthur removed a scarf from a hook and wrapped it about his face. The Swarsby children must be absent or he wouldn't have been summoned here like this. He followed the sound of an empty sequence being picked out on a piano, all the way to the living room where he found Clive Swarsby waiting for him.

Through the glass beyond Swarsby, the garden was gossamer with mist. The politician was garbed in a lemon-coloured shirt and grey slacks, looking far more comfortable than the last time Arthur had seen him. Arthur seated himself in the nearest chair and tightened the scarf over his face.

"You can take that off for a start," said Swarsby.

"I'll keep it on, ta."

"It's cashmere."

And wool was wool. Arthur's smile became a chuckle as Swarsby shut the fallboard over the piano, causing its wires to chime. The guy had that skull blubber that overweight bald or balding men get, a head-roll of flesh rearing up from the neck that tempts you to reach out and pinch it.

He'd done just that in June, pointing the cricket bat at Swarsby to make him stay put. Out had come Arthur's hand, surprisingly steady, given what it was up to, pincering the soft back of Clive's head between finger and thumb. He dropped the bent photographs of the man's daughter on his desk.

"These are what you want me to pay for?" Swarsby eventually said, leaning back in his chair, in the process knocking the calico blinds that were strung along the window.

"Or we send 'em to papers."

Swarsby let out a derisive burst of air. *Pffft.* So Arthur struck the desk with the bat, leaving a huge dent in its bevelled edge.

Swarsby cowered. *"But I don't have anything!"*

Arthur clouted the desk again, accidentally striking the lightbulb. Glass tinkered everywhere, raining over the three men.

Sound travels brilliantly in wooden-floored rooms. A kinetic energy sluiced through Arthur, and he had to take a moment to steady himself. This was surreal as it got. Swarsby's aftershave was pungent, and the study walls seemed as porridge-coloured as Arthur's life felt half the time. Dig deep for the miners. Arthur had Asa take hold of Swarsby's chair while he went to town on the filing cabinets. Useless manila folders were ransacked, discarded documents floating about the room like feathers loosened from a pillowcase until the Swarsby bank statements surfaced, which, lo and behold, proved there were no savings. The family were living at Threndle House rent-free.

Still, there had to be cash, credit cards or assets. *Something.* Arthur was about to say so when Asa pulled him into the corridor.

"Fucking what?" said Arthur.

"It in't working."

"No way we're leaving empty-handed."

"We've been too long already, what if someone comes?"

Arthur wasn't sure. He had a mind to set the whole of Threndle House ablaze. He batted Asa's arm away and re-entered the study, Asa trying to grab him.

"*Arthur!*"

Swarsby tentatively rose from his chair. "*Arthur?*" he said, "Arthur . . . this house isn't mine. You do know that?"

"But you've all this!" cried Arthur, whacking the desk for a third time. "He's having us on, it's his favourite thing. You must have summat, where's the jewellery, the fucking cash? I'll take that bloody jag off your hands, shall I?"

Swarsby was practically hyperventilating as he waved the photos at Arthur.

"*Think*," he managed to say. "Why would I have these if not for the same reasons as you?"

Arthur lowered the bat. He was drawn to, fascinated by, Clive Swarsby's breached iris, where a mysterious concourse had been created by the oil spill of his pupil. It was like a poker player's tell, only in-built, permanent: the bluffer's mark. And Asa must have seen it too. He swatted the pictures from Swarsby's hand, produced his NUM badge from his pocket and set it on the knackered desk. "All them families," Asa said. "All them jobs."

"Oh, what *bloody* jobs?"

Asa grabbed what remained of Swarsby's hair and used it to slam his face against the desk. Then he lifted him by the pyjama collar and cuffed him around the back of the head like he was some back-chatting kid.

Arthur had to break it up. Swarsby was bleating by then, stammering, confessing tearfully that a friend had taken advantage of his daughter. There was more dirt to come, he said. This Guiseley was worth a packet and likely to pay.

Arthur couldn't breathe properly through the tights. He put his forehead against the politician's and said "Like what? What you fuckin' got?"

"I'm not sure! But why not chance me finding out? I need someone to come in with me as it is," Swarsby said. "Keep me distant. No one will suspect you. I don't even know who you are . . . We can split the money."

"Fuck off," said Asa.

Arthur flapped him quiet. "How much we talking?"

"Put it this way," Swarsby said. "It'll be a lot more than the three thousand you came here for today."

A cessation then, one of those loaded moments where

something you knew all about is revealed to someone else. Realising his lowballing had just been outed and certain Asa would take the news thick, Arthur reached for the cricket bat. The red and white Grey Nicholls sticker was vertical against his eye.

"*Three* thousand?" said Asa quietly. "An' wi' the bat now, Art, n' all?"

"Listen, wait, *hang on a tick!*"

Asa snatched the keyboard from the desk, yanked it free of the computer, wire and all, and swung it broad as a plank at Arthur, who ducked. The keyboard caught Clive Swarsby in the temple, letters and numbers flying everywhere. Swarsby fell to the ground, pyjamas rucked at the shins and his stomach jiggling openly. Arthur stared at the scattered alphabet, the keys one to nine. At his feet was the number one, and above that fabled digit was an exclamation mark.

Oddly, that seemed to quieten things. Asa was shaking. He prodded Arthur in the shoulder, once, then stormed out of the room.

"Scanny!"

He didn't stop. Fucking Moonface. You tried to do a guy a favour. Arthur went to help Swarsby up. The daft bugger was about to have a heart attack so Arthur passed him a tissue and let him dab himself.

"Let's make call," he said, patting Swarsby's back. "This Guiseley. Get it over wi'."

"We can't. I need proof. Evidence. You need to give me until the election. I need more time."

Summer had crawled on since then. Picket after protest, relentless. Police on your doorstep, stationed on the outskirts of the borough and all over Yorkshire. A bunch of clowns are supposed to be funny; this lot were far from it. Stop and search every day. The whinny and whine of their animals, the chug and fume of their engines, their sirens busy and your powdery breath visible now that August had puttered away.

The TUC talks had finished, with the NUM of course left high and dry, and as per fucking usual, the Labour party was nowhere to be seen. It was the seventies all over again. And while they were kissing Thatcher's and Heseltine's arses, Scargill and Mick McGahey could get in line to kiss Arthur's too.

What a joke. The government were coming in hard, going after the union's brass, persuading two blokes from Manton to take the NUM to court over what they'd have been told to say was an illegal ballot. This whole strike was illegal, according to Thatcher and her cronies. A helicopter had been chartered to serve a writ to Arthur Scargill at the Labour conference.

Rejoice, Maggie.

Rejoice.

It was a low blow going after the union's brass, even a non-believer like Arthur could see that. So many families the NUM were supporting had nothing, really nothing, and the government still weren't satisfied. Sons and husbands were getting their heads split open every morning, wives and daughters were supporting them and everybody else and people were still losing their bloody homes. No electric, no heating, having to pick loose coal-scraps from the spoil heaps to burn or flog any way you knew how. It wasn't enough, no. Forcing folks back to work was the size of it. It was no wonder people were listening. In front of them was the Litten Path.

Arthur was almost halfway up it himself. His sulky wife

had driven him a good way along. Shell was such a let-down. So she'd had a horrid do down in Sheffield – she'd been making out like she'd been born under a bad sign way before then. For Lawrence they had to make a go of it; she just wasn't interested. Not in anything but herself. Every conversation Shell steered back to how she was feeling, the muck they'd been forced to eat for dinner that day, wondering what someone was saying about her in town. Arthur was constantly trying to make her feel better, cuddling her, kissing her and being told to leave off for his trouble. *Give me a break.* Gob full of catarrh. Carpeted into a strike you didn't give a fuck about. It was like being back at school, being told to stand during the national fucking anthem. Told to shut up and say the Lord's fucking Prayer. Arthur had never once kept his eyes shut during those incanted words. The teachers could try and make him as much as they liked, and they bloody well had done, but if the carrot hadn't worked then why the hell should the stick?

Shell had done the yard recently, her little project, and that was something. Plus she was reading the books Arthur lent her. That was something, too. She'd started to come along on the visits to Lawrence as well, although reminders over how to behave were all she seemed capable of uttering. Don't be out past curfew. Don't do 'owt you shouldn't. At least Arthur knew how to say sorry. At least he could relate to their angry son. He couldn't understand why Shell had to be so damn pig-headed.

Or ignorant. As for another matter Shell hardly ever noticed the mounting Hate Mail, or was refusing to discuss it if she did. A one-track mind she had, a one-way street Arthur always had to be the one to do the reversing up. The only thing to grab Shell's attention recently had been when he'd hinted at going back to work.

"You wouldn't give in like that?" she'd said, the first true question she'd asked him in many weeks.

"I dunno."

"Arthur?"

"I said, I dunno."

"Whole of Litten'll turn on us!"

That pretty face, so animated. She was lovely, Arthur couldn't deny that, nor could he deny that the passion Shell brought to everything still got to him. He'd win her back, make her happy and get them out of this shithole once and for all, soon as he had the money. Maybe then Shell could be who she wanted. He'd given her a lengthy look then gone walking on the moor.

Autumn here we come. Sat on the settee with the lord of Threndle House, Arthur could almost hear his ancestors laughing. Clive fucking Swarsby still towed the smell of aftershave around. Spiced stuff, sort of like you got in Catholic churches when they swung the thurible. Sloshing that shit all over himself when he was supposed to be skint. Swarsby was just another liar. Lying is as much of a choice as cowardice.

"You've lost a few pounds, our kid," said Arthur.

No reaction.

"Suit yourself."

He lit a fag and smoked it though the scarf.

Swarsby dragged over the coffee table and dropped some papers on it. They were stapled together in the top left corner. "These might help," he said, fixing Arthur with a flat stare. "Visual aids."

Arthur tried to work out if he was being mocked, decided

he was and logged the insult. "Let's have at it then," he said.

The first sheet was a photocopied image of the same thick-haired, heavy-set man as had been having dinner with Guiseley at the Savoy in the original set of photos.

"Recognise him?" Swarsby pointed at the face.

A gesture of agreement with the hands.

"*This* is our leverage."

"Fat as fuck paddy."

"Irishman is correct. It's taken a while but I can finally confirm that *this* is not the kind of individual our mutual friend should be meeting with."

"Guiseley reckons he's invincible," said Arthur. "What did you say he is again – a flaming duke?"

"A baronet, a peer and arrogant with it."

It paid to be underestimated. Arthur amped up the ee-ba-gum. "Lad's spit of us father-in-law o'er Leeds way," he said, examining the photograph theatrically.

"His name is Martin Doran. He's an intermediary of the Irish Republican Army . . ."

Jesus. Arthur cricked his neck.

"Or one of their subsidiaries, I'm not sure. Either way, he's been introduced to Guiseley by this gentleman, here."

Swarsby flipped the page and revealed a picture of a little man who could easily have been a jockey. Name of Sheehan, Swarsby said. "But it's Doran we're interested in. He's the one who'll help us apply our squeeze."

Squeeze. Prick thought he was in some spy story. Arthur could barely keep a straight face as he said, "Reight, what ah'll do is ring him up and say I'm wise to him. I'll go, listen, kid. How much is that peerage worth? Few bob or nay, fucking tell us."

The expression on Swarsby's face was priceless. Arthur cackled and punched the jumped-up little toad on the arm – he knew exactly where to aim to make it go dead – and waited for him to continue. The politician just cleared his throat. The two of them were stuck together now, Arthur knew, and there on the wall was that vein of subsidence. It reached the ceiling thanks to the empty ventricle of Brantford pit. The damage had travelled right the way here, cracked all the way through.

He spent the rest of the afternoon celebrating. You could rely on the veteran miners from the welfare to shout you an ale: men like Henry Evans, a former lampman, a pithy celebration of old bones in braces and a grandad shirt. In exchange for a pint all you had to do was listen to the stories, over-cooked as they were, tales of giving up the bacon and egg shift for the two till ten, dashing in for last orders and getting so hammered you missed your shift the next day and had to soot your face up to fool the wife as to where you'd been.

Arthur had stories of his own: nicking the keys to the steel case set in concrete and having away with the morphine, getting at the youngsters with some old shotfiring cable in the showers that time. But there were more pressing matters at hand: namely, how to explain away Skegness. When he felt himself getting too pissed he made himself scarce, gave a screw of tobacco up to Henry then went home to paper it over with Shell.

On the way back he stopped at the shop, stuffing a box of chocolates up his jumper while the girl behind the counter fetched him some fresh tobacco. It was late afternoon and already darkening.

He ate a peppermint before entering the lounge. "Here you are, pet," he said. "Sorry I missed beach."

Shell had been dozing on the settee. Arthur knelt by her side and handed over the chocolates. "I ended up last minute help for a mate who needed a lift wi' a set of drawers," he explained, taking Shell's hand. Her wedding ring felt so loose. "The buggers turned out too big for the stairs. I had to take 'em apart. By the time I got to Wolton the coach had gone."

Shell set the chocolates on the floor. "You'll have stopped in the WMC then," she said.

"Aye, popped us head in."

Shell sat up, rubbing her face. "There weren't time to leave a note. I left a message wi the barman. Did tha speak to him?"

"Aye, chap mentioned it. He were all right, actually. Decent fella."

There was a long period of silence before Shell lay back down. "I'm *tired*, Arthur."

"I said I were sorry, love."

"Well in that case don't worry about it."

You just never knew when you were going to drop in the drink with her. Arthur stood. "Did tha least have a good time? Bit of a break, wasn't it . . ."

"No I didn't have a good time."

"Well, what about Lawrence? You an' him get chance to talk?"

"He didn't turn up either."

There went the last flutter of salvation. Arthur picked up the chocolates. "I'll pop these on t'side for when you wake," he said.

There was no talking to Shell when she was like this.

On the front step Arthur sucked down a flood of air. He

could see the leaded windows, the gloom-obscured brick and pebbledash of the neighbouring houses, and of a sudden, a shape in the window opposite. It could have been a spectre formed by candlelight in the Cairns' house. David Cairns, beckoning with his head.

Arthur knocked-on. He'd always had time for David, so when he was let into the lad's house he tried not to show his dismay at the sight of the downstairs, which was completely empty of furniture save a deckchair in the front room.

David sat on the chair. An unlit Calor Gas camping stove stood in front of him on which a pan of spaghetti rested, a plastic fork buried in the slop. Circular beds of light ringed two or three patches of candles and piles and piles of letters were on the mantelpiece, under which some embers throbbed. Arthur could just make out what looked like a table leg protruding from the ash.

"Just you in?"

David nodded.

"Where's Cherry and t'kids?"

"Left."

"Anywhere nice?"

"*Left*, Art."

"Oh."

Arthur sat cross-legged on the carpet. David was a good ten years younger than him and had a boyish cow-lick and non-existent eyebrows, both of which were obscured by a woollen hat. David set the pan down, took his hat off and scratched his head. Some pictures the tots had drawn were in the kitchen, taped to the cupboard near where the fridge had been. He said, "Probably for best. Not fair on t'littluns, living like this."

"Who knows, after all this is finished . . ." Arthur trailed off.

David looked like the food he'd just eaten was off and had been all along. He fixed his gaze on the subdued fire and said, "I were sorry to hear about Het."

"What's sack-head got to do wi' anything?"

"If I'd known they'd go after him, I'd have doubled back."

"What you on about?"

"You not heard about us getting stopped?" David said, staring at Arthur as if he'd grown a second head.

"Apparently not."

David's duffel coat was hiked around the stomach. He undid it, smoothed it, picked the pan up and started tucking into the spaghetti once more. Speaking through his mouthful, a cave of wet string, he said, "Spotted after curfew on us way to picket Braithwaite. Busted on us way back. Someone's reported Het's car – they had his details on file. He were arrested. Now he's on bail."

A crump is a shake in a bed of stone when a gap closes and you get an almighty bang in the earth above your head. Arthur had a similar feeling now. David was a bright lad who was after becoming a ventilation engineer one day. Perhaps he could explain it.

"All of yous lifted?"

"Just him. Got any cigs?" said David. "I've started again." He gestured at the empty room as if to say, *why not*. Arthur handed over the tobacco.

"You've spoken to him?"

"Thought you might've."

Arthur snorted. "Y'know what us two are like."

"That I do," said David. He seemed really to be searching

for something as he put his tongue to the rolling paper and ran it along the gum. "Which is why I was surprised to see him on the coach to Skegness wi' your missus earlier."

And you're very keen not to make eye contact, so very careful now you've let the pin out of the grenade, David. Arthur made disbelieving noises that felt false, even to him, as he began to pace the room. He might have known. Of course he knew. He had always known.

"Before Cherry went to her mam's," David was saying, "she mentioned Shell and Het had been seeing a lot of each other. I been on picket more often than most, so hadn't noticed . . . Course *you* knew.

"*Anyway,*" David continued, before Arthur could respond. "I were on coach, sat minding us own at back. I thought it'd clear us head, the day out. Sea breeze, like. Well them two got on, one after t'other. Side by side. They went off together on t'sand."

"Reight."

"Shell weren't on t'bus back."

This was the emptiest house Arthur had ever been in. He watched the smoke unfolding up the chimney.

"I'm losing the place, Art," said David.

"I'm sorry to hear that," replied Arthur, or at least that's what he thought he'd said. He couldn't be sure with his brain fizzing the way it was, the keening noise in his ears, sort of like the sound they played at night on TV when there were no more programmes to watch. He felt sick.

"*Sure* you seen 'em?"

"Well, I couldn't reckon it up for definite, but I saw 'em side by side, getting all comfy, then they went off together. Like I said, only one of 'em were on t'coach home. I suppose I could have said summat on the way back, give Het chance to explain it away. I just couldn't for some reason. Shell had her head on his shoulder all the way there. I thought it best I say summat, Art. If it were me I'd want to know."

... A reckless spread of fern and gorse. A wolfhound emerging from the undergrowth with a conduit of blood trickling from its nose ...

Arthur snapped awake, trying to catch his breath.

... The hound leaping off the mountain, a hen harrier trapped in its mouth. Through the beating hail the dog's paws thumped the last of the burnt heather, pounding the Litten Path, the bird's blood sizzling as it dripped on the ground ...

Arthur slipped out of bed. Not a peep from Shell, lying there, this stranger he'd elected wife. He glared at her form, then felt terrible. He mouthed an apology, dressed and put his shoes on, left the bedroom and the freezing house.

His mam's front garden was silent and littered with decaying leaves. Nothing here was growing. It was all reduced to stalk, easy to snap, skeletal.

Helen had done very well for herself since Alec's accident. This house was so much bigger than the old place, the fraught terrace of Arthur's boyhood that had been laden with the smell of lard cooking, bread and dripping and lavender candles. The thinned upholstery of furniture had hosted decades of afternoon naps.

They used to go up Wolton Road washhouse when Arthur was little. It was his job to cart the laundry in the old pram. If he'd been good, his mam sometimes let him book a tub in the bathhouse. Sneaking next door, all but naked, Miss Starkey showing him where to go, her husband a pit deputy, she in white overalls that must never have been dry. Her prunish fingers ran the baths by turning the taps with the special key. Arthur always asked for his extra hot so he could have a proper soak, spending so long in the marvellous water that his mam had often to come and fetch him.

His wife was at it with his brother.

He gathered some chalky dirt from the flowerbeds, compacted it in his hand and chucked it at Lawrence's window. It came back and blew all over him. Some went in his mouth.

He tried again, catching the glass with light stones until Lawrence's head appeared speculatively out of the window.

"Kid?"

The head shot back inside.

"Please, Lawrence."

No answer.

Arthur still wanted Shell. He didn't know how to make her want him back.

"*Oh, come on.*"

Lawrence's gentle brow, the boy's fingers and nose, appeared at the window ledge.

"I'm in bed, Dad."

"I'll make it quick. I just wanted to explain, about yesterday . . ."

"Time is it?"

"Summat came up."

"I knew you wouldn't show."

"I meant to, I promise."

"Have you spoken to Mam?"

Talk? Arthur could barely look at Shell. And as for Het. He was some brother. This was some life.

"I want to make it up to you, kid. I thought we could go for a walk later. Have a chat, like . . ."

The expression on Lawrence's face made Arthur cover his mouth.

"Oh, stop trying to make us feel guilty all the time, Dad!"

"I'm not!"

Arthur had been copping it since day one and although his son had ruined everything for himself at school, he could still be helped in some respects. Arthur could do something for the only person he had left. "I expect you'll be busy wi' that Swarsby lass," he said, "but listen, this might not be the time or place, but, Lawrence, I've been meaning to tell you, well . . . I've heard stuff about this Evie girl an' I think it's only right I tell you what's what."

"Oh go home, Dad," Lawrence said angrily, retreating and hauling the window down, leaving barely a gap.

Arthur sat on the path, wishing Sam was here. His brother could have been the ignited piece of coal wrapped in a newspaper, a hot cob to rekindle a life's spent fire. There are so many ways to die and so few ways in which to live. The Litten Path was drawing in, a rent in the hills with the eyes of the wolfhound nearly up it. "Ask her about Guiseley, then," Arthur called up at the house. "Ask that girl what she and that lord got up to down in London then."

The window drew to, just above.

Arthur was able to thumb a lift from a milk dray. He didn't know where he'd go but sitting among the crates he happened to drive past Chris Skelly, Gordon Lomas and Darren Roach. They must be on their way to a picket somewhere, and maybe that was the kind of release he needed.

He knocked on the driver's window. The dray quickly slowed, Arthur jumping off and going after the others. Thanks to the street lamps, his reflection was clear against the wet tarmac and road markings. Arctic, it was. The zip on his coat was broken so he had to tug it about himself as he hollered at the lads to slow.

"Boys!"

Arthur met them at the bus shelter, where they said hellos, shared smokes and cupped hands around matches to guard against a moody wind and the beginnings of a light rain.

"You're out early," Gordon said.

"Just roaming about," replied Arthur. "I needed the quiet."

Chris Skelly nodded sympathetically. "Where you been hiding?" he said. "I were beginning to think you'd packed it all in."

"So were I. Had to clear us head though, you know."

"Fancy it tonight?" Chris clapped Arthur on the shoulder. "We're off to fetch car."

From his pocket, Arthur removed a bottle of juice he'd lifted from the milk dray, peeled the cap off and took a sip. It was tart, the bottle so cold it was uncomfortable to keep hold of. He didn't need to say anything.

They slipped out of town and headed towards Tockholes Farm, where Chris had his car stashed. All the way there they walked in the grass on the hill-side of the drystone wall, so that when a vehicle came by they could duck, and arrived a short while later, safe and damp.

Fortunately there were spare towels in the boot and Gordon had a Thermos of tea, so they warmed a little on the drive to Kellworth. Quiet and weary, the miners listened to the rain dropping on the car. It sounded like someone was scattering tons of grit at them.

At Kellworth they were admitting strike breakers into the pit at staggered times, so the NUM had instructed its picketers to correspond their arrivals accordingly – morning till lunch. Arthur and the others were a part of the second or third wave of protesters that morning.

They pulled in a fair walk from Kellworth's compound and navigated the tricky sump of sodden fields until they got to the scar of railway sidings cut into the pit itself. Five minutes or so down these tracks they heard a noise in the trees behind. They lay flat and tried to see over the embankment, spotting the flashing rods of many torches in the murk.

Police.

The percussive sound of boots did not stop or go away. The noise came closer, then closer still. Arthur and the others were forced to scrabble from the train tracks, heading through the field instead, in the direction of the pit's rear. They quickly got caught in an obnoxious lake of thick black coal slurry six inches deep. They waded through the muck to the west of Kellworth. Shit-stinking, legs filthy, they eventually reached the outer wire fence that they could follow in the hope of getting closer to the picket.

The pit lights were huge and alien and the fence, made of interlinked and criss-crossed metal cord, created a blanket of tessellated diamonds that sent mesh shadows on to the face of each man. Arthur and the others edged single-file along the fence until they could see the picket stationed by the main gates, the police lines in darkness way ahead.

A group of officers were conversing with the lead picketers by the tea hut, its tarp and brazier lending the proceedings a rich, satanic glow. Behind this group were larger numbers of picketers and way more police. Hundreds on either side.

Arthur nudged up front with Chris. They couldn't hear what was being said but voices were being raised. The lead police officer give a signal to some of his men to approach the tea hut. They did so, a small group carrying between them a large bucket. The men emptied the bucket over the picketers' brazier, which left the detached floodlights in the pit compound the only remaining source of light.

Beneath these unforgiving beacons the picket was set upon and men were beaten and arrested in the patchy glare. Shouting. Fragments of violence. Everything got mixed up until Arthur couldn't tell which side was bloody which.

He and Darren wanted to pitch in immediately. Chris and Gordon wanted to wait for the scab vans and the rest of the picket to arrive. As they bickered, the clomp of boots and hooves got louder. A centipede of reinforcements was coming, aiming towards the carnival of violence playing out by Kellworth's central gates.

This was followed by vehicles coming at the fracas, headlights blinding. Arthur broke free and ran towards the vans. He found a wedge of rock, and, imagining the lead vehicle was Het's face, threw the rock and managed to pop a headlight.

Unfazed, the van hurtled though the space created by the police, straight into Kellworth Colliery. Another van zoomed behind that, a car and motorbikes, then it was the turn of the riot squad. Some headed into the pit and the rest manned the gates as they scraped shut. These men went to beat up the picketers, the melee left battling outside.

Arthur kept on with the rocks, managing to ping a couple more policemen before Gordon tackled him to the ground.

He'd drawn the attention of some bobbies in nipple helmets, and they were heading this way. He and Gordon fled, Arthur's mind emptying amid the singular imperative of escape. He was in the woods now, alone, reflecting on all that had happened since he first jumped the wall at Threndle House. You tried to solve one problem and created a whole set of others. The moths were out of the rug. They were everywhere.

Scaling an incline, he ran headlong into a fresh batch of policemen who were preparing to attack the miners. Arthur hopped it in the opposite direction, tripping and jarring his midriff on a tree stump. Swearing, he made for open country, running for home, a fitful sleep and the forthcoming by-election.

Sure enough, the Free Press was full of the election in the weeks that followed. The days Arthur hardly registered, the nights felt like they were centuries long. He took to waking in the early hours, staring at the back of Shell's head, wondering if she'd have a face when she turned around again or if it'd just be her hair, no matter how many times he spun her. Smelling your wife's clothes, watching her leave for work, following her through town and if you lost her, enquiring as to her whereabouts, always taking her account of where she'd been with a pinch of salt, a cocktail of fact and fiction, parallel lines that would always be the same distance apart, like you and her.

Shell had played billiards with Arthur's head. His brother, too. Het even had the nerve to come round and offer to buy Arthur drinks one day down the welfare. Blood and treacle in a pint pot. Arthur nearly glassed Het where he sat as he was told that he should consider himself free, that he was off the hook for breaking into Threndle House in the spring.

Benevolent fucking Het, condescending to tell Arthur it might have been a mistake forcing him on picket. Het even suggested it was high time Lawrence was brought home, tarried back to Water Street to cheer up the same woman who'd driven him away in the first place. The arrogance of the man, not realising for a moment that Arthur knew all about what had been going on between him and Shell. The two of them at it. His brother and his wife.

On the night of the by-election, Arthur ticked the box next to the name Clive Swarsby. This is what they got when they told him what to do. Course the Tory candidate was heckled at the announcements, booed, some obscure independents plus Labour and Jennings: Derek Shaw's amanuensis, or whatever the piss he'd been while his old boss festered in office those thirty years, all of them finished above Swarsby.

Swarsby didn't even seem surprised. From the moment he was sent to fight this seat he'd known he'd lose it. So he set his plan accordingly, fashioned his trap. Arthur helped, making the call to Bramwell Guiseley a few days before Litten cast its vote. He sent the package by secure delivery. He was only supposed to include the photos of the Irishman Doran but he shoved the ones of Evie in for good measure: the whole lot plus the contact details of the editor of every major newspaper in the country made for a compelling case. The accompanying letter invited Guiseley to the post-election gaudy at Threndle House, where he was to drop the money off, behind the same bins the moth rug had been left in a lifetime ago.

The drop-off couldn't come soon enough because October had duffed the miners up and left them for dead. Fucking NACODS threw the towel in. Course they did. Bought off because everything could be bought – every single thing on planet earth – the NCB penning a blank cheque for the pit deputies and their under-officials. And now that the managers' union weren't coming on strike the effort was done for. It had all been for nothing, just as Arthur predicted.

The strike limped on, staggering into lethal November. In the space of three days, tasty pay-outs were offered to any miner who'd go back to work, and Labour leader Neil Kinnock stuck it in reverse, refusing to speak on his party's behalf at the NUM rallies with Arthur Scargill.

Soon after that some youngsters died, picking coal for their families on a winter spoil heap. Three lads, aged fourteen and fifteen. Around that time the greenlight was also given by Thatcher's government to slash the welfare for the striking families again. Arthur was reduced to grubbing for coal himself, filling compost sacks with shit-bits he could sell in the pubs to those with open fires. All you needed was a spade and a pickaxe for where the ground was frozen. He went on to watch the bank repossess David Cairns' house, and, after hearing about Asa and the girls, found his old friend down the Grey Grebe and offered to look after him as had originally been agreed, a cut of the Guiseley money as soon as the pay-out came. *Here me out, Asa. Here me out.* Trying to apologise, only to be shoved over, told where to go and called a shammer in front of everyone.

But it was coming to an end. Five grand was on its way, Arthur's half of ten. He could almost taste it. He kept visualising rocking home in the taxi, opening the door to Shell with his final surprise, one that'd work this time, win her back for good. He'd take her down the airport. Pack your bags, love, this is it. Have a gander at the travel brochure. Take your pick.

It had snowed the night before, only some of it sticking,

frost holding the parts together at the high points, dampness accounting for the rest. Threndle House appeared in view, almost feudal, the last bastion of the vanguard glowing against a hillside that was leopard-printed with slush. The house itself was neat and tidy: no sign of the Litten Path as yet, that cartilage of shattered rock that had broken from the crag. But it was out there: Arthur could feel it.

The air was brittle and parched and the gate was wide open. Music played and there were fancy cars parked outside: Rovers and Mercs stationary as crouching dogs. Amber fairy lights wound along the house's porch. A sweeping band of shifting hues stretched unbroken, miles above.

Arthur could hear the laughing guests. They were of no concern to him, all he had to do was collect his money from the side of the house and be on his way. His half of ten.

He didn't have to creep but did so anyway. This was a mad thing to be getting on with: a miner's lad from up Litten way, getting one over on the bigwigs from down south.

Here were the bins. Arthur lugged them aside. The ground was mossy and webbed with shit and leaves and the heat busted from him as he looked down.

Fuck.

Fuck, no.

There was nothing there.

. . .

He checked again.

Nothing was there.

. . .

Arthur knelt in the snow for a long time, then prowled the outskirts of Threndle House, checking for a holdall until he was sure the bastards had done him. It felt like someone else was walking this route, not him. His beard had dew in it. His hair was so much thicker since growing back after Shell chopped it all off. Never in a million years had anyone been gulled like this. Chilblains. Fondling. Shell kissing Het. Het kissing Shell. Her hands up that scar. Did Het make love with his glasses on? Shell's tongue all over Arthur's brother in his brother's flat. Up in the woods. In Arthur's bed. His wife and his brother in his bed.

No.

Arthur could see into the living room. Guiseley was acting as if everything was fine. Everyone had ironic looks on their faces. Masks. The lot of them were a bunch of fucking masks.

Then he saw Lawrence.

The boy no longer wore jeans and a bobbled woollen sweater. He looked smart, Arthur's son of such dense varieties who must have weighed no more than ten stone soaking wet. Lawrence had a rough smile, just like his mam, using the side of his mouth just like Shell did. He also had that same lack of eloquence that felt oddly verbose, that same talent for putting things. But Arthur was in there too. Lawrence had the same reluctance to comply as his doomed old man.

And that was it, wasn't it? At the end of the day your child was as alone and corporeal as you were. You couldn't protect them. Everything they went through, they went through because of you, simply down to the sheer fact of being brought into this world. Maybe they were better off deracinated. Arthur could have smashed the window and dragged Lawrence out. He could have done the same to Swarsby, any of them. But why wreck things for his son just because he'd run out of track? He thought for a moment that he could hear the blast charges of Brantford pit. He listened again. There was only the wind.

The next part was easy. Arthur headed into town to do what he should have done months ago. He knocked on the door of Clifford Briscoe, Brantford's pit manager, and told him he wanted to go back to work.

19

E VIE WATCHED LAWRENCE emerge from the iron-mongers. It was cold and her scarf smelt like peppermints. She blew against the cashmere, hot damp spreading across her face. Her first north winter and it was as cold as she'd expected. Mischief Night, not even November, the pavement ice pale and the Christmas lights suspended prematurely across the street in unlit colours.

Evie mimed a round of applause as Lawrence raised the glue tin above his head. He'd grown out that vicious skinhead and might even scrub up presentably for somebody one day.

She took his arm and headed towards the woods, where they were to meet Duncan. Her brother had gotten over the garden party better than she had. Right up to the faint Evie could recall, the flutes of champagne, the wisp of cigar and scotch fumes, acquisitive attitudes practically slathering off the walls.

Bram had just been *there*. How could that have been how he first saw Evie again? She thought of his esoteric good looks: he had a face like a leather briefcase, his shoes squeaking with every movement. Evie's mother loitered behind him, tutting about missing the speeches thanks to *another performance*. That same old paradigm of disappointment.

The afternoon sky was streaked with violet when they eventually arrived at the den. The elm tree's garlands were withered and its bunting was faded, the painted stripes up the neighbouring tree chipped and sparse. As the ground was wet and the chair under the tarp had long gone, Evie had Lawrence clean some stones for them to sit on. He'd been windbagging about something so she thought she'd better set him a task.

Presently she sat while Lawrence prised the lid from the tin with his house key and emptied the glue into the sandwich bag the way she'd showed him. They took turns huffing at the bag, trapping and exhaling the glue's fumes as if having panic attacks. Amid the whirl of solvent, Evie thoughts divided . . . her train ride north at five am, dosed on the Nitrazepam she'd stolen from her mother's bathroom, so out of it she had to be escorted from the train by the ticket inspector when she arrived in Litten . . . sleeping it off . . . awakening to Clive emerging from his study with a cut above the eye . . . Duncan . . . 'Please don't say anything' . . . lolling in the garden with a drink until Lawrence arrived, babbling about horses, in danger of crying and knowing neither of them would forget it if he did . . . sorry I wasn't at the woods . . . kissing her . . . letting him do it . . . Bram was . . . Fiona fixed . . . the season had flowed into August and beyond the trees, the trees, there was a gate . . .

"That was fun," said Evie.

"It's mad is what it is."

Evie snorted.

"What's so funny?" Lawrence said.

"Your lips have gone all blue."

"They haven't."

Evie let him kiss her cheek and put his arm around her, but soon grew tired and shrugged him off. Submitting to the designs of someone you pitied was just another act of self-harm. Bram had taught her that much.

She nudged the glue tin out of sight at the sound of her brother. When Duncan arrived, his eyes flicked to the sticky bag. His hair reached to his chin now. He was still some distance from attaining Lawrence's height, but was broader in chest. Evie had caught him doing press-ups only the other day.

"All set?" he said, pushing a sheaf of hair behind his ears.

"Born ready."

"What about you, Lawrence? *Mischief Night*."

"Looking forward to it," Lawrence said, glancing to his left, which Evie had read somewhere was a sure sign of a lie. She leapt onto his back and demanded a piggy-back.

They took the bus over the high road, through the police cordons towards Whitbeck. Passing through the checkpoint, the concertinaed roofs of the old army barracks drew into view. There was an assortment of police vehicles in the exercise yard: Transits, Bedfords and Leylands, cars, carriers, bikes, horseboxes and Range Rovers. Never mind the men. Evie pointed it all out to Lawrence, who didn't seem bothered.

He could suit himself. Out of the rear window, if it would do, was a suet and cinder-coloured firmament framing the spoil heap on the edge of Litten, and adjacent to that great false hill, by a few miles, stood the colliery's winding gear and chimneys. Evie was feeling kind; she would not remind Lawrence of the subterranean drama of alignments and networks that formed the citadel of his future, at least not today. He was watching a bird ghosting in flight outside, its tiny form leaving the emaciated shapes of industry far behind. Evie made eye contact with him in the window but could think of nothing to say.

The bus stopped ten minutes' walk from Fernside Grammar. Evie was beginning to feel the ping of the

Dexedrine she'd also taken from her mother's bathroom and supposed Lawrence must be feeling the fizz too. Duncan, none the wiser, removed three rubber masks from his bag: a witch, a vampire and a werewolf. "Vampire for me," he said. "And I think we can guess who gets what between you two."

Evie took the werewolf mask.

Fernside felt abnormally quiet. It had been such a long time since Evie was in a school. Since passing her O-levels well enough to get into college, she had decided to defer a year to 'figure things out.' She wouldn't miss the jostle for position, the obligations and insecurity of education. Her future in the real world would be so very different.

The masks fitted closely against their faces. Evie felt delicious in hers. Hidden from herself as well as others, she felt energised and alert, displaced. Or maybe it was just the amphetamines.

She followed Lawrence uphill to the sports hall. The new complex had just been completed, replacing the concrete tennis courts. Grundy, Fernside's headmaster, patrolled it daily, a pitted block of windowless concrete that had a green roof that lent it the appearance of a huge lunchbox.

They shook the cans of spray-paint and began to graffiti the outside of the hall. They had a colour each: Lawrence red, Duncan blue and Evie yellow, painting a massive crude jack-o-lantern on the brick and writing the name *Grundy* above it. They gave the figure a gross body with naked, lactating breasts and a pustulating cock and balls. At its feet they sprayed the corpses of children, trampled, prone. *Fuck off, Bastard, Twat,* Evie wrote, whilst sitting on Lawrence's shoulders.

Happy Mischief Night.

When the end-of-day bell clanged, the three of them made

themselves scarce, spraying the waist-high walls surrounding the school grounds as they went. The channels of painted colour were reminiscent of the marks left on the wall by the subsidence beneath Threndle House. The cracked lines of paint also extended along the panels and doors of every teacher's car parked along the road.

As the first pupils streamed outside, desperate for home, Evie and the boys hid from view. First one student noticed the hall, then another, then many more, until one ran inside to fetch a teacher. Grundy soon appeared, gawping at the ten-foot tall grotesque daubed on the side of his beloved building. Evie felt fit to burst and delinquent as her eyelashes caught on the eye-holes of her wolf mask. High, she tore out clumps of grass from the space between her legs and clenched them as hard as she could.

The headmaster had yet to notice the marks on the school's walls and teachers' cars. Vainly, he tried to clear the crowd as more and more children appeared. Lawrence reached for Evie's hand. "Not now," she said, absorbed by the commotion.

Duncan clapped Lawrence on the shoulder. "Aren't you going to say thank you?"

Lawrence lifted his mask and nodded at Evie. "You were right," he said.

"You make it sound as if sometimes I'm not."

The mask slid down his face, the witch's nose tilting at a forty-five degree angle. "There's Fenton," Lawrence said. "Loving it as usual."

"Which one's he?"

"Greasebag. White Dunlop jacket."

Dusting her mucky hands on herself, Evie said, "Well, what's stopping us going after him?" She looked to Duncan for her easy yes. It was a Mischief Night, after all.

They followed Ryan Fenton towards the main road once he'd split away from the other pupils. Mask ditched, Evie re-applied her make-up, then headed over the road to meet him as he swung around the bus stop, hand on the pole that bore the timetable, its plastic screen blistered with cigarette burns.

Fenton stopped swinging at the sight of her. His smile was the colour of dead grass, his hair shaven tightly at the sides of his head and left lengthier, gelled forwards on top.

He offered Evie the cigarette she asked for, then handed her a lighter. He'd done that thing where you remove the metal guard and fiddle with the fuel switch so that when the flint is sparked, the lighter's wick erupts into a figure of dancing flame.

"Watch your lashes," he said.

"Thanks."

Evie affected a toothy smile. Fenton's friends were watching nearby, after all.

"What's your name?" she said.

"My what?"

Were all the locals as bad as Lawrence? Evie repeated the question.

Fenton answered.

"Nice name."

He looked confused.

Evie cleared her throat. Lawrence was hiding somewhere, watching. "I'm not from around here."

"No." Fenton fiddled with the zip of his coat, the charming diligence of the action and its basic humanity making Evie hesitate. The plan was to lead this bully to The Carousel, a newsagent Lawrence had said could only be reached via an isolated track at the end of a cul-de-sac that led from a nearby estate. There Fenton would be stripped of his clothes, covered in spray-paint and left naked.

Feeling the pervasive rush of nicotine, Evie stepped closer to Fenton. It wouldn't do to fall at this hurdle, whether he deserved what was coming his way or not, so she opened her body language up to him and asked for directions to The Carousel. She was meeting a friend, she said. She'd only get lost if she went alone.

In the gravel passage between sets of houses, Fenton touched Evie's lower back as they stepped over a large, kidney-shaped puddle that looked like it was made of tinted glass. They were in the initial yards of the alley. The high walls of the alley were of concrete, an intricate roof had formed from a maze of creeper and branch, and there were bits of litter scattered everywhere.

They were out of sight, alone. Deciding to push things forward, Evie made a wet kind of eye contact with Fenton and bent to his height, her mouth open. It was always a surprise kissing a new person, the different methods they had. Fenton wasn't shy. He was a fleshy kisser, committing at a similar depth and pace as Evie, to the extent that although he hadn't questioned her actions, she still felt compelled to justify herself in some way. "Fiona," she said, pulling away. "My name's Fiona."

She was pushed against the wall. Kissed for the second time, Evie found herself unzipping Fenton's fly. Thank God for the sound of children, though, thank God for boisterous fuss. Because the noise from a nearby garden made Evie realise what she was doing.

She let go of the zipper. But Fenton was already scrabbling at her. He managed to hitch her skirt up and push his hand between her legs. Evie took far too long to remove him. Breathless, she felt breathless, high on Dexedrine and her own permissive nature.

"What's up?" Fenton said.

"Nothing's up."

There was no witch at the end of the alley.

No vampire.

Evie let herself be kissed again, zoning off completely. The only comparable experience she could think of was exercising, in that there is a point, when running, when watching your steps and controlling your breathing, that thought begins to disappear completely. Evie's exchange with Ryan Fenton quickened and became so urgent that she could do nothing but feel another body against her own and welcome it, enjoy it even, feeling the urge to stop anything disappear as she dissolved totally within the moment.

Her knickers were tugged down and then the surprise of Fenton was upon her and as easy as that, it was happening. Evie could see the top of his head. She could smell his hair gel and make out the dandruff freckling his red scalp. A part of her was saying this wouldn't matter. Another part was digging the uneven wall and shrieking. A final part, the significant part, was simply not there at all.

Then, as quickly as Evie had departed she returned, as rooted to the earth as ever. She juddered and let go, gasping. The moss under her fingernails was thick and unclean and some kind of twine was knotted about a branch by her head. The TV aerial of the house past the fence was shaking under the weight of a great gabbing crow. Evie felt despicable. A moment passed. She couldn't stand it. "What are you looking at?" she cried. "You've got what you wanted, now FUCK OFF!"

She swiped at Fenton's cheek, feeling a cool nab of flesh coming loose. Fenton didn't need telling twice. Clutching his bleeding face, he ran down the alley and disappeared.

It was a brief walk to The Carousel, where Evie saw her father's name in the Free Press's A-board propped outside. Dazed, she ran her hands through her matted hair. Just who the hell was she?

Footsteps. She opened her eyes. "Where were you?" she said, oddly calm.

"He took you a different route to the one I thought," Lawrence said. "Are you all right? I couldn't find you . . ."

"I'm fine. When you didn't turn up, I let him go."

These feelings would pass. They would have to.

Driving wet outside. Duncan was busy with his tutor so Evie and Lawrence were playing Monopoly, alone. Evie was winning comfortably: she beat Lawrence so often that sometimes she wondered if he just let her win.

After putting down her counter, the top hat, she said, "I want to ask you something. Promise me you won't laugh."

Lawrence took the dice and rolled his turn. "I promise," he said, without looking.

Evie snatched his battleship counter before he could move it. "You can't do that."

"What you on about?"

"Swear so fast without thinking."

"You said to promise?"

Evie dropped the counter and went to the window,

breathed on the glass and scratched a clear line in the haze of steam. She had been too troubled over the last few days not to speak her mind, despite her reservations, and Lawrence, she realised, was the only person in her life who she could to talk to.

"OK," she finally said, taking a deep breath. "This might sound weird but, Lawrence . . . do you ever feel like you want to disappear?"

Lawrence seemed about to get up, but stayed where he was. He *never* got things straight away. In the passageway with Ryan Fenton, consenting like that, a part of Evie had taken over that she hadn't been able to stop thinking about and was only just beginning to comprehend. She was trying to describe the pursuit of loss: the compelling minor deaths that come from sex.

Lawrence must have realised he'd behaved incorrectly because he quickly apologised. "You're going to have to explain."

Evie sighed.

"Lose myself?" said Lawrence.

"As in, go after a feeling you can't put your finger on. Like what's the point in not doing." She was nervous around him as she'd never been before. "Oh, forget it."

"No, hold on. Give us a chance."

He nodded for her to go on.

Evie's voice felt very tight. She wasn't sure what to do with her hands. "So the last few months," she said, swallowing. "Maybe the year before, I've been feeling, I dunno, like I've been opened up, like something's passed across me and now everything's changed. Do you ever get that? I mean, is it just me or does this happen to everyone at some point in their lives?"

Lawrence always seemed so quiet, even when he was talking. He said, "This year I've felt like that."

"So is this what it's like to be an adult?"

"I wouldn't know what adults are like."

"Have you ever wondered how it would be, following that feeling to its logical conclusion?" Evie felt tearful. She knew now that she wanted to dismantle absolutely everything. "Because I feel as if that's what I'm always trying to do these days, one way or another."

Lawrence picked up the battleship, and moved it to its destination: the chance panel. He didn't take a card. He simply reclined in his seat, twiddling a strand of hair for such a long, ponderous moment that Evie nearly reached out and tapped him on the knee. It was his eyes that kept her from doing so. Beneath their blinking hoods, Lawrence's pupils were swollen with the same distance Evie saw in everyone. She wanted so dearly to drift in the sap of another person's thoughts, to understand someone the way she thought she understood herself. But she knew she never would.

Eventually Lawrence spoke. "My family have this saying, right. Well, it's not a saying, exactly, it's more a thing we refer to. Dad says Gran started it – it comes from the way out of town – she just started going, one day, if you were caught daydreaming, like, Oh, he's taken the Litten Path. Meaning, you know . . ."

"You were miles away."

"Yeah. Then everyone started using it. Someone a few towns away wins the pools, he's taken Litten Path. Someone pops their clogs, they've gone up Litten Path, you with me? You've a choice to make, one way or the other. Path or safety."

"You take it or you don't."

"Yeah. It's a divide between one reality and the next. When things come to an end, you go up top. It's the route you take. It can mean all sorts."

Evie felt giddy with recognition. "And what's on the other side?"

"Oh, nothing. Like really nothing. But everything as well. My dad's obsessed with it. I think it's desolate. It scares me."

Evie remembered their first meeting in the forest, Lawrence's bald head, his muddy trousers. There had been a boy who had experienced poverty, not just in material terms but in all its myriad forms, and poverty can be a stigma you can't shake. She would never have thought the two of them would still be hanging around together all these months later. That she would come to think of him as a friend.

"See someone can come back from most places where there's life," said Lawrence. "But the Litten Path, if you take it, I mean *really take it*, the fog comes. That's it."

"Only footprints left."

"I suppose on the one hand if you really wanted to take it then you wouldn't want to come back, even if you could. Otherwise it would defeat the purpose of going in the first place. I guess I think sometimes people think taking the Litten Path is the only way, when really it isn't."

"Oh, Lawrence, it's the perfect way to describe it."

He almost folded in two. ". . .I always thought it were daft."

"No, no. It's quite beautiful."

The Litten Path. Evie murmured the words to herself and tried to visualise it, although picturing something so figurative was surely pointless. She had the idea of a line of pebbles showing the way in a hailstorm; another of stepping stones reaching to an endless island on the other side of an unknow-able lake.

"Your gran taught you all this?"

"My dad, mainly. Did you know my whole family's either a Capricorn, a Virgo or a Taurus? We're Earth symbols, all of us. Which star sign are you, Evie?"

"Aries."

"That's fire."

She picked up the dice and rolled her turn.

The rain had abated and now dusk had settled. Evie's feet seemed to make no impact in the furls of mud, the saturated grass. Unable to resist following Lawrence had betrayed the interest she had in him, an interest she hadn't been prepared to acknowledge up until now. She blamed their conversation earlier. It had slit holes in every part of her. She could now see her thoughts for the lost cleft of stones they had always been. She could see that life was really just a hike to a barrow built at storm height just for you.

Lawrence's spry figure made its way down the lane, and into Litten itself. His parka could have been a cloak. She could have been pursuing a highwayman in the eighteenth century. Evie wished she'd brought a coat herself.

Urgent blue flashed in the armada of rabbit runs and chicken coops that comprised Flintwicks Estate. Evie knew where the welfare was, the arcade and bandstand. She knew where the pit was, too. Living here during the miners' strike had been like flying above a tempest, even though she had be-friended Lawrence, who she now knew was from a pit family. Even though he had described to her the intimacies of the strike, his experience at Orgreave, Evie had been barely able to express anything beyond a plastic kind of shock as she reached for the next gin and tonic.

But that Litten Path. He was just like her, and so, at last, what was going on had become no integer, but a number and a half. There were additional values to everything, it seemed. Hidden decimals.

Lawrence must have been eighty feet away. He was a funny thing: loping and genial, and that pigeon chest! Lying on the sofa, slipping his top off, that time, Evie wouldn't have been surprised to see a downy bar of plumage across his breast. He looked so much like his mother. After he'd told her about Shell's affair, Evie had gone to have a look at the woman. Scones in a paper bag, a tired face, spinach-green tabard and netted homburg; the two of them had touched fingers as Evie received her change. Saturday lunchtime, full of the secret power of knowing things. Shell had no idea Evie knew about her. No idea at all.

Evie had also quizzed Lawrence about the family friend who turned up that night, the scarred man with ashen pinches in the crunches of his eyes that made him look like he was wearing mascara; Lawrence just said there'd been a falling out. Evie wondered what he'd say now if he saw her as they came to a strip of terraces. These houses were bigger than those on the Flintwicks estate, and were bricked or pebble-dashed. A clump of scruffy trees flailed outwardly behind them.

Evie kept her distance as Lawrence arrived at one of the houses and stuck his key into the door. She had come this far. She whistled as a tycoon might, causing Lawrence's outline to stop. He removed his key and stared at her.

"This is the big mystery?" she said, strolling over, nearly reeling at the thunderous expression awaiting her.

"What do you think you're doing?"

"I got bored of the Scarlet Pimpernel act?"

"You had no right to follow us!"

"Oh, *fine*, if you're going to be so precious about it."

Evie was about to sweep away when the door to the house opened. Lawrence's mother stood there wearing a coat and a scarf, holding a tea towel. "I heard the key in the door," she said. "Oh, hello."

"You must be Mrs Newman."

"Who's this, Lawrence?"

"A friend."

Some friend. Before she could protest, Evie was ushered into the Newman's candle-lit lounge, where Lawrence's mother tidied away a variety of papers from the settee. She seemed alone and highly embarrassed.

"Dad in?" said Lawrence.

"Upstairs."

Lawrence glared at Evie as if that was her fault.

Shell introduced herself by name. Evie did the same.

"So nice of you to pop round an' see your mam," Shell said to Lawrence, apparently wanting to hug him but unsure how. "I'd offer a brew but we've none, Evie. Do you drink coffee?"

"Oh, yes."

"How do you take it?"

"I like cappuccinos."

"We've instant. I can do it milky."

Mrs Newman left for the kitchen where she produced a carton of powdered milk from the cupboard. In the lounge there was no TV, no radio or furniture other than the settee and the armchair, a stuffed bookshelf and an empty minibar. A photo of Lawrence hung above a mantle beneath which a switched-off electric fire stood, its metal bars dusty. The floor in front of the fire had scratches on it and a bank of flickering candles offered the only light. The room would have felt cosy if it wasn't so cold. Beginning to realise the scale of her imposition, Evie tugged the hem of her skirt over her knees.

"You're always so secretive," she said quietly.

"Who do you think you are?"

"I don't." Evie shut her mouth. "I should go."

"You're here now. Have a good look."

"It's not like that."

But it was.

"I didn't realise. I mean, I thought you weren't even living at home?"

"I'm not," said Lawrence.

"Then why are you here?"

"I came to see us mam. That alright wi' you?"

"You're not being fair."

"That what you used to say to Lord Guiseley?"

There was a clattering upstairs.

Guiseley.

"Don't mind the racket," Shell said, entering the room with three mugs set on a tray. "That's just Lawrence's dad."

The lukewarm coffee was sweet and had discs of grease floating on its surface.

Guiseley.

"How's he doing?" said Lawrence. Not an inch. Not even the guts to look at Evie. She could feel her indignation growing.

"Fine, I suppose," said Shell.

"Pissed, then."

Was Lawrence blushing? He was!

Shell gave him a hard look, then diverted her attention to Evie. "Will you be eating, Evelyn? Is it Evelyn? I'm afraid we've not much in." She was nibbling a lock of hair. "I could run to the shop."

"Oh no. Thank you. I was just walking Lawrence home."

"You're sure?"

"Just stretching my legs."

"I wasn't expecting guests. If this one had said something, I could've tidied."

"Don't worry, Mrs—"

"Shell, please."

"Shell."

The woman was tremendously pale and unable to make eye contact with anyone. What must it be like to have such a sense of the done thing that to have your home even slightly out of sorts in company was this upsetting?

"For God's sake, Mam, *what?*" said Lawrence.

"Nowt." Shell faced the bookshelf. "Are you sure you won't stay, love? I've some Parkin. I work at the bakery. We've—"

"Mam, will you just leave it!"

"Well pardon me, Lawrence, I was only . . . Do you know, Evelyn, my son has never once mentioned you. In fact, I don't think he's even had one friend round, not in all the time we've lived here."

"Before you shipped us to Fernside I did."

"Aye, and we know what happened there, don't we."

Lawrence glowered whilst his mother pushed the long kinks of curly hair from her eyes. "I'm plain embarrassed," she said. "Here's me, all wrapped up, no face on an' tha's here for the first time and it's all . . ." Her hand went to her lips. "I've just thought. Are you not cold, love? I'm sorry. How

347

rude of me. Let's get a coat round them shoulders before a death is fetched."

"Oh, I'm fine, Mrs Newman. Don't worry—"

"It's no bother. And please call me Shell."

The poor woman was on her way to the kitchen when Lawrence swore, which made his mother stomp over and clip him around the head. The blow made a snapping sound.

"Watch your mouth when we've guests! Cursing like some flamin' paddy."

The sound of footsteps. A voice ricocheted down the stairwell. "What's all this racket about a fucking paddy?"

No one spoke. Lawrence's father stomped about upstairs, audibly complaining about not being able to find his boots.

"Arthur," Shell called. "Them boots are where they were left."

No response.

Arthur. Evie thought of the look on the man's face that summer. *No way*, he'd said. She hadn't thought of that in months.

"Evie's to be off," said Lawrence. "Remember your date, Evie?"

"Oh yes." She downed her coffee.

Guiseley.

"I've got a red hot date with the tub."

"Oh, I am jealous," said Shell. "But will you not say hello to Lawrence's dad before you go? Arthur!" she called, raising a single finger when Evie opened her mouth to protest. "Get down here an' meet us guest."

Arthur's booming voice made Evie jump. "Guest, what bloody guest?"

"You OK, love?" Shell said.

348

"I'm fine, thanks." Evie stood. "But I can't stay." Shell was wittering on about tea when it was dinner, not tea. Evie hurried from the room before anyone could stop her, heading out of the door and into the possible night.

Her dreams were full of bends in shape. Chrysanthemums in plastic wrapping, a creaking byre with a corrugated iron roof and wretched, collared birds fledging from the byre's eaves. The night, it wound about her. The smell of Ryan Fenton's hair gel, Bramwell Guiseley's desk adorned with antique pens, its green leather top. Eventually the night evolved into the radial of day and with that came Evie's father who sat opposite her, greedily buttering his toast.

"So you've finally noticed what's going on, and *now* you want me to take a look?"

Evie slugged back her orange juice. "It just occurred to me that you might make the campaign more convincing if you were to actually meet these people. You could even help."

"The campaign isn't supposed to be convincing. And if I was to go and kiss a few babies, I doubt I'd come back in one piece."

"Honestly, Clive, they're struggling."

"They're quite capable of going back to work if they want to."

"It's not as simple as that and you know it."

Her father was really launching into breakfast. He poured another cup of tea from the pot then spooned an entire boiled egg onto a dripping segment of toast, mashed it with a fork and sprinkled it with salt and pepper. "Look . . ." he began.

"All it takes is a phonecall. What's the energy secretary's name? Or the coal board? I bet you know someone."

"For God's sake!" Crumbs exploded across the table. "The vote's tomorrow, there's no point rocking the boat now. What's brought this on anyway?"

"Maybe I have an ounce of humanity in me?"

"Spare me the violins, Evelyn."

"I prefer the cello. It's a far sadder instrument."

Clive waited.

"I made a friend," said Evie.

"Ah yes, Duncan mentioned him. The local boy?"

"His father's on strike."

"They're all on *bloody* strike. What's his name? He's been helping with the posters and things, hasn't he?"

"Lawrence."

Clive demolished the remains of his food then carried his plate across the kitchen. "Well you've kept him well hidden, that's for sure. But you can bring him for dinner if you like. He can take a doggy bag home for his parents."

Beneath the hot tap, Clive's empty plate tolled against the Belfast sink. Even he must have realised how callous he was being, because his voice softened. "So the family . . . you've met them? I assume that's what's brought this plea on."

"I met the mother. She's a Litten Lady, that's what they call themselves."

"Ah, yes. Soup kitchen. Admirable women." Clive switched off the tap and patted his hands dry on his trousers. "And what about the father? Why hasn't he gone back to work if things are so dire?"

"Oh, *Arthur*, God knows. Lawrence refuses to talk about him but he's a bit of a character by all accounts. It was quite funny actually . . ."

She was reaching for the toast when Clive grabbed her by the wrist.

He didn't even give her time to put on shoes. Evie rubbed her bare feet while her father beat the Jaguar's horn and swore until the rusted old jalopy farted into life. They tore into Litten – it was lucky Evie remembered the way – then pulled in at the far end of the street where Lawrence's parents lived. Clive got out and wrote down the address. He seemed in two minds about whether to knock on the door, decided against it then came back and sat in the driver's seat.

"Describe him," he said.

"*Why?*"

"Evie, tell me what Newman looks like."

"You're hurting me!"

"What does he look like?"

"He's tall, short hair, beard! He has this mark!"

"Here?"

"Yes!"

Clive wouldn't say any more. He disappeared into the study the moment they arrived back at the house. All morning Evie could hear him oozing down the phone. She tried to listen in on the conversation from outside in the hallway but when she accidentally made a noise, Clive flew out and bellowed at her to make herself scarce.

She reverted to the sanctuary of her Walkman. Bored, lying on her bed, Evie wished for Lawrence but dared not go to him. At a loss, she retreated from questions and spent the day smoking the last of the grass she'd stolen from Clemmie Dallas until she fell asleep. Later she ventured downstairs and found Duncan in the living room. The lawn out of the windows was frozen and the trees had been picked clean by the winter.

"Where's Dad?" she asked.

"London."

"That's short notice."

"He had a meeting."

Evie scratched away the last of her nail polish, and was shocked to see a horrid smile carving its way across Duncan's face like a red wound.

"He's meeting with Bram," her brother said nastily. "Your boyfriend."

20

T HE FIELD WAS full of Canada Geese, a familiar sight in the gravel pits and down the rec. There were twenty of them now, absent wardens ferreting in the white. Lawrence leant on the fence to watch them go about their business. He always found in the natural world a reflection of the things he felt.

He was heading to his gran's along a slippery pavement embroidered with hexagons of frost. He'd be there within the hour. He blew on hands that looked frozen themselves they were so cold, gave them a rub and hurried on his way.

Tomorrow he'd be back on Water Street. He was far from struck on the idea but his grandmother couldn't afford to keep him anymore. He was just back from lying to his mam about the whole thing, explaining that it was by choice that he was moving home, and that if he was to see it through she'd to end whatever it was she had going on with Uncle Het. Arthur might be too weak to see what was going on. Lawrence knew very well. He just did.

Of course he was careful with how he went about it. He wasn't specific. He just said it needed doing. *It*. A stop put.

Seeing your mam go all quiet, go inside herself. "You know what I mean," Lawrence said.

"Heard you, love."

"I know what Dad's like. It's just . . ."

He stopped short of saying Arthur didn't deserve the betrayal he was getting.

"And you'll come home?" Shell said.

Lawrence nodded.

"Then it's settled. And that's the last any of us will say on it."

She'd been having it away all right. He would never forgive her.

The geese took to the air in a skein. They passed overhead, hooting. Lawrence watched them wink out and disappear. Cottonlea Retirement Home was in view, St Michael's weathercock poking above the adjoining cathedral of trees. What were their names? His dad would know. Ash, maybe. They loomed above an understorey of hawthorn. Lawrence stopped to twist one of the hawthorn's stubborn branches in half and jammed its spines against the fence. He couldn't believe what Evie had tried last night. She had trespassed all over him. She thought she knew his every step before he thought to take it.

He arrived at his gran's, the house enveloped in the smell of his goodbye dinner. She'd done him a pot of tea, boiled some ham with potatoes and cabbage, while dessert was jelly and ice cream. Gran didn't eat any herself, preferring to watch Lawrence enjoy his food, which he did, for the most part. He'd be dining at the soup kitchen soon enough. Chips, egg and beans on a trestle table, followed by more chips, egg and beans and the same again the next day. Christmas would be fun. Lawrence wasn't even thinking about his approaching birthday.

After he'd finished his meal, he planned to head upstairs so he could pack and be angry in peace, but his gran lay her hand on his wrist. Her skin was spotted and coloured by poor circulation. When Lawrence thought of her, this room was where she was, reading the newspaper, slippers tapping the chair leg, or dwarfed by the stove and surrounded by a bloom of steam and the melt-cackle of spitting butter.

"I shall miss thee," she said, "who will I have to peel us spuds and weed the garden when tha's gone?"

"Who's going to pay me for it as well as you do, Gran?"

Helen grinned. She had been good to him.

"There'll always be a place for you under this roof. But it's the right thing, you going home."

Lawrence nodded, although he couldn't say he agreed. The zip on his gran's apron had been replaced by a safety pin. He watched her play with it, up and down. A centimetre, up and down.

"Oh, look at that face. Tha's like tha father, lad. Chin up."

Lawrence didn't answer, he didn't move.

"Those like you see the deep streaks. Blots on clean windows an' even in the sunlight, sadness. It's not all so bad. All of this will be a footnote one day, you'll see."

Lawrence had only a sense of what his gran meant, yet still nodded. Usually he couldn't see through her Spitting Image face. Today was different. Smooth her cheeks out and also the forehead, reduce that nose of hers and those ears and the folded skin gathered like bedsheets around her neck, then add a bit of colour and there you had it: how she'd been when she was young. His gran believed in reincarnation, and Lawrence wondered, if she was right about all that, if she'd had the same face throughout all of her lives. She had once told him that people are born with their hands closed because they're holding onto their new souls; that they die with them open because they've released their soul to the next body. Perhaps that's why babies look like pensioners, he thought. He felt ancient himself, as if generations of his forebears were coursing through him to this day, long after they'd gone up the Litten Path.

"I don't know if I feel any better," he said. "Thinking that."

Lawrence lay under his covers the following afternoon, re-membering Orgreave. At the time he had worried he would never make it out of the shed he'd run to. Now he knew that in one form or another, he would always be trapped there.

More of a lean-to than anything, the shed had smelt of garden paint and wood preservative. He'd hid on a compost bag below a push-mower hanging from a nail. Powerless hours, every now and again peeking through the murky window at the crucible of Orgreave village: the eddying violence dragging anyone in who got too close.

Horses on the tarmac. Blokes dragged up the street by officers in double-breasted tunics. The boiler-suited officers were the worst. The others with their great round shields came a close second. Every person there had a sweat-marbled face, cop and picketer alike fighting through the bricks, the glass, the heat. The riot officers giving it that terrifying Zulu.

Landing that punch on Het had been almost worth it. Lawrence had tumbled down the hill and nearly fractured his collarbone, before retreating into the village where he found the shed, sneaking out later on when he thought it was safe. Two officers proved him wrong on that front. They charged him and knocked him to the ground. Kicked him and punched him. He'd thought he was going to be arrested but they left him alone once they realised how young he was. He'd ducked into a side passage and found three blokes there, hiding: Scottish lads who'd caught the coach south then the bus that morning from town. 15p to come and have a truncheon wrapped around your head. Bare-chested and bleeding, shirts nowhere to be found because they'd not had time to put them on when the cavalry charged. They'd never seen a shield unit deployed this way, nor those Orgreave horses, who had turned into foaming monsters rather than the trained sentinels they were supposed to be. Orgreave. Each man in that village snick promised never to trust a policeman after what they'd seen that day.

Orgreave.

Orgreave Lane.

Lawrence left the bed and was forcing on his shoes ready to go for a walk when he heard a knock on the door. It was Evie, dressed in a baggy leather jacket and a denim shirt, a yellow kerchief and sunglasses. Her hair was in a ponytail, this show-home girl of cryptic comments and casual flirtations.

He tried to shut the door on her but she stuck her foot in the gap.

"I'm saying it then," she said.

"Sayin' what?"

"Really, Lawrence?"

"Apologising means actually saying you're sorry."

She removed her sunglasses. Her eyelids were as green as they'd been the morning Lawrence first met her. "I've come to invite you to dinner," she said. "So how's that for an apology?"

"What dinner?"

"It's the by-election tonight. We're celebrating."

Lawrence had completely forgotten. "I know what night it is," he said. "What if I've plans?"

"We both know you don't."

"I could be busy."

"Well if you are then you'll never see me again," said Evie, and cocked her head. *There you go.* She made it a few yards down the street before turning around to call back at him, "And I am sorry, OK? I'll see you later."

Lawrence watched her go and wanted to follow. He shut the door.

No question of not attending. He owed it to the last months of trying to have another crack at Evie. It was a long shot but you never knew. She was the one who'd come all this way, and dressed up, too. That had to count for something.

It was just that Evie was the only girl Lawrence had ever got anywhere with, and whenever he was with her he became so clumsy that his every limb might as well have been wrapped in duct tape, his tongue made out of that coir stuff you made doormats from. She must have realised. She must have seen.

Girls could have anyone they wanted, it was so easy for them. Lawrence wondered what the fabled terrain of post-virginity would be like when he reached it. He had a fantasy of returning to Fernside after he and Evie had done it. He wouldn't have to say anything. Everyone would just *know.*

He went to the bog and had a cold bird bath in the sink, rinsing his armpits and squeezing the pimples on his shoulders and chest. Maybe he was wasting his time, considering the way Evie carried on. She wasn't bothered about a charity case, a novelty act like him.

Although, to be fair, he had got *some* of the way. He'd kissed Evie. Held her close. So maybe she did care. Maybe she cared so much that she was saving herself so that when it happened it'd be dead special. Apparently girls did that. Lawrence used the last of the talcum powder. Most of it dappled the bathroom carpet.

In any case it was confusing, especially with Evie's tactic of connecting then pulling away, making you feel like you'd done something wrong. That day at Conisborough Viaduct was a typical example. They'd taken the train to where Lawrence had visited one foggy morning with Arthur when he was a kid. Amazing, it had been. Twenty-one arches, brick caves of cloud, hundreds of feet of lattice girder spanning the River Don.

Both the Swarsbys were impressed. From the top of the viaduct, where the tracks used to be, they could see a changing valley, the approaches, the water necks and townships. They shared a bottle of brandy above Lawrence's North of industrial vestments, spiritual fetters and battered walls.

When they'd had enough of the view they moved on to a sun-washed glade where a rope swing had been rigged above the water from the low-hanging branch of a tree. A great find. The river here was as golden as chip fat and above it the twitch of blue cord had been looped above the natural over-hang. Lawrence and Evie took turns gripping the stick-handle knotted to the rope, and belted free above the water. Duncan sat on the bank because he wasn't in the mood to get wet.

Run up, career out, let go. Once Lawrence and Evie went at the same time, hanging onto a portion of the handle each, their damp torsos bumping against one another before they dropped into the river. It might have been one of the best days of Lawrence's life. He didn't know if that meant he'd led a sheltered existence, or what. There was just something about being the one to show others a special place that made the moment stick in the memory, gave it meaning.

While Duncan slept a little later, Lawrence and Evie sat on the bank to dry off, smoking some of the grass Evie had managed to get hold of. Although admitting it was against his instinct, Lawrence confessed he'd never tried weed before, and was thrilled when Evie said he was handling it well for a first timer. Enjoying the roving buzz of the grass, he'd imagined the trains carrying coal over the great disused viaduct: a clockwork kind of enchantment trundling over the Don and Dearne, a memory of the barracking passage of industry, the slippage of time.

Lawrence asked Evie about things he already knew of, mainly because he enjoyed the sound of her voice. What France was like; if she could speak French. When he asked why her family had come to Litten, she wouldn't say.

She'd been the one to move closer. Her bra and knickers had gone almost see-through and Lawrence's boxers left even less to the imagination. He'd clumsily reached for her, only she wouldn't have him for longer than a minute and he ended up setting a hand on her knee and saying, "Come on, Evie. Don't be tight."

Her response was an ambiguous smile that he instantly knew he would always question. She went to the rope-swing, launched herself over the water and splashed out of sight. Lawrence pulled his clagging t-shirt back on, noticing as he did that, to his horror, Duncan was awake and had witnessed the whole thing. He lay flat on his back and pretended nothing had happened.

He knocked on the door of Threndle House, and was met by Clive Swarsby himself. A robust man with his shirt open a button too far, Clive had shower-damp hair and a lobster-pink face.

He greeted Lawrence warmly. "Lawrence, isn't it," he said. "Here to celebrate Labour's victory?"

"Evie said dinner . . ."

"I'm joking, of course. Why don't you come in?"

Lawrence was ushered into the atrium, which had been swept and smelled of pine. He hoped he wouldn't be asked how he'd voted, because he hadn't bothered.

"And while a defeat is a defeat," Swarsby was saying, taking Lawrence's soaked coat from him. "What matters is we staged a campaign that didn't end too ignominiously."

"What was the count in the end?"

"Well, it's important to reflect on the turnout," said Clive. "Which, I *think* was something approaching twenty one percent. Pitiful, really, that the locals can't be bothered to vote. They forget their ward representative's an important figure."

Lawrence had only the vaguest idea of what councillors did. He craned to see around Swarsby into the living room and was pleased to see the table bedecked with various platters of food. He jumped when Clive clapped him on the shoulder and said, "But let's just say there'll be no need for a recount."

Evie chose that moment to show her face. She stepped downstairs pulling on a black turtleneck sweater, widening the neck hole with both hands and pushing her head through so her hair didn't catch on the sides. She wore a red skirt below a gleaming PVC belt. "Are you talking about the vote?" she said.

"That's why we're here, darling. And I believe you assisted with the campaign, Lawrence?"

It was time to concentrate on how he spoke. "Oh yes," Lawrence replied. "I lent a hand."

"Good man. I might be able to use someone like you one day."

"*Really?*"

Swarsby was no longer listening. His attention alighted

upon his daughter. He lifted his chin to Evie, and, to Lawrence's astonishment, Evie kissed his cheek. There was much to make of the act, all of it forgotten as she kissed Lawrence's cheek too. Excited, Lawrence was shown into the living room while Clive chattered on about how great Litten was. How sad he'd be to leave. Then again there would always be new challenges.

"I have found it invigorating," he said. "The dramatic air. It's Bronte country, plain and simple. The blank *pages* of the hills . . ."

Was he drunk? "It's got something," Lawrence agreed. "My dad's always up on the moor."

Swarsby gave the impression of trying not to react. It was like when someone pretends they haven't seen you. He clapped Lawrence on the shoulder and said "There is a romance to the land that's impossible to overlook. I have enjoyed exploring the lea these last few months."

Fat-arse didn't look like he did much walking. Lawrence wondered how often Swarsby had visited Litten proper. The bridge in Barnes' Wood now had anti-Thatcher sentiment sprayed all over it. NO PIT CLOSURES was written on one of the high street walls. NEVER GIVE UP was sprayed up the shutters of the shops in the arcade. No one went out any more. The stand in the centre hosted the brass band still, with its fucking tubas and maudlin horns, mud rivulet up your trouser leg because you'd stood on a wonky bit of pavement and the rainwater had squirted up all over you. Imagine the romance of *that*. Imagine Clive Swarsby wondering why no one had bothered to come out and vote.

"Sounds like you'll be wanting to contest the seat again," said Lawrence, nodding hello at Duncan, who stood by the piano with a pot of weird pink dip in his hand, breadstick reaching from his teeth to fingers, like a cigar.

Duncan answered for his father, "Why on earth would we do that?"

"Well, your dad was just saying how nice it was up here. And getting people to vote next time as well . . ."

Duncan put down the dip and offered his hand, opaque eyes suddenly alive. "We won't be staying in Litten, Lawrence."

Lawrence tried to grip Duncan's hand as firmly as his was being gripped. "You're leaving?"

"It's the prudent course of action," said Clive. "I made a few calls. We should be south again within the next couple of weeks."

"I didn't realise."

"Why would we stay?"

Evie arrived, her mouth heady with lipstick. She looked at her father. "Dad's negotiated our way home."

She never called him dad. Lawrence was going to ask where they were moving to. He wanted to take Evie to one side and tell her *he* was her reason to stay, she couldn't go, but a knock on the door surprised him into silence.

"Speaking of which," said Evie, departing from the room, Lawrence's enduring quarry. He willed her back. Elongated shadows.

Clive seemed confused. Duncan touched his arm. It was hard to believe that this pretty young man was a year younger than Lawrence. "I'll get the door," he said. "Lawrence, why don't you keep my father entertained."

"I'll do my best."

Lawrence accepted a glass of wine. It tasted reedy, a silly drink.

"So what do you do, young man?" Clive said.

Lawrence thought on it; there was no point dressing it up. "I'll be going to work at the pit."

"Yes, yes, important work. Skilled labour. Damn shame what's been going on. One hopes for a speedy resolution."

"One does."

The second guest was in the house. It was difficult to hear what was being said over the jazz playing in the next room, the umbrella being shaken by the door. Lawrence could hear its spokes, the material folding like a set of wings. He imagined the water beating the roof tiles as the winds of his approaching solitude howled outside.

An elegant man entered the room. He had scree-grey hair that was combed to one side, and he patted it to test its shape once he'd removed his leather gloves. The guest seemed to make Clive and Duncan go up a gear, and indeed Lawrence found himself touching his own hair, which was wet still. He turned to check himself in the window. His mop was a bit of a crow's nest but otherwise it seemed OK, as did the shirt he'd got for Christmas last year, his freshly-ironed school trousers. He couldn't make out the face. He was nothing but a blank oval.

The man's fey hands were behind his back as he surveyed the room for the first time. "Goodness, there's mother's piano," he said, pressing one of the black keys and producing a disquieting, minor note. "Many's the hour spent at this old thing. Many were the rainy days."

Duncan and Clive made consenting sounds. The guest could have been a magnate standing in the heather, annihilating grouse. A clever man who did things to insects when he was a boy.

After a loaded moment he seemed to look, not past Lawrence, more through him, at the large crack up the wall. He put his hand to it. "A new development," he said, caressing a line of subsidence so dark that it could have been made of obsidian. Whatever age this man was, Lawrence wouldn't have been surprised to hear it. Nor that he had gone up the Litten Path himself a few times, somehow managing to claw his way back.

"Clive?" the man said.

"It's just shown up." Clive chortled. He was well into a large glass of wine by this point.

"Subsidence," Lawrence offered. "From the pit."

The words had just popped out. The man straightened and regarded Lawrence. "And isn't that neat," he said slowly.

Clive Swarsby cleared his throat. "This is Lawrence. Local boy, Evelyn's guest. Done some sterling campaigning for me."

Lawrence held his hand out to greet the man. He could smell cooked meat, and out of the window thought he could see the outline of someone watching everything, a tall, malingering shape standing a few yards away in the snow.

"Lawrence," said Duncan, doing a great job of expressing a lot while saying very little. "This is Bramwell Guiseley."

You couldn't really have that good an idea of someone you knew by deed alone. From what he'd been told about Guiseley, Lawrence had been expecting someone a lot younger, more disdainful. He supposed the man had presence. A powerful chewer, Guiseley pushed great clods of nubile lamb into his mouth. He ate in sequence. First the carrots and then the greens, then the potatoes, eventually graduating to the roast beef. He hadn't said much all night, and now in the final plump stages of his meal, he continued to hold his tongue.

A few other guests had arrived to break things up, to none of whom Lawrence was introduced. An alderman and his jowly wife from Hoy-on-wold, another two Conservative councillors from the borough and their spouses. Lawrence sat next to Evie, who seemed to have lost the will to speak and barely touched her food. He asked her if everything was all right. She said it was fine. From time to time, glancing up the table, he noticed her and Guiseley catch each other's eye. He wasn't sure if it was a smile he saw, or if he'd imagined it.

After everyone completed their main course, Clive tinkled his plate with his fork and stood with his glass raised, the claret glowing in the light, his lips bruised a dim purple as if he'd been drinking something totally different to everyone else.

"These have been a few strange months, and not just in this fold, but all over the country, generally, and though it hasn't been easy, not for any of us." He glanced at Lawrence. "I know that as a party and a people we have the right amount of grist for the mill. It's certainly been a difficult time for many of us, but now that the ward for the borough has been selected . . . by its able populace." Clive flashed that plummy smile. "So my family and I shall be retreating to whence we came." He raised his chin in triumph and faced Guiseley directly. "And with my return to London and active party service imminent, I am reminded of some of the bard's lines, that seem fitting, indeed, for the occasion:

'The west yet glimmers with some streaks of day. Now spurs the lated traveller apace, to gain the timely inn.'"

"Macbeth," whispered Evie, pushing away her plate.

"So as I, the lated traveller," her father continued, "safely return to the timely inn, my friends, I would like to thank you all for coming. You are all so very dear, and more than welcome to visit us in the south. Hear, hear."

"Hear, hear," repeated everyone, even Guiseley.

As the guests resumed their seats Evie left the table without excusing herself. Noticing her brimming eyes, Lawrence untucked his napkin from his collar, set it on the table and went after her.

He had never been this far into Threndle House. It was exactly the disappointment he had been led to believe it was. The parched weft of the carpet and the faded walls said everything. It would be mad to live in, though, this place, to live a dream of something, just as his father had once said to him. That was true enough. This was Threndle House, not so much a bad dream as an old dream, one where you were stuck and couldn't control what was going on around you. All you could do was fail to run.

Lawrence searched for Evie, trying every room until he found her packing a bag on a double bed. A suitcase was open and clothes of all kinds were littered over the floor. Outside, through the window, were shapes. A gothic outline of this weather-beaten land.

"Is it seeing him again?"

"It's everything. If I have to listen to their . . . *sophistry* anymore, I'll scream."

"And that Guiseley. Bloody hell."

"They didn't say he was going to be here. He was once so . . . God, Lawrence . . ." She sat on the bed. "I can't even describe it."

"Duncan just said he were your boyfriend. I didn't expect him to be a fucking pensioner."

"Oh grow up."

"You never said you were leaving either! Were you just going to go without saying anything? I thought . . ."

"That's why I invited you, to apologise. I honestly didn't realise what you were going through."

Look at her, so unused to penitence. It still grated on Lawrence, Evie's presumptions. She had lived her whole life with no idea, all because she came from a different neck of the woods to him. All because somewhere along the way one of Evie's ancestors had stumbled upon a better opportunity than one of his.

It was no use going over it all again. "What's that tosser even doing here anyway?" said Lawrence. "If Duncan knows what happened, doesn't your dad as well?"

"*They invited him*," Evie said tearfully. "They've made some deal. Duncan said a man like that is better to keep in your pocket than set against you."

Lawrence was too shy to comfort her now. He could picture her big affair, the excitement in all its heaving moments and leatherette permutations. For all her spike and meanness, Evie was as vulnerable as any other young person. She had been joyridden.

"But why?" he said.

"I don't want to talk about it."

"Well where will you go?"

"As long as it's away from them, I don't care."

Lawrence glanced at her shyly. "How about the moon?"

Evie dried her eyes. "I'll buy a caravan."

"The moon in a caravan." Lawrence liked the sound of that. "I'll come with you," he said.

"We'll go up the Litten Path."

368

"That's it."

"I've ordered a taxi," said Evie, shutting her luggage.

"I wish I'd had one of them when I ran away."

The two of them hugged, about as close as Lawrence would ever get.

"What will you do?" asked Evie.

"Get a job, I reckon."

"You don't . . . Oh, Lawrence, why don't you come with me?" She showed off Clive's Mastercard. Her mascara was blotchy and the wind was really racing outside. It was to be a cavernous winter in this land of theirs.

Lawrence hadn't the words. Thoughts of his mother intruded, the cage she'd built for herself that for years she'd been too frightened to leave. He understood not just the cage now, but Shell. Litten too. What would he do if he wasn't here? Who would he be? When you weighed it up, surely you were better off where you belonged, rather than aimless with someone who didn't care for you other than as a friend?

"I can't do it," he said.

"OK."

They snuck downstairs. Evie opened the front door. "Lawrence, I was meaning to say, about your dad . . ."

He stopped.

"Tell him from me, that they know who he is. Just tell him that."

Unsure what she meant, he watched her go. Her form was caught in the twin headlights of the taxi. She was leaving his life as she had come into it, illuminated by the lights of a car.

The taxi drove away.

Lawrence could hear the guests in the living room, so thought he'd slip out of the house without them noticing. In the kitchen he found Lord Guiseley standing at the window: the hereditary peer and his profile. Precision had a smile for Lawrence over its shoulder.

"The miner's boy."

Lawrence foraged for his coat in the throng hanging from the hooks.

"Pup has left then, I take it?"

There it was. Lawrence put it on.

"I suppose she's said a lot about me, but take it from someone who knows, there are some choices in life you wish you could unmake." Guiseley turned back to the view, paused, then said. "Wait a moment, dear boy."

Lawrence went to the postern door, stopping at the sound of Guiseley's voice. The man was offering him an umbrella. "Here," he said.

Lawrence didn't move.

Guiseley always seemed to be smiling with his eyes. "My family owned Brantford once, you know. Probably employed a relative of yours at one time or another."

"Daresay."

"It's a shame. All the closures the government's planning. Far more than they've publicly said . . ."

Lawrence stepped out into the rain. Guiseley was eyeing him with deliberation.

"That got your attention," Guiseley said. "Tomorrow I'm going to the colliery. I suspect it will be the last time I shall see it, if you follow my charitable meaning. Let us hope for winter sun. I have a vision of the view. One advantage to the industrial age has been the sunsets: the most magnificent vistas come from smog."

"I could go papers about you."

"You could try."

Lawrence splashed to the gates. As he reached them, he turned back towards Threndle House. The gargoyle at its peak wasn't grinning at those who entered, as he'd always thought.

It was weeping.

Smashed glass woke him later. He sat up at the sound of another crash. He could hear his dad's voice, his mam in tears. It was five in the morning according to the bloody alarm clock.

He slung on his dressing gown, put on his slippers and went to face the disturbance in the living room. Lawrence found his mam chucking mugs at his dad, the floor coated in coloured bits of china. Shell was in her nightslip while Arthur was fully dressed and didn't look like he'd slept.

"I'm only just home and already the two of you are at each other's throats."

Neither of them were listening. Shell threw one last mug, which bounced off Arthur's cowering form, his unkempt figure looking more like a saturated heap than it did dad. The mug shattered on the ground with the rest of them.

Mam was in a right state. Moisture dribbled in brooks from her nose and eyes, meeting on her chin. "Your father," she said. "Has decided to ruin us!"

"He's *not*."

"Tell him, Arthur!"

"Tell me what?"

Arthur couldn't get a word in: Mam was too hysterical. Five in the morning, hysterical. Welcome home, son.

She said Arthur had told the bosses he was going to go back to work. She said he was going to scab.

Scab.

Shell tore the picture of Lawrence from the wall and threw it at Arthur. The frame was made of thick plastic so didn't shatter. Lawrence stared at himself on the floor in his grammar school uniform.

More insults. Arthur was a crust of tissue on the face of the community. He was a leach. A scoundrel.

A scab.

Shell rushed across the room and began to slap Arthur's shoulders and head. Lawrence had to pull her off. He had to force his mother on to the settee and pin her arms against her sides.

Scab, she kept saying, *he's scabbing*, the energy leaving her body. She ended up sinking on to her front, against the cushions, spent, breathing heavily, before eventually sitting up again, both arms wrapped over her eyes, head against the backrest, crying.

Lawrence didn't need to ask if it was true. His dad's face was death itself. Coarse, haggard, Arthur spoke. "We'll lose house otherwise."

Lawrence sat on the settee next to his mam. "Oh, Dad."

"It has to be done!" cried Arthur. "We've no choice." Someone had to save the family, he said. With the bonus he was getting, he'd put food on the table. *Proper food*. He'd pay the mortgage. Pay the debts. Opting out of this tribal nightmare was the right thing to do.

Mam was really crying. "Oh aye," she said. "The pay-out. His vulture money's the right thing. Arthur Newman with the right thing. You're a cheat is what you are, Arthur. A bloody traitor!"

"Aye," Arthur croaked. "And how about that."

Mam looked like she might spew. She bent down until her

head touched her knees. She gripped her ankles, her shoulders heaving.

Lawrence went to the window. At either end of the street was a police cordon. Already the crowds were gathering there, and two police officers were at the front door. Out of the kitchen he could see men in the backings, too, a man in the bloody yard by the bloody coal shed.

"Dad, when word gets out about this . . ."

"To tell you the truth, lad, I'm past caring about the word."

"Well what about us?"

Arthur's voice sounded full of rubble. "Best pack a bag," he said. "Both yous. Officers are on t'way. You're to sheltered accommodation for the time being."

Ever since they got the rug. Ever since then.

While Arthur left to get himself sorted, Lawrence went outside. There was a mob collecting at the end of Water Street, and they were starting to shout. He could see the sporadic flare of the sirens. He could hear the dogs.

"You all right, lad?" said a sympathetic voice, one of the bobbies guarding the house. He was a local copper, judging by that accent. "You're best getting inside. The car's on its way an' it'll not be pretty."

The brilliant sun teemed into view, a shimmering locus of heatless chrome. People emerged from the houses. The neighbours were staring – Shell's worst nightmare.

The clarion was set to emergency. Lawrence wasn't sure if the scab bus was coming with it, how this sort of thing was arranged, but something official was definitely coming this way.

It was just one car in the end: a white Rover SD1 with its aerial twanging back and forth. The crowd at the end of the street totally lost it when they saw the car park outside the

Newman house. Lawrence watched the people muddle and react, his dressing gown breaking open like an old cloak, the cold bouncing harmlessly off him, he felt that dazed.

Inside he called down his dad, who arrived in full work gear, in all his naiveté thinking he'd need it. There'd be thousands of picketers outside of Brantford pit by now. Brantford on their lips, Brantford on the brain, mining folk from all over Yorkshire, from all over the country, coming to protest Arthur Newman, the dirty scab.

Lawrence hugged his dad. "You sure about this?"

Arthur hugged him back, tight as anything. "Not really, no."

He was shaking.

"I've an idea. They put you in the car, you get straight out again. Easy."

"I wish it were."

Mam tried to block the door when the two police officers arrived. One of them gently pushed her out of the way and held her by the shoulders.

"You ready, Art?" the second said.

"Have to be, don't I."

A few people had managed to break through the cordon and were running towards the house, pursued by more police officers. It was Asa and Janice Scanlan and the Roaches. And there was Uncle Het.

Lawrence's mam fought free of the policeman. She was in the doorway with a face on her.

Go on, Mam.

She prepared to halt Arthur, even though she ought never to attempt a thing like that, because you could pluck every leaf from an oak tree, but at the end of the day they would

374

always grow back in exactly the same demented shape. The police readied the blanket to put over Arthur's head. Shell was blocking the path. "This is a picket!" she cried. "It's my wages gone to the union these months, so by my count that's me a paid-up member. *This* . . ." She indicated the limits of the doorway. "Is an official picket, Arthur, right here, and I am asking you as your wife, friend and comrade, not to cross it!"

It almost worked. Arthur found his courage and tried to turn back but the policemen threw the blanket over his head before he could utter a word. Lawrence watched the police wrestle Mam out of the way and speed Dad out of the front door.

A second later Arthur was in the back of the police car. The siren kicked into life and the car blasted him away down Water Street via a space cleared by force through the horde. If the land-speed record could have been set between fifty and sixty miles an hour down a hundred yards of terraced house, that car would have broken it. People tried to stop it. Then it was gone.

Lawrence ran upstairs and threw on some clothes. The moment he came back downstairs Uncle Het arrived, bursting through the front door. "Family," he was saying, "This is my family."

Shell ran to him and collapsed into his arms.

Lawrence left them to it. A couple more police officers had entered the house by then; he managed to slip past them. Water Street was a blur. Lines of police had surrounded the place. Eggs and mud bombs soared. They hit the houses and bounced off the slate roofs. Lawrence heard the smash as next door's front window was hit by a rock.

"Scab!" went the challenge. "Newman, Scabs!"

Down the road he ran, dodging the outstretched arms of a policeman, evading everyone. Someone tried to punch him as he pushed through. He was far too quick to for that.

Lawrence was on his way through Litten.

Edge of town.

Out of town.

And there it was, the late road. The watery run-down usually made this stretch of ground a bog, but after last night it had been frozen into crunchy ripples. Lawrence's weight didn't alter those shapes. Foot after foot, he struggled up the black frost until it became snow, dunes of powdery white. Now he was at the bottom of the hill. He could see the abandoned Land Rover ahead, which today was as good as a box of ice. He went to it, touched it. The ice crystals on his fingertips entered his mouth.

It had been a year of moments and culminations and now Lawrence was at the infertile part. This area was of nothingness, ice. He made his way as best he could, getting away from himself, at long last, slipping away. Higher ground. Peak ground. Snow-logged. At long last Lawrence could see what continually brought his father to this place. This was not the woodland; it was something far more final than that. He hurried into the untameable space. He knew now that the small world he had been born into had disappeared. His feet shed any hindrance, so too did his legs. He was navigating a crushed and buried land, making his way towards the sheer fell, and he would not stop, he would not look back until he had reached the summit. He could feel the elemental force running through him. And he would keep going until he was fused with it, and with the light. And again and again with the light.

ACKNOWLEDGEMENTS

TOTAL THANKS TO my family and to dearest Lizzy for all their understanding and support whilst I worked on the book. Thanks to Chris and Jen Hamilton-Emery at Salt for having faith and publishing me, and thanks, too, to Linda Bennett for her thoughtful editorial suggestions. Also, a quick nod to everyone at The Manchester Writing School at MMU, where this book was written, particularly Carys Bray, who provided invaluable steerage for the book in its earliest incarnations, and Joe Stretch, who supervised me as I wrote the bulk of the draft. You really helped me pin the voice down. Finally, sincere thanks to Nick Royle, who has been readily available for advice and support over the years. It was Nick's prose workshops that I attended way back in 2007, the feedback I received making me realise that maybe I could do this one day if I actually pulled my finger out and applied myself.

This book has been typeset by SALT PUBLISHING
LIMITED using Neacademia, a font designed by Sergei
Egorov for the Rosetta Type Foundry in the Czech
Republic. It is manufactured using Creamy 70gsm, a
Forest Stewardship Council™ certified paper from Stora
Enso's Anjala Mill in Finland. It was printed and bound
by Clays Limited in Bungay, Suffolk, Great Britain.

CROMER
GREAT BRITAIN
MMXVIII